for
whom
the # BALL
rolls

FOOTBALL FICTION
AND MORE

Ian Plenderleith

ORION

An Orion paperback

First published in Great Britain in 2001
by Orion
This paperback edition published in 2003
by Orion Books Ltd,
Orion House, 5 Upper St Martin's Lane,
London WC2H 9EA

ISBN 0 75284 257 9

Printed and bound in Great Britain by
Clays Ltd, St Ives plc

Contents

Acknowledgements

My gratitude to the following, who read at least some of my stories and offered me both criticism and encouragement: Conny; my mum and Carol; Dad and Roz (sorry, the dead dog had to stay); Tim Bradford; Ellen Thalman; Tanvisha Longden; Barb Staszewski; Andrew Isbester; Martin Morgan; Drew Whitelegg; Gerd Lotze; Sue Pukali; Dagmar Aalund; Lori Cuthbert and Mark Emon; Marcus Kabel and Theresa Waldrop. Thanks also to Mark Blacklock for research, and to Dukey for free taxi rides to Heathrow. And to Ian Preece for his intelligent editing and his belief in my work.

For Conny, Nina and Natascha

Football Fiction . . .

Save of the Day
(in a Small Scottish Village in 1974)

I DID NOT want to go to the village football pitch on my own, I wanted my dad and Uncle Tam to come with me. But that didn't happen any more. A couple of years back they would have kicked around with me in Uncle Tam's garden, now they said they were too old. Today they were already standing in the lounge drinking whisky and smoking cigars and it was only three in the afternoon. I knew there was no chance they'd come with me once they'd started drinking whisky and smoking cigars.

'Still a big football fan, eh?' Uncle Tam would say as he pinched my cheek and grinned. 'The Hibs could maybe use you at the moment, they're having a rough time of it.'

'He's a Rangers fan like his father,' my dad would reply. 'He wouldnae be playin' for the Hibs.'

'Aye aye,' Tam would say, and that was about it, because I was too taciturn to say anything myself. I worshipped them both – my dad because he was my dad, and Uncle Tam because when we'd visited the previous year he'd given me a Glasgow Rangers scarf from the 1950s – and didn't think that a nine-year-old could make a worthy contribution to their exchange. Then Tam would look at my dad and say: 'Can I get ye a wee somethin', Lawrie?' and my dad would rub his hands together and that was when the register of the conversation changed completely to the adult wavelength that caused children to switch off automatically and look for something else to do.

Uncle Tam, who was not an actual uncle but an old schoolfriend of my dad's who happened to be avuncular, and his wife Annie had three girls. I saw them once or twice a year when we drove up from our home in England for a week visiting Scottish relatives. I wanted nothing to do with them because two of them, Aileen and Alison, were older than me and very attractive and I was scared of the way they talked to me by leaning down and smiling and asking me straight questions, and their hair sometimes brushed against my cheek and I could smell their perfume. The other daughter, wee Corrie, was much younger and I considered it beneath me to have anything to do with her, given that I was going to be a professional footballer, not a builder of dolls' houses. So to look for 'something else' I had to get outside.

Uncle Tam's garden was big, but not the right place to play football, there were too many flowerbeds and no natural goalposts created by either trees or laundry poles. I always tried for a while, but it wasn't like being on your home turf, where you knew all the cracks and the bumps and the exact height of the neighbour's garden fence. Plus last time we had visited wee Corrie had overheard me commentating on the match and emerged tittering from behind a tree. But I always tried for a while because anything was better than going down to the local pitch.

Of course at the pitch there was endless space and real goalposts. That was great. The problem was that there were always other kids there. Scottish kids. And when you'd grown up in England that was always a problem, even when you tried to tell them that you were Scottish. 'Where's yer accent, then?' they would taunt. 'How come ye speak like a sassenach?' And although I didn't get roughed up on some pretext *every* time I went down to the football pitch (in fact I think it only happened once), it seemed to me that, as I walked down the hill clutching my ball, praying by miracle that the entire field would be empty, some sort of confrontation was inevitable.

Sometimes there was no one there, but only because in Scotland the school holidays often fell at different times to the English ones. Then I would play for hours just like I did at home, running up and down the field re-enacting whatever game I wanted, commentating out loud in pure Queen's English because all those local toerags were safely locked up in school and the brash Scottish wind carried my southern tones far away and out to the soft green hills of the border country. Then at quarter to four I would pick up my ball and sprint back to Uncle Tam's house before the gates to the local schools unleashed the kind of kid that liked to defend his territory against foreign invaders.

Today was hopeless, though. It was a Saturday, and there were always other kids around on a Saturday. But I had to risk it, I didn't want to head back inside and be ignored by grown-ups in the whisky and cigar room, and I didn't want to be anywhere near the girls because they were girls, and I didn't want to play in the garden because the grass was too long and every time I kicked the ball against the garden fence it shuddered and made a noise which threatened some kind of imminent damage, and that was preventing me shooting with the necessary full conviction. So it had to be the big pitch, and the chronic pre-match nerves that made walking the few hundred yards between Uncle Tam's house and the field were, I felt, at least necessary preparation for the day I would walk down the tunnel at Hampden Park.

When I got down there the pitch was in use by a group of older lads, but that wasn't all bad. I would rather have had a goalpost to myself, but I felt sure that I was far too small to be of any interest to a group of what seemed to me almost grown men of around fourteen or fifteen. I took off my tracksuit top and together with my transistor radio – brought along so that I could listen to the second-half commentary – improvised a goal on the large space that lay between the football pitch and the arable fields beyond. I started juggling the ball a little bit, which I always did when I started to play in a public place just to show anyone who might be watching that I possessed a little ball control.

I couldn't help but look over at those older lads, though, just because they were having a game, and watching a game that was taking place before my eyes was already something that came

5

naturally to me. If ever I was out walking with my dad at home over the weekend we would end up by unspoken consent at the town football pitch and be drawn into watching the abysmal locals fall victim to some superior side in the county League. I thought about just sitting down somewhere inobtrusive and listening to the radio while watching the lads flail about in their flares, their long hair and their laughter being somehow more inviting than my pathetic-looking goal. Then I noted that their game had stopped and that they were all looking over in my direction.

My first instinct was to pick up my ball and radio and run back to Uncle Tam's. But as they were closer to the gate than I was I knew I had no chance, besides the fact that there were well over a dozen of them, and all doubtless faster runners than I was, even allowing for the hindrance caused by the prevailing fashions flapping around their calves. Another thing was that they did not altogether look like they were pointing at me in an aggressive fashion, as if they were all going to charge over, pin me to the ground and demand money (I had three pence, which I was hoping to dispense at the sweet counter of the village shop provided the coast was clear). Could it be, I wondered, that they were quite impressed with my juggling skills, and perhaps one of them had a dad who was chief scout at Ibrox, or even the Hibs would do at this stage of my career . . .

The lads on the village field were no more interested in my juggling skills than they were in my future career. It was something more material which had caught their eye. My ball, a proper ball, still an old-style lace-up brown leather sphere which I was directed to smear in dubbin by my father whenever I had played in the wet. My watchers, in contrast, were struggling to control a flighty plastic balloon more at the mercy of the whistling air than the gifts of their feet. They wanted my ball, but they didn't want me, and this was obviously the issue at debate as they contemplated how to get my possession on to their pitch without actually having to tolerate my presence on the field of play.

A delegation of two began to walk in my direction. I tried to pretend I was not looking at them, but my attempts to nonchalantly continue juggling ended with such a pathetic lack of control that the ball squirted off my foot and directly into the path of the oncoming negotiators. There would have been nothing to stop them picking it up, turning around and starting to play with it. But one of them picked it up, lent it a probationary squeeze, and began to competently juggle it himself as they continued their way towards me.

'Ye want to come and play wi' us?' asked one of the lads, a tall, pallid youth with yellow hair and prodigious acne. They made no reference to the ball, but it was hardly necessary. I shrugged, which they took as a yes, and by the time I had picked up my tracksuit top and my radio they were almost back at the field, having kicked my football ahead of them. When I walked over to the pitch the game was back in full swing and they ignored me for the next couple of minutes. These lads were big, though, and I wasn't quite sure where I was going to fit in, so I was not unduly bothered other than feeling a little miffed that no one was making even a token attempt to include me in the proceedings.

Then when the ball had been blasted far out of play one of the lads pointed over at me and shouted: 'Jim, what aboot the wean?' Jim, a boxy youth who seemed to barge his way through tackles without ever looking like losing the ball, glanced over at me doubtfully. 'Can ye play in goal?' he shouted.

Again I shrugged, not wanting to betray my accent if at all possible.

'Billy!' yelled Jim. 'Come oot o' the goal and let yon wean have a game.'

I trotted over to the goalmouth happily vacated by Billy, unsure exactly how defending this vast space against a horde of half-men twice my size could qualify as 'having a game'. Plus, I wished they'd stop calling me a wean.

'Whit's yer name?' asked a lad playing in defence in front of me with curly hair and an open face. I liked the way he asked me in a friendly manner.

'Alex,' I croaked, attempting to feign a tint of Celtic tongue to my pronunciation.

'Hi, Alex, I'm Doug,' he smiled. 'Just do yer best, eh?'

I nodded, feeling a little sorry for myself and wondering what they would do if I picked up my ball (if I ever managed to get my hands on it) and walked away from the pitch. I was scared too of letting Doug down. He was nice, and I was afraid that if I let in a few soft ones he might turn against me. But as it turned out Doug was pretty good, and with the one-man superiority our side now enjoyed, we dominated the game so much that for ten minutes or so the ball never came near me. Then the other side managed a couple of attacks but their shots went feebly wide and I ran off eagerly to retrieve my ball, glad to at least show that I could do *something* (that is, run).

All the while in my head I was playing a game. My life at that time was in fact a series of mental football games. Even when I had been sitting in the back of the car that morning on our way up the A 74 I had nominated two separate makes of car to count as goals for one side or another. And whenever I was playing in the garden with a friend at home I was, in my head, always a goalkeeper making his debut for a Scottish Second Division side like Alloa Athletic, about to embark on a major career by keeping blank sheets in the nether-leagues. But flinging myself around in a boy's goalpost against the enfeebled shots of my contemporaries was a different proposition to facing boys who could blast it with the toe-end of their platform shoes towards a full-size net. Therefore in today's game I was still playing for Alloa Athletic, but away in the Cup against Celtic. That way no one would need to see a major defeat as a possible setback in my career.

I had nothing to do, but was beginning to enjoy prowling around my goalmouth, ignoring the taunts of the massed Glaswegian support behind me, which was becoming increasingly frustrated at the home side's inability to break down the minnows' stubborn defence (as I phrased it all in my head through the mouth of Archie McPherson). Doug there could go on to greater things, I thought, he'll soon be on his way to Parkhead after a performance like this. Then all of a sudden my thoughts were broken off as Celtic had a break on and there were these pairs of flares flying towards my goal at high throttle. The ball was played out left, there was a quick cross, and there was Jimmy Johnstone standing free on the penalty spot. As he swung his left leg to connect with the ball I felt relaxed, because no one could expect me to stop the ball in this situation. I even heard one of my own players saying 'No' in a resigned kind of way, as if someone had asked him: 'Do ye think the wean'll get a hand on this?' A goal here wouldn't matter much.

Johnstone fair caught the leather and it was already going well to my right when I flung myself at it, thinking, This is really going to hurt, and turned it round the post for a corner. I was right, my hand stung like hell, but that pain was a gleeful, singing sting of heroism supplemented by the shouts of surprise and delight from my team-mates, who all came up to me one by one and ruffled my hair.

'Whooooah, whit a goalie!' yelled someone.

'Fuckin' amazin', wee man!' said Billy.

Just one save and I'd graduated from a wean to a wee man! Even the Celtic fans behind the goal had reacted with a small wave of begrudging applause. No doubt Doug and I would be off up to Glasgow together, maybe we'd share digs and break into the national side at the same time . . .

From the corner someone headed the ball straight into my arms and I clutched my beautiful ball – my best friend which I promised to dub every Saturday morning from now on whatever the conditions outside – close to my chest before giving it a massive welly downfield to show that I could kick the thing as well. A few minutes later the game was declared over and everyone gathered in the centre-circle for a cigarette. I thought I should leave now, but Jim was using my ball as a pillow, so I could hardly kick it out from under him.

As I approached them Doug turned around and said: 'Hey, whit

aboot a round of applause for the wee man Alex here, whit a save!'
And everyone cheered in a fashion I later came to know as
'ironically' and put their hands together for a second or two. I
blushed deeply and sat at the edge of the circle.

'Do ye play in goal for yer school, Alex?' Billy asked. This was it,
I would have to speak now.

'No, I play centre-forward,' I said, and for some reason everyone laughed, but I was still afuzz with pride so didn't much care.

'Ye frae fuckin' England?' said Jim.

I contemplated saying 'Aye', but thought it didn't matter any
more since my save. 'Yes,' I said.

'Who do ye support?'

'Rangers.' More laughter. Would they care if I told them that I
was allowed to support Rangers because my mum and dad were
Scottish? I thought not.

'Aye, sure, but who do ye support at home, like?'

'Lincoln City.'

'Who the fuck is that?' spluttered someone and they all laughed
again, but they were just joshing around, it wasn't malicious.

'He's the man wi' everything,' said Billy. 'Look, he's got a radio
too, can we hear the fitba'?'

I turned on the radio, feeling important. It was tuned to 1500m
long wave, which was where the football commentary always
was. It was Man United versus Man City.

'Can ye no get Rangers–Celtic?'

'Er, I don't think so,' I said.

'Don't tell me,' said Jim. 'It's an English radio,' and again
everyone was in hysterics.

After that the novelty of wee Alex and his ball and his radio
wore off and they started talking on that switch-off level like my
dad and Uncle Tam; something about girls and a disco that night,
and I think there was even a reference to one of Uncle Tam's
daughters, Aileen. I got up to leave and Jim gave me my ball back
and a couple of people said, 'Thanks for the game, wee man.' I
walked off the field, soaking up the standing ovation being

granted me by the home crowd after Alloa's historic and unprecedented Cup shock.

I tried not to walk too quickly. I thought I had stayed pretty cool while sitting on the grass with the bigger boys as they smoked cigarettes, all the while managing not to boast about my one-handed diving stop. I didn't want to ruin this now by walking away too fast, thinking that my acceleration would be an obvious sign to them that I was bursting to get home to tell my dad and Uncle Tam all about how I had made a brilliant save against the big boys. My hand was still throbbing with a delightful after-sting, and I wanted to preserve this pain until I got back to the house in the belief that the right palm's redness might stand as testimony to my courage given the lack of eye-witnesses to the actual deed. I scrapped all plans to stop at the village shop, despite phantasising that I might go in there and be greeted by the man behind the counter with: 'Look, Morag, it's the wee man who just made the fantastic save doon at the park.' So I walked back up the hill with my head high and my ball under my arm and the radio held to my left ear thinking that when I got back to my school I would challenge Ed Weggle for the goalkeeper's spot in the school team. I was stoked with pride, and imagined the gasps of awe from the whole family, including Aileen and Alison, as I held audience upon my triumphant return. They would take a good look at me, drinking in the significance of the moment – the moment when everyone realised that they were in the presence of a future star.

I walked into Uncle Tam's house by the back door and pulled off my training shoes. I put the radio down next to the ball and braced myself for my big entrance into the living room. I walked into the hallway, wiping my hands on my tracksuit trousers, all of a sudden a little nervous. I could hear the buzz of conversation coming through the slightly ajar living-room door, and it seemed to be louder than was usual for a gathering of four adults, even allowing for the whisky. When I tentatively pushed the door inwards I was first greeted by a fug of wasted tobacco that made me gag and a crowd of indecipherable human beings whose faces seemed to be way up high in a blanket of cigar smoke. I had no idea who they were, perhaps neighbours or distant relatives or old schoolfriends of my dad's and Uncle Tam's who'd come round while I was out. They'd all certainly been punishing the malt while I was down at the park performing acrobatics to bring Alloa Athletic into the next round of the Scottish Cup.

I found my dad and Uncle Tam over on the far side of the room by the window with another man, all jocose and uninhibited like grown-ups only ever get at weekends and on holiday. I realised that I would not be able to tell my story, first because there would be no way of getting their attention, and second because I had no way to articulate the happening in a way that could make it interesting enough for them to think I had really achieved something of note. How could I describe the power of the shot? How best to describe the collective adulation of the older boys without seeming like a braggart, something from which I had always been strictly discouraged by my dad? How could I convey the length to which I had stretched myself, the lateness and the drama of the sprawling, wholly unexpected, single-limbed rescue?

I leaned against my dad's leg to make my presence known. Uncle Tam was in the middle of a story, and at the end of it they all roared. When the laughter had waned Uncle Tam pointed at me and said to the third man, a colossus with a terrifying red beard, 'This wee man's going to play for the 'Gers, he says.'

'Whit position, son?' said the red beard.

'Goalkeeper,' I said, and my dad said: 'Ach, rubbish, he's a striker.' For a second they all looked at me and that was my chance, but I had no clue where to start and I missed the moment. 'I'll get ye a refill, Lawrie? Ye wantin' a glass o' lemonade, Alex?'

I nodded, and reached for some crisps with my magic hand. Over in the corner wee Corrie was playing with dolls. She looked up and said: 'Ye wantin' to play wi' me, Alex?'

The Man in the Mascot

THE GIRL WITH neck-length strawberry-blonde hair and irides-cent eyes (the result, I later found out, of turquoise contact lenses) seemed to be under the impression that I was a professional footballer. What's more, she was impressed enough by this fact to have allowed her knee to settle comfortably against mine as we sat at the bar drinking beer after beer. Having come this far, I was not about to risk losing this contact by telling her the truth. After all, I had not even lied to her to start with.

'So what do you do?' she had asked unoriginally. She smiled when she asked, which was good, and she was pretty and open and was granting me some attention, so for me that was enough, not having slept with a woman for two and a half years. Normally, I would tell the truth at this point, slowly and semi-sardonically pronouncing the words in such a way to show the listener in advance that there was little they'd be able to offer by way of intelligent response. I let them off the hook, in short, spared them the indignity of having to falsely sound a note of being impressed or feign an expression that was attempting to contort itself into a shape that conveyed an 'oooh' of interest. I'm a loser, don't worry about it, now let's talk about something else if you can spare the time.

'Every Saturday I take the pitch with East Park Academy,' I said and waited for the reaction. For her to say, 'Come on, anyone can see you're too old to be a footballer.' Or to question my syntax and say: 'Take the pitch? What's that supposed to mean?' Or to comment that she does not recall my photograph in the newspapers, or to ask me my name and see if she can place it. Because anyone interested in football will know most of the names of the East Park Academy squad. What luck for me, though, because the girl did not seem to know anything about football, although she'd heard of Jean-Pierre Quentin, because he's got an exotic name and he's always either scoring goals or falling over drunk in the nightclubs of East Park, and barely a day goes by without his Gallic fizzog appearing on the front page of *The East Park Evening News*. When she mentioned his name I became, for the first time in my life, inexplicably jealous of a professional footballer and the reputation he enjoyed. 'Jean-Pierre's an arsehole, take it from me,' I told the girl with some authority. 'None of the other lads can stomach his arrogance.'

She giggled and said, 'But he's got a lovely French backside.'

'There's a rumour in the club that he prefers young boys,' I said, originating the rumour right at that second. Being 'in the club' myself I supposed that once again I was not actually telling a lie.

The girl pulled a face and said, 'That's disgusting,' and I felt a stupid sense of accomplishment at having turned her against him with the aid of just one slanderous and completely unfounded sentence. Although, looking back at it now, I wonder for the first time if she was being sarcastic.

What I did not tell the girl, named Sabina, was that I was Topsy the Toucan. That was my only job. It had been my only job for three years then, although at one point I was Rex the Rottweiler. That was when I first started, but Rex was withdrawn for 'conveying the wrong image of the club'. He was originally supposed to prove what a hard-tackling, fighting, biting, fearless team East Park Academy was, but the selection of footballers at that time was so toothless that the mascot turned into a mockery as we avoided relegation by the slimmest of points for two consecutive seasons. So Topsy was invented, a happy-go-lucky, smiling, pecking, tomfool of a bird, with no connection to either the tradition of the club or the town, but no one in marketing ever worried about trivial details like that. Topsy was a strategy to win back young fans and convey no longer that wrong impression, but the right one, presumably. I was the vehicle of that strategy, and I cavorted around the pitch's edge being prodded, poked and verbally abused while wearing a big plastic smile (thank God it really was plastic, I couldn't keep up a grin like that any more than Jean-Pierre Quentin could go ninety minutes without getting himself in the referee's notebook). I pressed a little button to make a cawing noise, which the marketers and manufacturers believed bore a close resemblance to the noise emitted by the real-life beast. Though I never met the true version of my ornithological alter-ego, so I do not actually know.

I am sure it will amuse you to know that I am a drama-school graduate. I once, like my contemporaries, harboured mist-tinged aspirations the day we came out of some grand ceremony clutching a crisp parchment which testified to little more than the fact that we had spent three years poncing about in costumes, sitting cross-legged on wooden floors saying 'Ya' a lot, and affecting to have nervous breakdowns because we thought that lent us an air of professionalism. As soon as we had let the parents have their photos, then slipped out of the fusty black robes, our manner towards each other became even more superficial than it had been for the duration of our studies. Must keep in touch, here's my parents' address, see you on Broadway, ha, ha (though the next three times I met people from the course were all at the dole office, and they all pretended not to have seen me). Now, graduated, we all knew that we were no longer friends, but competitors, in fact we had been competitors all along, so we all stopped keeping in touch with each other unless we thought someone could get us a part or a mention in the right circles. That doesn't work either, of course. I know, I've tried it, gritting my teeth and placing those phone-calls, hearing the distant tone of reluctance in the voices of those who managed a vague stab at success.

Before I became Topsy the Toucan the most successful thing I achieved was to appear in an advert for dog food. As dog food ads go it was quite revolutionary – I was the owner of a dog who crapped on somebody's lawn. The owner of the house came running out enraged, only to sniff the offending dollop and decide that it did not smell that bad at all (the turd was not shown on camera). He asked me, 'Hey, what do you feed your dog on?', and I, who had just been shopping for nothing but one tin of dog food, took out of my bag a can of Waggit and held it up to the camera, and then the owner's dog came bounding out of his house and tried to take it out of my hand, or something like that. Anyway, the ad got culled because the highest executive forces at Waggit decided that they did not want their product too closely associated with turd, even nice-smelling turd, and so I never appeared on television, although I did get handsomely paid for my trouble. The rest of the time I have struggled, or exited the struggle, by not doing anything at all but enjoying the freedom of inactivity until it turned to lethargy, but even lethargy was more attractive to me than the thought of finding real work.

It's funny how you can get to thirty-three and realise that you've done nothing with your life except lose your youth. It's gone now, make no mistake, and I cannot honestly say what I have done with it. Had a few girlfriends, but none I care enough to talk about any more. Haven't been anywhere, because I never had any money, though sometimes Topsy was allowed on away trips to set up a friendly rivalry with Benny the Bantam or Gordy 'Gator or some other alliterated, man-sized, bestial fabrication. I've watched a lot of television, I've drunk a lot of beer, fallen over at a few parties too, and accumulated a store of mildly amusing anecdotes relating to those times. I've got a flat with a lot of junk in and several piles of second-hand books, because I like going to jumble sales. I have two parents who tolerate me, but who since my thirtieth birthday have refused me any more handouts. They gave me a big parcel, which was unusual because I was accustomed to getting an envelope containing the usual cheque for a few hundred quid. Intrigued, I opened it up and found a pile of Jobs sections from selected newspapers. 'Unemployment's gone under five per cent, there's never been a better time,' said my dad curtly. 'Slice of cake, anybody?'

Now, when I was home and some old family friend was around, I extracted a great deal of pleasure from my job, about the only time I got a kick out of telling people what I did.

'What are you involved with now, Jacob?' Rodney or Hattie or Geoffrey would ask (not daring to ask anything as direct as, 'Where are you working now?'), and already I could feel my dad squirm.

'I'm still in the arts and entertainment field,' I would say affectedly.

They nodded, not sure whether that meant I was still unemployed, and were perhaps afraid to ask further. Sometimes they did, but even if they didn't I volunteered the information anyway: 'Yes, I'm Topsy the Toucan.'

'Oh,' said Rodney or Hattie or Geoffrey. Then, after a pause, they'd add, 'Pantomime at this time of year?'

'No, *silly*,' I'd answer, piling on a wedge of camp. 'Topsy's the mascot at East Park Academy, perennial mid-to-low-tablers of the English Nationwide Division Two. Fancy, Dad, they've never heard of Topsy the Toucan.'

And my father couldn't say a bloody thing, because I got the job from an advert out of one of the newspaper sections he so thoughtfully presented me with on my thirtieth birthday.

SO I SLEPT with Sabina on what I presumed was the strength of my profession. It was very, very good for me. Simply because she was a gorgeous girl, and I don't say that because I am recalling her exquisite contours or the combined odour of her perfume and her sex which filled my bedroom with an air that it probably did not deserve. She was so easy to be with, she didn't make any demands on me, telling me to show up here or there, to pick her up and take her somewhere, didn't want to know where I'd been the four nights of the week I didn't see her, she didn't pressure me into getting a better paid job . . .

Because she thought I was a professional footballer. It was odd that she did not want to know where my flash car was, or why I didn't have to go to training on the mornings where we would lie there during those first few weeks unhurriedly exploring the parameters of our sexual hunger. My previous experience of women was that once you had slept with them a handful of times (and I admit that I am only talking about a handful of women here), then they began to impose themselves on your timetable, and that any spare minutes not spent in their company had to be fully accounted for. This was a problem a lot of the time because, having no job, there were usually a lot of spare minutes to be accounted for, and most of the time I couldn't remember what I had done with them. 'What do you *do* all day?' one girl called Philippa screamed at me in exasperation when she found the dishes from the previous night's takeaway and that morning's breakfast still lying in my sink where she had put them on her way to work. *My* sink, let me emphasise, not hers, but it was enough to spark a crisis which wound up the relationship some hours later, shortly after midnight, because she could not be swayed from the idea that because I had not been washing those dishes then I must have been pumping my buttocks up and down all day atop a series of women whose identities remained a mystery to both of us.

The more I started to like Sabina, despite the feeling that she was mentally a little slow, the more I started to feel bad about lying to her. Then I thought, if I wasn't lying to her then I would not be together with her in the first place and besides, I wasn't really lying to her, I had still never actually told her I was a professional footballer. I was concealing the truth from her, that was all, but she had not come and asked me straight out what position I played in or what my career statistics were. In fact she barely mentioned the club and my job at all.

Instead we talked about lots of other things, and I found myself gradually revealing parts of my life, saying things about drama school, my parents and my youth which I think would have caused anyone else to make a few connections and observe, 'That's unusual, a professional footballer going to drama school. How did that work out?' No, the sole reference she made to the club was to occasionally ask, 'So how's my friend Jean-Pierre Quentin?' And I would just shrug and say, 'Still as big a prat as ever,' and then I'd be waiting for her to ask me more, because I had stored in my head a whole bootroom of anecdotes to tell her about the life and people of East Park Academy FC. But she just kind of tittered and moved the talk on to something else; mundane stories about her work as a dental assistant, which were fine because they were keeping the topic away from football and the possible unmasking I feared would end our relationship.

What Sabina did on Saturday afternoons I never asked, in the same way that she was gratifyingly unobtrusive as to what I did in my own spare time when she was at work. If we met on Saturday nights then she would ask me how the team had got on and I would tell her the score. If we'd been playing away and Topsy had not been required to make the trip, then I would stay at home and listen to the match on local radio so that I should have all the details in the evening should she suddenly choose to ask me for a more detailed rundown of the ninety minutes.

But she never did, she would just stroke the underside of my chin and say, 'Oh you look tired, poor thing. No wonder, running about that pitch all afternoon.'

I would shrug and say, 'It was a tough afternoon,' and more often than not, stuck inside Topsy the Toucan, it really had been a tough afternoon.

Topsy's job was to walk around the side of the pitch before the game and try to incite the crowd. I often wondered which promotional genius had determined that a trussed-up, failed drama graduate would be capable of causing several thousand people to start getting excited about a football match by jumping up and down, flapping his wings and pressing a button which made a distorted cackling noise. But that is what I did, week after week, and no one ever told me to do it differently on the grounds that all I managed to incite were proddings, sarcastic comments, profanities and a large number of half-eaten burgers bouncing off my frame, whose myriad ketchup stains prompted Shirley in the club laundry room to berate me for trying to eat fast food through a three-foot long plastic beak. Once they gave me a huge basket of boiled sweets to throw into the crowd, to 'encourage our younger fans'. It certainly encouraged them, but only to throw every single one back at me as hard as their little chucking arms could manage, and for twenty minutes I was subject to a hailstorm of confectionery that cracked against Topsy's artificial case. Topsy maintained his smile throughout, while on the inside I supped lager through a straw from the can I had placed within a small container I had fixed to the inside of my costume.

Here are some of the intellectual exchanges that Topsy enjoyed on a Saturday afternoon:

'Hey, Topsy, I hear Mrs Topsy's at home shagging the milkman this afternoon!'

(Topsy cackled.)

'Hey, Topsy, can you use that beak to give me a blowjob?'

(Topsy flapped wings.)

'Fuck off, Topsy, you fucking cunt.'

(Topsy waved happily to the crowd.)

'Hey, Topsy, how come we never fucking win – I thought you were supposed to bring us good luck, you useless cunt.'

(Topsy jumped up and down nonsensically to the tune of the club song, which crackled through the tannoy somewhat awkwardly: 'We are the Academy/The best team in the land/We are the Academy/Now give us a big hand.' No one applauded.)

'When did you last get a shag, Topsy?'

(Topsy took drink of lager, wondering how the hell they knew that it'd been over two years since he'd last slept with a woman.)

All the while I could see the faces of the people who were shouting these things at me. Some of them I knew already, classmates from my schooldays turned into grown morons, standing there with their sons calling a fake tropical bird the most slanderous of names. Some I got to know because they seemed to make an effort to come down to the front of the terrace or the stand every week to yell the same thing, either because they seemed genuinely angry at Topsy's presence, or because they believed their comments to be so witty that repetition was permissible. I muttered inside the costume: 'Ah, here he is, balding Mr Blowjob with the tight–fitting replica shirt and his fistful of burger,' and sure enough, seconds later he would ask me about the beak and the blowjob and then turn around to soak the approval of some invisible companions further back up the incline. Perhaps it was a bet, and he'd raise money for charity if he said it every Saturday for a lifetime. Also, there were kids still too young to curse (those under four years of age), but who instead were terrified by Topsy's cackle, so that whenever an eager mother carried them down to the front to see the entertainment they reached out tentatively to touch my beak, I pressed the cackle button, and they flinched back before bursting into tears. This was the most pleasing part of my afternoon.

These fans weren't all stupid, they knew when the club was trying it on, and they refused to be coaxed into a forced jollity, to be told by some prancing puppet when they were supposed to get excited. Why should they start getting worked up before the players are even on the pitch? Was the mascot's tomfoolery not a tacit admission by the club that the players themselves were incapable of pushing the crowd into the realm of emotion? Who ever imagined that the way to create an atmosphere in a stadium filled with 7000 British people was to let loose some jaded, lifeless loser in an over-beaked suit of multi-coloured, ketchup-spattered feathers?

These were all questions I had in store for the club's executives the day they decreed it was time for me to hang up my beak, but in the meantime I didn't want to lose my job as long as it was bringing me in a fair whack of cash in hand on top of my social security benefits (the money was always rolled up and placed inside the container where I put my can of lager). And there was something perversely attractive for a failed actor about this weekly humiliation gig. Of course the fact that they could not see my face made the abuse somewhat easier to bear, but there was a feeling that, somehow, I had at least reached the stage where I was performing, albeit in front of a crowd characterised by hostility or indifference. I wondered, nonetheless, how many of my drama student 'friends' had stood on a live stage and danced before such numbers. Especially while secretly drinking extra strength lager.

After I had pratted my way around the edge of the pitch it was my brief to stand in front of the players' tunnel and look highly animated as they jogged out on to the pitch, flapping my wings in delight as the latest eleven men whose job it was to haul East Park out of its mid-table slough ignored my repeated cacklings of encouragement in the same way that they blanked me before the game if they ever spotted me down in the tunnel area putting on my beaky head. These men were at least sufficiently focused on the task ahead to refrain from making witty jibes at my expense, although a substitute, perhaps bitter at being left out of the starting line-up, once whispered to me before they played a very hard but gifted Preston side: 'Give 'em lots of luck, Topsy, mate, they're gonna need it.' East Park lost 6–1.

A FEW MONTHS after we started seeing each other, Sabina decided that she wanted to come and watch me one Saturday as she had 'nothing on' that coming weekend.

'Oh, come on, you'll be bored as hell, sitting all alone up there in the cold stands,' I said. 'Besides, you're not interested in football at all, are you?'

She shrugged, and the subject dropped.

The next evening I rang her and told her I had picked up an injury in training and that I wouldn't be playing Saturday.

'Oh, I hope it's nothing serious,' she said, sounding genuinely sympathetic.

Shit, I thought, now I really have lied to her. 'No, just a bit of a hamstring,' I replied, hoping that would be enough to prevent further questioning.

'Ah well, maybe I'll come next time,' she said in a ponderous way which made me think that I wouldn't be hearing any more on the subject.

I began to think that if I wanted to hold on to Sabina I would have to give up my job as Topsy the Toucan and tell her that my football career had been brought to a premature end by a . . . by a . . . what? What sort of injury could sideline a footballer for life, but remain invisible to a woman he was sleeping with? Perhaps I could claim to be the first footballer to retire on the grounds of a pulled conscience, torn feelings and a ruptured soul.

ON CERTAIN DAYS, if I was in the right mood, I could actually get quite a kick out of being Topsy. That mood was usually induced by tanking up in the pub beforehand, where I sat watching *Football Focus* and downing neat vodkas to minimise the smell on my breath and reduce the need to have to go for a pee while I was trapped inside Topsy's shell. I saw the crowd differently then because I did not care about their pasty, fat-rimmed faces, their hateful jeers and their mindless, repetitious jibes. I started talking to Topsy inside. On vodka days we became good mates, and I said to him: 'Hey, Topsy, look at this fat knacker, what's the betting we can get him to call you a fucking cunt,' and Topsy sniggered and stood in front of the guy and tried to stroke him on the chin with one of his feathered arms and then he cackled and, sure enough, the man – embarrassed as his mates laughed at the attention he was receiving – jumped backwards and shouted, 'Fuck off, Topsy, you fucking cunt,' struggling to recapture his dignity while his mates yelled, 'That's the only bird he'll get a come-on from this weekend.' Ha, ha, caw, caw.

On vodka days I did not mind the gangs of hyper-grinning, poorly anoraked pre-teen boys who pulled and poked at Topsy's feathers, who pelted him with loose stones from the crumbling terrace and who practised their swearing on a figure they knew could not respond by admonishing them physically or verbally. Topsy playfully chased the boys along the terracing, cawing away, and for once the crowd even laughed a bit. Topsy always managed to corner one of the boys too, usually round the back somewhere in the toilets or behind the burger hut, and the bird's sadistic side was discreetly and briefly put on show as he belted the boy once, but firmly, around the ears with what was actually quite a heavy plastic beak. The boy was momentarily stunned, then cried and Topsy flitted from the scene, ready to claim in case of parental complaint that this was an unfortunate accident. Topsy and I laughed like hell as we ran away thinking that this job could be good fun if you were prepared to put a bit of effort into it.

When the game started on vodka days Topsy and I loved to linger around the edge of the pitch, instead of getting our arses down the tunnel and taking a breather like we were supposed to until half-time. As we strolled back around the perimeter, Topsy cawed and pushed his wings up in a motion intended to tell the spectators that they should start getting behind their team. I chose my vodka days when East Park Academy was up against a tough opponent, when I was pretty sure that they were going to lose. That way you had more fun watching the angry or disillusioned faces attempting to ignore Topsy as he cavorted away, blissfully forgetting that East Park were already 2–0 down after twenty minutes and that they were barely getting a touch of the ball. 'Get out the fucking way, you stupid fucker,' they shouted. 'We can't see.' Topsy was just a bird and didn't understand human language so cawed loudly and waved his wings, before eventually beetling up the tunnel to get another can of beer.

Once he got a cheap laugh by standing behind the linesman and making obscene gestures, but someone complained and I was told to leave the match officials well alone and that, indeed, I was no longer supposed to be visible once the game got under way.

Once, after East Park had lost 0–4, Topsy stood behind the manager, a dour Welshman called Cliff Ulwyn, who got the sack shortly afterwards, jumping up and down in glee as he explained to the television cameras why his charges had played even more miserably than the expression on his face. In many ways this was perhaps Topsy's finest moment – I watched it in a pub that night on *Sky Sports News* and it raised a decent laugh, unless they were all amused by Cliff Ulwyn's assertion that he was going to 'turn things around very soon'.

Once I was so drunk I vomited down the inside of Topsy and had to explain to Shirley in the club laundry room that I had eaten something bad for lunch.

'Is that right?' she said with more than a hint of scepticism.

Topsy, it was just me and you pal, against the bloody, bastarding world.

'FOR SOMEBODY WHO earns so much money you're a bit of a skinflint,' Sabina said as I handed her the restaurant bill, the coins from my share slipping off the five-pound note and scattering themselves across the table of the cheapest curry house in town. 'Not only do you take me to grotty places, but I always have to pay half.'

'I thought we'd discussed this,' I replied, retrieving a five-pence piece from under a half-eaten popadom. 'I am a feminist and believe that women should be allowed equality in all things. And just because I'm a footballer does not automatically mean that I should frequent posh joints, does it? You think just because I have the money I should spend it for the sake of it? I go to these places with the players on other nights of the week, I want to be somewhere with you where I'm not going to run into the others.'

'More like you're ashamed of me and you don't want them to see what a thick girlfriend you've got,' she said, half-joking, but looking down into her purse instead of into my eye.

'Come on, what are you talking about?' I said, getting worried at the turn the conversation was taking. It wasn't like her to make maudlin comments, although it did not surprise me she was finally noticing that, for somebody in the highest-earning category (if all we read about footballers' wages is true), I was an incredible cheapskate. 'It's what I like about you, Sabina. You don't treat me any different just because I'm a footballer. You don't expect things from me, you're not impressed by superficial things like wages and fast cars and fancy restaurants.'

'You don't even have a car, let alone a fast one,' she said grumpily.

'I explained that before, a lot of the players don't – it's part of a club campaign to improve relations with the local community by cycling to the stadium and showing we care about pollution and the environment.' The lies were becoming even more crass. 'And another thing, it's not true that footballers earn so much. It's only people like Jean-Pierre bloody Quentin who cash in big. The rest of us get peanuts to supplement the presence of a big foreign star in the side.'

'So how much do you get, if you don't mind me asking?' she asked, a little humbled, or so I thought.

'Ah, you know.' I hesitated. 'About a hundred and fifty pounds a week.' Actually, that seemed quite a lot to me at the time, but I was looking to lower her expectations of me taking her to a fancy restaurant. 'Plus use of a bicycle for free.'

Sabina started laughing, spontaneously, but only for a brief second, then she stopped herself and took my hand. 'Oh, you poor thing, that's less than I earn. OK, I'm sorry I mentioned it.' She handed me the fiver back. 'Here, let me get this one tonight, you must be needing this.'

As it happened she was right, I really did need that fiver, and I really did take it back off her, though I went very red as I took it and rushed off to the toilet to hide my shame.

When we left the restaurant she asked me: 'By the way, how's your injury coming along? I kept forgetting to ask. It must seem sometimes like I'm not at all interested in what you do.'

'Ah you know, the physio said it'll be a few weeks, it's taking longer than he thought.'

'That's a shame, I really wanted to come and watch you before the season finished,' she said, almost wistfully. We walked along for a while in silence, heading back towards her flat.

'Sabina,' I said, as we approached her front door. 'There's something I think I need to tell you.'

She looked up at me and said, 'Wait!' Then she kissed me long and hard and the smells on her neck rendered me verbally impotent and we went through her door and straight at it on the floor of her hallway.

YOU'VE PROBABLY GUESSED by now that Sabina knew all along I was a fraud. She was playing up too, acting out the ditsy role, intrigued from the start that somebody who looked so obviously old and unfit as myself would pretend to be a professional footballer. Then she was fascinated further by the fact that I attempted to spin the lie out into a relationship over the course of several months.

'In a way I was flattered that you were prepared to go to such lengths to keep me interested, despite the fact that I was pretty brainless,' she said as we sat on a park bench one spring day. She had arranged to meet me here in her lunch-hour to finish it off because, she said, she did not want to see my dignity sink any lower through the execution of lies which were becoming ever more ludicrous.

'I did not think you were brainless,' I said, still lying a little bit. 'I liked you like that, you weren't too intrusive. I liked being with you, Sabina. I still do.'

She laughed again. In fact she was finding the whole thing too bloody funny for my liking. The keen rubescence of her lipstick added a superior, mocking quality to her face, and it was only then it occurred to me that dental assistants did not usually wear lipstick to work, nor suits with shoulder pads and platform-heeled shoes.

'You're not a dental assistant,' I said dumbly.

'God no,' she said, still laughing. 'If you'd ever asked me anything about my job then you might have found that out, but even when I made up stories about my co-workers and the patients you never seemed to respond much. I'm what they call a *marketing executive*. With Howard & Oberflach.' She looked at me questioningly, smiling as if that should mean something to me.

'Never heard of them,' I mumbled. Why should I care now who the hell she worked for? At least the way she had said *marketing executive* was making it easier for me to walk away from her without any regrets.

'We do the marketing for East Park Academy FC, Jacob. Your club, remember? We design your shirts, get you sponsorship, promote your image within the local community, something which, by the way, does not involve players using bicycles to promote saving the environment, though the idea got a good laugh at a meeting the other day.'

'Oh, right,' was all I could say.

She leaned across my body, close to me, and for one second I thought she was going to kiss me, and I think that at least half of me, probably more, would have gone for it. But then she looked me right in the eye and said, 'Other things we do include pro-motions and pre-match entertainment. For example, Topsy the Toucan. Did you know that was my idea? I come to every home match just to see my creation warm the crowd up before the big game!'

I got up and began to walk away, leaving Sabina on the bench in a state of hysteria. But then she came running after me, though I never wanted to see her again.

'Oh come on, Jacob, laugh a little. It was the bandy legs sticking out the bottom of the costume gave you away!'

'Fuck off, Sabina, leave me alone,' I said, walking faster.

'Don't go too fast, you might aggravate the hamstring, Jacob, and Topsy's got a big game Saturday – relegation dogfight against Cardiff City. Aren't you surprised a dumb girlie knows that, Jacob?'

'Fuck off.'

'Oh come on, don't be so bloody stiff, Jacob. The truth is that I really do like you too. When you're not lying.'

She had finally stopped laughing. I stopped on the pathway. We looked at each other long and serious, as if we were both weighing up how a relationship that had been an utter sham for its first six months could possibly go on. Then I said, 'I could never forgive you for inventing Topsy the fucking Toucan. Plus, I don't like your new hairstyle and the fact that you wear shoulder pads.' And then I walked away, feeling better if not good.

'I slept with Jean-Pierre Quentin!' she yelled as I reached the park gates. 'It's not true that he likes little boys.'

THAT SATURDAY TOPSY the Toucan was removed by police officers from the premises of East Park Academy FC for gross drunkenness, using foul language in the presence of minors, attempting to incite violence among opposing fans and simulating defecation in the goalmouth. Without their good-luck toucan East Park lost 3–1 to Cardiff City and were relegated to Nationwide League Division Three, where a series of stringent financial cutbacks necessitated the abolition of a club mascot.

The Right Result

WHEN OUR CHAIRMAN, John Bickell, opened the briefcase stuffed with brown envelopes, the usual pre-match banter stopped within a second. It wasn't that we had been stunned into silence, because I don't think that any of the lads were really that surprised. In fact, I think some of us had been half expecting Derek Wapping to try something like this. It was crude, but then what other way was there to go about it? It wasn't like any of us had offshore bank accounts.

No, it was a contemplative quiet which fell over us and put a stop to the customary Saturday rituals, the murmur of Terry Gulliver's prayers, the hiss of heavy metal seeping from the headphones of Sandy Tring's Walkman, the slap slap slap of Bobby Deller's embrocation (rubbing it in, like the rest of us, he considered bad luck), Gary Garforth's compressed heavy breathing exercises he'd learnt by taking diving classes, and my own superstition, slowly humming the Polish national anthem, which I'd picked up on a pre-season tour to Warsaw a couple of years back, when I'd scored seven times in three games, and which I now considered my talismanic threnody.

We were all contemplating one thing. The money. Or, rather, how much. The envelopes looked pretty fat, but then there was no way of knowing what denomination the notes were. They could be filled with blank paper for all we knew. With Wapping you never could tell, he was a crook. That was why he had so much money to throw around. That was why he had bought our opponents today, debt-ridden, Third Division mediocrities

Hansford Town, a team he declared would be gracing the fields of the Premiership 'within five years'. And that was why he was buying us too, another bunch of debt-ridden Third Division mediocrities, but he was only buying us for the day.

'Just a little end of season bonus, lads,' said John Bickell, a little nervously. 'Pick it up after the match, as long as we get, er, the right result today.'

We all knew how we were supposed to interpret his words and that there was no way the club could afford to pay us a bonus of any dimension, let alone a briefcase full. Besides, we had done nothing to deserve it, we'd been terrible for the past three months, and not much better before. Today was the last game of the season and we were in seventeenth position. For us today's result was meaningless, which was why Derek Wapping didn't think we'd mind throwing it away. After all, we'd already thrown away enough games in the past nine months, even without the incentive of a brown envelope stuffed with used twenty-pound notes.

It was simple. Hansford Town needed to beat us 3–0 today to gain automatic promotion to Division Two and achieve their first goal on the way to their new owner's Premiership vision. He had already spent so much cash on his club that a bribe here and there wasn't going to make much difference to his bank balance. He'd bought big-name players and an even bigger-named manager, and within months the newly assembled team had hauled itself up to the edge of promotion. The only surprising thing was that he had bothered to bribe us at all. The team he had assembled could probably beat us 3–0 with its now heavily sponsored bootlaces tied together.

There was a long, long pause, until finally Kevin Fyffe had the courage to ask: 'How much?'

'Twenty thousand pounds each, including the three substi-tutes,' said John Bickell, apparently relieved that somebody had asked. Gathering confidence, he went on quickly: 'And I feel obliged to tell you that an anonymous benefactor has also agreed to put a large amount of investment into the club which will ensure our survival for at least another season. I'm sure that those of you whose contracts are due to run out at the end of June will appreciate how important such a contribution might be.' And with that he closed the briefcase, picked it up and left the changing room.

Again nobody said a thing for the longest time. There were fifteen minutes until kick-off, and normally by now we would be out on the pitch stretching our muscles before coming back in for one final pep talk. But what was the point of warming up today? Besides, if you wanted to keep the money but maintain a half-clean conscience, a pulled hamstring in the first five minutes would be the perfect way of disclaiming some measure of culpability.

Kevin Fyffe was once more the brutally honest breaker of silence. 'Well, lads, let's just hope for the right result today, eh?' he said, but he couldn't look anyone in the eye; he was leaning down and tying his bootlaces. All the same, his observation curried a general murmur of assent and we all began to complete the strapping of shinpads and the priming of flesh.

Twenty thousand pounds. Just to lose a football game. I mean, who wouldn't? You could see the effect that the chairman's veiled threat had had on most of the players. Some were getting on a bit now, and some were never going to get better than playing in the Third Division. Without tax that was well over a year's wages, that was a good summer holiday before pre-season training started, that was insurance against unemployment, that could finance a period of retraining to do a proper job. And then at the other end of the scale were the teenagers, lads paid a pittance by government training schemes. One of them was playing in the first team for the first time today. There were two more on the bench. Sixteen years old and about to get twenty grand for sitting on a wooden bench for ninety minutes. Provided of course we got 'the right result'.

We trickled out on to the pitch to go through the motions of warming up. There was barely a cheer from our home support, and I soon realised that our ground had been colonised by travelling Hansford Town fans, who were loudly celebrating the names of their new signings as they were read out over the tannoy. Even our announcer, Harry Trewick, a loyal fan for nearly sixty years, sounded like he was behind the visitors. 'At number nine, Frankie Holding!' he almost shouted, heralding the appearance of a man who had been tempted by the Wapping money to drop three divisions at the peak of his career. The away fans responded jubilantly. I began to wish the afternoon over and done with as quickly as possible. Why couldn't we just forfeit the game now and be done with it?

I was trying to touch my toes when I heard Kevin Fyffe whisper in my ear above the noise of the Hansford fans: 'Willie, Willie, where's Tom got to?' I stood up and looked around our half of the pitch. Our captain Tom Hungerford was nowhere to be seen. It was Tom's last game. He was thirty-seven years old and was about to retire after making over 600 appearances for the club. Both teams were supposed to be forming a tunnel of honour for Tommy when he came out last on to the pitch, but with all of our thoughts on brown envelopes we had almost forgotten that this was supposed to be his big farewell. Maybe he was just waiting in the changing room so that he could savour the moment all the more.

'I'll go check he's OK,' I said to Kevin, and ran back down the tunnel to the changing room, although I was beginning to feel uneasy. Tom was our centre-back, and he was being asked to give away three goals in his last ever match. What a way to be remembered.

You don't get pros like Tommy any more. At least that's what all the old codgers in the crowd said. A one-club man, loyal and solid, played out of his shirt every second he was on the pitch. All the fans loved him, even though he'd had an awful season. But he recognised when it was time to pack it in and everyone respected him for that, and so no one really minded that in the last few weeks he'd just got too slow and had given away a lot of goals. It wasn't like it mattered much any more this season.

The changing room was deserted, no sign of Tommy. I was about to close the door again when I thought I heard a noise from the shower, the grate of stud on tile. I clacked across the floor and peered around the corner of the blue-tiled wall separating the showers from the changing room. And there he was, sitting in the corner, his head in his hands.

'Tommy?' I said.

He looked up at me. Poor bugger had been crying. I walked over and sat down next to him, put my arm around his shoulder. 'What's up, Tommy?' I said.

Tommy shook his head. 'I can't do it, Willie, I can't bloody do it.' He sniffed. 'It's me last bloody game. I couldn't have done it anyway, I don't reckon, but not in me last bloody game.'

I didn't know what to say to him. When I did think of something it wasn't that bright.

'Couldn't you use the cash, Tom?' I ventured.

He shook off my embrace and stared up at me, his watery eyes now lighting up with passion. 'Of course I could use the fucking cash,' he said. 'I don't have any cash, Willie. I never have. As of tomorrow I have no fucking idea what I'm going to do with my life. This money's four times more than my fucking testimonial brought in!'

I had never seen Tom lose his temper, he was normally so placid, the archetypal gentle giant: tough on the pitch, amiable and forgiving in the real world. I had never heard him swear either, not once in five years, despite all the effing and blinding the rest of us indulged in at every opportunity.

'Why don't you pull out if you don't like it, Tom? Say you've been carrying an injury and you don't think—'

'Yes, you'd like that Willie, wouldn't you?' he sneered. 'That way no one will stop us getting *the right result*. This is my last game, so fuck you, I'm going to play.' With that he stood up and walked into the changing room just as the other lads were coming back in for the final pep talk.

But there was no pep talk today. Our manager Jeff Troy had

gone temporarily AWOL, maybe too ashamed to show his face. We just hung around for another couple of minutes shaking our thighs (except for Tom, who was now warming up vigorously), and then when the referee knocked went back out again and formed a tunnel with the Hansford players for Tommy. Harry Trewick said the right things over the loudspeaker and there was warm applause all round for the big man when he ran out and saluted the crowd. Some chick handed him some flowers and he had his pic taken for the local rag. But by that time the rest of us had lined up for the kick-off and all we were thinking about were the figures. Zero-three, then 20,000.

We let Hansford come at us from the start. There was nothing suspicious about this. We were crap and they were good, and they had to win by three goals. But they weren't getting very far. It wasn't just Tommy who was putting in his tackles but our left-back Trevor Gee as well. He's not the brightest lad, Trevor. And we all realised there was something wrong when he went sprinting after a long clearance from Tommy out of defence, caught the ball by the touchline, beat two men and smacked a cracking shot against the Hansford cross-bar from thirty yards. An opposing defender cleared for a corner and Trevor held his head in his hands at his bad luck.

'I'll have a word,' said Kevin Fyffe as he ran past me. And he whispered something in Trevor's ear at the corner, and Trevor's face was a picture of enlightenment as Kevin presumably put him straight on what was meant by the right result.

But even with Trevor now on board, and despite all our best lack of efforts, Hansford could not find a way through. Their fans, who had sung encouragements from the start, were now getting quieter with nerves, and it was affecting the players too. Then just before half-time they scored, twice, and both goals were Tommy's fault. The first was a cross he let Kevin Holding beat him to in the air, the second his lack of pace let him down again as Holding sprinted past him, placing his shot carefully past our keeper Neil Hamilton. The ball hit the post, but Tommy was tracking back so desperately to clear it that it bounced off his shin and into the net. Tommy sat in the back of the goal with his head in his hands, while Neil patted him on the back and said, 'Never mind, Tom.'

The Hansford fans went wild and the ground was filled with the sound of 'Going up, going up, going up.' It wasn't much fun to have to listen to that, but then you can't expect money for nothing. At least we got some respite at half-time.

Not that the interval offered much by way of comic distraction. We all sat in silence again, staring at our feet, except for Tommy who had his head in his hands again, and dumb Trevor Gee who was grinning: 'I didn't realise, lads, I thought—' but Kevin Fyffe shushed him sharply and all we could hear was the distant cry of 'Going up going up going up . . .'

Jeff Troy edged through the door. Again nobody wanted to look at anybody else. He walked slowly over to Tommy, put his hand on his shoulder and said: 'How about a rest, eh, Tommy?'

Tommy shot up and hissed: 'Fuck off, Jeff!' which on any other Saturday would have meant an immediate fine, substitution and suspension. But Jeff just shrugged and left it and again all we had to wait for was the referee's knock.

Playing centre-forward in the second half was a doddle for me. First they had two big lads they had just signed from the Premiership at the tail-ends of their careers, but still too good for Division Three. Second, the ball hardly got as far as me anyway, and if it did I just tried to dribble past them. I had no chance, every time, but I must have looked like I was putting in some effort, especially as I gestured angrily at my midfield for their patent lack of support. The only problem was that they couldn't get the third bloody goal, and the more they tried, and the fewer obstacles we put in their way, the more chances they missed. Again things got tense. Tommy was still giving it 100 per cent, but his age and the fact that he was playing for the whole team meant that he was tiring even quicker than usual.

Then, with about five minutes to go, Kevin Holding was put clean through one more time. Tommy chased back and clattered him from behind in the penalty area just as he was about to shoot. Penalty, no question, and if it hadn't been his last ever game I'm sure the ref would have sent Tommy off. Maybe Tommy would have been happy, because then he would have been spared the sight of a gleeful Kevin Holding blasting the spot-kick past Neil Hamilton. Once again the ground was filled with the chant celebrating Hansford's imminent promotion.

So that was it, surely. All they had to do was keep possession, and there was no chance that we were going to try to take it off them. The final minutes faded out to the sad sight of us scurrying around half-heartedly as Hansford stroked the ball across their back four, like schoolkids against pros. Occasionally they knocked it back to their keeper, the away fans cheering every touch. And then their centre-back mishit one and their keeper had to chase it but he couldn't stop it going for a corner.

A few of us reluctantly shuffled upfield to make it look like we were interested. Tommy was up for it too. Trevor Gee went over to take it and I saw Tommy whisper something to him as they passed each other on the edge of the penalty area. The Hansford fans were whistling like crazy, the ninety minutes must have been up. Trevor put a perfect corner right on to Tommy's head, and from there it took a further microsecond to pin back the net in the top corner of Hansford's goal. Our few hundred remaining loyal fans went mad, their folk hero had scored and they'd denied promotion to the arrogant nouveau riche. Tommy went hell for leather into the crowd and they all jumped up and down together while the referee blew his whistle and decreed that the game was up.

The Hansford players must have known we'd been paid to throw it because when we tried to go through the motions of shaking hands they muttered 'Bastards'. I heard Kevin Fyffe say to Trevor Gee, 'What the hell did you do that for?' and Trevor said: 'He told me to put on his head and that he'd make sure it went over.' And Kevin threw up his hands in despair and we all went over to our fans to make it look like we were happy for Tom.

But Tommy didn't give a toss about us any more, the fans were carrying him shoulder-high, singing: 'Ooh Tommy Tommy, Tommy Tommy Tommy Tommy Hungerford!' By the time they did a lap of honour we were all back in the shower, the Hansford fans went off to wreck the town and, we later heard, Derek Wapping stormed out of the stadium without waiting to exchange niceties with anyone from the home club.

There was another happy team that day, Brygate Rovers. They went up to Division Two instead of Hansford Town. That summer Tommy Hungerford got a job there as youth coach.

For Whom the Ball Rolls

GREG FURT-TREVIS' wife knew exactly where she would find him when she came home from work. Lying horizontal on the sofa with the curtains drawn and the television on. That was depressing enough for a woman who worked a fifty-hour week for a mediocre wage, and who had once complacently expected the inevitable arrival of staple centric principles such as children, comfort and friends.

More depressingly, she knew not just that her husband would be watching television, she knew exactly which bit of television he would be watching. Nothing on the normal daily programme. Even an Argentinian soap opera would have been better by comparison than Greg's televisual obsession; his one remaining video which eventually warped or woozled and would then be replaced by a new one of the same name. Of the three and a half hours of footage upon that video he was interested only in sixty seconds or so, though if he fell asleep at night then the tape took advantage of the rare opportunity to run its course, rewind fully and then pop exhaustedly out of the machine's rectangular lips.

As she unpacked the shopping in the kitchen Andrea Furt-Trevis could, as always, hear the familiar tones of John Motson coming from the front-room. 'Just sixty seconds to go in extra-time of what has been the most exhilarating Cup Final for, well, possibly decades,' bubbled the ecstatic voice, still as hyped as it had been at kick-off over two hours earlier.

Greg always listened to the tape at an incredible volume, as if he wanted to let the atmosphere of the stadium that day reverberate throughout the whole house. Neighbours had, of course, complained that he had succeeded in recreating the atmosphere for the whole street, so now he only listened to the tape loud during the day, and then with the headphones on at night. Consequently his hearing was shot, but it didn't matter much, there was nothing more Andrea could say to Greg anyway other than that his dinner was ready; and there was nothing more he wanted to hear besides the howling crowd and the excitable commentator.

Andrea did not bother popping her head round the door to announce her arrival home, in the manner of conventional couples. She had tried that a few hundred times in earlier years but no response had ever made it through her husband's lips or along his limbs, so she had given up, letting it fall along the wayside next to all the other methods of communication she had attempted and then discarded since the day of the Final. She just unpacked the shopping bags and went about preparing dinner, which was a welcome diversion that took up a further hour of time before she had to face Greg's vacuous expression.

'What an afternoon it's been here in north London!' gasped Motson. 'It's 3–3 and it could have been eight apiece! And I think you'll agree that the goals we've seen here today have all been of remarkable quality!'

She had to make two different meals now, seeing as Greg refused to touch anything besides steak and chips, his pre-match meal from his playing days. Andrea could barely endure the sight of red meat now, so she spiced and grilled Greg's steak on autocook without thinking about what it actually was, while making herself fish or pasta. Greg actually came through to the kitchen from the living room for dinner, something Andrea had mixed feelings about. It was good, of course, that for the only time in his day he took a break from the television, but it saddened her that she had to waste half an hour in his company. Conversation was impossible, though sometimes she mono-babbled about her day at work just to fill the air with a human sound while Greg determinedly ate his steak, staring at the plate in front of him as if he was building up mental and muscular strength for the big game in a few hours' time.

Andrea would rather have read a book or the newspaper at the dinner table, but Greg's mere presence put her off, so more often than not they ate without speaking, each encased in their own solitude. She could not even switch into her own thoughts, for she knew what Greg was thinking about and thus began to think about it too. How different our lives would be now, if only for one small thing, if only one small clod of grass had not been in that place at that moment, right in front of the on-running Greg Furt-Trevis.

'Legs are starting to look very tired now and it's not surprising when you consider how much ground they've covered this afternoon,' Motson went on. 'But now the ball's with the substitute Bollingham on the left-wing. Maybe this Final's got one more surprise left for us yet.'

Andrea had wondered at first whether the makers of the video had got John Motson to add that bit on afterwards. Considering what happened just seconds after he had spoken those words they seemed uncannily prophetic. Greg had once told her that happened a lot, and that when clubs were bringing out videos they would often ask the players what they wanted the commentator to dub over one of their goals. Thus run-of-the-mill full-backs in years to come could play their grandchildren a tape saying: 'Now let's see what Smith can do from here . . . oh! That's amazing! Sir Bobby take a bow and Pelé eat your boots!'

But the more she listened to that line (and she had listened to it many thousands of times), the more she became convinced that it was just the sort of thing Motson would say any day of the week. You could almost taste the boyish optimism on the edge of his tongue, the hope that the Final would be finished with a dramatic last-second winner in the final minute of extra-time and he could explode into hyperbole along with 90,000 people beside him and several million more at home. And that whenever people watched again that historic goal they would hear his hysterical voice in accompaniment.

Andrea remembered fondly the days when Greg would come home with stories like the one about the video dub-overs. Although football had been his profession he still could not take it as seriously as anyone at the club he played for, or indeed as earnestly as the many thousands of fans who, while perhaps not adoring him as much as they worshipped the more flamboyant team members, at least gave him a wave or shout of recognition when they were seen out shopping in town on weekday afternoons (Andrea liked that – it wasn't intrusive and it made her feel secure and accepted). He had come home and laughed about defeats and the attitude of team-mates who had sat in the dressing room for hours after a match, kits still on and heads locked deep into their palms. He mimicked the theatrical, storming managers, the finicky coaches, and the pompous, over-weight club executives who tried to tell him how to play the game. And he had been different from the boisterous, cocky players in the team whose society Greg would tactfully spare her from on Saturday evenings at the club when things started to get out of hand.

'Bollingham's beaten Witt for pace with some ease there and has a big space opening up before him. Now, what can he do with it . . .'

Greg had been different. Not radically so, but different enough for it to be noticed. He had got good results at school and then while he was a young player had done a correspondence degree so that he would have something to fall back on when his playing days were over (the irony!). The others called him the Prof, and when he couldn't give them an answer to a clue in *The Mirror* crossword within a micro-second sneered that there hadn't been much point to all that book-studying, had there? He read a proper newspaper and liked classical music. 'Eh-oh, the Prof's listening to Mozart again, ha, ha, ha,' they'd say as he donned his headphones at the start of a tedious away trip. And the double-barrelled name. And the puns on 'Furt'. Good-natured joshing, of course. Or tiresome, repetitive banter, if you looked at it in the context of the same remarks every second Saturday for seven years, though it had never seemed to bother Greg.

'. . . and he's got round Henderson too!' squeaked Motty in amazement. How many times had Andrea thought to herself: 'If only that useless git Henderson had put a decent bloody tackle in.' He had come charging across and then slid at Bollingham's feet, and the latter, who had only been on the pitch twenty minutes, just sidestepped him and skipped onwards towards goal. Worse still, Henderson had in his desperation vacated his centre-back position and left Greg Furt-Trevis completely free in the middle . . .

'Now Greg Furt-Trevis is completely free in the middle!' Not for the first time Andrea's thoughts had been anticipating Motson's exact words, but she was no longer surprised or alarmed at this. Through many full moons they had kept her awake at night, peeling round her head like the worst kind of sleep-stopping pop tune. But now they were just there, always there, like the yellow, wood-chip wallpaper in the kitchen.

All of her friends and family had asked her at some point why she didn't leave Greg. She was firm on this, she wasn't going to leave Greg, she told them, although she did not mention there wasn't a second in the day when she didn't wish to find his self-stilled body on the sitting-room floor with the video frozen at the crucial moment. But leaving was out of the question. Greg had no one else to look after him, and leaving him would in no way liberate her, she would just be thinking about whether or not he was dying from neglect and starvation. Why do so many people stay together with people they no longer love, she asked her friends and family? It's simple – because it's easier than leaving.

Andrea didn't believe that this could go on for ever. Something had to break soon. But then after four years it was probably too late for Greg to snap out of it. Even if he did, what chance that he could walk down the street without the taunts which had greeted him in the weeks after the Cup Final? People yelling: 'Now Greg Furt-Trevis is completely free in the middle! Bollingham crosses and he must score!' Inconsiderate, heartless people who

----

considered themselves high-priests of wit, and who went down to the pub and told everyone they'd seen that Greg Furt-Trevis in the street and so, guess what, they'd yelled out, bla, bla. Such incidents could bring on a relapse.

On the other hand, Greg did not even seem to have the motivation to commit suicide. It was Andrea who controlled all the money, Greg's only expenses being the occasional replacement of the warped Cup Final video; though now she had four spare copies in storage after he had once started crying uncontrollably when the tape had broken and he was left with nothing to do for several hours while she went out to the shops. So he would never get the cash together to go out and buy a gun or a cyanide tablet, and how would he ever organise his head enough to face the outside world and actually leave the house? He wouldn't know where to start even if the idea occurred to him in the first place.

The sentence 'Bollingham crosses and he must score!' is interrupted by a short silence. A silence of utter disbelief. A silence, just a second long, shared by the whole stadium. Even Motson was lost for the smallest of syllables. Greg had missed, of course, but this was the mother of all misses, two yards out, right in front of goal, the keeper stranded on the edge of his six-yard box after trying to cut out the cross. Bollingham's pass had been too hard for the keeper, but it had been too hard for Greg too and had sliced off his shin and out for a goal-kick. Not just wide, but spectacularly wide.

'Oh I say, he's missed it! Oh I say!' Motson mouthed, dumbfounded but at last finding suitable words to reflect the feelings of several million people at once. There was nothing else you could add to that, really. Oh I say! Greg, his head in his hands, knelt down on the ground and wept as the final whistle went.

'Greg Furt-Trevis!' the commentator pointed out to the masses, just so they could remember that name for ever. 'This man has missed a golden chance to go down in Cup Final history!' Then, almost spurting it out as if he'd just thought of the cleverest, most apposite concluding line to the whole afternoon's drama, added:

'The man with the double-barrelled name has had a double-barrelled miss!'

One bum bounce on the normally snooker-smooth Wembley turf and that was it – years of unrelenting depression and psychosis.

Or at least Greg maintained afterwards that the ball had bounced badly, but Motson didn't point this out. Neither did any of the match reports the following day. Neither did the slow-motion action replay seem to back up Greg's theory, no matter how many times you watched it. Greg told everyone who wanted to listen that the ball had hit a bump just before he was about to slip it into the net and that was why it had skidded off his shinpad. Cussed luck of the lowest degree. And, as Motson said, while hammering home the point, witnessed by 'literally millions' of people across the world in 132 countries. Live.

Andrea wrote to John Motson a few weeks after the Final and asked what he had meant by 'a double-barrelled miss'. It was a short, bitter and pedantic letter which in a couple of paragraphs more or less accused him of ignorance and inarticulacy. 'For a shot to be a double-barrelled miss it would either have to have come off both legs or it would have had to miss the goal twice, or there would have to be two footballs on the pitch at once, both of which my husband would have had to have shot wide of the goal,' she wrote. 'As not one of these three scenarios was the actual case, I suggest that your metaphor was ill-advised and was intended only to poke cheap fun at my husband's surname.'

She had felt bad as soon as she had posted it. It wasn't Motty's fault that her husband had missed the easiest chance in the history of football at the most inopportune moment. She fired off another letter apologising for the first one, which she posted the next day, but Motty never wrote back, and who can blame him. What was he supposed to have done? Ignore Greg's blunder as if it had never happened?

After Motson had made the point about the 132 countries Greg wound the tape back again. In quick-time all the players ran backwards up the pitch. Andrea had a feeling that this was the part Greg enjoyed most, going back to the moment right before his life changed. As the players and the referee got closer to the halfway line there was almost a hint of serenity in his face for a few seconds, though as soon as he pressed the play button his face was dominated once again by the usual tragic furrows. Maybe it was this rewind respite that allowed him time to recuperate and face the action once more.

Greg Furt-Trevis' wife also wondered whether he hoped that just one time he would play the video forward and that it would end differently. Just like in the nightly dreams which had forced her into the spare room, where he sat up in bed and yelled, three or four times a night, 'Yeeeeeeeeeeeeeeeeees!' In his dreams the ball, cruelly, always went in. In his dreams there was no replay the following Thursday, with Greg on the substitute's bench never getting a look-in as his team-mates lost 1–0 in a scrappy shadow of the first match. In his dreams there was no following crash of confidence where he performed so badly in training and pre-season friendlies that the club put him on the transfer list to save him the savage chanting of opposition fans. Away at Northwich Victoria, in the middle of July on a Monday night in front of 200 people, and still there had been a loud and long twenty-minute singalong:

> *'He's got a double-barrelled name*
> *He's had a double-barrelled miss*
> *Old Greggy Furty-Trevis*
> *He must be bloody pissed!'*

In his dreams he did not sit around at home hoping and waiting in vain for offers from lower division clubs. In his dreams he was not untouchable, neglected by former friends and team-mates, unwanted by stigma-scared teams across the country. In his dreams the club did not suffer a slump in form which saw them relegated to the Third Division in successive seasons alongside numerous flirtations with bankruptcy. In his dreams people did not cite Greg Furt-Trevis' miss at Wembley as the turning point downwards in the club's fortunes. In his dreams he did not walk out to WH Smith's one day and buy a video of the Cup Final in question and then begin to watch and rewind, watch and rewind . . .

While Andrea was making dinner the video replayed around fifty times. She opened the living-room door and said: 'Dinner's ready.' She always waited to announce dinner until the phrase about the 132 countries tuned in live. Greg turned off the machine and Andrea realised how much it dominated the house, how much of a relief it was to be surrounded by silence for half an hour, even if it did mean having to sit in the company of her fossil-faced husband.

They both sat down, though for once Greg looked at her before he started eating.

'It got a bad bounce, you know,' he muttered, then looked down at his plate and began to slice his steak in silence.

The Man Who Forgot What Football Results Meant

DR POULTER WAS driving as fast as he could to John Trestle's house because it had sounded like an emergency. 'Dr Poulter,' John Trestle's wife had screamed down the telephone. 'Get here as quickly as possible. It's John. I think he's lost his mind!'

Dr Poulter occasionally drank a pint of beer with John Trestle when he went to The Laughing Antelope. Dr Poulter didn't drink there that often, but when he did John was always there at the bar, and he always liked to chat. About one thing, which was football.

That was OK by Dr Poulter, for although he had little interest in the game, it made a change from the usual medicinal queries, when middle-aged men approached and apologised for disturbing while you're off duty, but I've had a bit of a pain here, and a bit of a twinge there, and something's hurting somewhere inside, I'm not quite sure where, and it only comes once a month. And he was supposed to stand there over his pint and diagnose the problem just like that, then suggest a cure to set it all right.

Dr Poulter never did that, though, simply because he couldn't. He always said, 'Make an appointment with my receptionist next week and I'll take a closer look,' and they nodded, looking almost reassured that he had not immediately called an ambulance or told them they had cancer. 'Thank you, Doctor, thank you very much,' they said, backing off with their pints, although he had done absolutely nothing. And they never bothered to make an appointment.

But old John there, he had never bothered the doctor with some piffling ache, even though it was clear from the indisguisable cascade of his paunch that he was hardly a perfect model of fitness. He drank at twice the pace of Dr Poulter, and the doctor had no doubt that once he had left the pub after two pints, John Trestle continued drinking until the bells were rung and all the glasses had been gathered, rinsed and stacked. And all the time he drank he talked about football, and Dr Poulter nodded along and switched off and often found answers to problems he'd been trying to solve for weeks. He didn't think that John noticed he wasn't paying attention, and if he did he was either too polite to say so or was happy just to address a face which absorbed his hackneyed sporting wisdoms.

Dr Poulter pressed a little harder on the accelerator. He might not have taken Jessica Trestle's exhortations so seriously if it had not been Saturday afternoon. But her phone call had come in the middle of the football results. They were being announced on the radio when the phone had rung. He was not paying attention to the results, of course, it was just a background noise while he worked on his matchstick model of Worcester Cathedral. But after he had laid down the receiver, he thought: If John Trestle is not concentrating on the football results at this time on a Saturday afternoon, then something must be seriously askew.

Jessica Trestle opened the door and stood on the threshold, wringing her hands in worry even before Dr Poulter had turned off his engine. As he walked up to the front door she began to skip up and down, her whole face gurning in anguish. 'Please come quick, Doctor,' she simpered, and he trotted the last few steps and followed her inside as she ran ahead of him into the living room, her left hand gesturing him onwards.

In the living room John Trestle sat staring ahead of himself. When he saw the doctor he turned slightly and said: 'Hello there, Dr Poulter, we're sorry to bother you.' But his words sounded ominous rather than apologetic, and he looked almost like a shock victim who had escaped unhurt but traumatised from a serious crash.

'What's the problem, John?' asked Dr Poulter.

'It's the football,' intervened Jessica Trestle.

'The football?' said Dr Poulter.

'Yes, the football,' she confirmed. 'He's forgotten what the results mean.'

There was a short silence while Dr Poulter digested the symptoms. He didn't really understand what she was getting at, so he played for time. 'How did you, er, find this out?' he asked.

'Well,' said Jessica Trestle, taking a deep sigh. 'I was in the kitchen making tea while John was watching the results. He always has a cup of tea after the results, he usually needs it to calm him down while he takes them all in. But today I heard a huge roar, and he's shouting out, "Jessica! Jessica!" and I come running in and he's standing in front of the set yelling, "I don't understand, what are they talking about? Plymouth Argyle 2 Oxford United 0, what the bloody hell does that mean?"'

Jessica paused and looked at Dr Poulter expectantly, but he still had no idea what to say. John just continued to stare ahead.

'Here, I'll show you,' she whispered, and taking the remote control from her husband's limp right hand she turned on the television, then found the Teletext page where the afternoon's results could be read.

John remained immobile for a few more seconds, but soon became agitated, muttering to himself and fidgeting. Then he began to curse out loud, and turned angrily to his wife and the doctor. 'Jesus, what is this all about? What on earth are they trying to say here? Torquay United 2 Leyton Orient 1? I mean, you what? How can that possibly be worthwhile information? Two what? One what? Who the hell is united behind Torquay? What the hell has Leyton got to do with the Far East? Will you two just fucking well tell me what all this is about?'

'John, John, please calm down, control your language in front of the doctor,' said Jessica, switching off the television. Then, turning to Dr Poulter, she said, 'I'm so sorry for my husband's profanity,

Doctor. He doesn't normally behave like this, I really must apologise.'

The doctor raised a hand to assure her that everything was fine. Then he took her by the arm and led her out of the room into the hallway. John Trestle had calmed down a little, and was sitting backwards in his chair, but was still talking to himself at speed.

'Mrs Trestle,' said Dr Poulter, solemnly. 'I'm afraid that I have some very bad news.'

'What is it, doctor? Get it over with as quickly as possible,' the woman pleaded, tears materialising.

'Very well, then. I'm sorry to tell you that your husband is suffering from an overdose of Insight.'

'What does that mean, Doctor, what does that mean?' she whispered, echoing the very words her husband had cried upon the appearance of that afternoon's football scores.

'It means that he has suddenly and dramatically discovered that football results are intrinsically meaningless,' Dr Poulter explained, gravely. 'Which would not be a problem if he had not spent the past forty years of his life engaged in little or nothing else.'

'But Doctor, he doesn't seem to have *discovered* anything. It seems to me that there is no understanding there at all any more,' said Jessica Trestle.

Doctor Poulter held up the bottle of pills and smiled. 'Don't worry. Basically your husband is beyond help and his life is beyond significance. Pop a few of these into his bedtime drink and he will spend the rest of his days in his armchair, motivated to move solely by the need to evacuate his digestive sytem, or to fill it back up again at the dinner table.'

The worry was wiped from Jessica Trestle's face and she beamed unflinchingly at the doctor. 'Oh thank you, thank you, Doctor,' she said. 'What would we do without men like you? Would you like a cup of tea before you go?'

'Most certainly,' said Dr Poulter, returning the smile.

Where Mothers Cease to Tread

UNAWARE THAT HIS mother was lying dead in the room next door, thirty-one-year-old Carston Hicks awoke one Sunday morning in late April aflutter with nerves at the prospect of what he believed was going to be the biggest day of his life. For the first time ever he was going to be playing in a cup final, and although it was not a cup final that many people beyond the participant two teams were going to give a toss about, it was, relatively speaking, important enough to get Carston straight out of bed and on to the toilet before he had even so much as had time to rub the remains of weariness from his morose and verdant eyes.

It can only do me good to get all this out of my system, he thought to himself while shitting. I'll be able to run faster now. He was convinced that this was true, just as he had been sure that going out jogging every night during the preceding week might somehow enhance his performance on the field today. But no matter how much waste he evacuated from his gastro-intestinal system, and regardless of the number of pavements he forced his awkward and unathletic frame to huff along, Carston Hicks would remain an improbable footballer, whose side, the Kelloway Kickers, had reached the Gulley Flats Cup Final despite him rather than because of him.

Other sides in the Gulley Flats Sunday League would probably have found a way to get rid of Carston Hicks, perhaps by substituting him every week, or by dropping the odd unkind comment in the changing room, or by swearing at him when he made mistakes on the pitch. The Kelloway Kickers, however, was a notably unambitious footballing combo consisting of mainly occasional hackers and which usually finished bottom of the table and never progressed beyond round two of the Cup. Carston Hicks was exceptional within the side in that he always turned up, and in this sort of league on a Sunday morning that was already an achievement. Carston made up the numbers. He also played left-back, not a particularly popular position. And if he did not always make his tackles, at least he sometimes got in the way. Furthermore, he had been playing for the Kickers since he was nineteen, far longer than any of his team-mates. Nobody would have dreamt of dropping him.

In spite of his distinguished service, Carston was never put forward to be captain or treasurer or the one who was in charge of kit. He wasn't that sort. He was taciturn, removed, always focused on the contents of his tatty, dark blue sports bag before the game, nodding hellos, then always straight off again after the game, never hanging around for a beer or the full Sunday lunchtime six-pint session enjoyed by the rest of the team. That might have been understandable if Carston had a wife and kids waiting for him at home. But he didn't, he lived with his mum.

Many new players over the years had remarked upon Carston's quietness. The others shrugged. There wasn't much point Carston staying behind for a beer; they wouldn't have known what to say to him. Once a cocky newcomer said to the others: 'He's shite at football, he doesn't want to stay for the beer. What the hell does he play for?' Nobody laughed, Carston was too much of a fixture for that. Carston was not disliked, and no one made fun of him because he was too harmless. Soon after the cocky newcomer found another side to play for.

There was a simple reason why Carston never stayed for a beer. His mother had always cooked Sunday lunch. Even if he had ever once said to his mother: 'I'll be staying on for a beer with the lads,' she would just have replied: 'You can't, lunch will be ready at one,' and that would have been the end of the matter. He did not know what would have happened if he had stayed on at the pub and rolled in at four to watch the afternoon game and fallen asleep in the armchair, smelling of ale, gut rising and falling in time with his snores. He did not know because he had never tried it.

When Carston got off the bus which took him home from Gulley Flats and walked along the road where he lived, he knew that his mother would be waiting at the window. She disappeared behind the curtain as soon as he came into view, just like she did during the week when he came home from work at some time between a quarter to and ten to six. She believed that Carston did not know she looked out for him, but he had seen her back disappearing often enough and the curtains wavering in her wake as she bustled off to the kitchen to put his food on to a plate. By the time Carston came though the front door, that plate was on the table, and he would begin to eat as his mother hung up his coat. On Sundays she would join him at the table and they would eat a small roast joint together. Wordless, until she begrudgingly asked him how they had got on. His one escape into leisure during the week and she resented it, pointing out to no one in particular each Sunday morning, 'I don't know how you can be bothered, especially in this weather.' It didn't matter what the weather was doing, it was never, in the opinion of Mrs Hicks, right enough to play football in.

'We lost 4–0, Mother,' Carston might say, but she was not interested in the score, not even when he had begun to show some traces of animation a few weeks earlier at their unprecedented progress in the Cup competition. 'We might get to the Final!' he had said, as if this was the news she had been waiting for for the past twelve years, as if this would vindicate his turning out on all those days when it had, in her opinion, been too rainy or too sunny or too hard underfoot. But she was no more interested in the Kelloway Kickers' freak winning streak than she had been in their decade of defeats. In fact it was worse, because a good Cup run meant more matches, that much she understood, and that meant Carston spending even more time out of the house.

Carston may have been aware that he lead a lonely, trapped life, incarcerated by his mother's unspoken need to have him there as a substitute for his dead father, incapable of speaking to or adapting to the world beyond. On the other hand, he was so hamstrung by his dependency on all his mother did for him that he would not have had the faintest idea how to go about changing his life. He never thought: I'm thirty-one, I should move out, because he did not know what that meant. Where to? How? Carston Hicks' mother did everything for him. He would not have known what to do in front of a washing machine, or confronted by a gas bill or a rental lease. His mother took care of all that, without question. That was the point behind her life, to do those things. Carston's point, on the other hand, was to be the recipient of her unquestioning servitude, but at the price of sacrificing any attempt to live a life beyond the paralysis of mundanity.

Except for football on Sunday morning on Gulley Flats. Carston spent the week at his position behind the counter of a hardware shop thinking of little else, replaying every mistimed tackle of the previous Sunday's match through his head a hundred times, vowing to do better next week, certain that he was not as bad as his last performance had indicated and that he was still improving his game, could still reach the level where a team-mate or an opponent came up to him and said: 'Well played, mate,' something he had tantalisingly heard while trudging off the pitch on countless occasions, but had never himself experienced first hand. He had even tried saying such words to the wingers and attacking midfielders it had been his job to stop, but they never returned the compliment. One bloke had muttered quietly under his breath, 'Well, it wasn't exactly difficult,' and after that Carston did not say, 'Well played, mate,' to anyone again.

The past week at work had gone so slowly, because instead of thinking about the previous week's game Carston had been thinking ahead to the Final. For every waking second of the day. He had not been thinking realistically, he had been day-dreaming, and his boss, Mr Terry, had remarked upon this several times. Not that it affected Carston's job, he could have done that in a coma he had been there so long now. Mr Terry was not a bastard boss at all, he had just been pulling Carston's leg. 'Big day Sunday, eh, Carston?' he'd say, nudging the worker out of his reverie as he gazed at drawers full of nails as if they contained the answers to all his dreams. This was about as light-hearted as the banter got. Mister Terry didn't make jokes with Carston, it hardly seemed worthwhile, he'd never seen the boy crack more than the thinnest of smiles in all the fifteen years he'd been working there. Carston, meanwhile, would quickly lapse back into a world whereby his thirty-yard screamer impregnated the net in the game's final minute, the cap to his battling, ferocious performance and half a dozen crucial goal-line clearances. Then amid all the furore of the celebrations, a man in a long coat quietly lured him to one side and said, 'I like what I saw, son, how do you fancy coming up to Villa Park for a chat this week?' More often than not Carston forgot that he was thirty-one years old.

AFTER HE HAD finished in the bathroom Carston got dressed, which took a long time as he put on his full kit and then wore a tracksuit over the top. It was still early, and therefore quite absurd that he should be putting his shin-pads on a full three hours before kick-off, but professionals have pre-match rituals and superstitions, so why shouldn't he? There was no way he was going to break the tradition which had helped the Kickers reach the Final just because he was getting changed a couple of hours earlier than usual. Then he had to go back to the toilet again, so he sat there with his tracksuit trousers and shorts around his ankles, his socks and shinpads making him feel overdressed in this sanitary environment. Imagine if someone would take a photograph of me now, he thought, as he often did when he was in positions which most would not have considered even slightly compromising. But no one was going to take a photograph of Carston Hicks, not here, and not smiling on a beach or drunk in a pub. The last extant photo of Carston was taken when he was six years old, playing football in the tiny back garden with his father.

Carston could tell there was still something to come out of his body, but time was moving on and he wanted to eat his breakfast before it was too late. He'd done that a couple of times before, been sick on the pitch after not allowing his sausage, bacon and eggs sufficient time to be properly digested. Both times someone or other had grinned and said: 'One too many last night, eh?' because every week at least one person chundered on the pitch as a result of excess drinking the night before. He left the bathroom a second time and tiptoed (needlessly, of course) past his mother's bedroom and downstairs to the kitchen. He put the frying-pan on the stove and turned on the radio. He knew that he was not at all hungry, but needed to make the breakfast to try to distract himself from his chronic nervousness and give the morning an air of normality. The nerves became so severe that he began to wish his team was not in the Final, after all, but was about to battle out the customary pointless end of term hack-around to decide who finished in seventeenth place. He threw in the sausages and bacon and watched them sizzle gently. He boiled the kettle. On Sunday morning Carston always took his mother a cup of tea before he went to play football. It was the one and only thing that he physically did for his mother in the household. On Sunday she always lay in bed until eleven o'clock reading the paper before getting up to start Sunday lunch. This had been the case for as long as Carston could remember, and the only domestic chore she had ever taught him was how to make himself a fried breakfast and a cup of tea. If he was ever left alone at least he would survive on tea and bacon and eggs until the dust choked him.

It was twenty past eight. Carston wondered if it was too early to take the tea and paper up to his mother. Usually he left it until after nine o'clock. He decided to eat his breakfast first and then boil the kettle again for his mother. He picked the meat out of the pan and put it on to a plate and then began to fry two eggs. Great energy food before playing football. The fat was a little too hot and the eggs spat at him, and he stood back a pace after a globule of lard burnt his arm. Just think if that had hit him in the eye and he'd had to miss the biggest game of his life because of a drop of bacon fat! He turned the heat down and studied the eggs as they turned to white and then began to burn at the edges. Then, after scooping a little fat over the top to turn the surface of the yoke from yellow to pink, he lifted the eggs on to the plate with his sausages and bacon, put the plate on the small kitchen table, fished the stewed tea-bag out of his mug and threw it in the bin, poured some milk into his tea, opened the newspaper at the football pages, got the brown sauce from the cupboard and sat down.

Not hungry.

Despite distracting himself for twenty minutes with the food, the truth was that he could not eat a thing. He might as well have been faced with a plate of turf. His stomach had placed a huge lead barrier at its entrance, locked it and then announced that it was closed, permanently, and Carston really did feel that he was never going to be hungry again. This was such a deviation from his Sunday routine that the plate of food began to terrify him, so he picked it up and put it in the oven. He began to wish that the day was over, that the Cup was won, that he was . . . doing what? What would he do if the Kickers won the Cup? Come home to Sunday lunch and then watch television for the rest of the day? Tell his mother, 'We won!' and then hear her say, 'Well, I'm glad the season's over, perhaps you can spend some time with your mother on a Sunday now.' God, would he really just come home and have lunch if the Kickers won the Cup? Then this question seemed so remote from his current crisis of nerves that he decided to defer it until the event of a victory. That was easier. Maybe he should take his mother her tea and paper and get out of the house and down to the flats nice and early to go through an extended warm-up routine. Inspect the pitch. Get himself used to the atmosphere. Run off the butterflies.

His hand shook as he poured the water from the kettle into his mother's china cup. He picked up the newspaper in his left hand and then the tea cup with saucer in his right, but it was rattling so much that the tea began to spill over the edges so he had to put it back down again. He took the newspaper up the stairs, left it outside his mother's room, came back down again and picked up the tea cup with his right hand and the saucer in his left. He made it without spilling anything. Outside his mother's room he knocked gently, as he always did, put the tea cup back into its saucer and opened the door, the newspaper tucked beneath his arm.

Carston was concentrating so intently on placing the tea cup safely down on his mother's bedside table without further spillage that at first he did not notice that she was lying on her back with her mouth open wide, blue in the face, eyes goggling up at the ceiling, her body stiff as an unwashed paint-brush. When he turned around, though, even he, who had not seen a dead body since the day his father had died twenty-five years earlier, could tell that she was dead and that expiry had occurred some time ago. His first thought was that he should call the ambulance, but given that she was so obviously dead there seemed little point. He thought how embarrassing it would be to get an ambulance hurtling down the street with its siren blaring, only to be sworn at for diverting resources from a real emergency when they found that his mother had died several hours previously. So he would call the police. But what was the point of that, when there had been no crime? My God, he thought, who are you supposed to call when somebody dies? Why did no one ever tell him that?

Carston stood staring at the body of his mother for quite some time. Like most people in such a situation he had not yet properly grasped that his mother, who so far had been alive and present and living in the same house as him for every waking moment of his life, was now dead and would not be coming back. He could only think of the body in terms of a problem which had suddenly arisen and had to be dealt with somehow. Before, he would have turned around to his mother and said, 'What shall I do now?' and she would probably have known the answer. 'Get me to a morgue, Carston, for God's sake.' Or perhaps, 'Call up your Aunt Geraldine in Cromer and tell her that her sister's dead.' Neither of these ideas occurred to Carston as he stood impotently before his mother's corpse. He began to get scared and then he needed the toilet again so he rushed off to the bathroom.

I've been in this bathroom twice already this morning, Carston thought to himself. Why was that? He had a vague recollection that he had been nervous about something. He looked at his watch for help, having lost all concept of time. Quarter of an hour before nine. There was something happening at eleven, something which he could not miss. Not under any circumstances. The bloody Final, he thought. Mother's gone and died on the day of the bloody Final. And he started to weep like a small boy made to go to a girl's birthday party while his dad and older brother headed off for the match.

At a quarter past nine, a full half-hour later, his sobs began to subside as he embraced the unfamiliar feeling of having to think about something for himself. Clearly it would not do to sit here crying while his mother lay there dead in her bed and the match took place without him. I should ring Benny and tell him that I can't make it 'cos me mother's died, he thought, but could not imagine in what tone of voice he would say this. And wouldn't it seem odd that on the day your mother died you would have the presence of mind to phone someone up about something as trivial as a football match? Not that Carston thought the match was trivial, but he knew how other people viewed the game of football, especially at the kind of level of the Gulley Flats League. No, I won't ring Benny, he ruminated, that would be wrong, they'll just have to get by without me. In the Final. The biggest game the team has ever had. The biggest game in twelve years of playing for Kelloway Kickers. The biggest game of his life.

Carston got up from the toilet and flushed it and washed his hands and dried them very slowly, and then he went into his mother's bedroom and, without looking into her bulbous, death-stretched eyes, picked up the now cold cup of tea and left the room again, closing the door behind him. He went down the stairs very slowly, focusing on each step as if he was carrying a twenty-tier wedding cake, his right hand shaking just enough to cause the cold tea to brim over the cup's time-battered ledge and on to the saucer below, but not enough for a single drop to besmirch the worn, fawn carpet. No evidence at all, he thought. No evidence at all that I carried my mother a cup of tea this morning. Then back in the kitchen he diligently scrubbed the cup (so thoroughly that it was cleaner than it had been for years) and the saucer and dried them and then placed them back in the cupboard. He then opened the bin and pulled out the teabag and wrapped it inside the plastic packet he had earlier taken his bacon from, and then he placed the packet of bacon inside a plastic bag from the supermarket, which his mother normally used as bin-liners. Then he scrunched that up as small as it would go and shoved it down into the bin and covered it up with the debris of the previous two days.

Then Carston forced himself to eat his cold fried breakfast. It was like eating a tasteless, neutral substance that wasn't really proper food but nonetheless somehow digestible. It reminded him of going to McDonald's, something he did often through lack of imagination. He put his plate into the sink, feeling ill. Then, to try to make himself feel better, he said aloud: 'I don't think I'll disturb Mother this morning with her cup of tea, I think she deserves a proper lie-in, I'll just leave it.' Then, as he packed his football kit, laid out on top of the washing machine by his mother, aired, dried and ironed, he continued to talk out loud in an unnatural fashion which would have instantly raised the suspicions of anyone hiding in one of the kitchen cupboards. 'Mother makes a wonderful job of washing my kit,' he said. 'I don't know how I would turn out so smart on a Sunday morning without her.'

One thing about his mother dying. His pre-match nerves were gone.

CARSTON ARRIVED AT the flats way too early. There was still an hour and a quarter until kick-off, and he knew that most of his team-mates would not turn up until five or ten minutes before the game was due to start. Carston could not remember a game ever starting at exactly eleven o'clock, but that did not stop him always arriving on time. He checked the black-board at the entrance to the changing rooms to see which pitch they were playing on. GULLEY FLATS CUP FINAL, KELLOWAY KICKERS VERSUS SURREAL MADRID. PITCH 16. This should have sent a jolt through his bowels, seeing the juxtaposition of his team's name with the words 'Cup Final', but it had no effect, as if he was coming to watch the last game of the season as an outsider, as he sometimes did. He walked across to Pitch 16, ostensibly to check the state of the grass, although there wasn't much grass left on Pitch 16 at this time of year, or on any of the other pitches for that matter. On Pitch 16 the corner flags and nets were already set up; that was a privilege of playing in the Cup Final, you didn't have to put up your own nets for once in the year. It only now occurred to him this was the reason his team-mates always left it so late to turn up. There was always someone like Carston who was early every week to do tasks like that.

Four kids were playing in one of the goalmouths, presumably delighted by the idea of having a goal with a net. All of a sudden Carston felt enraged and, extraordinarily, took action. 'Hey, you kids,' he shouted. 'There's a Cup Final on this pitch today, clear off! Go play in one of the other goalmouths.'

The kids stopped for a second, then continued playing. Carston marched towards them and continued yelling imperatives. One of the kids, wearing a Man United shirt, said: 'Fuck off!' and Carston waltzed right over, picked him up and pinned him against the goalpost.

'What did you say?' said Carston, but the kid was a sneering, hard-faced little bastard and he repeated, despite struggling for breath: 'Fuck off, I said. We're just having a kickabout, there's nothing says we can't.'

And then the other three kids started kicking him in the calves and saying: 'Leave him alone, you bully,' and he suddenly lost all conviction and dropped the kid, who spat at him, but he didn't react because he was at a loss to understand what he was doing standing there in the first place yelling at kids and picking them up by the collar. He turned around and walked away and the four of them jeered and called out the usual threats about how their fathers would desecrate Carston's manhood.

He walked away and picked up his kit bag from the side of the pitch where he had dropped it, and as he walked off and the catcalls faded he began to sob gently and say to himself: 'Oh Mother, oh Mother', and he knew he should have gone straight home, but instead he went into the changing room and wiped his eyes and began to meticulously remove his trainers and tracksuit and put on his boots. He remembered the hundreds of times he had done this when things had been normal, and tried to recapture that Sunday morning routine to clutch back a sense of solidity, the regular ritual of applying the pungent muscle-warming cream he slapped on his thighs, which was actually superfluous because he could not run fast enough to pull a muscle. He'd once asked his mother to buy it from the chemist's and she had never questioned why or whether it was worth it, but when one tube began to run out she would always buy another and put it on top of his freshly laundered kit and say, 'There's your football cream.'

And I never once thanked her, he thought.

He walked out of the changing room with his bag. There was still no one around, though he could see Wes, the caretaker, pumping up some footballs over by the boot of his car. He thought about jogging round the field a couple of times to warm up, but he didn't want to leave his bag unattended, stuff was always getting nicked here on Sunday mornings. He took out his wallet and thought about jogging around the field holding his wallet in his right hand, but that would look absurd, and those kids would probably see him and start to laugh. He was about to do some stretching exercises, but just at that moment a couple of lads from the other team walked around the corner and nodded at him and then sat on the bench outside and started to talk about the previous night's *Match of the Day* and he felt too self-conscious to warm up in front of them.

It was five past ten. Fifty-five minutes until kick-off. Not long, really, but now it seemed like an eternity, and he needed distraction otherwise his thoughts would start wandering to the stiffened corpse of his closest blood relative lying in her bedroom back at the house. Carston didn't believe in God any more than he believed in anything else, but he wondered if his mother was somehow looking down on all this, if she had seen him abandon body and house and head off to play football, that stupid game, instead of notifying whoever it was you were supposed to notify when your mother died in her sleep (he had still not worked out who that was supposed to be). If he met her later in the after-life it would only take one second to determine from her face whether or not she knew what he had done on the day she died. And she would never forgive him, that he knew; for all eternity she would have that tight little expression on her face. It wasn't like in real life when he could make that expression good again. That face, which had always appeared when it had looked like he was threatening to stay away from the house for longer than two or three hours. Once he had ventured the possibility of going to Margate for a weekend with the football team. She had not explicitly said no, because he had not explicitly asked for her permission, he had just said he *might* be thinking about going. But the expression had said no, and it was followed by the ailments, all the aches and pains and possible lumps suddenly afflicting her at once, and then he had said, 'I don't think I fancy that weekend in Margate, after all, it'll only be the lads getting drunk and falling over by the seaside,' and the look on his mother's face melted away as quickly as her sore knees, the aching back, the dizzy spells on the stairs and the nascent brain tumour.

Well, if she *was* looking it was too late to go back now; the act of disloyalty, the preference for football over breast-beating sorrow had been perpetrated, and it would not matter to his mother that Carston had run away because he was scared and helpless rather than because he really really wanted to kick a football about for ninety minutes. That pinched and unforgiving expression would haunt him across the celestial landscape from the day of his death and down into timelessness, any compromise rendered impossible by his irreversible act. Carston went all cold, his body felt like it was freezing on the spot and he could not move and he thought he would never even get himself on to the pitch let alone be able to kick the ball.

'Nervous before the big one, eh, Carst'?' said a voice, and another one laughed and added, 'He's gone fuckin' rigid!' and his team captain Benny Tull gave him a hefty but comradely slap on the shoulders and Carston snapped out of the after-life. Now that Benny and Selwyn Puttell, their goalie, were here, things seemed to swim back into perspective. It was Cup Final day, there were ten other people coming here who didn't give a toss about his mother's corpse, who wanted to win this game of football and then drink beer out of a big silver cup until they were sick in the gutter and then they wanted to drink some more.

It would have been difficult for the other players to notice that there was anything wrong with Carston even if they had been looking. Normally he was grimly taciturn, and that was how he looked today. Even if they had seen that he looked more withdrawn than normal, they would simply have attributed it to the imminent game, although few realised how important Gulley Flats football was to Carston in the context of the mundane, mother-centred drabness that passed for his life. Besides, some of them were a little preoccupied with their own nerves too, reflected in the atmosphere of spurious conviviality that gradually dominated the changing room as the rest of the team arrived – greetings were unnaturally loud, thumps on the back were bordering on the painful, and there were yips and yelps and meaningless, raucous asides which made the place sound more like a classroom of pre-adolescent children getting ready for their end-of-term party.

Carston sat detached, endlessly unlacing and relacing his boots. His stomach was still dragging his whole body down, but he no longer had any idea if this was to do with his mother's death, which part of him was still refusing to believe had happened, or because of the game, which his body and mind were still conditioned to thinking was important, even though it no longer was. Perhaps. The game, he kept thinking. The game is about to really happen. When everyone started getting up and leaving the changing room he followed them like a lamb, though by now his head was spinning like he was suffering from concussion and his legs felt curiously light. He was floating on to the pitch. During the warm-up someone accidentally belted the ball against his leg and said: 'Sorry, Carst', mate.' But he didn't feel a thing. In fact, he was just starting to wander off the pitch to go home when Benny Tull stopped him and said bemusedly, 'Where you going, Carst'? You're at left-back, not right-wing.' Carston walked over to where Benny was vaguely pointing and then the referee blew his whistle to start the game.

And then the next thing he knew it was half-time and they were 3–0 down. It was like the pros always said in *Shoot!* about the Cup Final at Wembley, that it all went so fast that you couldn't remember a thing about it.

They all sat around in a circle on the pitch and drank some water. Most players would have had a cigarette at half-time, but this week no one bothered. 'We're not doing badly, lads,' said Benny, then looking straight at Carston: 'We've just got to tighten up in defence. We've had a few chances.'

As usual, everyone then started talking at once, each with great conviction, none with the remotest idea of which tactic was required to turn the game around. Only Carston said nothing, he was staring at a blade of grass which was much longer than the others thinking: 'I wonder how long I will live.' He only snapped out of it when Benny said, 'How about taking a rest, eh, Carst'?'

Carston had little idea that all three goals had come from the wing he was supposed to be defending, and that several more might have resulted if his team-mates had not bailed him out. Until now he also had little idea that for once the Kelloway Kickers had a substitute. He could not ever remember a day when twelve players had turned up, more often than not they only had nine or ten. But, of course, on Cup Final day everyone made it somehow. He wanted to protest but could not find his voice. He looked up at the bloke who was taking off his tracksuit top. Was that Gerry Hoxley's brother? He had only ever played once or twice before. Wasn't he quite useful, played a couple of times for Nuneaton Borough, or something? And now he was going to take Carston's place in that Cup Final he had been waiting for all his life which was already half over and he didn't even know how. Carston felt like the grass was sinking below him and that he would be swallowed up by a swamp of despair. Until, Nick Little said: 'Hold it, Carst', I'll have to come off, the old knee's buggered.' Benny Tull was annoyed that Nick had waited so long to say this. He'd hated having to tell Carston that he wanted him to come off.

His left-back was, however, born again by the reprieve. His head was wiped of its mental fog and before him he suddenly saw a football pitch. Better still, he kept seeing the ball, which once play restarted seemed to come towards him unproblematically, rather than past him hopelessly as it had done during the previous forty-five minutes. He smote it back in the general direction of the opposing goal as if he possessed a previously latent natural gift. 'Nice one, Carst',' Benny Tull shouted a couple of times, and Carston felt a momentary bulb of pleasure welling in his guts. Even a few pro-Kelloway voices from the steadily mounting crowd yelled 'Yes!' when he cleanly belted out a couple of clearances.

And Gerry Hoxley's brother was indeed pretty useful. A big, stonewall dribbler who seemed cumbersome, but who slowly but surely barged past opponents who just could not quite dispossess him. He set up Jim Lichen for two goals and scored one himself. The friends and wives of the Kelloway Kickers began to yell and, as the game wore on, more and more players from teams whose seasons were over ambled up to the pitch and found themselves unable to turn away again.

Surreal Madrid had taken up the second half in the complacent belief that the game was won. When the equaliser came they seemed to buck up too, and began probing for the winner. The Kickers could no longer find Gerry Hoxley's brother as their defensive clearances became ever more rushed, the ball getting regularly wellied off the sideline. The Surreal pressure was unrelenting for the last ten minutes, and many questioned whether the Kickers would stand much chance if the game went as far as extra-time. But even that would be something, to have taken the game to extra-time, and Benny Tull exhorted his waning men to keep on sticking in there.

In the last minute of the game Surreal got a corner. Carston went to stand on the goal-line as usual (he was never sure why, he just knew that was where full-backs were supposed to stand), but Benny Tull waved him away and said, 'Let Gerry's brother stand there, Carst' he's big. You pick up the man on the edge.' Carston moved towards the edge of the penalty area where a short but skilful Surreal midfielder, who had caused problems for the Kickers throughout the game, was confidently lurking. 'We'll fuckin' get you,' the player hissed in Carston's ear. Carston prayed that the ball didn't come anywhere near them. But when the corner came a Surreal forward headed it towards goal, Gerry Hoxley's brother headed it off the line and the ball looped out towards where Carston and his cocky opponent were standing. The little guy nipped away from Carston but misjudged the bounce and it went over his head. Carston was now in space, but this was such an unfamiliar situation he had no idea what to do. 'Whack it out, Carst'!' someone yelled, so he swung his leg at the ball with all his might and connected.

It was only then that some of the Surreal players realised that their goalkeeper had quested for glory and come up for the corner. The defender who had seen his number one stealing up at the last minute had yelled at him to get the fuck back, but by then the ball was already back in play. As it soared into the air from Carston's clearance the Surreal players commenced their yelling at the keeper turned hunter. Perhaps they could already see from where they were standing the projection of Carston's wild swing. The ball, meanwhile, went far above the head of the one remaining Surreal defender and bounced halfway inside the Surreal half. It had not rained for three weeks, and the bounce was true. It took the ball way beyond the possible domain of the retreating centre-back, but then lost momentum as it entered the penalty area. People were screaming like crazy. Carston stood staring but not quite believing that the ball would go in until it trickled across the line a few micro-seconds before the defender could throw himself into the back of the net in a failed attempt to clear. Then Carston felt the full weight of an entire football team smothering him into the dried ground and hollering like savages.

'Grass and soil,' he thought. 'You can *smell* them.' And then he began to cry again.

The Day FIFA Came to Lincolnshire

BOB STARLING SAVED his biggest announcement until the end. They'd solved the problems of kit clash, winter kick-off times and where the Stolen Pig was going to play its home matches next season. He could see that people were beginning to get restless to leave the committee room and replenish their empty pint-pots. So he stood up, cleared his throat of phlegm and spoke slowly and formally the following words:

'One more thing. I am proud to announce tonight that no lesser body than the governors of world football, FIFA themselves, has chosen the Kesteven Village Pub League as the testing ground for a radical new law to the game of football.'

The captains of the eight teams represented in the League stopped fidgeting in their seats and stared up at Bob Starling, League secretary.

'Yeah sure, Bob,' said Gary Inkling, captain of the Ferret's Snout. 'And the League winners qualify for the European Cup next season too, eh?'

The others laughed and again made to leave the room, but Bob Starling snapped at them, 'Look at this!' and held up a piece of paper with the FIFA logo clearly visible at the top. Again the men hesitated and now they peered at the document, although they were all too far away from the front to read it.

'Come on, Bob, stop messin' us about, will yer,' said Ollie Grain, representative of last year's League winners, the Hounds and Slaughter. 'Some of us are gettin' ower thirsty 'ere. What has FIFA really got to say?'

'I knew you buggers wouldn't believe me,' said Bob Starling. 'But it's true. I've even rung 'em up to check. Spoke to their top fella there. They've chosen us to try out a new rule and they're even comin' all the way ovver from Switzerland to see 'ow it goes.'

Ollie Grain tried to take the piece of paper out of Bob Starling's hand, but Bob held it back and said, in a slightly hurt voice, 'Well, do you believe me or not?'

The pub captains looked at each other. There was no good reason why Bob would tell them a lie, he wasn't exactly renowned as a prankster. In fact for this level of football he was considered around five hundred times too officious, but he got everything organised, right enough. It was Gary Inkling who spoke next:

'All right, Bob, we believe you, if you must. Just one little thing, though. What exactly would this new rule be?'

This was going to be the difficult bit, Bob knew. He felt himself blush and was suddenly no longer quite so proud.

'No tackling,' he almost whispered. And seven of the eight captains laughed so long and loud that several regulars came up from the bar downstairs to find out what on earth was causing such hysterics at the Kesteven Village Pub League annual general meeting.

DOWN IN THE bar the men all read the letter from Zurich several times over, shaking their heads again and again and squeezing out the last millimetres of amusement. Bob Starling stood around uncomfortably, wanting to take his letter and leave before one of the men became aware that they had not actually taken a vote on the issue. It seemed that they were gradually coming to terms with the introduction of the new rule, albeit reluctantly, with the resigned air of men used to taking on board ludicrous conditions imposed by distant authorities. If he could just get out of the pub without too much further questioning then he could go home with his letter tucked safely into his briefcase then phone Zurich in the morning to confirm that the League members had given the go-ahead for the new experiment. His head began to fill with visions of VIP box appearances at future World Cup finals.

' 'Ere, Bob, 'ow comes we got chose then?' asked Tim Bennett, captain of the Punctured Rabbit. 'I mean, 'ow come these blokes at FIFA 'ad 'eard of the Kesteven Village Pub League, eh?'

'That's a point,' added Ollie Grain. 'Not even many people in Kesteven 'ave 'eard of our League. Seems a bit strange you gettin' a letter orf this Platini fella out of the blue like that.'

'I've no idea,' said Bob truthfully. He hadn't really thought about it, so seduced had he been by the official FIFA logo, and so excited had he been to talk to Michel Platini personally on the telephone. He had just vaguely assumed that word of his efficient stewarding of the Kesteven Pub League had somehow reached high places, and that they had deemed him worthy of overseeing this crucial testing. On the phone Mr Platini had wooed his head with wonderful words about the integrity and beauty of football, preserving the tradition of gamesmanship and outlawing the brutal, skill-shy hackers whom he said had dominated for too long. Bob had agreed with everything he said before asking what the law would mean in practical terms.

'It is quite simple,' Platini had told him. 'Anybody attempting to execute a tackle will be sent off. The game can be played as it should be – passing, shooting and dribbling skills exhibited without interference from the butchers at the back.' It had sounded wonderful.

'And another thing,' said Ollie, before Bob had a chance to explain his theory as to why the pitches of Kesteven had been chosen to host such a radical experiment – namely, that his reputation as League Secretary had gone half-way across Europe. 'What exactly will this mean when we're playin'? I mean, I'm a central defender, always 'ave been. All I can do is tackle. What's the point of me playing at all any more?'

The others murmured assent. Bob hadn't the guts to tell Ollie that he would probably be sent off in the first minute of the game, so he grabbed the letter, told them he had to leave and on his way out the door said, 'I'm going to clear up the practicalities with my FIFA contacts. Just remember to warn all your players at pre-season training. I'll keep you abreast of developments.' And off he went.

'Pillock,' said Percy Klibbett of the Pint and Pissoir. 'My bleedin' contacts at FIFA indeed. And since when have any of us bothered with pre-season training?'

The captains all laughed again, then somebody noticed that Rod Tilley was strangely silent at the end of the bar. Rod's team, the Brace of Pheasants from Kesteven's best-kept village, Teelby, had come bottom of the League the previous season, having failed to pick up a single point. The other sides, made up chiefly of farm labourers, mocked them as a puffed-up parade of posh-heads whose main efforts were geared towards being immaculately turned out in bizarre pheasant-coloured silk shirts. They were crap, but nobody minded having them in the League; they were good for boosting your goal difference and when they were at home they always laid on a massive spread with free ale afterwards.

Rod had been about to leave. He had been feeling even more uncomfortable than Bob Starling all evening. Now he was being asked what he thought of the new rule.

'Yeah, come on, Rod,' said Gary Inkling amiably. 'Your lot never put a bleedin' tackle in anyway so it in't gonna make much difference to you.'

Everyone guffawed anew, but quickly fell silent in anticipation of Rod's answer. Inkling had been horribly close to the point.

'Well,' Rod began awkwardly, 'it's maybe not such a bad idea as it sounds to start with.'

The whole pub had gone silent and Rod began to sweat under the scrutiny.

'I mean, some of these games can be rather rough.'

There was a second's silence before the pub almost exploded with derision, and then the players present began to reminisce about games the previous season when they had kicked the

Pheasants off the field. 'You remember when Chopper Harker took out "Lord" Monty Mallinder, haw, haw, haw?' 'Ah, you should 'ave been there when we played 'em. I 'eard *Sir* Charles Baxdale offering the ref fifty knicker to blow for time ten minutes early 'cos they'd already 'ad three toffs stretchered off and he was scared he was goin' to be next!' And with that Rod Tilley slipped out, muttering to himself: 'Well, let's see what the League table looks like at the end of this season, you oiks. And you can forget the bloody free ale.'

'BUT, LADS, I'VE been reffing your matches for twenty-five years!' pleaded old Willy Linnett.

He was a heartbreaking sight, standing there in his antique black tracksuit free of fancy stripes and corporate logos, all held together by a single strip of zip and an elastic waist band scrupulously renewed each close season by Mrs Linnett. His whistle hung redundant round his neck, his massive, battered old leather boots stuck out sideways like penguin feet. Willy had been making baffling and infuriating decisions in the Ferret's Snout home games now for two and a half decades, but he was such a genial duffer that no one had the heart to tell him he was the worst ref in Lincolnshire. He even came along to away games because more often than not they had failed to arrange a ref and Willy stepped in gleefully. And if they had someone then he would just create havoc down the line instead. But one thing about Willy, he was always there, never missed a game, even the time he shot himself in the foot trying to bag partridge. He got his son, a simple lad, to push him around the pitch in a wheelbarrow.

'Sorry, Willy, you'll 'ave to sit this one out,' said Bob Starling. 'FIFA's sent their own ref ovver. Mr Wuehlschlaeger. 'E's Swiss. And they've got two blokes 'ere to check up on 'ow it goes out there. We can't send 'im all the way back now, I'm afraid.'

The eleven men of the Ferret's Snout remained silent. They felt sorry for Willy, but at the same time thought it would be nice to have a proper ref for a change. Although Willy's decisions averaged out over the season, the games they had lost due to his eccentric interpretations of the law stood out in their memories much more than the ones they'd won. And even they were quite excited at the prospect of being observed by FIFA representatives. One of the blokes they'd sent had once played for Finland, nine times.

Willy, though, was choked. 'OK, lads, enjoy the game,' he said, barely forcing the words out, then took off his whistle and laid it carefully on the bench where he normally left his car keys (Willy didn't need to change, he always came in full kit and drove his car in his boots). Then he left the changing room and trudged disconsolately up to the pitch to offer the men from FIFA his services as a linesman. But before he could get there he saw three fully-equipped officials, and a fourth reserve official, trot out of a FIFA mobile caravan. He went and sat on a tree stump instead.

'Right,' said Bob Starling, as everyone looked out of the window at the four officials limbering up professionally. 'I need to go through this with you one more time.' The players groaned.

'We've got the picture, Bob,' said Allan Morgan, the Ferret's Welsh left-back. 'No tackling, no contact, no breathing on another player. It's going to be a bloody interesting game, I can tell you. Is there anything left we actually can do?

'Pass, dribble, score, entertain . . .' began Bob, repeating the Platini speech from his phone-call, but the players had all heard his little speech too often by now and began to jeer him.

'Shut yer boosh, Michel,' said Frank Nicholl and they all ran out on to the pitch before Bob could get started again on Provisional Rule 648, Paragraph A.

Bob got in his car and headed off to check on the Stolen Pig's opening fixture against the Punctured Rabbit.

Today's opposition was the Fookin' Ale, captained by Phil Yorrick. It was a traditional opening fixture, followed by an almighty piss-up in the Ferret's Snout to inaugurate the new season. The Fookin' Ale was a pub in Bowsby Hill, the next village up the road, so most of the players knew each other and had even been known to swap sides at half-time if the game was a bit one-sided. Phil and Gary shook hands in the centre-circle at one minute to three.

'Awright, mate?'

'I'm awright, Phil.'

'Awright, Mr Woolschleger?' said Phil.

'I am very well, thank you,' said Mr Wuehlschlaeger. 'But it is a bit of a contrast from the UEFA Cup Final which I had the honour of officiating at the end of last season in front of 63,000 fans in the Munich Olympic Stadium!'

Phil and Gary swapped glances with eyebrows raised. 'Sorry, mate, all we've got is old Willy Linnett,' said Gary, pointing at the redundant ref still sulking on his tree stump and smoking a cigarette. 'Though Fred Brown usually comes down for the second half.'

Mr Wuehlschlaeger looked at him askance and said: 'Pardon, I do not understand.'

'Dun't matter, mate,' said Gary, and then his glance caught sight of the two linesmen and the reserve official meddling with the goalpost down at the bottom end of the pitch. 'Eh up, wot the fook are they up to?'

The two captains trotted down the pitch to the goalmouth, where they found the reserve official shaking his head measuring the right-hand post. The Norwegian linesman looked up and said, 'I am sorry, we will have to delay the kick-off slightly. One goalpost is being higher than the other.'

Gary Inkling chuckled. 'Dun't worry about it, it's always been like that,' he said. 'It's ower boggy on that side of the goalmouth cos it's nearer the river. Just leave it, you can't put it right.'

'But the post is one centimetre below FIFA regulation height!' explained the reserve official, who it turned out was from Kent. Poncy southerner, thought Gary automatically. Talks like bloody Rod Tilley. 'And it gives the side attacking the other goal an unfair advantage because this one's smaller.'

'Perhaps we could place a stone inside the hole to hold the post up,' said the second linesman, a large serious blond guy from Denmark. Gary told him exactly how many stones they put down there every season. 'They just sink into the mud, mate,' he pleaded, 'and the goal always slips back down. No bugger cares that much, if you want the truth.'

By this time both teams were standing round the problem, most of them grinning at the unfolding spectacle. The Ferret's Snout's lopsided goalpost was a part of League folklore and was the subject of many an anecdote where players who had blazed the ball metres wide claimed to have been thwarted a legitimate goal. Goalkeepers always kissed the post at its right angle before the match began, while only full-backs under the height of five foot eight could safely man the post at corners without endangering their skulls in the event of a possible goal-line clearance.

The two FIFA officials arrived and were briefed on the problem. 'Mr Platini wants to see bigger goals, not smaller ones,' said the man from Finland grimly.

'Then tell the bugger to send us one,' said Frank Nicholl.

'No, I am afraid that would take too long, and we are already late for kick-off,' said Mr Wuehlschlaeger.

'Well, get Willy Linnett to lift it oop a bit every time there's an attack at that end,' said the Ferret's goalie Bob Marshall, and everyone laughed. Except the FIFA officials who, once they had heard a full interpretation of the quip via a translation from the reserve official, thought it was a great solution and called Willy over. Willy was delighted to be playing any role whatsoever, so stationed himself next to the post and, after a couple of practice lifts, showed he was equal to the task.

The FIFA officials went and sat back down at the desk they had installed on the touchline and picked up their pens in readiness to take notes during the great experiment. Mr Wuehlschlaeger insisted on staging a toss-up, even though the two captains normally said all right as we are, with the away side kicking off. So Phil called heads, lost, and the two captains said 'All right as we are', and the away side kicked off.

The Fookin' Ale passed the ball all the way back to their defence like they always did. The Ferret's forward line advanced slowly, unsure what to do. Fookin' Ale centre-back Martin Munton stood on the ball, unsure what to do either. 'You can't tackle me,' he said to Frank Nicholl, who was advancing towards him. 'I know, I know,' said Frank. 'Well then booger this,' said Martin and ran past him, and past the rest of the Ferret team too and all the way down to the other end of the pitch. He was a terrible finisher though and managed to scuff his shot well wide with only the goalie to beat.

The Ferret's Snout took a goal-kick and Gary Inkling got the ball in midfield. He decided he might as well try what Martin Munton had tried, and he too ran forwards with the ball. But Kev Bright, a massive lad in the Ale defence, crashed into him and robbed him of the ball. Mr Wuehlschlaeger's whistle was heard across the whole village and in Bowsby Hill too. He ran across to Kev Bright and, arm rigid, flourished a red card in his face.

'Ah come on, ref, it was a fair tackle,' Kev protested.

'No tackling!' said Mr Wuehlschlaeger. 'Off!'

'You fuckin' cunt,' said Kev Bright.

'I do not make the rules, I only carry them through. Now off!' repeated the referee, his voice rising.

Kevin Bright marched towards the sidelines and sat down, his face red with anger. 'What was he supposed to do, ref?' asked Phil Yorrick. 'Their man would just have run straight through to goal.'

'He could have shown him a channel,' said Mr Wuehlschlaeger, and somebody said: 'What the fookin' hell does that mean?' But by then the Ferrets had taken the free-kick, strolled forward and scored. Nobody cheered, especially as a few seconds later Ale went back down the other end and equalised. Two minutes gone, 1–1 and a red card.

Passing was too risky, it was best just to run with the ball, then you could guarantee that no one would take it off you for fear of punishment. But with the score at 4–4 after ten minutes Ferrets midfielder Harry Lord whipped the ball off the toes of an advancing Ale forward. Again Mr Wuehlschlaeger advanced with red card held high.

'But ah never fookin' touched him,' Harry Lord said, incredulous.

'A tackle is a tackle,' said the referee.

'Ah fook off,' said Harry walking off the pitch. 'It's fookin' boring anyway, I'm off 'ome.'

'Yeah, me an' all,' said Martin Munton, and began to follow him.

'You cannot leave the field of play without the referee's permission,' shouted Mr Wuehlschlaeger.

'Fook off,' said Martin Munton, and Mr Wuehlschlaeger snatched on the opportunity.

'Dissent!' he said, and waved the red card at Martin Munton.

'I'll have one of them an' all, ref, you fucking cunt,' said Allan Morgan, making to follow the other two players, at which point the remaining players joined in the chorus of abuse and began to walk towards the changing rooms, having effectively red-carded themselves. 'Wait, wait!' shouted the Swiss ref. 'What are all your names?'

The two men from FIFA were meanwhile running towards the retreating players with their hands held in the air. 'Go back! The experiment must continue! We have an agreement with your League secretary,' shouted the former Finland international. The players ignored him and continued to walk. 'Stop, we insist! Otherwise we will ban you. Your League will be banned for ever. None of you will ever play football again!'

'Ah don't bloody want to if it's gonna be like this,' said Gary Inkling.

'Jumped-up bugger. Let's gie 'im a taste o' the Lincolnshire mud,' said Kev Bright, still fuming at his red card. The players all turned as one, sensing the cathartic brilliance of the idea and, hollering loudly, ran towards the officials, who along with the referee, the linesmen and the reserve officials, turned and raced towards the official FIFA caravan.

The pub players were not exactly fit, none of them having played for the best part of four months, so the officials easily outran them and locked themselves in the hut. But once the two teams had surrounded the cabin their collective weight was enough to start rocking it heavily backwards and forwards while singing, 'Bring back the tackle! Bring back the tackle!'

Inside the threats had changed to pleas as the six men were thrown around like jumping beans. After a couple of minutes Gary Inkling ordered a halt before somebody got injured.

'Please, please let us out now, we are feeling sick,' came a voice from inside.

'Only if you withdraw that threat to stop us playing,' said Gary Inkling. 'We woz quite 'appy 'ere with our tacklin' and wonky goalposts before you lot came along.'

'Yeah, and we'll let you out if you promise to bugger off back to Switzerland or wherever and leave our League alone,' said Allan Morgan.

There was a murmur of assent, and muffled consultation from within the hut. The man from Finland gingerly opened a window and stuck his head out to ironic cheers.

'It is not up to us, it is up to our boss, and your contact too,' he said tentatively.

'What, Bob Starling? We don't need his bloody permission for owt,' said a voice from the other side of the hut.

'No, not your Mr Starling, the other man. The man who arranged all this. Mr Tilley.'

There was an outbreak of protest at this name. 'Rod bloody Tilley, what's he got to do with this?' asked Gary.

'He was the man who came to Zurich, many times, and arranged everything with Mr Platini.'

Gary Inkling looked at Phil Yorrick. 'In the cars, everyone, and off to the Brace of Pheasants, I reckon.' And they all turned again and ran jeering towards their cars as the relieved FIFA officials emerged shaken and slightly stirred from their hut.

*

LATER THAT NIGHT they returned triumphantly to the Ferret's Snout to tell the story. In Teelby the Brace of Pheasants, the only team to practise the new law in pre-season training, had been leading the Unspoilt By Jukebox 14–0 when the Ferret and Ale players had driven up, invaded the pitch and pinned Rod Tilley to the ground. They had soon forced him to admit that he had brokered the deal in Zurich with FIFA while there 'on business', and that a tidy sum had been paid into his special bank account in the city for his troubles.

When the FIFA officials observing the Pheasants' match complained about the disruption, Bob Starling declared that today's games were all void, because there had been no vote to implement the new rule in the first place. He tore up the contract with FIFA and declared, 'Sue us if you like. The League's assets currently stand at £4.57.'

Calls had then been made to the other pubs across Kesteven and soon the whole League was cramming out the Brace of Pheasants, with Rod Tilley footing the tab, until they'd drained every last keg of ale in the house. Most of the FIFA refs and officials decided this was the only freebie they were going to get, and after half-wasting themselves confessed that they too thought the abolition of tackling was a crap idea. When the beer ran out the boys from the Ferret's Snout made it home to their local for a last couple of pints.

They crashed noisily into the bar, which without its regulars was almost deserted except for Willy Linnett, still in his tracksuit, and drinking on his own in the corner of the pub. 'Eh up, wot's the matter with our Willy?' said Gary Inkling. Josh Tankett, the Ferret landlord, explained: 'Poor sod reckons 'e'll never get to ref another game again.'

'Willy, come ovver 'ere,' said Frank Nicholl. 'Ah've got summat for you.' Willy looked up, as if he would never trust anyone in the world again. 'Come on,' said Frank. 'You've got yer job back, the FIFA thing's off. I just want to give you a present to 'elp you out this season.'

The lads went silent, as Willy's face began to brighten. 'You mean ah can ref again?' he said, standing up with his drink and tottering over towards the bar.

'Yeah, but on one condition,' he answered, handing Willy the copy of the official FIFA rules that he had stolen from one of the referee's bags at the Brace of Pheasants. 'You read the bloody rules first.' The merriment kicked back in and the evening ended with an impromptu and extremely raucous quiz on the laws of the game. Willy, to the delight of all, came last.

The Return of the Falcon

WHEN 'THE FALCON' signed for PSV Wacker Rotzwil the fans and the press, naturally enough, went wild. The Falcon! Playing here in Rotzwil! A man who has played at two World Cups will physically be present and playing football within the four small stands that constitute the Winzigrund stadium, capacity 9800. And not just once as part of some celebrity turnout charity condescension, but week after week in our very own starting line-up. And that for a team which regularly struggles to gain mid-table respectability in the Swiss league and which is more or less unheard of in the footballing metropolises of Munich and Milan, both less than four hours' drive away.

Why the Falcon should come to play for Rotzwil was a matter between him, his agent and the club president and benefactor, Otto Friess. In the dressing room we realised not only that he would automatically be placed in the team at the expense of a regular, but that he was obviously earning several times more than anyone else on the club's books. He certainly was not coming to bale us out of obscurity from the goodness of his heart or a latent love for the town of Rotzwil, as non-descript a town as you could hope to find anywhere in central Europe. No, the Falcon was thirty-three years old, and, although his career was impressive – at least up until a couple of years ago – everyone knew that his pay days were numbered and that he was out to get the best deal he could on the basis of his reputation.

Friess was taking a gamble. He claimed the Falcon's very presence would boost attendances from their average of around

5000 to a guaranteed sell-out crowd, week in and out. And his goals and his experience would lead us up the table to a place in Europe for only the third time in the club's history – previous appearances: UEFA Cup, 1969–70, first-round exit at the hands of Jugo Traktor 54; Cup Winner's Cup, 1992–93, preliminary-round exit, 7–2 on aggregate, against a Scottish team whose name I can't remember but who went out 8–1 to a Spanish team in the next round. It could have been argued that with such a track record we were better off staying at home than heading beyond the safety of the Swiss border, but no one would openly express themselves so negatively, at least not among the people like me who were dependent on Friess for a living.

So, the Falcon was coming to Rotzwil! Three thousand fans turned out to cheer his official unveiling at the Winzigrund, though his name had been leaked a few days before, otherwise the place would have been empty. The Falcon held before him the statutory club shirt with his name on the back, that same bogus theatre all new signings are forced to go through, smiling like the club colours really mean something to them and professing that they will be giving their all and that they really are very happy to be here. In Rotzwil. Where there was a giant mineral water bottling plant (owned by Otto Friess) and a small professional football team and not a lot else bar an annual competition to judge which cow in Switzerland possessed the most beautiful udder, an event of no value other than to alert foreign journalists based in Berne to climb in their cars and come to write a laconically toned feature for when their newspapers back home had nothing better to print.

After the signing ceremony, the Falcon was quick, however, to lower expectations. He told one of the larger Swiss newspapers that people should not expect him to go out and score a hat-trick in every game straight away. He had not played a competitive game for six months as he had been out of contract, and before that he had not been a regular for the team from the Greek league which, for reasons nobody in the club was discussing at this time of euphoria, had let him go. By way of background the newspaper nonetheless pointed out that the Falcon had scored only twice for that Greek club in twenty-two appearances. And prior to that he had played for an unhappy year in the French league, where he had netted just three times for a side in the second division. Certainly, his high-scoring years in the Spanish and Italian leagues, and his captivating World Cup goals for his national side, were what had made his name well known to supporters across the globe. What nobody really wanted to mention, though, was that his good years were going back some, and that he had not performed at his peak for four or five seasons. But football people are capable of an excessive myopic optimism which gives the game its charge and charm. Why else would PSV Wacker Rotzwil bother starting a new campaign every year?

When the Falcon was introduced to the lads he shook hands with everybody and said, 'Nice to meet you,' in English. Swiss dressing rooms tend to be multinational, but in Rotzwil we were mainly Swiss nationals because, unlike the Falcon, no one from abroad could be persuaded to come here. So everyone got by with either German, dialect, French or Italian. Most could speak a few basic English phrases, but apart from me, no one could speak it with anything approaching fluency. The Falcon didn't speak anything but English, and didn't even ask the lads if that was OK, he just talked to everyone like he'd walked into the Leeds United dressing room. If somebody shrugged in miscomprehension then the Falcon just ignored him and turned to someone else. It was clear from the start that as well as a late-career pay cheque the Falcon was interested in one other thing. Respect. Even Roberto Gambini, who claimed he could not speak a single word of English bar hello and goodbye, came to know the word 'respect' like a native annunciation. 'Give the Falcon some respect,' he would say as he walked around the dressing room, jostling other players in the back and throwing their kit on the floor. Though only when the Falcon wasn't there.

At first we bent over backwards to give him his bloody respect.

None of us complained about the language thing, or that he got the number nine shirt, even though the number nine shirt had been Uwe Ferkel's for the last three seasons (poor Uwe got wind that something was up before the season started when he got the number 23 shirt, while the number nine remained unallocated). Or that he seemed to be absent from a lot of training sessions for someone who was meant to be regaining match fitness, or that his wife was allowed to come on overnight away trips when ours had to stay at home. 'By order of the president,' said our trainer Willi Held when someone mentioned the Falcon's special allowances, and refused to discuss the matter further, though you could see he wasn't that happy about it himself.

But in truth the respect we afforded him at the start was genuine. None of us had ever played on the same side as a man of this reputation, and we were somewhat awe-struck by his star billing. That he was aloof and arrogant did not strike us as completely unnatural, even if it did get on peoples' nerves. And when he trained for the first time he smacked the ball into the net with a power and regularity we were not accustomed to. 'He's still got it,' our right-back Freddi deNeuve whispered admiringly as we stood and watched him belt the ball past our hapless stopper (Freddi had never scored a goal in nine years as a pro). If he could do that on the pitch then any resentment would be quickly forgotten as we cashed our win bonuses and enjoyed the unfamiliar feeling of being high up in the League.

The funny thing was that we were not doing badly when we signed the Falcon. We were unbeaten after six games, having won two and drawn four, including a 2–2 tie at Grasshopper, the first time we had not lost there in six seasons. In a League of twelve teams we were in fifth place, and although it was very early in the season, there was an unfamiliar confidence in the side which the Falcon's arrival went some way to disturbing. Uwe had scored four goals in those six games and was playing better than I'd seen him play in my five years at the club. Perhaps he had been extra motivated by that vacant number nine shirt and was sure that as long as he kept scoring goals then number 23 would remain as the striker's shirt until the end of the season.

Next game Uwe was dropped. Presumably by order of the president. There was a case for playing Uwe alongside the Falcon, but not a very good one as they were similar types of player. Bulky, good in the air, opportunist pouncers from close in. It was hard to imagine Uwe running on to the Falcon's flick-ons, or vice versa. So Uwe started on the bench and the Falcon made his debut, away at Servette, who were third.

By the time Uwe replaced the Falcon after an hour we were 3–0 down. Our new star was pretty much out of it, although he smashed a shot against the cross-bar after about twenty minutes. It was unfortunate that this was the closest we came to scoring during the match because everyone said the Falcon had created our only chance. In fact the match reports were remarkably lenient considering what the rest of the side had tactfully adjudged as his 'unhelpful' work-rate. The press seemed to think that his near-goal augured well for the future, while our now broken six-match unbeaten run was forgotten amid talk of the poor service that the midfield had provided to our lone striker. But it wasn't the Falcon's work-rate which pissed us off so much as his remarks to Swiss television after the game: 'Yeah, there's some potential in the side if they just believe in themselves a bit more and we maybe sign a couple more players,' he said, like he was the club's new owner or something.

On the following Wednesday night the Falcon made his home debut against FC Zurich, a side like ourselves, perennially struggling against mediocrity and low budgets. Otto Friess' hope for a season of capacity 9800 sell-outs was not even fulfilled on this first night, although there were a couple of thousand more than usual, and there was a big fanfare before the game as the Falcon waved to the crowd, who cheered back at the exhortation of the announcer on the tannoy system. Perhaps the number of people in Rotzwil who were interested in football was stuck at 7000 or so, and even Pelé or Maradona would not have filled the Winzigrund to capacity. Or perhaps after our 3–0 defeat in Servette the novelty of the Falcon's arrival was already wearing thin.

Uwe was left on the bench again, and although he hadn't said anything yet he was looking increasingly disgruntled at the way things were turning out. Luzern had already shown an interest, but that was a bit like leaving Rotzwil for Rotzwil, in footballing terms, and he had just bought a house in the area and settled his young family. When the team sheet went up on Wednesday morning a couple of the lads patted him on the back and said, 'Stick in there.' Uwe didn't say anything back, but you could see he was thinking plenty to himself. In training there was a new determination to his play, but he was trying too hard to emulate the star signing – he wanted to skin the leather off the ball every time he shot and his attempts were ending up all over the training ground.

At half-time we were one-nil down. Willi Held said to the Falcon: 'You're supposed to be holding the ball up but you're running away from it. We don't have the players here to lay on sixty-yard through balls. Show yourself, hold it up, lay it off short, and then run.' Willi turned to me and said: 'Translate, can you?' I did, as best as I could, and I saw the Falcon's eyes light up in anger. He didn't say anything, he just sat there smouldering. He'd done nothing the first half, barely touched the ball, and it was for exactly the reason that Willi was saying. The thing was, while Willi went on berating the rest of the team, the Falcon sat there glowering at me like it was me who had told him what to do. I felt intimidated, and found myself saying to him quietly: 'Willi says you're doing great, but the rest of the side is limited. It's like, you've got to bring yourself down to our level a little bit.' He nodded at this and looked slightly happier, but it obviously didn't sink in because in the second half he played even worse.

Willi took him off again after an hour and gradually we came back into it. Five minutes before the end Uwe got the equaliser, a great strike from the edge of the box, and we all mobbed him. Uwe, however, looked furious, and, as we walked back to the halfway line, was staring at the bench. I could see he was about to make some defiant gesture so I grabbed his arm and said, 'Leave it, Uwe.' He glared at me a second, and after the game stormed out of the dressing room without taking his leave. He wasn't the first to go, though. Apparently the Falcon had walked straight off the pitch, got changed and left the stadium with his wife long before the end of the game.

The game had been poor, so the press focused on the striker question, naturally enough. 'Mr Held, you seem to have two angry strikers on your hands, what are you going to do about it?' a journalist asked him after the game.

'Neither of them's as angry as me,' he replied. 'As they will both find out tomorrow morning.' And next day he invited them into his office for a ragging that shook the ageing stanchions of the Winzigrund. I don't know how much the Falcon understood (this time Willi didn't ask me to translate) but he must have got the general gist, and at the end the coach made the two shake hands and then train on their own together.

After training I was sitting on my own in the canteen with some lunch when the Falcon came in with a pile of newspapers, sat down at my table, shoved the newspapers towards me and said ungraciously, 'What do they say about me?'

I had already read the match reports that morning (although I wasn't mentioned in any of them except by one reporter, who pondered where I had been to allow such a huge gap to open up in midfield just prior to the FC Zurich goal. I had been afraid someone would notice), and knew there were few kind words for him. I picked up the papers and looked at them as if for the first time, frantically fabricating appeasive words in my head.

The first paper I looked at said: 'The Falcon was out of shape, out of form and out of the game. The only surprise is that he was not substituted earlier.' In the mass circulation *Blick* they were even harsher, and under a banner headline FALCON FLOP, FALCON STROP, condemned the striker not just for his performance but his petulant behaviour too. I looked up and looked the man in the eye. His gaze had not left mine for a second.

'They say that you need a few more games to adapt to the Swiss style,' I ventured, but he immediately flared up.

'What do you mean, Swiss style?' he said, again as if it was I who had written the words. 'There is no *style* in the game here. There are no players here with style. They have to adapt to me, don't you see that?'

He was leaning ever closer and all I could think was that the sweating forehead that was just inches away from my own had once put a bullet header past Gianluca Pagliuca in a World Cup quarter-final. 'But that's what this paper is saying too,' I said, grabbing the first one that came to hand, which happened to be *Blick*.

'What is this paper?' he said.

'It's the paper that everyone reads,' I said. 'It's the only one that matters, all the others are written by intellectuals and read by nobody.'

He smiled slightly and said, 'Yes, we have papers like that at home too. Now what is this here, why is there a five next to my name?' He pointed to the chart where *Blick* ruthlessly marked the players according to their performance: '1' was 'world class'; '5' was 'inexcusable'.

'They mark players up to five according to their performance,' I said shamelessly. 'You're the only one with top marks.' I had been given a '4', which meant 'worse than mediocre', along with many other players.

The Falcon grinned. 'I like this newspaper, it gives me respect,' he said. 'From now on I will bring it to you every day.' Then he got up, taking *Blick* with him, and left the rest in a pile on the table without even saying goodbye.

This pattern repeated itself so often over the coming weeks that I became a habitual liar capable of rolling off grandiloquent praise without even thinking about it. I wondered if *Blick* would give me a job when my playing days were over. Every week the Falcon played the same way, despite the express instructions of the coach, and every week *Blick* gave him a '5'. Their reporter's opinion that 'the Falcon is still nowhere approaching match-fit and is clearly hampering the rest of the team' became 'the Falcon once again showed why he has starred at two World Cups while his hopeless team-mates flailed around him.' The judgement that Willi Held 'should drop him immediately until the team finds its way again' became 'the only person that deserves to be in Rotzwil's starting line-up is the Falcon. The question is how can Willi Held find ten other players to line up beside him.'

He did manage a couple of goals. One was a penalty, where he grabbed the ball before our designated penalty taker Christoph Suess could get to it. The other was a tap-in from two meters which, as *Blick* put it, 'not even the Falcon in his current miserable form could miss'.

'What did they say about my goal?' he asked feverishly, thrusting the rag into my hand in the canteen. I answered: 'The Falcon's finishing was typical of his predatory instincts which are the foundation of his global reputation, and capped off a superlative, scintillating performance.' Never mind that we had lost 3–1.

The star would sit there grinning and nodding his head and slapping me on the back as if I was personally responsible for the words. Which of course I was. But I was not spoon-feeding his giant ego and its need for respect just because I was intimidated by his reputation and his temper. I was actually, or at least so I tried to convince myself, contributing to team harmony. The Falcon no longer stormed out of the stadium when he was replaced by Uwe. He started grinning and shouting out 'Goooooooal!' whenever he scored in training (which for some reason was still much more often than during an actual game). He started to even say hello to his team-mates in the morning, not that they cared much any more, most of them couldn't wait to see the back of him. But that was not going to happen given the amount of money we were probably paying him. I felt I was doing the club a favour because it seemed clear that as long as the people's paper, and thus the people too, thought he was 'world class', then that was all that

----

mattered. And as long as he stayed at the club I deemed it better that he was slapping us patronisingly on the back than throwing prima donna tantrums.

'Why's he always so bloody happy when you tell him what's in *Blick*?' Freddi deNeuve asked me one day.

'Ah, he knows it's just a gutter rag, he thinks it's funny what they write about him,' I said.

Now I was lying effortlessly to my team-mates too. Freddi looked at me sceptically but said no more. In fact the others stopped bitching about the Falcon in my presence because they seemed to think that he and I were becoming great friends.

The team, meanwhile, was not doing well. We were mainly losing, sometimes getting a draw, and twice scraped a couple of wins against teams which were even worse than us. Attendances actually dropped below the previous season's average and the papers, *Blick* included, called upon Otto Friess to confess he had made a terrible mistake and to end the Falcon experiment, regardless of cost. Poor Willi Held, still under orders to pick the Falcon every game, tried everything, including playing him up front with Uwe from the start. But the two men played as if they were on opposing sides, and the scheme was dropped when they almost came to blows on the pitch. My translation of *Blick* to the Falcon needless to say blamed the whole episode on poor Uwe, who, in fact, had merely remonstrated in exasperation with the former for shooting (wide) instead of passing when Uwe had been much better placed to score.

However, the spurious harmony created by my falsely inter-preting the negative headlines of the popular press was, I felt, only going to last so long. After all, it only needed the Falcon to actually reach for a dictionary and look up the word 'inexcusable' to discover that I had been lying to him all along. Or perhaps, by chance, he would one week play a blinder and be alarmed to open up the paper and discover that he had been awarded a '1' by the *Blick* correspondent. But such eventualities were pre-empted by a surprise invitation to dinner with his wife, which the Falcon passed to me and my girlfriend, Angela. And although I was vague in responding, because I did not want to go at all, Angela was dead eager, having never met anyone famous in her life, and she pressed me to accept. 'You're always talking about him,' she urged, 'and, besides, what other perks do I get from my boyfriend being a professional footballer? I hardly call free tickets for the game against Aarau something to brag about to my friends and family.'

And so one Saturday evening, after a soulless 0–0 home draw against Lausanne (crowd, 3600), we followed the Falcon and his wife in their car from the stadium to the flat they were renting on the outskirts of town. I've no idea if he was paying the rent himself or if the club was footing the bill, but I had never seen luxury on that scale in the Rotzwil area. The ludicrous thing was that they were obviously travelling light, and the place was bereft of any personal touch bar, of course, a plethora of trophies and framed pictures featuring the former international striker's finest moments, which formed a kind of shrine on and above the commode in the dining area.

Angela gushed and oohed and aahed at all the silverware as the Falcon stood there beaming with pride and his wife cooked in the kitchen. I shuffled around with my hands in my pockets, but the two of them spent so long admiring his achievements that after taking in the view from the balcony and then studying the twenty or so CDs in his collection, I was forced to mosey over and participate in the general obeisance.

'My friend, my one good friend in this pathetic town,' the Falcon said, slapping me on the shoulder. Even though I knew this was baloney, his charm was such that I could not help but feel flattered by his words, and for a few seconds felt well disposed towards him. Until he added: 'I know that as a good friend you will not mind me saying that you did not play well this evening.' He gestured towards the metal and pictorial embodiments of his achievements in the game. 'You know that you will never be able to stage a display like this one, but people like you are the lifeblood of the game, even if you rarely touch the levels of skill and excitement that make grand crowds of people go wild.'

'Not much chance of that in Rotzwil,' said Angela giggling, and the Falcon laughed long and hard and put his hand on her shoulder too, ostensibly for support. She made no effort to shrug it off.

I was coloured a humiliated red, but was incapable of saying anything. Looking back, I should perhaps have told my host there and then that his performance that day had not exactly sent the masses into raptures either. He had bustled and elbowed his way around the penalty box, missed two clear-cut chances and been taken off the pitch after seventy minutes with nothing more than a yellow card for persistent and unnecessary fouling.

'Did you hear how the crowd booed the trainer for taking me off?' he said suddenly, turning to me as if he had read my mind, wondering as I was about how he had interpreted the catcalls and jeers emitted by some fans as he had left the pitch. Nonetheless, a majority of those who turned up seemed to be still granting him some leeway, as if at some point a player of his talents must be bound to produce a display worthy of his reputation. 'Yes,' I answered non-committally, looking past him at some Golden Boot or other. His wife appeared at my shoulder and said, 'He's a fantastic player, isn't he?' and once again I assented, being too hungry to tell them now what I really thought and risk missing dinner.

I would have gladly missed dinner, though, if I had known that I would be occupied listening not to the Falcon, but the Falcon's wife, telling me what a truly phenomenal talent her husband possessed (she used the present tense, unlike the Swiss press). At the other end of the table, I tried not to take any notice as her husband flirted openly with Angela, talking low and smooth to her and even taking her hand while she sat there lapping it all up and giggling and occasionally the pair burst out laughing, presumably making more jokes at the expense of Rotzwil and its deficient footballing talents. I could not exactly hear what they were saying because Mrs Falcon's questions to me were loud and direct and demanded frequent responses (such as: 'Yes, I agree, his goal against Italy surely ranks as one of the finest ever scored in a major international tournament'), as if she was deliberately trying to distract me. Her husband's manner with Angela appeared not to disturb her one bit, but during dessert I think that she finally noticed how distracted I was, and how I kept trying, without success, to involve the other two in our conversation. She leaned closer to me and said simply, 'Great men have certain needs that others are not burdened by.' And then looking at me in a knowing manner she began to clear away the dishes.

As soon as she was in the kitchen I said to Angela, sharply, 'We must go. I'm tired from the game and have a splitting headache.' And then, looking at the Falcon: 'Besides, we have training tomorrow.'

'Not me,' said the Falcon, laughing. 'I've got a sick note for that dodgy ankle of mine.' He winked at me unblushingly. 'Come on, stay another hour or so, we're having a good time.'

'No,' I said as firmly as I could, annoyed that I had almost given in at the first attempt, still unable to banish from my mind the image of that stupid bloody goal he'd scored against Italy. 'We have to go. I'm sorry.'

The Falcon's wife stalked through from the kitchen and said, as if grossly insulted, 'What's going on here? You want to leave already?'

'Most ungrateful,' said the Falcon, still laughing, but not quite as kindly as before.

'What does the young lady say?' asked the Falcon's wife, sounding like a school matron.

'Oh, I'd love to stay a little longer,' she purred, avoiding my eye.

'Angela!' I said.

'My husband will drive her home later if you really must go now,' said Mrs Falcon.

'I'd rather that didn't happen,' I said, although the Falcon, curse him, did not touch alcohol so I could not use that as an excuse.

'Oh come on, loosen up, don't be such a . . . such a Rotzwiler!' said Angela. And she and the Falcon and the Falcon's wife laughed like that was the funniest joke ever told (although it was probably the funniest one Angela ever told).

'OK, if that's how you want it,' I said, and walked out of the door without saying good night. As I left the building I was hoping for Angela to come running out after me, and thinking that if she did not then we were through. But as I went to my car all I could hear was more raucous laughter coming from the open window of the Falcon's flat on the second floor. I drove home in a fury and was fortunate not to kill myself or someone else.

AT THE WINZIGRUND the next morning, minus the Falcon, the team was made to sit through a video of the previous night's horror show. The Falcon had been right about one thing, I really had played abysmally, but I was not the only one, and Willi gave us all a true bollocking. When we saw our star international's missed golden chances you could tell what was going through everybody's heads, that we were dying to say something, but because none of us had played any better we didn't really have the right. The missed chances provided for me the only pleasure from the whole sitting, a deep sense of *schadenfreude* rippling through my veins at the memory of the previous night's entertainment at his flat. This pleasure was quickly decimated at the other image I couldn't get out of my head – one of the Falcon pumping away between Angela's splayed legs while his wife looked on in satisfaction. Angela hadn't returned last night, though it was possible he had driven her to her parents, who lived close by to his flat.

At the ensuing training session I was so fired up that Willi had to warn me three times to take it easy after I had flattened a couple of team-mates with some robust challenges. God, how I wished that my special friend had been playing there that day, he'd have gone home with more than a dodgy ankle. Willi's warnings were not enough to calm my rushing, though, and I was carried off the pitch, ironically, with torn ankle ligaments. 'That's you out until after Christmas,' the physio, Marco Garelli, pronounced grimly as I lay on the treatment table.

I was gutted. No, not really, that's just what pros always have to say. Mildly disappointed would perhaps be nearer the truth. No more training and away trips until after Christmas, all the time drawing full pay. I fancied some Balearic island and getting laid and legless, like those model English players. Stuff you, Angela, you can stay and enjoy your celebrity three-in-a-bed-ins with Mr World Cup Superstar.

'Marco, between you and me, what's up with the Falcon that stops him training so often?' I said to the physio as he packed ice around my ankle.

Marco sighed. He was an ex-pro himself, an honest man who had been with the club for ever because for some reason he loved it. He had played sixteen years in the first team in the 1950s and 60s.

'You won't say anything about this?' he said.

'Not a word.'

'There's nothing wrong with his ankle. He gets special dispensation.'

'By order of the president, by any chance?'

'Those are your words, not mine,' said Marco. 'As far as I'm concerned we never had this conversation.'

'It only confirms what we already suspected,' I said. And then I badmouthed the Falcon for as long as I lay on the treatment table, but Marco remained silent apart from the occasional hummph. After a while he said that I'd need treatment for at least two weeks if I wanted to make a quick recovery. Without telling him that I didn't want to make a quick recovery I pleaded for him to let me go and 'rest' for a fortnight. 'It's personal, Marco, I've got to get out of here for a while.' He asked if it was to do with Angela and I nodded and he said he'd sort it out for me. 'But two weeks today I want you back on this bench,' he said sternly, before putting my ankle in a support and advising me on the light exercises I could start within a few days. I hobbled out to the car park and went straight home and packed a case.

I heard nothing from Angela on Sunday evening and made no attempt to contact her. Instead I phoned a journalist from *Blick* and held a very long conversation with him. On Monday morning I got up early, drove to Zurich and got myself on the next plane to Ibiza. The copy of *Blick* was burning a hole in my hand, especially when I glanced at a picture of the Falcon on the front page, but I deliberately waited until I was sitting comfortably on the plane before I unfolded it to see what had been the result of my chat with their senior sports correspondent.

Next to the striker's picture, which showed him missing one of his easy chances on Saturday, was a headline, in English: LETTER TO THE FALCON. Then, in German, subtitled: HOW ROTZWIL'S STAR WILL LEARN WHAT WE REALLY THINK. Plus: THE FALCON'S FAKE INJURY, AN INSIDER REVEALS ALL.

The whole of the front page of the sports section was taken up with an open letter to the Falcon, on one side written in German, and juxtaposed with a translation into English. It read:

The *Blick* has learned that Rotzwil's international superstar striker, aka the Falcon (this season: eleven appearances, two goals, eight times substituted), does not understand a word of German and has thus far been unable to read the less than flattering reviews which have greeted his less than goal-laden performances for PSV Wacker Rotzwil since his big-fee signing in August.

We also understand that a team-mate, terrified of the great man's huge ego, has been falsely translating our match reports to make him believe that the *Blick* has been giving this monstrous underperformer rave reviews.

Blick will tolerate many things in our society, but not lies and distortion.

So, Mr Falcon, here is the bad news. Every time you've taken to the pitch this season *Blick* has given you a rating of FIVE.

That, for your information, does not mean 'world class', as you've been lead to believe, but 'inexcusable'. It is the WORST possible rating in *Blick's* marking system, and gives you the WORST rating of anyone in the entire Swiss League.

We think it is inexcusable that someone of your talents should perform so poorly.

We think it is inexcusable that you have come to our country to make money out of a poor club before your playing days are over.

We think it is inexcusable that you should pretend to be injured while your team-mates train (see page 2 of this section).

And we think it is inexcusable your arrogance is so inflated that you cannot see when you are playing badly and blame it instead on your team-mates.

The message is loud and clear. We can see it in Rotzwil's falling attendances and its falling position in the League.

Go find somewhere else to play out your twilight years, you overpaid, overrated, malingering fraud.

I had to stifle my laughter as I read the open letter again and again, delighting in the bombastic righteousness of every phrase. I had wondered how they would print something that the Falcon would be unable to ignore, regardless of the language, and translating the editorial into English had been a neat stroke. My only regret was that I could not see his face when he read it, nor gauge his reaction and the damage he might do to the admin offices at the Winzigrund.

As the plane began to taxi I turned to page two of the sports section, and was surprised to see my own picture prominently featured. The headline read WHY THE FALCON'S A FRAUD by Wacker Rotzwil's long-serving midfielder. The article was written in the first person with my name in bold letters at the top. I told all about the false translations, the fake injury (directly quoting Marco), the bad feeling in the team and that Willi Held was under direct orders from the chairman to play the Falcon every week, regardless of his performance. I didn't mention Angela, but I did intimate that his wife procured extra women for him, quoting her phrase about his special needs.

'The sick bag is in the back of the seat in front of you,' the air hostess said to me. I must have been looking very pale. I had spoken to the *Blick's* reporter on condition of absolute anonymity and that he did not mention Marco's name either. 'No problem,' he had said, 'no problem.' Not exactly a promise in itself if you analyse it, but at the time I had not analysed it. Now I had been betrayed.

It no longer seemed important how the Falcon would react because I suddenly knew that my career at Rotzwil was over, and that Marco and maybe several other people who were valuable to me would never speak to me again. Not necessarily for what I had said but the backhand way ('backfannied' way to use the more appropriate translation of the German) I had gone about it, blabbing like a petulant schoolboy. You might think that ending my career at Rotzwil is no big deal, a second-rate player in a second-rate team. But it was all I knew, it was where I grew up, and football was the only thing I could do in a half-competent way.

For the record, and because if you've bothered to read this story you will want to know how it ended, the Falcon really did go berserk. But not in the way I had expected. While everyone at the club was waiting for him to explode, he said nothing. He turned up for training every day that week, and then on Friday evening in Lugano scored three cracking goals like the ones he tended to score in training. The following weekend, with over 8000 in the Winzigrund, he scored two more against Neuchâtel. I was watching on television, having just arrived home from two miserable weeks pondering my future and my personality. Angela had taken all her stuff and I never saw her again, though I learnt she had moved back in with her parents. I had a letter from the club suspending me with immediate effect and putting me on the transfer list.

As I was reading that letter, my suitcase still unpacked, I could hear the home fans cheering 'Falcon! Falcon! Falcon!' He waved back in acknowledgement, smiling lazily.

Fitchie Gets the Point

'SO THEY DREW again, huh?' said Sadler, as we came through the door and into the living room of our rented terrace house. He was anchored in the same armchair where we had left him four hours previously.

'Yeah, but what a game!' blurted Fitchie, still thriving on a guts-load of thrills left over from the match which, via some nerve strands connected to the last part of his brain not clogged by an Iliad of football uselessness, was causing a pre-school grin to split across the facial areas where his cheeks used to be. 'We scored twice in the last four minutes!'

This news did not prompt Sadler to spring from his seat, embrace Fitchie with a whoop and join in the celebrations. Sadler was not interested in football, except for the possibilities it offered to wind Fitchie up. On Saturday afternoons he stayed at home and read books, almost deliberately, as if he wanted to emphasise to Fitchie that while he had been out ululating on the terrace like some primitive earlier mutation of *Homo erectus*, Sadler had been sitting here counterbalancing the backward steps that his flatmate was taking in evolutionary terms. In short, Sadler had been sitting here all afternoon just getting more and more clever.

Fitchie never gave up, though. Every Saturday morning when we went down to Arthur's Café for breakfast he would say to Sadler, 'Fancy coming to the game this afternoon?'

Sadler would always say, as if genuinely poking out the hope that he would come, 'Who you going to see this week?'

Fitchie would grab this slender query and pump his answer

with enthusiasm. 'Down Brisbane Road to watch Orient. Should be a good game. Against Chesterfield! Come on, mate, you might enjoy it – it's only a twenty-minute bus ride, you'll be back by five-thirty. It'll be a laugh, won't it, Frog?'

I shrugged, knowing full well that Sadler had no intention of coming, and knowing too that going to watch Orient was many things, but seldom 'a laugh'. In fact, I only went because Fitchie went. I would hardly say that I woke up on Saturdays looking forward to it. On weekends when he wasn't around I didn't bother. I kind of missed it then, though I'm not sure why.

'Orient versus Chesterfield?' Sadler would then say, masticating sausage and egg and looking up at Fitchie from his newspaper, eyebrows slightly raised, like this billing was the one he had been waiting for all these years before finally committing himself to ninety minutes of live football.

'Yeah, should be a good crowd today, bit of atmosphere. Chesterfield are eighth and the Os are tenth, so they've both still got a chance of making the play-offs.' Fitchie always thought there was the 'chance of a good crowd', because he couldn't understand that the rest of east London was not looking forward to the match quite as much as he was. Factors such as a sunny Saturday morning in Walthamstow (where we lived), an Orient away draw the week before, a new signing from Southend United – Fitchie could invoke any of these things to back up his prediction that the people would be flocking up and down the Central Line to a Third Division fixture. 'We'd better leave early today,' he always said. And so we'd end up standing more or less on our own behind the goal at quarter past two, me reading the *Leyton Orientear* (Fitchie wouldn't read fanzines, because he said they were always criticising the club), and Fitchie saying, 'I reckon it'll fill up a bit more later.' And he wasn't wrong – most of the people who came seemed to turn up at around five to three and got in no problem.

So there we would be, sitting in Arthur's, and Sadler would say again, 'Orient versus Chesterfield. Now tell me, Fitchie, why in the name of our good Lord would I want to go and watch Orient versus Chesterfield?'

At this point all Fitchie's hopes were deflated as even he realised that there was a familiar pattern here, that every time Sadler would tease him into thinking that he might just come along to the game – and Fitchie was genuinely convinced that if he came just once he would never miss another home fixture – only to find out that, guess what, Sadler had been stringing him along the whole time.

'So,' said Fitchie sniffily, unable to answer the question, 'what are you gonna do all afternoon?' As if there could be nothing else worthwhile.

'Ah, you know. Things,' he would say, wearing a crooked little smile of intellectual superiority. Then he would go back to his newspaper and I would keep on reading mine, and Fitchie would eat his breakfast in a huffy silence until he decided to turn to me and say: 'So, you reckon they'll play Harvey and Coops up front today?' Which was a stupid question because they *always* played Harvey and Coops up front, but I suppose it was intended to make Sadler feel left out rather than an attempt to discuss the intricacies of Orient's attacking tactics.

But Sadler would just butt in with something like: 'Coops? Is he really called "Coops"? Or is his birthname perhaps "Cooper", and this abbreviation is another example of stunning terrace nickname wit?'

Such was Fitchie's fervour, though, that this was all forgotten by the time we got home, and Sadler's laconic observation on this particular day that Orient had got 'another draw, huh?' was sufficient to make Fitchie believe that his friend was again really interested in what had gone on.

'You should have been there, Sads,' bubbled Fitchie. 'We'd just about given up, 2–0 down with four minutes left. Some people had even left the ground!' That, to Fitchie, was reason enough to be locked away in a secure institution for a very long time. That was worse than not coming to the game at all. Then he proceeded to tell in great detail exactly how the goals had been scored and by whom and how everyone had gone apeshit (I felt a bit embarrassed at this, and caught Sadler stealing a wry glance in my direction, as if he could not imagine me doing something so spontaneous). 'You should have been there, Sads,' he reiterated. 'Maybe next time, eh?'

Sadler ignored this and said, 'Tell me something, Fitchie, though do correct me if I'm wrong. Is it not true that when you came home two Saturdays ago you told me that the team had earned a 1–1 draw?'

'Yes,' said Fitchie, blithely unaware that there was danger ahead and gulled into believing for the thousandth time that Sadler actually cared. 'Against Wigan. Me and Frog—'

'And is it not true?' said Sadler, interrupting him, 'that you came back from that game in a state of some disappointment?'

Fitchie said: 'What?' Then he looked like he was thinking hard, like he had already forgotten. 'What do you mean?'

'Look,' said Sadler, putting his book down, sitting up and looking animated. 'You always get one point for a draw, right?'

'Well, yeah, but . . .'

'And I distinctly remember you and Frog walking through that door two weeks ago and you swearing and cursing at the unfairness of it all because Wigan had got an equaliser in the last minute.'

'Oh, yeah, that's right,' said Fitchie, slowly remembering. 'Terry Howard lost the ball on the right side of defence—'

'Never mind that shit,' said Sadler harshly. 'What I want to know, as a non-football fan, is how you can come home angry with one point one week and ecstatic two weeks later but with the same single unit of points? I mean, how does that work, Fitchie?'

'Well, you know,' said Fitchie, getting a little flustered, 'it's different because this week we equalised so late, you know, it was kind of unexpected, me and Frog had given up—'

'Yes, yes, yes, I realise all that,' said Sadler impatiently. 'But at the end of it you get one point. How can a point be bad one week and good the next? How can a point send the fan home angry one Saturday, but overjoyed the next? Where's the logic in the points system if the same result produces such wide variants of emotion?'

I could see what Sadler was doing. He didn't care about the logic of the points system any more than he cared about Orient's League position. He just wanted to ruin Fitchie's football-induced good mood.

'You don't understand!' said Fitchie exasperated, to which Sadler chuckled and said: 'Oh I think I do, Fitchie, I think it's all too easy to understand. The points system does not work. It fails to reward the sentiments of the people who, or at least so you're always telling me, are the most important people in the game. The fans. What good is a system that toys with your feelings while at the same time exploiting your blindness? Wake up, Fitchie, you've been done, mate!'

'You don't know what the fuck you're talking about, Sadler,' screamed Fitchie and ran up the stairs to his room, where he slammed the door. A few moments later came the thud of loud music through the ceiling.

Sadler sniggered and settled back down to his book. He cocked an eyebrow upwards at the ceiling and said, 'I'd rather listen to that than all about the bloody game.'

Drunk on Success

THEY ALL WENT out and got plastered the night before, the stupid little bastards. Not one of them older than thirteen and they all, every man jack of them, got completely slewed on cider and lager mix, and some of them even had vodka, though my lad kept off that, thank God, or I'd have taken another strip off his hide. I don't want to harp on about the youth of today and all that, but you wonder what kind of gratitude they're showing these days to parents who put so much into this club for them, giving up our free time on Sundays and having committee meetings and selection meetings and fund-raisers for new kit, and driving them all over the bloody county for away games. The more I think about it the more it baffles me, it really does.

And who was to blame for all this nonsense? What was the excuse for breaking a twenty-two-match unbeaten run and failing to make a new league record of twenty-three consecutive wins? After all the vomiting, the falling over and headaches, can you believe who they tried to scapegoat as the supposed instigators for the whole self-poisoning tomfoolery?

'It was a communal decision, Dad,' said my son, Keith, after he had finally arrived home from the match late in the afternoon, not looking anything like as guilty as he should have done.

'Communal bloody decision? Who taught you language like that, lad? Is it that bloody English teacher with the beard again?'

'No, Dad,' he whined impatiently. 'We all decided together, as a team.' He faltered here, and when he uttered his next sentence I knew why, because even he must have sensed how weak his words were. 'We were just sick of winning.'

Sick of winning! I belted him right there on the spot and he ran off to his room and slammed the door. What can you reply to a son who tells you he's through with success at the age of thirteen? I had to let him know in the strictest terms how much baloney he was talking, and shouting would have done no good, so I just belted him because that way the message gets through quicker sometimes.

My wife, Jen, came running into the sitting room to see what was going on.

'Jeff, you hit him again!' she yelled.

'Is everyone going completely bloody mad around here?' I shouted back. 'Did you hear what he said to me? Do you want to know why your own son and his so-called friends filled themselves with alcohol on Saturday night and then fell about like a bunch of clowns on Sunday morning? Apparently they were "sick of winning". Sick of bloody winning! The poor little tots, the suffering they must have gone through winning week after week, the stress of leaving the field victorious after putting another ten past hapless Hattington Rovers. Oh, why didn't we see it coming before, we should have had therapists at the side of the pitch to help them off the field and aid them in coming to terms with Repetitive Victory Syndrome. Why, we could have scrapped the very idea of a team if we'd known that winning the League would prove so bloody stressful that it would turn a dozen pre-pubescents into alcoholics.'

'Jeff,' she said, 'you know it wasn't really about that. If you'd just listened to him for a second.' She was looking very bloody determined, I must say, defending her son who had been out slugging snakebites twenty-four hours earlier, five years before he was legally allowed to. 'It was not that they were sick of winning, they were sick of the way they were winning. There was no enjoyment in it any more, and you know exactly why there was no enjoyment any more.'

'That's bloody nonsense,' I snorted.

'I don't really care either way,' she said, coming close up to me in a manner that took me so by surprise that I did not at first know how to react. You're not used to surprises after sixteen years of marriage. 'But stop hitting him because, if you do it again, me and him and Clara are leaving, do you understand?'

She turned around and flounced out the room.

'Jen, love,' I said, but when she didn't react I got angry too and stormed out of the front door and took the dog for a walk. To the pub.

IT WAS TREV'S idea, which is a bit fresh when you think about it, because Trev doesn't have a dad, and his mum never comes to watch, but we were all in on it, especially those of us whose mums and dads take such an active part on the touchline. And though not all of us thought it was such a good idea with the cider and that, we all agreed that something had to be done.

'Couldn't we just, like, you know, talk to them?' I ventured. 'Just ask them to calm down a bit?'

*'Listen, Keith, when was the last time you talked to your old man?' said Trev. 'How many of us here sit down and talk to their parents, and if we do, how much do they listen?' For someone without a dad, Trev was pretty well sussed on what it was like to have one. 'They'll either pat us on the heads and say, "Yes, lads, of course, now get out there and hammer them!", or else they'll tell us that if we don't want to win then we shouldn't be playing at all. You've seen what they're like, as soon as the game starts they're at it, they're like little kids who can't help themselves. Besides, how else do we do it? Storm the selection meeting and demand an audience?' He paused, a little dramatically, and took the lack of response as a cue to his final sentence: 'No, it's **action** we need, the kind of action that will make them sit up and take notice.'*

Someone else suggested just throwing the game, but Terry Weals pointed out that it wasn't that easy. 'With all due respect, lads, I think some of those teams we've been up against this year, well, I don't think we could lose against them if we tried. We've really got to incapacitate ourselves.'

There was a silence. It was a good feeling, sitting out on the school field in a closed circle, no non-players allowed. Not everyone wanted to get drunk, you could tell, but we were close, and we knew that no one would let the side down.

Eventually Chris Ebitt said: 'Er, well, has anyone here actually got drunk before?' We all sniggered. It was exciting, I won't deny it. Getting the drink in, then finding somewhere we could all meet to down it. Plus finally finding out the answer to that question: what's it like getting drunk?

'It's no big deal,' said our goalie, Frank Trewliss, and everyone went 'Ooooooooh, Mr Cool,' and he laughed.

'And when did you imbibe alcohol, young man?' said Trev, and Frankie said, 'At Christmas, my dad gave me a beer,' and three or four lads chorused sarcastically, 'Wow, one beer!' and Trev said, 'Well, you must have been wrecked after that, Frankie, but we'll be hoping for a slightly larger consumption on Saturday night.'

Frank went red and everyone laughed, like they had known all along it would take more than one beer to get drunk. Then the bell went for afternoon lessons and we all walked back to the school building together, some of us walking in twos and threes with our arms around each other and that felt pretty good.

WHEN I WALKED into the pub there was no one there except, would you believe it, Keith's bloody English teacher with the beard. Might have known that he would be the sort to be out drinking on his own on a Sunday evening. Smoking too. I tried to ignore him and was hoping that I could chat with Willie behind the bar, but he didn't seem to be around and some decorative girl served me without a word. So there we were propping up the bar together, and me trying to avoid his eye and wondering how I could safely get to a table without it looking too rude, and him looking at me and just waiting to say something, I could tell.

'It's Keith's dad, isn't it?' he said, as I was trying to pretend that I was preoccupied with the dog.

'That's right,' I said abruptly, but I knew now there was little chance of avoiding a conversation.

'We met at the parents' evening,' he said cheerfully, and reached forward with his hand extended, and protocol dictated that I shake it. 'Brian Walsh, Keith's English teacher.'

'Nice to meet you again, Mr Walsh,' I mumbled.

'Brian, please,' he said, a smile suggesting that he thought it absurd I had addressed him by his surname.

'Er, are you all right for a drink?' I gestured at his pint glass, which was three-quarters empty, expecting him to say he was OK, but typical bloody teacher, he said he wouldn't mind another pint at all, and I summoned the baby-skinned bargirl, more concerned about looking moody and sophisticated than pouring a decent pint, and she duly went through the motions.

'If I remember rightly you were concerned that Keith had only come third in the class in his pre-Christmas class test,' said Walsh. Again his way of saying it gave you the feeling that you had been an idiot for suggesting that your own son might have done better in class. I didn't see why I should be defensive about that.

'Yes, I was,' I said roughly. 'So, is he doing any better?'

'Well, I don't think test results are that important at this stage of tuition, do you?' said Walsh smugly, and you just knew he was one of those teachers the kids loved because he was so bloody cool, man, but I bet they never got any work done in class because they were too busy talking about whether nuclear energy was a bad thing or should lads be allowed to wear ear-rings to school. 'We do not really place children according to achievements in one-off tests, and I only told you Keith had come third because you had insisted on asking. Besides, coming third is no mean feat, he's in the top class for his year, you know.' Yakkity yakkity yak.

'Well, he achieved something pretty good last night,' I said, eager to deflate his patronising tone and his banal praise for my son's average classroom performance. 'He was so sick from alcohol that he spent half of the night vomiting into the bathroom toilet.'

I waited for Walsh to say something but he just looked down at his drink with this knowing little half-smile on his face and I felt like I wanted to punch him in the mouth. You could tell he did not think there was anything remotely wrong with such behaviour. No doubt he thought drinking snakebite to excess should be an obligatory part of the curriculum. 'Well, teenagers all go through that for the first time at some point in their lives,' he said. 'I guess you and I must have done it too, eh?'

'As a matter of fact I do not think that this was the kind of behaviour that a thirteen-year-old kid should be indulging in,' I snarled, though the more aggressive I became the more this bearded prat seemed to be enjoying it, as if everything I said confirmed his image of "old-style" parental discipline. 'He cannot do that legally for another five years, and even when he can, I'll still roast his backside if he comes home vomiting through the night again.'

'And in your day you were all tucked up in bed on Saturday night after doing your Latin homework, eh?' said Walsh, still with the disarming cheerfulness of someone who knows he's in the right. I walked over to him and picked up the pint he had not yet touched. 'I'll tell you what,' I said. 'I'll take this away and drink it myself seeing as how you would obviously not want to degrade yourself by accepting a pint from someone employing such defective and old-fashioned parental techniques. And, anyway, I don't care about bloody English, he's going to study science.'

'That's not what he told me,' Walsh murmured as I marched over to a table in the far corner of the pub with my two pint glasses, the dog slouching in my wake. I pretended not to have heard him and sat there stewing over my drinks, in such a foul mood that I did not want to be here or home or anywhere in particular. At times like this I wished I smoked a pipe to keep my hands occupied.

Walsh ordered another pint, and annoyingly caused the moody girl behind the bar to laugh long and loud as he was doing it. The girl, probably some pupil or ex-pupil he wished he was fornicating with, cast a quick glance in my direction. Then some of his teacher colleagues, having of course spent all weekend indoors preparing their classes for the coming week, joined him, and every time someone new came in he would lean over and tell them something and they would laugh and then try to cast a discreet glance in my direction. There they were, the people responsible for my son's education, getting ready for the week ahead by smoking and drinking. England, bloody England.

TREV KNEW A place, of course. Or rather he knew how to get into a place. He had somehow procured a key to the pavilion of the local cricket club, which was completely unused at this time of year. 'The best thing about it, lads, is that the beer and cider are already there, down in the cellar. Unlimited supply, no questions about buying it under-age, and no one's going to find out that we were even there until the new cricket season starts in May. All we have to do is get there under darkness and sit down in the cellar, though you might want to come well-clothed, it's pretty cold down there. I'll sort out some music. All you boys have to do is think up a good excuse to your parents why you're going out Saturday night.'

'My mum and dad are off out Saturday night,' said Sean Wickes. 'Just say you're coming round mine to watch a video. If any of them ring up there we can just say the phone's in the other room and we had the TV up so loud that we didn't hear it.'

No one had a problem with this except Hudd Anyan, who had to go to a family wedding. 'Easy,' said Trev, 'you can get blasted right under their noses, they won't even notice they'll be so far gone themselves.' Hudd didn't say anything, like he didn't believe it could be quite so easy to get drunk in front of your parents. 'Maybe I'll try to sneak out,' he said.

Come Saturday night it was Hudd who broke our vow of secrecy, but as it turned out nobody cared. We had been sitting in that cellar for two hours, listening to Trev's bloody awful country and western tapes, trying to get drunk. To me the snakebite was virtually undrinkable, so I moved on to the vodka instead, which warmed me up at least. It was all a bit forced, and the thrill of the deviancy was long since worn to tedium by the chill and a perhaps creeping doubt that this was not such a good idea when Hudd turned up with his three cousins in tow. Female, teenage, beautiful (or so they seemed in that light, after that much drink) and half-

cut cousins, happy to escape the numbing family occasion in the town hall half a mile away on Hudd's promise of a trip to an illicit drinking den in a dim cellar. Hudd, who was beaming like Santa Claus at the orphanage Christmas party, had even stolen a compilation dance tape from the DJ. Trev said a token, 'Hey, I thought no one else was supposed to know about this,' but he was ignored and I think he realised that Hudd had saved the evening.

The alcohol kicked in with a collective wave of intoxication as we boys, who had, seconds before, been slumped on beer boxes, became fast-talking paragons of wit with something to say and something to prove. The girls – Esther, Tilly and Louise – were surrounded and chatted to and danced with for another two hours without anyone really bothering to ask them who they were or where they came from. Their looks were enough for us blabbering virgin drunkards to make us think we had landed in another country. Who needed football when you had girls and drink? The three cousins laughed at our jokes and danced and drank a little too, though they wouldn't let any of us get close enough to touch. It's possible that at least two of them were a good couple of years older than us, though I can't remember exactly and I never asked Hudd about them again.

When Hudd dragged his relatives back to the town hall before it was too obvious that they were missing it was almost eleven. We all sat for another hour, drinking like seasoned sozzlers, talking animatedly, all of us secretly fantasising about where our lips wanted to be right now while affecting only a quasi-macho interest in the girls' physical attributes. We straggled out of the cricket pavilion at around midnight, giggling and puking and falling over, and by one most of us had received a sound bollocking from our parents before crashing out in bed, oblivious to newly administered thick ears and the forthcoming disciplinary measures because we were all in love, more or less, for the first time.

I'D NEVER HEARD Keith talk to me like that before, which was why I hit him when he came home on Saturday night. I was trying to bring the lad to his senses, though he was so drunk he didn't even seem to notice. We'd been sitting up all evening, worried because we'd rung up Sean Wickes' house and there was no answer, so then I went round there in the car and the place was completely dark, no sign of anybody watching a video at all. Lying little bastards. And then we were just about to call the police when we heard him trying to get his key in the front door, but he was too far gone to manage it and so I swung the door open and he almost fell into the hallway, but just kept his balance in time before staggering past me.

I bombarded him with reproaches and questions, demanding to know what had been going on, who had been responsible, where they'd got their drink from, but he was too insensible to react. I wanted to know right there and then, so that I could make phone calls and get straight to the bottom of this thing and deal out the necessary punishments and then put this whole stupid thing behind us. I admit that despite my anger I was already thinking ahead to the game the next day. I didn't want us to miss out on that League record after all the hard work we had put in, and I didn't want my son to be the one who let the side down. Little did I know that the entire team was in as bad a state as he, and that they had indulged in this excess purely with the aim of sabotaging their own chances of going down in district League Under-14 history.

His distant, glazed and thoroughly indifferent look induced by the quaffing of unfamiliar liquids was already annoying me intensely. He was too drunk to be properly registering my parental anger and concern, and I wanted him to know how important this episode was in terms of his indiscipline. Then he started making his way towards the staircase while talking in this smart-arsed, all-knowing tone which I'd heard some of his friends talking in before and after their football matches. 'You're getting worked up, Dad,' he said, 'just like you do on the touchline every week, shouting at those young referees and those parents on the opposite side of the pitch, going red in the face about every decision given against us like it was the most important thing in the world, much more important than third world starvation, oh yeah, a free-kick against us eighty yards from our own goal in a

Treswick U-14 District League match, that's *really* important, Dad, that is.'

I grabbed his shoulder and swivelled him round. I was too livid to speak and demand the apology that I knew was rightfully mine, but he just looked at me and said, 'Leave me alone, we're all sick of you parents and your pathetic tantrums. Why don't you do something worthwhile with your lives?' And so I walloped him around the head and he fell over, then he sprinted upstairs to the bathroom and I was going to follow him when Jen pulled me back and said, 'Just leave it to the morning. Besides, you'll wake Clara.'

We went upstairs and we could hear him vomiting into the toilet, and I waited until he came out and stood there watching him, waiting for some flicker of acknowledgement of his wrong-doing, but he just walked straight past me. '*You're* the one who's pathetic,' I said, and he snorted and went into his room and slammed the door. A few minutes later when Jen went in to put a bucket by his bed he was already unconscious.

WHEN I WOKE up the next morning I wished we hadn't done it. It wasn't just the hangover, though that was bad enough. My stomach seemed to weigh a ton, and my head was hammering like there was some kind of piston inside there relentlessly knocking a spot on my cranium just behind my eyes. I felt like I did not know which part of my body to try to move first, and as I lay there I mouthed my debut vow to never let myself get that drunk again. I could not imagine how I was going to get my body on to a football pitch, and spotted a big flaw in our plan. How could we lose the game if none of us could actually make it to the ground?

The physical discomfort of the hangover was overriden by the fear of my father and the vivid memory, despite the drink, of how he had looked at me the night before, just before he had swung his arm around my head with such force that I could still feel its consequence on my swollen left ear. I knew this night was not going to be casually written off as a youthful mistake, that there would be groundings and fines and all the rest of it. But that was not bothering me because we had all expected that as part of the price to pay for our protest. What bothered me was the conflict ahead. The feeling that he wasn't going to understand why we had done this, and that even such an extreme protest was going to be futile. They would not see the reason for the protest, they were just going to concentrate on the drunkenness and condemn us for that alone. Evading the issue, as my dad is always so quick to scream at politicians on the evening news.

And who was I to make him see the point of all this? How could I out-argue my father, who wouldn't listen anyway, as Trev had pointed out? How could I explain, without hurting his feelings or making him go off the handle again, that I found it embarrassing when he stood there shouting at referees, a man of his age? Well, that's irrelevant, his age, I mean. It was the loss of respect I could not stand, after looking up to him for so many years, after believing for so long that everything he told me was the truth, and that all the advice he gave me was right. Then this season he was all of a sudden interested in my football team and I was so pleased that he would be coming along to watch and then . . .

What are they thinking of, my dad and Sean's mum and dad and Hudd's parents too, and even Chris Ebitt's granny, for Christ's sake, these people who from the time shortly after we came out of nappies laid down the law to us on good behaviour day after day, who taught us to say please and thank you, to step aside for strangers, to wear our school ties and not answer back and a million and one other little nuances of protocol whose breaching would apparently tear society apart. There they were, delighting us one day by helping us to form a football club and organising it all, then the next day standing there raving and shouting like lunatics at complete strangers on the other side of the pitch. Every week, even when we were winning. Actually threatening people, and then one week, which must have been the week that Trev got his idea, a real fistfight, and not one of them adult enough to break it up until they kind of realised how ludicrous the whole scene was and they backed off a bit, although that didn't stop them mouthing off at each other until the final whistle. We won 8–2.

Lying there with my hangover thinking about all this gave me the strength to get up. I knew that Dad would be glaring at me over the kitchen table at the very least, that there would be more comments about my irresponsibility, my ingratitude, my immaturity, all those words they throw at you to try to make you turn around and apologise and grovel for forgiveness and then promise never to be a bad boy again. Oh no, Father, I will study every night until I become a pillar of society like yourself, standing publicly swearing at men and women from the next village because their son might have fouled my son on a football pitch.

Ah, who cared about all this? Surely there were more important things in life. Like Esther, Tilly and Louise.

I showered and washed my hair and that seemed to clear my head a little bit, but there was no way I could eat breakfast. My dad made a big show of making me a huge plate of sausage, eggs and bacon and placing it in front of my nose. 'The usual pre-match meal,' he said shortly, and then, when I wouldn't touch it, he added, 'Oh, so we're not hungry this morning, what a surprise.' Then the phone rang and it was Mr Wickes. Word had somehow got out that the whole team had been party to the previous night's bevvying and now the parents were ringing each other up and shaking their heads and collectively deciding that 'we' would first play the match and then see what happened and what the consequences would be.

As planned, we were truly terrible, we had no choice. Everybody looked as rough as shit, and during the first half three players ran off the pitch to vomit next to the touchline. The other team were loving it, having expected the usual hammering. We'd beaten them 12–1 at their place earlier in the season and you could see by their looks when they turned up that they were not anticipating anything much better in the return fixture. When they went 1–0 up they didn't celebrate much because you could tell they thought it was a freak goal, although if they'd looked deeper into the eyes of any of our players they would have seen that we had not just started sluggishly but were suffering a more deeply ingrained malaise. When they went 2–0 up they shouted a little louder, especially their parents on the touchline, who sensed that maybe today was the day for an upset. They missed a lot more chances to go further ahead, despite our best lack of effort, but when they scored a third just before half-time they went completely mad, mobbing each other and diving on the guy who'd scored, and their stupid mums and dads jumped up and down and even ran on to the pitch too.

The home parents had stood huddled together on the other touchline, subdued and brooding, making no gestures at the referee and barking no oaths at their adult counterparts. I couldn't help but spend more of the first half looking at them than at the game itself. I hardly touched the ball because I wasn't quick enough to get to it before my direct opponent. Another thing was that I kept looking towards the gate of the field where we played, somehow hoping that Hudd Anyan's cousins were going to turn up. I avoided looking directly at my dad, who had not spoken to me all morning except to make sarcastic comments about my failure to eat breakfast, and we had driven to the game in loaded silence. But he was not looking much at the game either – there seemed to be an impromptu committee meeting on the touchline.

The opposition's third goal not only triggered off wild celebrations among the away contingent, but saw the entire mass of our parenthood walking towards their cars and driving away without a word. There was something comical about this sight, while at the same time relief surged through my body that my dad was no longer standing there. At half-time we walked across to the touchline and found the water bucket and sponge just lying there, together with the keys to the changing room. We trudged into the changing room and some of us immediately stuck our heads under the cold water tap among a general groaning and heaving. Our substitute Kev Beetings got seven offers to come on, but he was happy to sit it out for the rest of the morning, looking just as pale as the rest of us.

Trev meanwhile was rushing around emptying sachets of white powder into the orange beakers we usually drank our half-time cup of tea from. 'I thought this might happen,' he said. 'Now everyone drink one of these and let's take it easy for the first ten minutes until our stomachs are settled. Kev you take one too, there are sure to be one or two of us too hungover to react to the antidote.' We sat sipping reluctantly. 'No, that's no good, gulp it down in one!' Trev said, and we did as we were told, and then he said, 'Well, what the hell are we waiting for, let's get out there and thrash this lot. Come on, they're useless!'

'But I thought we wanted to lose,' said Chris Ebitt.

'Not any more,' shouted Trev like he was explaining it to a five-year-old. 'They've gone!'

We scored our seventh just as the final whistle went, and Trev spread his arms out and started running around the pitch making aeroplane noises, and we all did the same until we landed in a big heap together, then we lay on our backs laughing and laughing and laughing as the spring sunshine bathed our faces and the churned turf beneath us smelt of the hope and happiness ahead in our young lives.

'Shall we tell them?' said Sean Wickes.

'No,' said Trev. 'Let 'em read it in the paper next Saturday.' And we all laughed again.

Furlington Welfare's Last Great Orator

ALF WANGERMAN WAS ostensibly a fan of Furlington Welfare, and it's true that he never missed a home game. On cool late-summer Saturdays or frozen winter Wednesdays, Alf stood solid in his long black, buttonless coat and terrace-worn hobnail boots, his hands only emerging from his pockets to toss a mint mouthwards or to roll a cigarette, a feat he managed effortlessly on even the windiest of days, while never for one second taking his eyes off the game.

Alf was not really there for the football, however. He was there for the referee. More precisely, he was there to *hate* the referee, and in this respect you could not doubt his passion and commitment. Every week he hated the referee from the moment the latter stepped on to the Welfare's scruffy turf at Lugdale Lane until the time around two long hours later when he disappeared back into the refuge of his changing room, Alf's huge, prickly jaw bumping up and down and casting the last of his colourful curses at the nape of the hapless official's head.

You could find Alf shortly afterwards at his regular table in the corner of the club bar with half a pint of stout and a black, hard-covered notebook. It was not advisable to approach Alf at this point in time. He would be mumbling to himself, writing quickly but assiduously, pausing occasionally for a toke on his roll-up and a sip of his beer. Sometimes the referee would step into the bar in his civvies for a post-match drink and look over apprehensively at Alf, and then around the bar, as if looking for guidance on whether or not it was safe for him to stay. As far as Alf was

concerned, however, the game was over, the referee's performance had naturally been an absolute disgrace, and that was that.
He would simply ignore the official, as if to say he had wasted
enough breath on him for one day. More important now was the
documentation of the arbitrator's failings, though to what end Alf
was compiling this volume of incompetence was anybody's guess.

Many referees complained about Alf to both the club and the
committee of the Lexington Waste Management League, as it was
known back then. Some requested that they should never again be
asked to whistle at Lugdale Lane, while others demanded that the
club take action against Alf by either gagging him or banning him.
The club refused, saying that when you were up to your neck in
debt and nurturing an average home gate of 150 you could not
afford to ban a single person from the ground, as that meant a loss
of £2.50 per week. The League, meanwhile, was inevitably run by
a bunch of spineless nobodies who never got round to making a
decision on the matter before the issue resolved itself.

Many speculated that the real reason behind the club's inaction
was that they were scared of Alf. He was not really the kind of
man you wanted to alienate. He was big and loud and he didn't
look people in the eye unless he was saying something unpleasant
to them. You could quite easily imagine him taking revenge by
dropping some kerosene and a match underneath the club's tatty
wooden stand. Or late one night after a midweek fixture confront-
ing one of the directors in the patch of dark waste-land that
qualified as the club car park.

For others, though, Alf was as good a reason as any to waste
an afternoon at Lugdale Lane. The man was a powerhouse of
oratory. It wasn't just that he could go for two whole hours without throwing the same insult at the referee. No, Alf had gone for
years without falling into repetition. He was a true original, who
could bellow wordy rhetoric while looking at the same time as
though he wanted to murder the man in black for the perceived
injustice of a petty foul awarded against the home side in an
entirely undangerous position. He monopolised ref abuse so

much that any innocent who came for the first time to Lugdale Lane and shouted, 'Where are yer specs, ref?' would find himself the object of one of Alf's terrifying, prolonged stares.

Alf had no sense of humour, even though he must have made hundreds of people laugh in his time. He was deadly serious about insulting the referee. It was very, very important to him. But Alf did not smile unless something comical happened on the pitch, like the referee getting smacked by the ball in the bollocks, or the referee falling over on an icy pitch while running backwards. Then he would emit a scornful, rather than spontaneous, staccato series of ha ha has. Once, the referee at a Furlington Welfare game pulled a hamstring and had to leave the field just seconds into the game. Alf jeered him with a huge grin all the way to the tunnel, shouting, 'It's as well you left now, I *know* you were going to be crap. Even your *hamstring* knew you were going to be crap, that's why it did you the favour of pulling before you made an utter pilchard of yourself, you bastard son of a syphilitic freemason.' And then, in the same breath he turned to the linesman – a slender man who was preparing himself to replace the referee – and bellowed, 'And you'll be no bloody better, you ginger-bonced stick insect. You'll be knackered just from blowing your whistle.'

That was all relatively mild. Alf was no doubt sparing with his invective on the grounds that neither of the two men had, as yet, made a decision that was, in the eyes of our friend, utterly execrable. Once the game got going, though, there was not a referee in the land who stood a chance of escaping Alf's noisome contumely, and he followed the game up and down the east side of the pitch, which was bordered by a few deteriorating, weed-littered concrete steps that passed for terracing, barking vitriol that would only be stemmed by a home goal for Furlington, an event marked by a small cheer and some polite applause. Once the game restarted, so did Alf.

'What about your positioning on that corner kick, referee?' It did not need an actual wrong decision for Alf to commence barracking, he had his eye on everything that the man in black was up to. 'How the hell were you supposed to see any pushing in the six-yard box from where you were standing? What sort of positional sense do you have when your missus tells you she wants to do it standing up? I bet you're out in the garden pruning the bloody roses!'

Writing these words now, I do not find them particularly amusing, it's just the memory of Alf while he was shouting them that brings a smile to my face, and the glorious pointlessness of those afternoons spent as a young man in my twenties with no responsibilities, and nothing better to do with my life than watch non-League football with a couple of mates and have a few beers. What the hell was he on about, pruning the roses while his wife was waiting for a shag? It was this slightly surreal obscurity which seemed to make his harassment all the more delightful for the other spectators, because you never knew what was going to come next.

'You harlot, you politician's tart, you big referee's blouse, you should be at home with a darning needle making hotpot for your weak-kneed husband!' he yelled once at a referee whom he had deemed to be slightly effeminate because of a wavy, bouffant hairstyle. The bloke fancied himself a little bit, that's true, but that was thread enough for Alf to grab and tug and turn into his theme for the afternoon. 'Was it a blow-dry? Did Angela ask you how the kids are doing at school while she took the curlers out? Did you swap recipe tips with Gloria while you were sitting under the dryer, you la-di-da-di, teatop-toting, handbag-hugger. Did Lionel Blair show you his pink silk underwear? Gerroff the fucking pitch and back to your boudoir, you skirt-wearing trollop! And that was not a foul, that was NOT a foul, but you gave it because you are a woman and do not understand the laws of a man's game!'

Another afternoon, as the two captains were shaking hands, he took one look at the referee's name on the teamsheet and declared: 'Mr Perry Tarkington-Smythe of Russet Mills!' The poor guy, who looked as regular a bloke as they come, did not stand a chance. 'Oh, I say, what a privilege to have such a fine and dandy man at humble Lugdale Lane. I do hope that the changing facilities were sufficiently comfortable, and that the club butler was able to provide for all of your needs, Mr Perry Tarkington-Smythe. Now, don't worry, we had the pitch sterilised before you ran out, and these gentlemen will be on their best behaviour throughout the ninety minutes . . .' Once the game started, naturally, Mr Tarkington-Smythe was treated with less mock respect, and more of the fuck-off-back-to-your-country-mansion, Tarkington-Ponceworth, though Alf expressed it with a greater linguistic flourish I can no longer exactly recollect.

Some players left the club because they claimed that Alf disturbed their concentration. The fact is, though, none of these players were good enough to make it worthwhile trying to persuade them to stay. 'If you can't ignore a single spectator on the side of the pitch you'll not be much cop in front of 90,000 at Wembley,' they were quite rightly told. One thing's for sure. Most of the referees were so unnerved by Alf that their performance just got worse and worse as the game went on. They hesitated too long before making decisions and then usually made the wrong call. The further the referee deteriorated, the more excuse Alf would have to get on his back, and then some of the crowd would start to groan too, firing up Alf to increase his vitriol.

Alf's reputation began to spread in certain circles. Referees' assessors would come especially to Furlington Welfare to see how officials coped with the one-man hostility show. They probably worked along the same logic as the club did with those wantaway players – if you buckle under the pressure of a single heckler, then what chance do you stand against a partisan crowd in eastern Europe during a big UEFA Cup tie? This was unfair in a way. Everyone in a ground like Furlington's could hear every word Alf said. The lucid words of this standalone foghorn must surely have been more difficult to ignore than the white-noise, massed whistling of 40,000 Red Star Belgrade fans. Then again, if any referee was capable of ignoring Alf, then they were surely marked to move to grander and grassier footballing plains.

Others must have heard of Alf's reputation too. With increasing frequency, those sad, speccy ground-hoppers would come to Lugdale Lane to tick us off their list, but would spend most of their afternoon within gaping distance of Alf. Groups of stupidly grinning students started turning up and standing close by him, sniggering in that highly irritating student manner, while never daring to get close enough that Alf might reach out and take a swipe at them. They'd look around at the rest of us, as if to say, 'What a laugh, eh?' Alf seemed to be completely unaware of them, which was good, although few would have stood in his way had he decided to take a good run and stick his hobnailed right boot up their smart undergraduate arses.

This was around the time when football was all of a sudden a topic that could be mentioned in polite circles. Every week a new glossy magazine appeared on the newsstands laddishly proclaiming the invention of a sport called football. On the radio everyone was allowed to ring up and bore the nation with their trite and poorly informed opinions on every aspect of the game, while on television the Friday night encounter between Port Vale and Swindon assumed the mantle of being the most important game in the history of both clubs, if not the history of the game itself. Flimsy, garish football shirts were placed on racks at almost metaphysical prices. And publishing houses, eager not to miss out, razed whole forests in the name of rushing out prejudiced fan- bile, scrappy club histories and memoirs of fat-bellied former 'legends' with nothing new to say, but with the copyright to a few after-dinner anecdotes now deemed interesting enough to be laid down in print, bound within a hard cover, and presented to the public as a tome worthy of both their time and their money.

At the zenith of all this vacuous tripe was a weekly television programme called *Total Footie!* It took all the worst aspects of the above-named media and edited them down to what the programme's founders had presumably stipulated to be a 'punchy' style, but which merely had the effect of making you want to punch the programme's frontman, the smugly faced Simon Mellis. This odious careerist bore an all-knowing expression which was meant to slam home the message during the entire hour's running time: 'Hey, kids, it's all ironic, eh?' Armed with this same expression, and a microphone and a cameraman, he turned up one week on the terraces at Furlington Welfare interviewing fans along the lines of 'Why would anyone want to come and watch this crap when you can watch Man United at home on TV?'

The club had allowed him in on the grounds that he was supposedly doing a documentary on the trials and struggles of a small and mostly unsuccessful non-League team. However, once he had reeled off a token couple of questions about the psychology of Furlington Welfare watchers, he slipped in a seemingly innocuous query whose full intent only later became clear. 'Who would you say is the club's most loyal supporter?' he asked. And just in case we unsophisticated thickies had not understood, he added, 'I mean, who comes every week and never misses a game, and gets really worked up and shouts at the referee and that kind of thing?' So, this top investigative reporter had been tipped off about Alf and had sneaked in on the pretext of doing a club profile. Smart journalism.

Gradually he moved along the terrace towards where Alf was standing. The game had just started and Alf was already haranguing the ref, who that day had the misfortune to be modelling a new line of shirt that could best be described as 'flushing pink'. 'Hoi referee, you took your wife's night-shirt out the wardrobe by mistake! And she's sitting at home in bed watching the afternoon film on BBC2 in a thick black top, whistling at all the film stars and waving yellow cards at them when they act out of order!'

Normally there would have been a ripple of laughter at this, but everyone was distracted by the camera crew moving towards its prey, and the sound of Simon Mellis shouting: 'Ha, ha, ha! Very funny!' Then he tapped Alf on the shoulder and said, 'Excuse me, could you say that again facing towards the camera?'

Alf turned around and looked at Simon Mellis as if the man had just asked him to stare down the barrel of a shotgun while he tried out the trigger. He didn't say anything in reply, he was too baffled, although he did briefly glance at the camera before resuming his stare at the reporter, who said, uncertainly, 'Well, er, never mind . . . er, well, just keep on shouting at the ref as if we weren't here!'

Alf turned away from the microphone and leaned on the fence that surrounded the pitch, rolling a cigarette. There was a long silence as the regular fans waited to see how Alf would react to the camera's scrutiny. Mellis stood stupidly, his microphone still sticking out before him, until he whispered something to the cameraman, who then pointed the camera back at the game. An unusual quiet hung over the ground, and even some of the home players took their eyes off the game every now and then to see what had happened to Alf. But Furlington Welfare's most regular visitor had been stunned into silence and seemed to have gone off into a dreamy, distant state of mind.

Right then a Welfare forward was put through clear on goal before an opposition defender took his legs away about ten yards outside the penalty area. Alf jumped up in excitement, then began to rage as the man in pink only showed the defender a yellow card. Instantly, the camera turned on Alf and Mellis proffered his mike, and just as instantly Alf was silenced again. Under normal circumstances such an incident would have fuelled a fifteen-minute attack on the referee and a detailed dissection of the laws to prove that the official had erred. Today, looking bewildered, Alf froze up and seemed to stretch backwards, like a cornered animal, staring with genuine fear at the microphone like it was a bloodied dagger in the hands of a psychotic foe.

'Tell him to fuck off, Alf,' somebody yelled helpfully.

'Come on,' exhorted Simon Mellis, 'it's only a camera. Say

something funny about the ref again. Come on, he gave a yellow card there, it should have been a red, eh?'

At this, Alf's expression changed and he started leaning forward, his roll-up in the corner of his mouth. 'What the fuck would you know about it, you little creep?' he growled. Then, to the cheers of the spectators, he grabbed the mike, flung it to the ground and began to stamp on it, his heavy footwear rendering it useless in seconds. 'Keep filming!' Mellis ordered the cameraman, no doubt excited that his story had a new angle, THE WILD MAN OF FURLINGTON WELFARE. Alf, though, grabbed the camera, yanked it off its protesting operator, and raised it over his head before dashing it on the terrace with a roar. A large piece of concrete came loose, which Alf then used to pummel the thing until it buckled. He tore out a video tape and proceeded to unreel it and rip it, while the rest of us cheered him on.

If the two men had boasted an ounce of brain between them they would have left at this point, but the pompous frontman, perhaps believing that his status as a BBC worker had propelled him to untouchability, proceeded to yell at Alf and demand that he *hand back* (those were the words he actually used) the broken equipment immediately. Instead, Alf picked up the reporter, lifted him on to his back where his dangling, black-jeaned legs kicked in comic struggle, carried him up to the top of the terrace and deposited him head first over the wall and on to the road below.

It wasn't a drop of more than ten or twelve feet, but we all ran up to see if the bloke was OK, except the cameraman, who had picked up the remains of his tool and was running towards the exit. Mellis lay groaning and writhing on the pavement, and somebody dashed towards the main stand to call an ambulance. Alf, meanwhile, stomped back down to the front of the pitch, but though he tried to catcall the ref on a couple of occasions, he had lost it, and around twenty minutes later was arrested by two police officers on a charge of actual bodily harm. Those not tending the injured reporter watched in melancholy silence as Alf left the ground for the last time.

There was a huge fuss because it was the BBC, and as all the tabloids splashed the story in glee the club had to take action and ban Alf from the ground, although he had to serve a short prison sentence too. They might as well have boarded up the club on the same day, because attendances dwindled to almost nothing within months, the club dropped out of the Lexington Waste Management League to the league below, and the following summer merged with a club nearby and sold Lugdale Lane so that someone could build a garden centre on top of it.

The newly merged club kept the Welfare part of Furlington's name, and then after two years discreetly dropped it without a murmur of protest from anyone. Because by then, nobody cared.

Behind a Common Cause

JAS HILL FELT suddenly disheartened as he looked at the long day's schedule he had been handed at the door of the convention centre. What the hell am I doing here? he thought. Why did I have to get involved in this? He was the kind of person who volunteered for things either impulsively or because he found it impossible to say no when asked. He even managed to seem genuinely keen when he raised his hand and said, 'I'm up for it, no problem, count me in.' Then afterwards, often within seconds, a feeling welled up inside him that he was not going to be at ease again until the task he had impetuously volunteered for was over.

Jas was only twenty-five, and prone to irrational memberships, joining up with hobbyists of all hues in that search for extracurricular fulfillment. Over the past few years he'd enjoyed transitory membership of all kinds of clubs and societies, but none of them held his attention for long, and in between he would lapse back into his usual pastimes of drinking and football. Then, after a few months had passed, and sensing that drinking and football, while eternally enjoyable, were not really getting him anywhere, he would come across some *new thing* in which he could not but help get himself involved.

The problem with clubs and the like, Jas had discovered, was that they loved new members. They devoured new members. They were so bloody keen to get you to join and stay that they put you off right from the start. And the reason was that all clubs had a small selection of tasks that no one wanted to do. It was usually the position of treasurer. Be they ramblers or revolutionaries, they always needed a treasurer, and they offered you this position almost as soon as you walked through the door, as if it reflected the greatest privilege, as if it was a symbol of their immediate trust and acceptance of you. Jas had learned never to accept the position of treasurer, because unless you moved to another country you were burdened with it for all time.

Three weeks earlier, in a fit of raised consciousness, Jas had joined a political party called Socialist Solidarity. He had bought a magazine from a bookshop in Camden called Socialist Standard, and then, as he was reading it in a café nearby, had been approached by a friendly, graying man in his forties called Barry who wanted to know what he thought of the journal, and several other issues too. Jas was vaguely left-wing in the kind of way that many young people who live in north London are – a *Guardian* reader who tuts in all the right places while reading it, then goes out and drinks beer and watches football. He realised that this was not good enough, and for some years had been meaning to do *something about it* but was not really sure where to start. Barry was the catalyst he had needed to become active, and before Jas knew it Barry had left the café and he was left holding a life membership card (cost: £1), having promised to attend his first meeting the following Tuesday.

Socialist Solidarity met above the Pickled Liver in a room that seemed far too small to reflect the grand goals of the party which Barry had outlined to Jas the previous Saturday. The only person there when Jas arrived was a sour-looking woman with straight, dull hair. When Jas knocked tentatively on the door and went in she looked at him like he was the last person she wanted to see.

'Yes?' she snapped.

'Er, Barry told me there was a meeting here,' he said, already wishing that he had not come.

But when it dawned on her that he had not come into the room by accident her face brightened, realising this rarity of a new recruit had to be welcomed into the brotherhood before he slipped away like so many before him. 'Come in, sit down,' she bubbled.

She came towards him and extended a small, tight hand. 'Kate,' she said. 'I'm second in command to Barry.'

Jas smiled back nervously. 'Jas,' he said, and then sat down in the front row of four chairs (he was surprised to see that only twelve chairs had been put out).

Kate then grilled him on his political views in exactly the same way that Barry had done on the Saturday before. She sat and nodded thoughtfully, her mousey nose wrinkling itself involuntarily from time to time. He made all the right noises anew, slagging off Blair and the Labour Party, dropping the word 'sell-out' in time and again, and emphasising his trade union membership as evidence of his political credentials, although in reality he had been in the National Union of Journalists for only six months and had never attended a meeting of any description. In the meantime a bearded man in a shabby parka shuffled in and sat down at the back and listened. Kate ignored the new arrival as Jas talked until he had apparently satisfied the criteria for remaining in the room and the party. He half expected her to ask him if he wanted to be treasurer. There was a silence until the man with the beard stood up and introduced himself as Chris. 'New member?' he asked in a Birmingham accent, and when Jas said yes he was sure he saw a smirk momentarily flit across Chris' face. Still Kate did not even look at Chris.

'How many branches have you got in London?' Jas asked, and Chris let out a small snigger and Kate looked at him for the first time with the same expression she had worn when Jas had first come into the room.

'This *is* the London branch, mate,' said Chris with a wry smile.

'Oh,' was all Jas could say, but then added, 'And what about the rest of the country?'

'Birmingham, Manchester, Newcastle, Leeds, Glasgow, all over,' said Kate quickly, before Chris could interrupt, listing off the cities like a saleswoman.

'Don't forget Bristol,' said Chris, and, looking at Jas, mouthed the words 'one member'.

Kate saw this and shouted: 'Just shut the fuck up, will you, Chris? You'll soon be out of here, so just don't stir it.'

'We'll see how the vote goes, won't we?' said Chris, and went and sat down at the back again, grinning. He took out a newspaper (Jas was surprised to see it was the *Independent*) and Kate sat staring moodily at the table until Barry arrived with a pint. It was already quarter to eight, and the meeting had been scheduled to start at seven-thirty.

'Right. Let's get started, shall we?' said Barry cheerfully, winking at Jas. Jas thought he was joking, that there must be other people down in the bar getting their drinks in, that at least the twelve paltry seats would be filled up. But no, this was it, and Kate read out the two items on the agenda.

'Item one. The motion to expel Chris Ninion from the party. Item two. Nomination of delegates to attend the conference: *Socialism into the Next Millennium*.'

'OK,' said Barry. 'Shall we take a vote straight away or do you want to defend yourself, Chris?'

'I've nothing to defend myself about,' said Chris. 'I just came to watch the circus. I see you've given new membership a grand boost though to maintain the party numbers.' Addressing Jas, he said, 'Good luck, mate, though don't dare to question the good intentions of Sendero Luminoso.'

Jas looked at Barry questioningly. He had no clue what Chris was on about. Barry then read out a lengthy indictment charge which, as far as Jas could make out, meant that Chris was to be expelled for expressing views on the Peruvian Shining Path guerrilla cell which had been contrary to Socialist Solidarity's 'total and complete' support of the movement. When he had read the charge Barry and Kate voted to expel Chris. Chris voted to remain in the party. When Jas failed to raise his hand for an abstention Barry looked at him and said, 'Come on, Jas, adopt a position.' Jas had not realised that he was allowed to vote already. For a second he thought of voting with Chris in an attempt to get himself expelled as quickly as possible but, as he had no idea what Chris was actually supposed to have said, he told Barry that he would rather abstain at this point.

Chris left the room, but not before placing his hand on Jas' shoulder and saying slowly and sardonically, 'All the very best of luck, mate.'

When he had gone Barry muttered, 'Good riddance, reactionary bastard.' Kate announced that it was time to move on to the agenda's next item.

Now that Chris had left, the platform of Barry and Kate at the front table was left addressing an audience of one, namely Jas. The two spoke, however, as if the room was full of people. He wondered what they would be doing if he had not turned up. Barry droned on about this conference that was coming up and the line that the party would be taking on the topic of socialism into the next millennium. Jas suddenly felt very tired. He'd slept badly the previous night and had had to get up early that morning for work. He was a bad listener at the best of times and quickly got bored, and when he was tired found it impossible to resist sleep. But tonight he could not forget that he was the sole listener, and that it would be embarrassing to drop off, especially as he was supposed to be at the peak of his commitment to the party he had only just joined. He tried to focus again and again on Barry's voice: '. . . absolutely no compromise on any of the fundamental tenets of Socialist Solidarity's manifesto . . . absolutely crucial to make others understand why Sendero Luminoso is the pivot upon which international revolution shall be ignited . . . absolutely . . .'

The next thing Jas knew Kate was cradling his head and slapping him gently on the cheek. He opened his eyes and she said, 'Are you all right? Barry's gone to get some water.'

'What happened?' said Jas, feeling awkward that his head was in Kate's lap, but too shy to jump up too quickly.

'You fell off the chair and hit your head on the floor.' She smiled. Her front teeth were a terrible brown colour. At that second Barry came back into the room with a glass of water and said, 'But not before we had voted to nominate you as one of our two delegates

to the Socialism 2000 conference. Congratulations, young man!'
Jas sat up and drank the water, while Barry and Kate beamed at
him like proud parents watching their son taking his first drink
out of an open-top beaker.

The conference was scheduled for October 9th. As he sat
downstairs in the bar of the Pickled Liver with Barry and Kate
Jas tried to remember what the hell it was about that date.
Something was supposed to be happening that day, besides this
absolutely crucial conference, of course. He prayed that it was
something that would reprieve him, like a family wedding or a
christening, the kind of occasion he normally dreaded. Then
again, he could hardly see Barry and Kate showing much understanding for a wedding or christening as an excuse. 'It's absolutely
imperative that counter-revolutionary Christian ceremonies be
abolished in the fight to . . .' Barry would drone on in the same
voice which had put Jas to sleep, a voice curiously lacking in the
fire and fervour of great orators of old, and much at odds with the
fighting content of his speech.

He was still feeling dazed from his fall, and wondered if it
would perhaps not occur to him until the next day. He also
wondered whether Kate and Barry had taken the vote on his
attending the conference before they had checked whether he was
all right or not. Perhaps a late party member had sneaked in and
clobbered him on the back of the head, as this was the only way
they could persuade people to volunteer, by voting for them while
they were unconscious. But Jas knew that he would probably have
volunteered anyway, simply because he would have felt too
embarrassed to have said no.

Kate and Barry were assassinating Chris' 'bourgeois' character traits when Jas remembered and involuntarily blurted out:
'Shit!' The other two looked at him and Kate said: 'What's the
matter?'

'Sorry, nothing,' said Jas, reddening. 'Just something I forgot to
do at work today.'

Barry and Kate resumed their political obituary, and Jas thought to himself shit, shit, shit. October 9th. How could he have forgotten? Sweden versus Poland.

OVER THE NEXT three weeks Jas reconciled himself with the fact that he was going to miss the game. It didn't matter. This was a new era in his life, he was going to be too politically involved, and, of course, motivated, to think about football. It was just ninety minutes of football between two foreign nations. It wasn't even England, even though the game's result would decide whether or not they made it to the Euro 2000 play-offs. When he thought of it like that he realised how pathetically unimportant it sounded in the light of . . . well, he thought of all the usual facile comparisons. Compared with third-world hunger, the evils of capitalism, la-di-da-da. OK then, Jas thought, compared with the future of socialism in the new millennium. That was very important, and it was important that he was present when leaders of the leftist movement were there to discuss it. No dispute. And he felt momentarily quite righteous that he would not be watching Sweden versus Poland.

As the day approached Jas was, nonetheless, undeniably depressed. He tried to convince himself that the depression was rooted in some other cause besides the oncoming convention – his lack of a girlfriend, maybe, or the tedium of his job as a sub-editor on *Kitchens and Interiors* magazine and the cretinous journalists who bawled every time he moved a comma in their copy. But he had to concede that the depression seemed to be accentuated by the phone-calls from Kate. Kate was the second delegate to the convention, and she was eager to discuss the party line with Jas almost every evening, at extraordinary length. She sent him piles of old *Socialist Solidarity* newspapers (they could have done with a ruthless sub-editor too), which lay unread by his bedside, because every night when he tried to mentally penetrate the intense rhetoric he immediately fell asleep. He started going out in the evenings to the cinema or, on two occasions, to watch the Monday night game down at the pub to avoid the calls from Kate. As he watched the game he held a copy of Lenin's *What is to Be Done* in his hand, but he could not take his eyes off the game long enough to get through the opening paragraph. Southampton 3 Derby 3. A bit of a thriller, he had to admit, even as an ardent Marxist who now probably had to view Monday night football as part of a ploy to divert the working classes from erecting barricades around Westminster.

'We've absolutely got to push the line that US imperialist vilification of Gaddafi has to end immediately,' Kate rasped when he foolishly answered the phone that night at eleven-thirty, six pints of bitter sloshing around his gastric system. He had even forgotten to go for a pee when he came in before he picked up the receiver. 'Yeah, right,' he said, and then stood with his legs crossed in agony for half an hour before she got off the line. When she finished the conversation she would break off in mid-sentence and say, 'Look, I've really got to go now, Jas, goodbye,' and slam the receiver down, like it was Jas who had rung her at a really busy and inconvenient time.

On the Saturday of the convention, however, Kate greeted Jas with a radiant smile when they met outside Embankment Tube station. She even, much to his embarrassment, linked her arm with his as they walked along, jabbering enthusiastically about the impact they were going to have on the day's events and, by consequence, on the history of the twenty-first century. She was wearing dark blue slacks and her hair looked as though she had not washed it since Jas had last seen her at the Pickled Liver. God, what if someone from his work saw him, or one of his friends, and thought that was his girlfriend? When they passed a newsstand he uncoupled himself from her on the pretext that he needed a packet of mints. He hoped she might follow suit to temper the foul odour that came from her mouth every time she looked up at him and spoke, but she just waited for him on the pavement. Why am I spending my Saturday in the company of this woman? he thought as he looked at her hunched little figure waiting patiently, then felt an inexplicable sense of compassion towards her, as if he had to protect her. This evaporated when he walked back towards her and she saw that he had bought the *Guardian*. 'Liberal, bourgeois lies!' she spat, before railing against half a dozen of its journalists and their ideological misdemeanours in such detail that Jas got the impression she must buy the paper fairly often herself. Then just before they reached the convention centre she snatched the paper off him and dumped it in a waste-paper basket, saying, 'Sorry, but we don't want the other parties seeing us with that in our hands.'

'Mint?' said Jas hopefully. Kate declined.

Inside the convention centre, which was actually a hall in a student union building conveniently placed next to a bar, Jas felt a catatonic depression descend. First of all, it reminded him of his student days, and so did some of the people who were hanging around – over-haired Trots who thought that wearing scruffy jeans gave you prole credibility, or fiery-faced crew-cuts who thought that short hair and a bovver-boy attitude could either mask or make up for their greenbelt origins. There were not many women, and those present were mostly in the Kate mold, with round glasses and bad trousers. Jas thought it lazy and reprehensible to think in types, but that did not stop him doing it. He could never stop himself thinking when he saw a gathering of Christians that they were all ugly and wore glasses and badly patterned jumpers. It wasn't true, but somehow it was.

Here you could walk in off the street and spot a leftist convention in a second, he thought. You could tell that they loved the atmosphere of the building, that they all wished deep down they were still students. Jas meanwhile wished that he was in bed, a feeling enhanced by the tedium of the opening – and sparsely attended – debates, and the fact that Kate kept pressing her leg up against his no matter how often he attempted to shift his position. When she talked to him sometimes she adopted this strangely simpering, girlish attitude, like she was a teenager on her maiden date. This was punctuated by seething indictments of the other speakers whispered into Jas' ear along the lines of, 'This creep is a reactionary fucking reformist bastard.' Or 'Middle-class feminist bitch.'

Despite her severe judgements on the fellow delegates, Kate was reluctant to stand up and say her piece on Sendero Luminoso or the absolutely pressing need to bring Colonel Gadaffi back into the international fold. Perhaps there was not the right moment, but Jas could not really tell, because he was not paying proper attention. He started using as many excuses as possible to go and get coffee or go to the toilet. He thought about leaving altogether, just walking out. If it had been sunny instead of the customary London grey he would probably have done it. Yet he knew that Kate would be on the phone half the night demanding to know what had happened, where he'd gone. He wanted there to be a clear break from the party. He wondered if Chris had deliberately provoked the debate on Sendero Luminoso in order to free himself of further party-related obligations. Maybe he had seen this convention coming up and had wanted to get out of it.

Jas was queuing for a coffee, hoping that the queue would go very slowly, when Chris himself tapped him on the shoulder and said: 'All right, mate?' They got talking, and Chris admitted that he had now joined Workers' Action. They went and sat down with their coffees in the bar area. Jas looked longingly at the pint taps. It was twenty-past eleven.

'So why did you leave Socialist Solidarity?' asked Jas. 'And why did you join Workers' Action?'

Chris laughed, like he seemed to laugh at everything. 'It's a kind of compulsive hobby,' he said. 'I know it's a waste of time, but I love it. I'm fascinated by the debate. This is the fifth party I've been in, I got expelled from the other four. You know, you get sick of meeting in the same pubs, hearing the same clichés, so you move on for some different ones. But there are some genuine people in these parties, and some good talk.'

'I haven't seen much of that in Socialist Solidarity,' Jas muttered, feeling a bit like a traitor.

'No, and you won't get any,' said Chris cheerily. 'Socialist Solidarity is just Barry and Kate. They live together. They claim there are these other branches, but I never met anyone from them. I don't want to put you off or anything, mate, but they're nutters.'

Jas sipped his coffee, feeling foolish for not having realised that before.

'Why isn't Barry here today?' he asked.

Chris laughed again. 'Why don't you ask Kate? Listen, I'd better get inside there again and show me face. Plus, if Kate sees you talking to me she'll rip your balls off. Catch up with you later.' And with that he got up and left.

At lunchtime, as they sat in the bar area, Kate really started to get on his nerves with her cattiness, especially when she spotted Chris guffawing with his new comrades from Workers' Action, all of whom wore black leather jackets and looked more like a bikers' posse. 'Treacherous scumbag,' she hissed. 'He's a political tart, jumping from party to party then leaving when it suits him.' Jas wanted to point out that he had been expelled, but kept quiet. He was more worried by the fact that she wouldn't keep her bloody leg off his. He moved his right thigh decisively away and turned his chair so that it was facing almost away from the table. Then he crossed his legs so that there was an unbridgeable distance between the two of them. 'Where's Barry today, then?' he breezed innocently.

'He had to meet the comrades from Manchester. It's confidential. He might be in a position to talk about it when he gets back,' Kate said snappily.

Jas had the feeling she said it too quickly, as if the excuse was pre-penned. 'It must be very important, because this meeting is supposed to be very important too,' said Jas.

Kate looked at him waspishly and said merely, 'Yes it is, actually.' Then she clammed up and shut up, which was fine by him. He only wished she hadn't thrown his paper away, but there were plenty of partisan leaflets around to peruse.

Jas decided to get a drink. 'Do you want a pint?' he asked Kate out of courtesy. 'No,' she said curtly. He shrugged, and she saw fit to add: 'What if the revolution started today and we were all drunk?'

'It would probably be more fun,' said Jas, and Kate said: 'Yes, well that's just the kind of attitude that will pen us back into the middle ages for ever, I'm afraid, Jas.' Jas went to the bar and got a pint of bitter.

Could she really be so pissed off because he had pulled his leg away, or was it because he had spent so little time in the hall actually listening to the morning's proceedings? Whatever, a couple of pints would loosen him up and give him plenty of reason to go to the toilet during the afternoon.

The place seemed to be filling up, though, and there was a buzz around the bar. He drank his pint and went back for a refill, but it was difficult to get to the front. When he finally did he realised the reason why. People weren't moving away from the bar. The television was on. It was quarter to two and there were Ray Wilkins and Stuart Pearce talking about the game. Jesus, he thought, satellite TV in a student bar, what's the world coming to? And then he grinned and said, 'Excellent!'

All of a sudden Jas didn't give a toss about the afternoon's schedule, due to begin at exactly the same time as Sweden versus Poland was going to kick off, with a talk entitled 'World Revolution Before 2005?' The cherubic face of Wilkins and the humourless, neanderthal mug of Pearce were such a welcome sight to Jas, it was as if he had found what he had been looking for all morning. He became so focused on them, even though the television was not loud enough to be able to hear what they were saying, that he almost forgot where he actually was. He clutched his pint delight-edly, his depression salved by the miracle cure, straining to ease himself into a better position before kick-off. He thought that the bar area might begin to clear, but if anything it seemed to get busier the nearer it got to two. Just as he had made a little niche for himself between two groups of drinkers, he felt a little tug on his jacket.

'Jas, come on, drink up, we have to get back in now,' Kate whispered insistently.

'Oh, er right, I'll be back in a few minutes, there's something here I have to see,' Jas replied vaguely.

'Who?' she said, thinking that he had said 'someone' and not 'something', because what kind of something could you possibly want to look at behind a bar? 'You shouldn't go fraternising with people from other parties, you know?'

'I thought that was the whole point of this,' Jas couldn't help himself saying. 'Aren't we supposed to be building a united socialist front for the revolution?' He said it very loud, the beer already starting to take effect, and several people looked around at them with bemused expressions.

Kate, however, looked incensed and continued to whisper, angrily: 'Half of these people are counter-revolutionaries and government agents, they'll be the first to go once the revolution starts. Now come on, let's get a good place near the front, you've got to back me up when I start heckling those fascists from the International Leninist Brigade.'

Jas realised that watching the match was not going to go down as a viable excuse with Kate, so he said that he had to go to the toilet and that he would join her in there. When he was sure that he had seen her disappear back into the symposium he ordered another pint.

The game was five minutes old, and the crowd at the bar had become so dense that it was almost impossible to struggle to the front and get served, when a man in a beard, who had been chairing the morning's proceedings, appeared at the door of the hall in front of the bar with a megaphone. 'The debate "World Revolution Before 2005?" is about to begin. Will all comrades please clear the bar area and make your way into the hall.' Despite the volume at which this was announced, the man was largely ignored, aside from a couple of drinkers at the tables next to the bar who had genuinely lost track of time. One delegate took a look through the doorway, shrugged, and came back to resume his position near the television screen. 'Come on you Swedes!' somebody yelled.

The man with the megaphone slowly realised what was going on and announced, testily, 'Will the bar management please turn off the television set so that the afternoon's programme can commence?'

This time the reaction was far greater, with cries of 'No way!' and 'Leave it on, Harry, eh?' Harry, the deadpan bar manager who was overworked on the pint-pulling front, ignored the request from the megaphone man, who eventually tore through the crowds and pushed his way to the bar, landing right next to Jas. 'Hey!' he shouted at Harry. 'Please turn the TV off, we are about to begin the afternoon's programme!'

Harry looked up at the man with the beard and said deliberately, 'I am the manager of this bar, and the television is staying on.' There was a muted cheer, although many comrades were feeling a little guilty about watching football rather than debating the date of the forthcoming global revolt.

The beard got more worked up and said, 'We have hired this facility for the afternoon and I order you to turn off the television or I will demand that you close down the bar area.'

'Fascist!' somebody muttered at the end of the bar.

'Who said that?' screamed the beard, so apoplectic that Jas' heart began racing. He hated violence and shouting, and at that second realised that even in the unlikely event of a revolution, he would more likely be running in the opposite direction for fear of getting hit by a stone. But the bearded man was now pushing people aside to get round to the other end of the bar and confront his accuser. 'Who called me a fascist?' he roared. 'Come on, own up, who the hell was it?'

At that moment Sweden came close to scoring and there was an ooooooh from those at the bar who were managing to watch both spectacles at once. The bearded man looked up at the television and yelled, 'What the hell is this anyway? A bloody football match! You're meant to be revolutionaries, for Christ's sake. This is opiate fodder to keep us in our place, this is pointless conflict on the sports park to sap us of our revolutionary fervour, to make us channel our energies and frustrations against arbitrators and fellow proletarians.' There was an embarrassed silence until he looked up at the screen and said: 'It's not even England playing!'

Once again there was an oooooh, this time a sardonic one. 'We're internationalists,' said a voice, again from the other end of the bar. 'We'll watch comrades play football from around the world.'

This threw the bearded man right off the edge. 'This is serious!' he screamed. 'Move, move, move!' He started trying to shove people away from the bar, but had unfortunately arrived just at the spot where the leather jacketed crew from Workers' Action had their seats. A burly hand grabbed the bearded man by his jumper and threw him to the floor. Jas felt inexplicably sorry for him as he lay there, momentarily stunned, but he was back on his feet in seconds, and with the help of a few other organisers who had emerged from the hall began to berate those still standing there refusing to move. Whether by misfortune or sabotage, the satellite connection suddenly went down, and with a resigned collective groan people began to troop back into the hall for the afternoon's debate.

There was something flat about the debate on the timetable for the millennium's coming revolution. About an hour into proceedings Kate stood up and delivered her piece about the absolute necessity of backing Sendero Luminoso, taking time to splutter out vitriol at the reactionary, counter-revolutionary, CIA-loving policies of at least six other splinter parties. She was largely ignored, especially by Jas, who sat there sulkily wondering whether Sweden had yet penetrated the Polish defence. She was just about to indict the International Trotskyite Cell for its failure to back Tamil separatists when the door to the hall opened and Harry the barman announced: 'There's been a goal.'

'Get out of this debate!' yelled the bearded man, but one or two people at the back were whispering to Harry, 'Who scored, who scored?' to which Harry responded, now grinning widely, 'Why don't you come and see, the TV's back up.'

There was mass scraping of chairs and a run to the door which this time could not be stopped by the dictatorial exhortations of the chairperson. Jas stood up too, but Kate yanked his jumper and said: 'Stay here! Or you're out of the party!' At that second Chris, who was about to leave the room too, turned away from his new comrades and said, 'That's rich! Come on, Kate, tell Jas here where Barry is this afternoon.'

'Fuck off, Chris,' Kate screamed, angry for the tenth time that day. Jesus, she really is nuts, thought Jas, thank God I'm about to be kicked out.

Chris was happy to fill in the necessary information. 'Barry never goes to political events on a Saturday, Jas. Barry's too busy with other things. Barry has a season ticket to Gillingham, and wouldn't have missed this afternoon's crucial home game with Wrexham, even if it had meant missing the Queen's execution at the hands of a socialist firing squad.' And with that he turned tail, giving a little skip as he heard the cheer coming from the bar area which surely meant that it was the Swedes who had scored.

Kate sat down and hung her head and then began to cry. Ah, even revolutionaries have feelings, thought Jas. The man with the beard, alone on the podium at the front of the room, was sitting with his head in his hands. Jas dropped his pile of pamphlets on to the floor and said, softly, 'Goodbye, Kate.' She didn't look up, so he walked quickly towards the door in case she had another fit. It was going to be a riveting last half-hour, with the Poles chasing that equaliser.

The Night Football Wrecked My Life

THERE ARE THREE kinds of mates. Real mates, work mates and football mates. With real mates you can talk about anything, right down to genital herpes and premature ejaculation. With work mates you bitch about your boss and about the other work mates who couldn't make it down the pub that night. With football mates, well, it's a bit limited. There's only one thing to talk about. But what a thing. And with this kind of mate you may share some of the most intimate and emotional moments of your entire life.

You may not know where your football mates live. You see them at the stadium, or in the pub before the game, or on the train home, and there's never any awkward silences, there's so much to have an opinion on. And then when you wave them goodbye on the station forecourt you don't care which direction they're going in, or whether they still live with their mums or in a sad little bedsit together with a thousand empty pizza boxes, or, even worse, with a girl. These details are superfluous. Because football mates are fine, but they're not the sort of people you'd want to have a relationship with. In fact, a lot of them you don't even want to find yourself next to at the game. Like Stasher.

I never found out Stasher's real name, or why he was called Stasher. We both supported Colchester United, and knew each other by sight from the pubs and the terraces and away-day coaches to miserable places like Hartlepool and Rochdale, but I tended to exchange nothing more than a nod of acknowledgement with him. He was a bit of a nutter, though not in the traditional sense of being a hooligan. I never saw Stasher getting physically violent. He was just a bit too intense, even for a fanatic, as I discovered the one time I was sitting next to him in the coach back from a midweek League Cup tie at Darlington.

I was tired and had been hoping to sleep all the way home, knowing that I wouldn't make it into my bed until four in the morning. But there was no chance of sleep when you were sitting next to Stasher. Even though the game had been a thoroughly unremarkable 1–1 draw, he wasn't happy until he had unleashed a biased and bilious attack on the referee, both linesmen, all eleven members of the Colchester side, and the manager too (who had been in his job for just three games at the time). He replayed incidents from the game which I had already forgotten, furiously citing mishit passes and ill-timed tackles which inevitably constitute around ninety per cent of the game at that level, and which every spectator groans at for a second before continuing to follow the game in the wayward hope that something good may come to pass. In the end, you surmised that if all Stasher was saying was true, then a real and just scoreline would have been Darlington 0 Colchester 8, despite the fact that the entire team deserved to be tied by their feet to a horse-trailer and dragged around the Essex countryside, there to be pelted with rotten sugar beet by locals every bit as angry as Stasher himself.

'The Darlington goal was a fucking mile offside,' Stasher railed. I didn't bother telling him that I had been standing in line with play and that the goal had been perfectly legitimate. That would have been perfidy as far as Stasher was concerned. And like most people who watch the game, I don't think he really understood the offside law in any case. Besides, you couldn't get a word in edgeways when the lad was in full flow, and all I managed to contribute to the discussion on the way back to Colchester were nods and grunts of assent, wishing with all my body that I was back home in my bed and wondering why I had bothered to undertake this trip in the first place (actually, I can remember the reason – I had never been to Darlington's ground before and for some reason at that point in my life thought it was important that I did so).

After that I made sure I avoided sitting next to Stasher on away trips. The team was, as usual, performing lamentably, so there were usually only one or two coaches going to away games, and I started turning up at the last possible moment in the hope that Stasher had already boarded and found some other unfortunate to regale with his rantings for the duration of the trip. A year or two later I left town to go off and study and my life became sufficiently fulfilling to remove the necessity for Fourth Division away travel. By the time I had settled down in London with a job in my mid-twenties, I started to watch the Arsenal and only went to watch Colchester if they came to play Orient or Brentford or if I was back home visiting my parents. Stasher was still around, of course, dressed and tattooed all in blue, and if we caught each other's eye he would still give me a nod, as if he saw me every week just like in the old days. God knows what he would have said if I'd told him I had a season ticket for Highbury.

In my parallel life I had done pretty well for myself, getting a business degree and then getting work at a major-name management consultancy. I was earning enough to buy myself a terraced house in Crouch End and was together with a steady girl called Stephanie I'd met through work. I mention this not by way of boasting (I've lost it all now), only by way of background to indicate how straightforward my life was before the night I went to watch England play Germany in the semi-finals of Euro '96. If that night represented another night of so-near, so-far heartbreak in the hearts of millions of Englishmen and women, for me it marked the beginning of a steep decline which saw me lose, in turn, my job, my house, my girlfriend and, to some extent, my love of football.

I had tried in vain to get tickets for the match but like thousands of others had missed out and was resigned to watching it on the big screen down at my local. Then my boss called me into his office two days before the game and handed me three tickets. 'You're a football fathead, aren't you? Here, take these on Wednesday and make smalltalk with Samuel Finch and Freddy Hettering from

Waring Bros. They're going to be in town to sign a fat contract with us Thursday, and they need to be entertained. Take them up West afterwards and give your expense account a good thrashing.'

I was initially thrilled at the thought of going to the game. The seats were not unadjacent to the royal box and they weren't costing me a penny. And what better way to celebrate England's passage to the final than heading up to Soho and drinking the night away on the company's account and even having a good excuse for turning up to work the next morning with a hangover? But in business there's no such thing as a free ticket to Wembley, and the thought of having to be on my best corporate behaviour while attending England's biggest international match since the last time they'd encountered Germany in a major semi-final was nagging at the back of my mind as a possible downside to the whole trip. How would I react if I was sitting between Mr Finch and Mr Hettering, neither of whom I had ever met in my life, and Teddy Sheringham put England 3–2 up in the last minute? And the two were perhaps politely applauding and already getting ready to leave while all I wanted to do was hug someone and scream the turrets off the twin towers? Well, I supposed I could worry about that when the time came. In any case, wasn't the whole of the country mentally sucked up in football meaningless-ness this week? Wouldn't any red-blooded Englander be sticking his chest out for love of Blighty, regardless of whether he appreciated the game or not, simply from fear of missing out on that rarest of fests, a no holds-barred English love-in?

As it happened, I was so busy at work on the day of the game that I barely had time to anticipate the evening's main event, although an occasional roar from the pavement below my office, where early starters had already begun to imbibe themselves outside the Sotted Hack, served to remind me that I was really not where I wanted to be at that moment in time. In fact, when I look back on it, I do not understand how I lasted in that job for more than a day. I could not really even describe to you what I did all day (should you be bothered to ask) because I can no longer recall, or perhaps I've blotted it out, the shamefully useless function I served in a company that existed purely to provide a service that the world could easily exist without. My 'real' mates asked me what had happened to the supposed anarchist sentiments that I had harboured while at university. I would just grin fecklessly in response, too complacent to think that I needed to provide them with a cogent answer. When you're earning much more money than you really need, why do you have to justify anything?

So at four o'clock the boss stuck his head around my door and told me it was about time that I headed off to the Dorchester to pick up Mr Finch and Mr Hettering. A flutter of nerves gripped my digestive system for a second, although I'm not sure if that was because of the England game or because I was, for the first time, being given the responsibility of entertaining two such important clients on the evening prior to them sealing a big contract. Previously I had been only on the periphery of corporate entertainment, and had always maintained a low profile as the older men spent a couple of hours droning business-speak before lapsing, under the influence, into the realm of hopeless humour – long, boorish jokes with crude and predictable finales. I didn't know any jokes. I hoped that tonight the football would pull us through.

Outside the Sotted Hack there was already spew and broken glass on the pavement, while a lagging rendition of 'Three Lions' held out the promise of a long and weary evening for the barstaff. Yet somehow I felt that I would prefer to be spending my evening in such an atmosphere than in the stadium bound by the restraints of corporate etiquette. I was half tempted to walk in, sell the three tickets for a decent price, then take my clients out for an early meal before accidentally losing them in a crowded pub with a big screen. This plan was countered by the thought of my boss's expression the following day when he inevitably learned the truth, and the possibility of missing, live in the flesh, one of England's greatest moments in international football. And that against the hated Hun.

At the Dorchester I asked the receptionist to call the two gentlemen. I sat down watching people come and go and, after about ten minutes, a tall, besuited man in his fifties with a stiff walk and an even stiffer expression walked out of the lift. He wore glasses and sported a mop of brown hair which looked so unnaturally perched on his pate that it had to be a toupee. I prayed that this was not to be one of my accomplices for the evening, but already felt fated to be spending time with this hard-nosed boardroom bore, a feeling confirmed when he muttered something to the girl at the front desk and she pointed over to my seat.

I immediately stood up, mustered my phoniest smile and strode across to the gentleman in order to shake his hand. 'Lance Tiller,' I said. 'And you must be Freddie Hettering?' I don't know why I plumped for Hettering. He simply looked more Hettering than he did Finch. 'I am Mr Finch,' he said remonstratively, emphasising the 'Mr' like master to schoolboy, while unsmilingly granting my outstretched palm the briefest and limpest of contacts. 'Mr Hettering cannot be with us,' he added curtly. 'Something important has come up. And Mr Griel?' he asked, enquiring after my boss. 'Where are we meeting him?'

I felt like saying that something important had 'come up' for Mr Griel too, which in fact it probably had. We all knew that he often delegated evening socials to his minions in order to shaft his mistress from marketing, Anna Clove, while having an alibi for his statutory spouse in London's outer edge. But Mr Finch did not look like he would be impressed by such an excuse, and all I could stammer was that Mr Griel had a late business appointment this evening and that I would be 'taking care' of him.

'Oh,' was all he said.

'We're, er, going to the football match,' I added weakly.

'Oh,' he said again, looking like he would rather have gone to a greasy café in Seven Sisters. 'Whereabouts?'

Jesus Christ, he didn't even know that there was only *one* football match on in the whole country tonight. And when I told him England versus Germany at Wembley he did not register a flicker of recognition, rather looked as if I'd held up two tickets for Sutton United versus Tooting and Mitcham reserves. Then he sighed and said, 'That would have been more up Hettering's street. Do we have to go?'

Maybe some remnant of humanity in his soul perceived the flash of panic and alarm in my eyes when he said this, and I stammered, 'But we have the tickets already, some of the best in the stadium.' I fished the tickets out of my jacket pocket and held them up as proof, hoping that he would perhaps catch sight of the price on them. 'In fact we've got an extra one now. Some people would probably give up a fortune to get their hands on that today.'

'Yes, yes, OK,' he said brusquely. 'I'm sorry, it's just not what I was expecting this evening.'

'We'll go out and eat straight after the game,' I said, but he didn't answer, and I secretly hoped that he was already thinking up an excuse to get out of that one. Presumably he'd had in mind an informal chat with my superiors going over some of the contract's final details, although he didn't look like the kind of man who spent his time telling businessmen jokes. He certainly wasn't going to get much out of me about the deal with my company for I had done very little work on it, and even if I had done it would have been the last thing on my mind this evening.

Mr Finch, however, had other ideas, and seemed determined that if he was going to have to go to a football match, then I would at least have to spend the evening lending my ear to his philosophies on business and management.

We had hardly settled into our taxi when he commenced holding forth on strategic integrated personnel destructuring systems, or some such shite, and although I knew enough to bluff my way through such a conversation, my greater difficulty consisted in masking the misery I was feeling at going to such an important football match with one of the last people in Europe I actually wanted to be with, or who wanted to be at the game itself. I thought of all the people who deserved a ticket more than he did.

I thought of all the people that deserved to be *alive* more than he did, the miserable, deadpan, tedious, grim-jawed mogadon.

'Enjoy the game, lads,' said the gruff, big-eared cabby as he dropped us off at the bottom of Wembley Way, though I am fairly sure he was being sardonic given the nature of the conversation which he had just overheard. As I paid I raised my eyebrows to him and gave him an inflated tip in the hope of winning back some credibility, as if it mattered. He drove off smirking.

As we walked up towards the stadium the swelling mass of chattering fans, the bellowing cockney vendors, the optimistically lofted, billowing flags and the preponderance of colour might not have existed as far as Mr Finch was concerned. When I bought an England scarf to help our suits try to blend in with the surroundings a little more he didn't pause for a second in outlining the prospects for increased profit margins at Waring Bros. based on the indicators in the first quarter results the firm had just thrillingly announced. As we reached the stadium we became caught up in a posse of sweaty, chanting German fans walking in the opposite direction, but that did not prevent him from telling me that, 'Of course Farnham's has got the better technical know-how, no denying it, but we have the better strength in depth in terms of sales potential.' In fact the only thing to interrupt the flow of spectacular inanities was Stasher, who was somehow suddenly standing right in front of me half yelling: 'All right mate?'

I didn't recognise him at first because I had never seen him out of the Colchester blue, and he'd had his face painted with the flag of St George and a Union Jack bleached into his close-cropped hair. He was wearing a replica England shirt, offensively patterned knee-length Hawaii shorts and two England scarves tied to his wrists in the 1970s style. For a second I was baffled, until I spotted a tiny CUFC lapel pinned to his collar. I realised that I hadn't seen either him or United for at least two years.

'Oh, all right mate,' I said, not wanting to say 'Stasher' in front of Mr Finch in case he thought I'd just bumped into my drug dealer. I was not sure what to make of this meeting. Although Stasher, psychotic as he was, made a refreshing antidote to the droning executive in my wake, he was hardly the kind of person you wanted to be recognised with when entertaining an important client. Had I asked Stasher if he wanted to come for a burger with the vice president of Waring Bros., the well-known Bournemouth-based manufacturer of tunnelling equipment, I'm pretty sure he would have turned round to Mr Finch and said, 'Bournemouth? Ha, we stuffed you 2–fucking–0 down at your gaff last season, cunt!'

The problem of what to say next was taken out of my hands. Stasher, as it happened, was not 'all right', and had perhaps been waiting to bump into anyone he knew to offload the story of his chronic misfortune. 'Can you believe it? I've lost me fuckin' ticket!' he wailed. I believed him, or he was a very convincing fraud, because he genuinely did look upset enough to have come by such a mishap, and men like Stasher do not, as a rule, walk around with watery eyes. 'I had it on the fuckin' train this morning and then I went to the boozer and when I got there it was bleedin' gone. I backtracked to the station three times, not a trace. Some bastard's going to the game tonight on my ticket, can you believe that? I tried the ticket office here but no cunt will believe me, and eventually they got the fuckin' pigs to drag me away.'

'Well, we have a spare ticket.' It was not me that said this, but Mr Finch. I do not believe that he felt sorry for Stasher, or that he wanted to spend the next few hours of his life with him either. It was a pragmatic solution to a problem scenario, as he would probably have said in one of his business reports. I had harboured no intention of telling Stasher that we had a spare ticket, even though I felt sorry as hell for him. 'Yes, but we're still expecting someone along,' I said hastily, shooting a glance at Mr Finch, who came nowhere near interpreting it in the manner intended.

'No,' he said insistently, 'I already told you in the hotel that Mr Hettering is ill-disposed tonight. Why not give the man Hettering's ticket if he has lost his own?'

Stasher gave me a look that was half contempt for the lie and the betrayal of a fellow Colchester fan, and half dogwagging hope because I represented his last chance of getting into the stadium. I took out the ticket and handed it to him without a word. He looked at it for a second, but then his face fell and hope rose once more in my heart. 'Ah shit, I can't afford this mate, I'm sorry,' he said. 'Jesus, I didn't even know a ticket could cost this much.' He was about to hand it back to me when his new benefactor intervened once more.

'Don't be silly, man,' said Mr Finch impatiently. 'This chap gets them for free from his company; it won't cost you a penny.'

Stasher looked at me and looked at the ticket, as if he could not conceive of such a thing. 'You sure, mate?' he gasped, and I nodded and Stasher broke into a huge grin and said, 'Fuckin' 'ell,' and then said, 'Listen, gotta go, see you in the ground,' and ran off jumping in the air, and then Mr Finch said, 'Of course you're only as strong as your weakest sales rep,' and I wondered what the chances were of Stasher losing two tickets in one day.

I CAN NEVER quite celebrate with my normal abandon when my club or country scores a goal in the first minute of the game. Even as my arms are raised in the air and a long 'yeeeeeeeeeeaaaaaaah!' of delight emerges from my lips, I tend to look around me with a sense of detachment at the jumps and grins of disbelief nearby which seem to say, 'It's only the first minute and we've already scored! We've already won it! In fact if the game goes on like this we're going to win 90–0!' And no matter how often this turns out not to be the case (in the experience of Colchester United, almost always), nothing can blunt the unthinking optimism of a fan who has just witnessed his or her side scoring a goal. In that moment they are ahead, and celebrating, what could be better? The manager's game plan is working a treat, they got the early goal. Until the more fatalistic among us sit down thirty seconds later and say to our neighbours, 'I wish it was the ninetieth minute.'

So when Alan Shearer put England one up against Germany in the first minute of the game I did not feel like it was going to be

England's night, unlike the jubilant huggers and dancers around me. Actually, to say that they were 'around me' is not strictly accurate, because they were all a block or two away; the gentlemen sitting around me were more of the Mr Finch persuasion, politely applauding on their feet like at the end of a speech at the Royal Overseas League, bar the odd barmy exception, like Stasher. Whereas outside the ground we had looked out of place in our everyday work costume, it was the scarf-wielding, face-painted loony who looked the misfit in the pricier seats. Not that Stasher cared, he was screaming, 'Kill the fucking krauts!' at the top of his voice before turning to his visibly flinching neighbour and shouting, 'The boys are gonna do it, they're gonna fuckin' do it!'

We had got to our seats while the national anthem was on, myself having blagged our way into the Wembley restaurant by bribing the head waiter in order to keep Mr Finch happy for the hour we had to spare before kick-off. I was motivated by my own near starvation and the hope that a meal before the game would absolve us of the obligation to go out together afterwards. But the meal presented its own problems, the least of which was Mr Finch's continued business bletherings, and the worst of which was when he asked for the dessert menu ten minutes before kick-off.

'Er, there's probably not going to be time for that,' I ventured. 'The game's about to start.'

Mister Finch looked around as if he had forgotten that he was even in a football stadium. 'Can't we watch it in here?' he said.

When I pointed out that we could not see the pitch, he merely gestured at a television screen high up above our heads.

'The problem is,' I said, 'if we're not in there at the start they won't let us in at all.'

'Ah, like the theatre,' he said, and placed the menu back on the table and made to get up.

When we came into our section I could already hear Stasher singing 'God Save the Queen' above the self-conscious murmur around him. As we moved down the row towards him he turned and grinned and pointed down at our two empty seats like we couldn't work it out for ourselves that we were sitting there, then continued bellowing, 'Long to reign ooooooover us,' as flat as a flounder. Mr Finch had finally shut up for a minute or two and I could only hope that the crowd and the occasion might keep him mute until the final whistle.

When we sat down again after the anthems were over and the teams finished warming up, Stasher said to me, with thinly disguised reproach in his voice, 'So, ain't see you down at the "Us" much lately.'

'No, no,' I said. 'I live down in London now, don't get much chance to make it these days.'

Now that he was safely inside the ground, and perhaps recalling my earlier reluctance to give up the free ticket, Stasher was frank in his assessment of my current status. 'Fucking yuppie now, eh?' he said with a sneer, looking my suit up and down. I winced, not knowing what to say, but at that moment the game got under way and Stasher turned around and aimed his invective at the Germans instead.

After the Shearer goal, however, Stasher was a little better disposed towards me, and said eagerly, 'That's it now, eh? We'll get revenge for 1990 now. Fucking Nazis!' I looked at Mr Finch, who had been the only Englishman in the ground not to stand after the goal went in, something which, happily, had escaped Stasher's attention. I wasn't sure how I would have coped with Stasher leaning over and saying, 'Wot's up with 'im – 'e the fuckin' Bosh or somefin'?'

For the remainder of the first half I divided my attention equally between Stasher, who had a tendency to grab my shoulder and swear copiously every time the Germans came even slightly near the England half, and Mr Finch who, unbelievably, had begun to say just a couple of minutes after the Shearer goal, 'As I was saying before, when we opened the Boscombe plant revenue went up by eight per cent over the first nine months . . .' Stasher seemed completely unaware of Mr Finch, and Mr Finch was mutually ignoring the torrent of foul language coming from two seats to his left. It was a typically English scenario, with everyone for twenty rows around more aware of Stasher than they were of the game, but nobody daring to say anything about it, except for one man who leaned forward and tapped him on the back and said over his shoulder, 'Excuse me, but my wife is not accustomed to hearing that kind of language,' to which Stasher, barely turning his attention off the pitch, snapped, 'Then take her to the fucking opera.' I feared, or maybe hoped, that the offended man might go and fetch a steward to have Stasher either warned or ejected, but his Englishness prevented him from taking further action.

I was little able to focus on the game itself. How can you watch a game like that when somebody on one side is saying things like, 'You're probably aware of the market changes in the tunnelling equipment sector over the past five years,' while on the other somebody is almost tearing your arm off while releasing a torrent of xenophobic rage every ten seconds? While on the one hand I disliked the kind of support that Stasher was lending his country, it was certainly no worse than the general passivity of those who were sitting around us who, for the most part, did not look any more comfortable in a football stadium than the man to my right and his one-man tunnelling equipment show. Yet if I sided with Stasher now and began vociferously exhorting my countrymen to stuff the Hun and ceased to nod in Mr Finch's general direction as if I was actually listening to him, what sort of impression was that going to make on a professional level? The price on that ticket left me in no doubt where my duties lay.

Yet I was simmering with resentment at the two men on either side of me; against Finch because he had cast an iron straitjacket around my natural emotions, and against Stasher because I was genuinely jealous of him. Jealous that I could not behave as naturally as he was able to, and jealous that I could not, even in normal times, support my side with such unbridled fervour regardless of who else was sitting close by. Instead, I developed a kind of inner support, muttering, 'Yes, yes,' under my breath when England were going forward, alternating this with a louder, 'Yes, yes,' for Mr Finch's benefit whenever he outlined some stunning new point on drilling and boring mechanisms. I figured that if England could just win tonight then I would watch the Final Sunday night all alone in my house but for a four pack of draught Guinness and a packet of cigarettes, with some bubbly chilling in the fridge for afterwards to quaff with Stephanie.

At half-time Stasher barged past us to go to the toilet, while Mr Finch stood up to stretch his legs and for the next fifteen minutes actually stopped talking, except to ask me whether this was a World Cup match or the Champions' League. When I explained, in some detail, how the European Nations' Cup was structured and how we had come to reach the semi-final, he said, 'Ah,' and remained silent until the resumption. All around us, however, people were engaged in his kind of talk, and instead of chatter about the game you could overhear words such as 'contract', 'trade' and 'tender'. When Stasher reappeared at the end of our row just as the second half was kicking off Finch leaned over to me and said, 'Here comes your friend,' but in such a way as to suggest he knew exactly what sort of a lout I was in my spare time and that I wasn't fooling anybody with my suit and tie and title. I began to fear that he would tell the story to Mr Griel the next day, who would somehow interpret it wrongly and think that I had invited Stasher to take the spare ticket in the full knowledge that I would be exposing an important client to an obstreperous, blaspheming yob. At this point I even considered taking Mr Finch out of the stadium and apologising for the whole thing over a drink before talking earnestly for a couple of hours about the technical aspects of the Canary Wharf Tube extension.

But the second half had started and I couldn't keep my eyes off it.

And Mr Finch started up again too, only he seemed to have exhausted some of his theories and now wanted to know mine. I answered him as best as I could, and as curtly, speaking out of the side of my mouth so that Stasher would not hear what I was saying. But just as he asked me, 'So what would you say are the five core competencies offered by your company?' Stefan Kuntz equalised for Germany and I let out an involuntarily, 'Oh fucking hell.'

'I beg your pardon?' said Mr Finch.

I waved towards the pitch. 'The Germans have equalised,' I moaned.

Stasher, meanwhile, was leaning forward with his head in his hands, letting out a long wail of, 'Noooooooooooooooooooooooooooooooooooo!', his body rocking backwards and forwards. 'You fucking kraut Nazi fucking bastards!' he almost wept when he recovered the power of speech. Finch looked at him long and hard, as if registering him properly for the very first time that evening. I was too upset to speak, though I wanted to cry out in frustration too. When the Germans come from behind they always win. Yes, I could feel it, the Germans were going to win. It was that kind of evening.

'Anyway,' said Finch, blandly, as the game began again, but you could hear him louder now than before because the stadium, apart from a few jeering Germans far away, had lapsed into a resigned and mournful silence, 'I believe that we were talking about core competencies.' I didn't know what to say. I could not bring myself to answer that question right at that moment in time. Then Stasher intervened on my behalf and leaned across, hissing: 'Will you shut your fucking mouth, Mr hoity toity bloody bollocks, and watch the fucking game!'

Finch stood up. 'Well, I never—' he began, but Stasher stood up too, and then I stood up and pleaded with them all to sit down and just watch the match, and they did, Stasher muttering manically to himself, Mr Finch in broody silence. I prayed that he would not stand up and announce that he was leaving as I would have felt obliged to follow him and miss the rest of the match. England were going to lose, of course. But then again maybe they wouldn't . . .

During the final twenty minutes of the game, Mr Finch sat rigid and without voice, while Stasher fidgeted and swore almost constantly, although now his oaths were reduced to whispers of desperation audible only to those sitting right next to him. In the face of Finch's muteness I was finally focusing on the game, and my body language began to echo Stasher's, hands spread over eyes, jumping up and down out of my seat twenty times a minute, even gripping Stasher's arm in moments of minor drama. In fact Mr Finch's presence receded to the point that when the final whistle blew, I turned round to him and said, completely forgetting who he was: 'Jesus, now it's sudden death!' Stasher echoed my words: 'Oh fucking Christ, sudden fucking death.'

Mr Finch more or less ignored us, indeed he was standing up, brushing down his jacket and was about to make for the exit.

'Er, Mr Finch, where are you going?' I asked.

He turned and looked at me sternly and said in the tone of someone who has seen more than enough for one day. 'It's over now, isn't it?' apparently oblivious to the fact that no one else was leaving the stadium bar a few bodies skipping to the toilets.

'Ha ha, no, no,' I said brightly, 'it's 1–1, you see, so in order to determine who goes through to the Final someone has to score a goal.'

His face was granite.

'But, look,' I rushed on, 'as soon as someone scores then it's all over, then we go!'

'What if nobody scores a goal?'

'Well, after thirty minutes then there's a penalty shoot-out,' I said, still sounding like I was trying to sell a kids' adventure holiday and that this was all going to be great fun. Then I explained exactly what that would entail, and what a penalty was. Mr Finch stared at a point somewhere around three rows ahead. When I had finished, however, his expression changed, and he looked for a second at Stasher as if some idea was germinating in his head that, for the first time in several years, had nothing to do with tunnelling equipment. 'OK, extra-time it is,' he said, but there was, or at least seemed to be, a slightly lighter tone to his voice for the first time that evening.

You don't need me to tell you here what happened during extra-time. Least of all to remind you that Gascoigne missed putting England into the Final by a slither of a millimetre. After staring at this in disbelief for a couple of seconds Stasher turned around, knelt down and began headbutting his seat, emitting a strangled howl of pain and exasperation. Finch observed him with a superior contempt, although there may have been a hint of a smirk behind his vice president eyes. Stasher stayed in this pose until the end of the thirty minutes, his hands held in prayer and his eyes averted to the ceiling of the stand and asking me, constantly, 'What's happening, mate, what's happening?' I would assure him that there was no current danger and that he could turn around, but he just said, 'No, no, this is their best chance, if I'm not looking.'

When the penalties started Stasher had manoeuvred himself back round again and was standing like everyone else, even the suits. By now he was so wired he was no longer capable of speaking. He watched the England penalties and went, 'Neeennngh!' or something similar, and pumped his arm backwards and forwards. But he couldn't watch the Germans, and turned away, though he could tell from the crowd noise when they'd scored and would kneel down and beat on his seat furiously with his fist. I was going through the emotions too, my stomach as clenched as the rest of the nation's, but I was worried about Stasher and that he was really going to freak out if England lost. When Southgate missed I wailed with the rest of them, but straight away looked at Stasher.

I needn't have worried. He just crumpled into his seat and said, 'That's it,' and little-boy tears came down his cheeks and on to his sweat-stunken replica shirt.

'Come on, Stash,' I said, suddenly eager to revive him, 'the Germans might miss one too.' He shook his head, brooking no doubt. I turned to the pitch and concentrated on Andy Moeller. 'Miss you bastard, miss you bastard,' I whispered. 'Just this once, just let us win this once, miss, miss, miss, please bloody bastard miss.'

When Moeller scored there was the customary numbed silence all around us. Until Mr Finch leaned across me and, his face just inches away from Stasher's, said slowly and deliberately, 'Ha. Ha. Ha.' Stasher looked up, his face not seeming at first to understand what was going on, again like a little boy, perhaps about to be punished for a misdemeanour he has no idea of having committed. He half smiled through his tears, and then the first stirrings of a reaction began to register in his face, a renascent need to defend his pride manifesting itself in the creeping furrow of his eyebrows, the pre-violence puckering of his lips. But I thought, Why Stasher? Why should he suffer? And the anger I felt at Andy Moeller was all released in one terrific butt of my head against Mr Finch's nose, which bled spectacularly as he slumped over the seat in front of us.

Stasher looked at me in astonishment. 'Nice one,' he said. Six stewards in orange vests moved hastily towards us.

. . . And More

Straight is the Gate?

AT THE NEW Evangelical Forum we are always glad to see new members, and we welcomed Derek in an open and friendly manner – as we do with any other human being – even though one of the first things he confessed to us was his homosexuality. There was an awkward silence until Derek explained that he was coming to the group to find some answers, and that he wanted to find a cure for his affliction, and when we realised that he needed our help of course we welcomed him because that is our Christian duty, and if I was in the same position today I would do exactly the same again, although I would certainly be wary of some of the lessons we were taught by granting Derek membership.

No one introduced Derek to the forum, he just showed up one Friday night at one of our handshake and hugging sessions after the weekly service. We had advertised extensively for new people and there had been a good deal of interest, so we were perhaps a little bit carried away by the rate at which the group was expanding and failed to exercise correct judgement in allowing him to participate. As a rule you don't have to already know somebody within the group when you join, but we like to know a little bit of background so that we can best assess a new member's capacity to take on board the central tenets of the New Evangelical Forum's philosophy. I can tell you straightaway what those tenets are – love, sharing and kindness through Jesus Christ.

We are now a country-wide organisation loosely attached to the C of E, who let us use their churches for our Friday night services because they cannot attract any young people to the church themselves any more. We have staged some beautiful Friday night events, swaying and singing and celebrating the life of Jesus, and I shall never forget seeing previously sceptical friends for the first time falling to the floor for Christ, joyously weeping as they have let themselves go and realised the fundamental importance of the man who died for all of us, and thereafter pledging themselves to the NEF and its principles.

After the service we break up into the handshake and hugging discussion groups mentioned before and go to sit in various corners of the community room. Many of us need to wind down for a while after the intense spirituality of the church service, and we play trancing-out tapes to create a relaxed, informal atmosphere. Then once we have drunk some water and eaten some sandwiches we talk about how Jesus has helped us through the previous week, and talk through any lapses into sin, or wicked doubts which the devil might have caused us to entertain.

And it was during one of these sessions that we first met Derek.

I was the discussion group leader, and was a little nervous because this was the first time I had taken on such a responsibility. Brian, our branch captain, had told me the week before that he thought I was ready after I had told my discussion group how I burnt some filthy pornographic magazines I had found beneath my older brother's bed. I had been so proud, and fellow-member Rachel (towards whom I was beginning to feel an attraction) and I went out and celebrated with a pizza and she hugged me very closely when we said good night at the bus stop. When some drunken louts started cat-calling at us from across the road I could feel Jesus' strength course through my body and hugged Rachel even firmer than before.

That evening as I led my first discussion group things started well. Ellie, for example, told us that she had been serving a customer in the shoe shop where she worked and that the customer had wanted to try on dozens of pairs of shoes and had then left without buying anything. Ellie had been annoyed and wanted to shout something after the woman, but then she thought how Jesus would have reacted in such a situation and calmed down and got through the rest of the day with a smile on her face. Then everybody in the group shook Ellie's hand and hugged her, which is the custom, although I already noticed then that the man who later introduced himself as Derek was holding back. But that's not unusual for new members, and we do not force anything on anyone.

Then Everton told us how his grandmother had passed away that week and we all said a prayer for her. It had been a long illness through breast cancer, which had developed into cancer of the liver. Everton's grandmother had been very brave, he said, and he had provided her with hours of comfort on her deathbed telling her how she was going to meet Jesus. We all agreed that Everton had been noble to sacrifice so much time to such a good cause and everyone shook his hand and hugged him. I looked at Derek and he looked back at me, and I nodded at him and he leaned forward and he also shook Everton's hand and hugged him, if perhaps a little shyly. I was feeling great at this point, everything was in hand, and I could hardly wait to tell Brian how I had induced a brand new member to start hugging at only the second confessional.

'Tell me, brother, what is your name, and why have you come here tonight?' I said to Derek.

'My name is Derek and I am a homosexual,' said Derek. 'I've come to find God.'

There was a silence, and I knew that people were looking to me as group leader to say something, but I could not find the words. Then Everton let out a kind of repulsive sound, like yeeeeurgh, and stood up and said he was going to the toilet to be sick. 'That jabber just hugged me, man!' he exclaimed.' Then to Derek: 'Scuse me, man, but God don't like your sort of people,' and off he ran out of the hall.

Derek didn't look too disturbed at this, and luckily he began to explain why he was here, because I was still unsure what I should say next. I agreed with Everton, but thought he had been a little tactless, and decided to have a word with him afterwards. After all, he was probably still upset about his grandmother going through such a long illness. While Derek was talking Everton returned from the toilet, and sat down in the circle with an aggressive expression on his face, glaring all the while at Derek.

The latter had been passionately explaining his need for redemption, about how he wanted to escape the devil's iniquitous lusts inside him, and when Everton returned said to him, almost in tears, 'You are quite right, Everton, and God is quite right not to accept my filthy, unnatural habits. That's why I have come to you. I need your help, all of your help to enter Jesus' inner circle, to achieve the enlightenment necessary to become a good and proper Christian.'

Normally at this point in an individual's speech the group leader would lean forward, shake the speaker's hand, and then hug him or her. There was a long silence again. Then I remembered, I was group leader! I had been thinking about Derek's words so carefully that I had clean forgotten.

'Derek,' I said, 'please join our group and we will do all we can to cure you of your disease. We will say a prayer for you,' and with that we all bowed our heads and I improvised a prayer, asking God to purge Derek of his terrible habits and to save his soul. When I finished I looked up and asked if anyone else had a story to tell of the week just gone, but Derek interrupted me and asked, 'Don't I get a hug and a handshake?'

It was rather impertinent to put such a question at your first meeting, and I had rather been hoping that with the prayer we could all forget about hugging Derek. Maybe it would have been wise for me to have told him that we did not hug new members at their first meeting. But instead I leaned over from my floor cushion, shook his hand briefly and then hugged him lightly, although he clung on to me for longer than I would ordinarily have wanted, and squeezed me on my back in a manner I found far too forward for a new member. But I had set the precedent and everyone else did the same, although I suspect it was easier for the girls. Everton, however, said, 'I ain't hugging no pooftah. If he gets cured then I might think about it,' and he stood up again and walked out of the hall.

Brian was worried when I told him afterwards that I had let Derek join the group. 'I wish you had asked me about this first, Gideon,' he said. 'You've only just become a group leader, you know. You shouldn't start getting ideas above your station.' I felt dreadful and apologised profusely, until Brian said, irascibly, 'Yes yes, OK, but next time come to me first with something like this.' I had never seen Brian irritated before, and I went home feeling miserable and couldn't sleep that night, I was so worried that Brian was annoyed with me. I prayed and prayed and prayed, and I admit that I also prayed for Derek not to turn up the following week.

I LOOKED OUT for Derek during the church service the following Friday because I wanted to see how heavily he was into our style of worship. I thought that if he failed to prostrate himself at the foot of the altar, or if he tried to sing and sway with the crowd and was not displaying sufficient conviction, then I could gently try to recommend to him that he find himself a new place of worship, and that perhaps the New Evangelical Forum was not really the right platform upon which to redeem himself from his filth and sins. Then again, there was a part of me which really wanted him to come along and make a successful stab at turning him into a normal, loving Christian, and then I could have shown Brian what I was capable of as a group discussion leader, and that it had not been a mistake to let Derek join the church.

I had telephoned Brian a number of times that week for advice and to ask his forgiveness for failing to consult with him before allowing such a reckless sinner to mix in our ranks. He was a lot more conciliatory and apologised for having snapped at me the previous Friday. That was more like the Brian of old, the inspiring, gentle branch captain who had first initiated me into the Forum when I was at a very low point following a series of exam failures at school. I asked him if I should let a more experienced group discussion leader take Derek into their group and he said firmly no, Derek was my case now and he would be following with interest the progress I made with him. We agreed, however, that Everton should be moved to another group, and Everton was apparently only too happy to swap with Sammy, an altogether more tranquil character; or at least he had been since overcoming his crack addiction.

So the following Friday I was looking for Derek during Brian's inspirational service, but got caught up in the singing and began to feel the Lord taking over my mortal marrow and I was swaying wildly thinking about a prostration at Brian's feet because I hadn't done one for weeks, and I still felt like I had to make up something to him. But there were a lot of people prostrating that evening and I wasn't sure if there was room down at the front, so I craned my neck forward from my pew and then I saw him, red-faced, right in the middle at the front, howling, sweating and gyrating for Jesus. Derek, his eye sockets almost turned inside out, was freaking out like a true born-again, and really giving it what we in the Forum call Extra Commitment.

At this point I felt terrific, and I prayed that Brian was taking it in, even though he had his eyes closed and was leading the singing up to the climax of his sermon. I knew then that it had not been a mistake to take on Derek and I felt sure I was going to increase my profile at the church (and with Rachel!) when everyone got to know how I had helped turn a man of vile propensities into a believer firmly walking the Byway of Rightness.

I was almost floating at the discussion group afterwards. Derek looked exhausted and lay back on his cushion with his eyes closed, trancing out, while the rest of us told our stories from the week just past. I was particularly encouraging in my handshakes and hugging that week, all the while conscious that there was no awkwardness because Derek was lying back with his eyes closed and so wasn't hugging anybody, which I thought was for the best all round.

When everyone had spoken I was getting ready to wind up the session and go through to the reception room where people gradually take their leave when Derek sat up and said, 'I have sinned terribly this past week. I need to tell you my story.'

A silence struck the circle, which I broke a few seconds later by saying, matter-of-factly, 'Well, I'm afraid we've run out of time for this week, Derek, perhaps you can come along next week—'

'No, no, I need to get this off my chest, I need your understanding and forgiveness,' he begged with a passion from within. I could hardly wind up the group then, especially as there were still three other circles in session. Still, I was annoyed because I had been so in control up until that point and was feeling really good about myself. I quietly told Derek to proceed with his story.

'On Wednesday afternoon I was in a public toilet near Crosswell Park,' Derek began, and I was already gripped with dread. 'I was standing at one of the urinals when I noticed that there was somebody behind me. I turned around and there was a man slightly older than me standing with his genitals exposed, and he looked over towards me, and I looked back at him, and then he reached out and grabbed my penis, and I didn't stop him, and soon my penis was erect too.'

There was a short, disgusted gasp at this description, and several of the group looked at me to stop Derek going any further, but I was suddenly lost for words, my voice-box frozen in repulsion at the words my brain was being forced to hear. Derek was unperturbed, however, and pressed on with his story.

'The man said to me, "Fancy a wank?" and I replied, "I can give you a blow-job if you like," and he said, "OK," and so we went into one of the cubicles and I leaned down and took his penis in my mouth, and then a third man who had been sitting in the next cubicle asked if he could join in, and I said, "You can fuck me if you've got a condom," and so he put one on and ripped down my jeans and began to bugger me ferociously . . . oh, I'm so sorry, Lord Jesus, what could have led me to this? Please, please, please forgive me and convert me and stop me sinning so again!'

All the time Derek was telling his story I wanted to stand up and shout him down and declare the session ended, and then tell him to leave the hall and never come back to our church again with his squalid pornography. But the problem was that I could not stand up. The devil, that ubiquitous evil, had entered my own body, had entered my own underpants, and was pulling at me, trying to drag me down the same tunnel of sin where Derek was stuck in the mud of depravity. I looked up helplessly at the other people in the circle. The boys were all looking down at the floor, presumably in embarrassment, while the girls were still sitting there with the same O-shaped shock on their lips, staring at Derek like they could not fathom what they were hearing. Ellie looked over to me for a signal, for guidance, pleading with me via her eyes to make him hold his foul tongue. I, meanwhile, was trying to purge the devil from my body by thinking about Jesus on the cross, what he suffered for us, but the devil clung on hard and only with the most determined effort could I rid my head of the shameful scenes that Derek had described in such awfully graphic detail.

When Derek stopped speaking we all sat in shocked solitude for a few minutes while Derek hung his head downwards, apparently snivelling. In the end I said, 'Well, Derek, it doesn't look like you've progressed very far in saving yourself from this time last week. I'm afraid that you only get a hug and a handshake when you've done something worthy of receiving them. Perhaps next time we could hear a little more about how you struggled to resist sin rather than the full lurid details of the actual act. I can see why poor Everton ran gagging to the toilet last week!'

Derek looked up at me, his eyes seemingly red from crying, and said exasperatedly, 'But no one's giving me any guidance. Where was God when I was down in that toilet? Where were any one of you when I needed you? What's the good running away from the problem? I don't even know where to start looking for the answer?'

I felt sorry that I had reacted so pompously and unsympathetically, and particularly regretted making the remark about running off gagging to the toilet. I moved over towards Derek and said in a much gentler voice, 'You have to find the answer in Jesus, Derek, you have to look for Jesus and seek him out and learn to love him.' To show a lead to the others I even put a hand on Derek's shoulder. 'Then you have to let Jesus lead you to the answers. You have to pray a lot and sing a lot and read the Bible and you have to recognise your sins and do something about them. Jesus will help you resist temptation, but we promise we will help you find him, won't we?'

I turned to the others with an encouraging smile and to my delight they responded heartily, shouting lots of encouragement like: 'Jesus is in you, Derek, you just have to feel him!' and 'Let the Lord take you, Derek, we know he loves you!' Soon the feelgood was riding high in the circle and one by one we hugged and handshook Derek with a lot less apprehension than the previous week because we could tell that he meant it and that he wanted to find the good path and dance on down it smiling with his new brothers and sisters. Nevertheless, when I hugged him I was alarmed to feel the devil creeping back into my body, but took it as a sign from the Lord not to get too physical with the sinner until he had been properly cured.

I felt good about the progress we were making with Derek, and felt so sure that he would not relapse into depravity that I told Brian we were well on the way to redeeming Derek's soul. In fact, I might have overplayed my own role in all this a little bit because Brian seemed to look slightly annoyed when I persevered in giving him every detail of Derek's confession and how I had forced him to see his own sin and reduced him to tears of remorse (I did not feel it necessary to add that old Nick had impinged himself upon me in the shape of rancid sexual desire).

Indeed Brian was as irritated with me as he had been the previous week and said, tetchily, 'Yes, very good, Gideon, but Derek isn't the only new recruit in the Forum these past couple of weeks. I have other less perverted people to worry about as well.'

I shrugged, not feeling as bad as the previous week when he had admonished me, and supposed that it was due to my own climbing confidence as a group discussion leader.

Afterwards I went for a coffee with Rachel, and I suppose again I was maybe talking a little too much about my role as group discussion leader because at one point she cut me off in mid-sentence and said, pointedly, 'How much Bible-reading did you do this week?'

'What sort of a question is that, Rachel?' I asked warily.

'Well, all night you've talked about group discussion this, homosexual that, Derek the other. Then there were all these calls with Brian all week long. I mean, I just want to make sure you're not losing focus on Jesus and what we're about, Gideon.'

'Well, of course, I've been reading the Bible,' I lied, realising at that moment that I had failed to pick the good book up once all week. I had been meaning to, but I had been busy at work and then in the evenings there had been, like Rachel said, lots of phone calls. 'But saving someone else is what we're all about too, Rachel. If we can save Derek from the devil then surely that's worth much more than me sitting around at home reading the Bible. We can't just read it, we have to act in a Christian manner too!'

Rachel sat in silence for a while, looking into her coffee cup. She was building up to say something she was finding difficult to get out, I could tell.

'But remember,' she said after a while, a little uncertainly and a lot more quietly. 'Remember that you've only just become a group discussion leader, and that has to be reviewed after three months; you may not even make the grade.'

'What are you saying?' I snapped uncharacteristically. 'That you don't think I'm good enough to be a group discussion leader?'

'No, Gideon, please don't get me wrong,' she exhorted. 'I'm just saying this because I care about you. I don't want you to get too arrogant just because you make one convert.'

Rachel took my hand in hers underneath the table. Two or three weeks ago I would have been astounded and delighted by this development. But she was annoying me with her edicts on Bible-reading and hints that I was getting ideas above my station, so I withdrew it straightaway and stood up.

'I can't stay, I've got some things to do,' I said, and left the café without looking back.

I GLOWED WITH vindication the next Friday as Derek began his account of how he had been on the track of Jesus. He mentioned me several times, as we had talked on the phone every day, and I had given him help on where to look while making it clear that he must not moot an appointment with ol' Beelzebub. He quoted several passages from the Bible, and all of us whooped with joy a little when he told us how he had felt a process of rebirth as he had prostrated himself at Brian's feet that evening and he knew he had rid himself of his unnatural desires as long as he had Jesus by his side. I was just about to give the nod for a hug and a handshake when Derek looked over to me and said, 'Not yet, Gideon, there's one thing I have to tell you all before I can get on with the rest of my life with Jesus.' I was floating so high I felt sure that he was going to tell the group that it was all thanks to me, and was already picturing the expressions on Brian's and Rachel's faces when I repeated the quote.

'On Tuesday night I was at a party with some friends from my former life,' Derek said. 'I wanted to take leave of them, tell them I wouldn't be hanging around with them any more, maybe even persuade one or two of them to come along here on Friday night to find Jesus.'

Derek stopped to take breath for a second and then looked down and I began to fear the worst. 'I think somebody must have spiked my drink with something because the next thing I knew I was dancing with this guy called Paul who was wearing nothing but a small, sweaty, grey vest and a pair of lycra cycling shorts. We danced and danced and danced and I was thinking about Jesus and how I wasn't going to say yes to temptation, and then I went to the bathroom to urinate and I must have forgotten to lock the door because next thing I knew the door was opening and there was Paul and soon we were kissing and I peeled off his lycra shorts and my trousers were already down from urinating and soon he had me up against the wall, buggering my arse as hard as he could until we both came together and I ejaculated all down the bathroom wall—'

'Urrrrggh! Gideon, get him to shut up!' screamed Ellie.

'Yes, er, that's enough, thank you, Derek,' I said, still in a state of confusion, having been carried away listening to Derek's latest ugly episode, the devil once more inveigling himself into my licentious regions and mercilessly taking control of my reproductive organ. 'Really, really, let that be the last of these stories now that you've saved yourself, please.'

I must have sounded a little feeble because Sue, another girl in our discussion group, said, 'I don't want him in this group any more, he's filthy! Tell him to go get off somewhere else.'

'That was the last one!' insisted Derek with a profound passion, tears washing his cheeks. 'I'm free now! I know I'm free, you have to believe me, but I had to offload this last sin somewhere, and where better to do that than here?'

'He's absolutely right, Sue,' I said with a little more conviction, wanting to keep a firm grasp on my convert, although I was wishing that he had just kept his last sin to himself and not bothered the rest of us with it, especially as it just seemed to attract Old Nick towards our discussion group. 'I feel that Derek has come through the worst and has purged himself of all his excesses by finding a cathartic outlet in both Jesus and the discussion group. We must continue to support him and help him because come the day when Jesus' army has to take on the devil we're gonna need as many on our side as we can possibly get!'

Without realising it my voice had risen during the course of this short speech, and by the final words had peaked to such volume that all the discussion groups in the hall went silent until I had attained my zenith. Then there was such a whooping and clapping and shouting that I thought I was going to be lifted away by the whole wave of volume which crescendoed across the congregation. Soon the groups broke up and they all began to come and hug me and handshake me, and I was feeling really good about myself, although I noticed that in the far corner Brian and Rachel were talking earnestly, seemingly oblivious to what was going on around them. Well, I supposed Rachel was sore that I had rejected her advances and Brian was just a little envious about all the applause I was getting because it was becoming ever clearer to me that if all the prostrating was not taking place at Brian's feet then he tended to get a little bit peeved in a manner I would not label entirely Christian. Well, flipping blow them, I thought, it's me doing God's hard work here, not them!

I SPENT A lot of that weekend on the phone to fellow members in the Forum because we are encouraged to liaise across the groups and not just keep in touch with people in our own discussion group. All of the people I talked to congratulated me on my speech and said how inspirational it had been to them and how they would say the same thing next time some cynic cast doubts on their deeply held beliefs. 'You've got such commitment!' said Harold, another long-term member like myself. In fact the word commitment came up again and again and I thought that it would be a useful term to bring up next time Brian or Rachel confronted me with snide comments about me becoming too big for my boots. I asked Simone, who had joined the Forum at around the same time as me, if she thought that Brian was still as committed as he had been at the start.

'Oh, why, don't you think he is?' she asked, a little shocked.

'Absolutely,' I said, 'no doubt about it, Brian's one hundred per cent committed to the Forum and to Jesus. But I've been talking to a lot of people this weekend and I've been getting a few signals about him not being as involved as he used to be, that he's a little distant from some of the members, and a few even seem to think he's become a little unapproachable.'

Simone was quiet for a few minutes, and then she said, 'You

know, perhaps I have noticed something. He doesn't seem to hug me as much as he used to at the start.'

'Really?' I said, full of astonishment. 'Oh, Simone, this is actually quite worrying, there seems to be some sort of a trend going on here. We perhaps have to do something about this. Do you have any ideas?'

Simone had no ideas because she never had any ideas, which was why I had been promoted to group discussion leader even though we had both joined the Forum at the same time. 'Maybe,' I ventured, 'you could ask around, very discreetly, gauge feeling among the members and get back to me. Don't tell them that I asked you to ask, because people might get strange ideas now that I'm moving up the hierarchy myself. But we need to help Brian and if we can identify the problem then we can approach him and see if we can work out a solution and get him back in touch with the membership.'

Pliant as she is, Simone swore herself to secrecy and agreed to help me out, promising to phone as many people as she could before the next meeting.

THE FOLLOWING EVENING I happened to be walking near Crosswell Park when I noticed the public toilets which had been the venue for Derek's first lurid confession. They were the old-fashioned, shabby green, wrought-iron public toilets still common in our country, and instinctively I decided to go inside and take a look. Perhaps it would help me to work out the devilish dilemmas inside Derek's head if I could more vividly picture the place where his sins had taken place. As I went down the stairs into the dingy, low-lit basement where the urinals were I suddenly felt my heart begin to thump and I began to secrete a little sweat from under my armpits. When I reached the sordid, smelly basement I knew that I wanted to get out of there as soon as possible and that coming down there had been a mistake. Even worse, as I remembered Derek's appalling story, the devil remembered me, and once more I found myself fighting off his insidious attempts to take hold of my body. There was nobody in the toilet, and I knew that the best way to shake off Old Nick was to go back up those stairs and take a flipping good run across Crosswell Park, but just as I was about to leave I heard footsteps behind me, so I dashed into one of the cubicles and bolted the door lest someone should see me and get the wrong idea about what I was doing there.

I sat down on the toilet seat, trembling and fearful lest the devil made further inroads, but my organ was pulsating with hateful lust, and no matter how hard I tried I could not get him out. I prayed for the man to leave again so that I could get out as quickly as possible, but I sensed that he was still present at one of the urinals. Then I noticed there was a peep-hole in the toilet door, so I looked through and there he still was, he seemed to be taking an age to finish with urinating. The top of his buttocks was visible and I had to close my eyes to shut out the sight of this vile, male flesh, and then the next time I looked a few seconds later, to see if the man was finally finished, he had turned round, and there was Derek, his trousers unzipped and his right hand caressing his unmistakeable tumescence, grinning in my direction (he seemed to be looking straight through the peephole), and from his lips I heard the words, 'Well, well, well, fancy seeing you here!'

At that moment the devil had me, I was no longer in control, and Old Nick caused me to spume his disgusting seed down the inside of my trouser leg. I had wanted to jump out of the cubicle and save Derek there and then, but before I had the chance I had been paralysed with evil desire in this sordid hell-hole and it needed the strength of more than one to take on the forces of darkness. I wondered what Old Nick, disguised as Derek, had in store for me next and I prayed for something to save me. As always, Jesus answered my prayers. I realised that Derek had not been talking to me, but that there was a third person in the toilet there with us, though by now I was in such a state of shock that it took me several seconds to realise that the man passionately kissing Derek in front of me was none other than our branch captain himself.

I do not see fit to describe in detail here the lewd acts which took place between Brian and Derek in that doss-pit, although fortunately they smashed the light-bulb over our heads and I was not forced to witness in its entirety this vile spectacle, and I spent the minutes praying and praying and praying for it all to be over and for me to get out of there. Eventually, when Old Nick had satisfied his sickening, craven lasciviousness all round, they left the toilet and eventually I was able to make my way home. I ran most of the way because I had a heck of a lot of telephone calls to make.

BRIAN WAS BOTH surprised and annoyed to find that George Rutkin, a member of the Forum Central Committee, had come along to the meeting without Brian being informed.

'What's going on? I'm supposed to be branch captain here,' said Brian, his red hairs almost visibly bristling as I introduced the two.

'George is here tonight to make an important announcement,' I said. Brian glared at me, then said quite openly in front of George, 'I've got a few things to say to you after tonight's service.'

'We'll see about that later,' I said mildly, and turned away from Brian quite deliberately, leading George around and introducing him to some of the young worshippers.

My task was made easier by the fact that Derek turned up, although I had not been relying upon it. I took him to one side and said, 'Derek, I want to ask you something very important. Do you by any chance have a confession to make this week? Some sinning you feel you need to get off your chest?'

He looked down at the floor. 'Actually, I do,' he answered truthfully. 'Am I that transparent?'

'No, no,' I assured him. 'It's just that if you don't mind, I want you to make your confession during the service instead of at the discussion group afterwards. I know there will be a lot more people listening, but we have someone very important here tonight from the central committee and he wants to see how we are coping as a church with a difficult convert like yourself.'

It sounded a bit lame, I admit, but it seemed Derek was only too keen to tell all before a larger audience. I was not sure if he would be naming names, but I was ready to step in as the star witness at the appropriate moment.

Poor Brian never even got the chance to start his sermon that week. George Rutkin stood up and brushed him to one side and introduced Derek, who not only told the story exactly as it had happened in the public toilet at Crosswell Park, he informed us gleefully that he was not a Christian at all but an actor and a dramatist, and he was going to put everything he had experienced here into a play that would be performed at the town hall in a few months' time. I'd been expecting one of his tearful, hair-tearing remorseful gigs for better effect, but this performance more or less did the trick, even though I was angry at myself for not having spotted he was a fraud. At least I was going to be portrayed on stage! Brian ran out of the church to the sound of jeering, only to be photographed by the hacks from the local paper whom I'd tipped off beforehand. And all around me I could hear the sound of people saying to each other, 'I knew there was something wrong with Brian all along.' Simone had done a good job. There only remained the task of appointing someone as Brian's successor to lead that night's sermon in a storm of swaying and singing and hugging for our good Lord Jesus.

I AM BRANCH captain and engaged to Rachel. I have appointed Everton as my deputy, with the strict instruction to swiftly eject any perverts who ever again see fit to sniff round our hallowed church door.

Older and Wiser

IT CAME AS a surprise to Art Molder that his daughter had undergone a character transformation after a term away at college. Her cropped hair, second-hand chic and assertive poise all reflected a welcome lean towards the radical, and Art was quietly pleased that she had shown herself receptive to new influences. Although she was more precious to him than anybody else in the world, she had always been a little bit too straight and bookish at school, and he had been slightly alarmed at the general lack of moody adolescent angst which his contemporaries had ceaselessly bemoaned in their own offspring. He remained taciturn as they exasperatedly chronicled unscheduled all-nighters, experiments with intoxicants, late-night encounters with the law, and academic under-achievement. He felt obliged to remain silent because he certainly wasn't going to crow, 'Well, Andrea's teetotal, gets straight As and she never stays out beyond ten o'clock.'

And what a relief that she had dragged home a boyfriend, 'Hig', a shaggy-looking creature attempting to cultivate a shadow of down on his chin who smoked roll-up cigarettes and was eloquent on jazz, the blues and twentieth-century French art and literature. That was all a pretence, Art knew, but he'd much rather that than an engineering student in Tesco's jeans who wanted to talk man-to-man about the mechanics of automobilia. He'd wondered for more than a decade how he would react when Andrea brought home her first boyfriend, but had got so fed up with waiting that it had finally turned out to be nothing more than an immense feeling of relief. He made a big effort with 'Hig', and was pleased that Andrea had not resented how well the two of them had got on.

'Hig' had gone home now after a week and he was looking forward to spending Christmas with just Andrea. They had not had the chance to talk to each other properly for months and he also wanted to spend a couple of evenings reading books like they had done in the past few years, one or the other occasionally looking up to articulate some outstandingly good or poor paragraph they had just come across. Andrea's new, harder-nosed exterior had already relaxed a little since they had taken 'Hig' to the train station that afternoon, and he found himself flattered that in her boyfriend's absence she still liked to cling on to him a little and had stroked the back of his neck that evening as he had been making dinner in the kitchen. They enjoyed an amenable supper and sat down in the living room with the remainder of a bottle of wine and their books spread out on their laps. Outside it had been windy all day and Art felt warm and comfortable sitting in his chair, across from his daughter on the floor cushion. Then the doorbell rang. Andrea told him to leave it, but Art was already half-way towards the door.

Art would normally have been pleased to see Terry Hiddell, indeed he had been especially grateful for his company over the past three months since Andrea had left home, during which time he had been feeling lonelier than he cared to admit. But, although he did not betray it, tonight he wished he had not bothered going to answer the door. Now Art was annoyed with himself for letting his curiosity lose him an evening of easy relaxation in favour of one where he would be obliged to open the Scotch and talk big themes. Terry was an interesting, wholehearted character but Art didn't half wish he could sometimes give the major issues a rest and talk about his favourite way of making lemon soufflé or something.

Worse still, Andrea nearly always went up to her bedroom when Terry arrived, making excuses that she had to get on with schoolwork. Art knew this wasn't true because she always did her homework the minute she returned from school, but he never dared ask her what she had against Terry. Still, his friend was so thick-skinned that Art doubted whether he even noticed that Andrea snubbed him within minutes of his arrival every time he came round. Or perhaps he didn't care, and was more than happy to have Art to himself to discuss manfully the main socio-economic topics of the day.

'Here's a little something to warm you up for Christmas,' said Terry, smiling as he crossed the threshold, forcing his bulky frame into the small hallway. Art felt guilty about wishing he hadn't answered the door as he unwrapped a bottle of his favourite malt. It was good of Terry to bring the bottle, he knew that Art couldn't afford this stuff on his weedy salary. Mind you, he'd have to open it now because it was all the whisky he had apart from Sainsbury's own brand, and he knew there wouldn't be much left by the time Terry stepped back out into the night again. Still, what the hell, he thought, as he went to the kitchen to get two tumblers, what's it there for if not to drink, and he chided himself for the meanness of his thought patterns.

'Ah, the wandering student returns!' he heard Terry exclaim as he went into the sitting room. He knew this exclamation alone would be enough to send Andrea scurrying upstairs, but was surprised to hear the murmurings of a conversation as he took the glasses from the cupboard and gave them a quick rinse. Then, as he was about to turn off the kitchen light he heard Andrea call brightly, 'If it's whisky you're having, Dad, then bring me a glass too.' He shrugged to himself, called out: 'OK!' then turned and went back to get a third glass, wishing he'd thought to ask her in the first place.

'So what have they been teaching you at this so-called educational institution that we taxpayers are funding?' Terry boomed at Andrea, as he settled back on the sofa and imbibed such a generous gulp of whisky that Art had to refill his glass immediately. 'A bit more this time, Art, if you don't mind,' said Terry, winking at him, then to Andrea, 'Always a bit of a tight-arse, your old man.'

Art winced, again convinced that such a crass observation would inevitably precede his daughter's exit from the room. But she just ignored the comment and said to Terry, 'Well, Terry, as *you* are the taxpayer, what sort of things do *you* think we should be learning?'

Art marvelled inwardly at the assured sarcasm of his daughter's riposte. She would never have spoken to Terry like this three months ago, and he noticed with pride how her answer momentarily wrongfooted his friend, who turned towards him and said, 'Oooooh, I say, I think we can already tell what she's been learning, Art. Clever-cleverness and disrespect for her elders!' He was only half-joking.

'No more disrespectful than calling my university a "so-called educational institution", Terry,' she replied. There was a hint of waspishness in her tone, but she was smiling, therefore Terry could not take real offence.

'OK, OK, fair comment,' said Terry, holding up his hands in submission, but still clearly a little taken aback at the change in the normally timid Andrea. 'Still, you haven't really answered my question. I mean, genuinely now, Andrea, what have you been learning since I last saw you?'

Art knew that this was a prelude to an attack on arts degrees. Andrea would say that she had been reading works of fiction, and Terry, as he had already done in the summer when Art had first told him what Andrea was going to study at college, would explain why such degrees were a waste of time and money for humanity, and why weren't our universities used for finding a cure for cancer and teaching young people how to run their own businesses. Just like Terry did, and—

'. . . I became successful quite nicely without picking up some useless piece of paper while poncing about in a black gown!'

There, argument over as far as Terry was concerned. The figures proved it. If you went to work at sixteen instead of sitting around for five or six years reading books then you would be richer. Nothing or nobody would ever convince Terry otherwise. But Andrea had something more to say.

'Do you and Leah ever go to the cinema?' she asked mildly.

'We go once a week at least,' said Terry. 'Last week we saw—'

'And do you watch dramas and feature films and sitcoms on television?'

'Well, yes,' said Terry, becoming aware that the questions were leading somewhere and were not in fact a polite enquiry as to his extra-curricular activities with his spouse. 'I suppose we do watch quite a bit in the evenings. But—'

'And do you suppose,' Andrea continued, 'that the people who made these programmes studied business at college? Do you think that all the ideas for the plots and the characters and the pathos and the comedy came while people were sitting around working out the best way to achieve a fat plus sign at the end of their balance sheets? Do you think that Shakespeare would have written *Macbeth* if all he had wanted was a big house in the suburbs to show off to his friends? And another thing, if you're such a successful businessman, how come you're always making people redundant?'

Art had been impressed further still by his new, dauntless daughter, but only up until that last sentence. Terry had been on the rack and struggling and casting nervous smiles Art's way in what had almost seemed like an unspoken appeal to help him out of his corner. But the way she delivered that last sting had not just changed the focus of the argument, it had been more than a little spiteful and personal too. Worse still, it had provided Terry with the perfect material to fight back.

'Oh, I see!' he triumphed. 'That's what they've been teaching you there – socialism! Well, what a surprise, off to college the innocent little daddy's girl and back home in a red blaze of Marxism!' He was turning her sarcasm back on her and getting much too big a kick out of it for Art's liking, who was also annoyed by the comment about Andrea being a daddy's girl. Mind you, not as annoyed as Andrea, judging by the sudden glint in her eyes. Or was it just the effects of the whisky? Art poured new tumblers all round so that he could continue to avoid taking sides. Terry meanwhile gassed on.

'It's wonderful to know too that Marxism is teaching you so well about the rudiments of good business,' he said. 'Because if I was a *bad* businessman, well, then I wouldn't be making people redundant. I have to make people redundant to keep my business in *good* shape, to keep the business efficient. You can't afford to be sentimental in business, young lady. Though I don't suppose that's the sort of thing you can read about in Charles Dickens.'

'You can if you read *Hard Times*,' she countered.

'Well, I bloody haven't,' laughed Terry, 'but I know that if I'd sat around on my arse reading books half of my life then I'd be experiencing a few *hard times* of my own!'

Neither Art nor Andrea laughed at this. The discussion was too bitter to be enjoyable, and although Andrea had relished the chance to finally take on a man she had disliked for years, both she and her father were now regretting they had lost the evening they could have spent alone together. Terry meanwhile held forth at great length on why socialism had never worked and could never work and why competitive capitalism may not be the perfect system but . . .

Art wasn't listening because he realised he'd heard it a hundred times before, while Andrea was staring distractedly at the floor, like she was thinking of 'Hig' or wanted to be back at college among her own, where she gathered with her friends and the lines between good and evil were so lucidly delineated that there was rarely the need for cantankerous ideological debate. In the end she looked up wearily and said, 'Yeah, Terry, you're probably right,' just so that he'd shut up, and he promptly did.

There was a long silence and Art became lost in thought, realising that Andrea's passionate debating style, followed soon afterwards by apathy and indifference when she could no longer be bothered to argue the toss, closely resembled that of her long dead mother's. He became melancholy and automatically reached for the whisky bottle. He offered it to Terry, who said, 'No thanks, Art, I'd better be going.' This was surprising as he hadn't stayed for longer than half an hour. Usually he stayed until one or two in the morning, but Art wasn't displeased, realising that he could save his evening with Andrea after all (not to mention the fact that the malt bottle was still two-thirds full).

'Are you sure?' said Art, praying that Terry wouldn't change his mind. But to his relief Terry heaved himself off the sofa and made for the hallway, saying, 'No, it's OK, Art, best be going, got a busy day ahead of me tomorrow, unlike some.'

This wasn't Terry's last comment before he left, though. Thinking that he had effectively out-debated Andrea he patted her on the shoulder as she came out of the living room to see him off and said, 'I don't blame you for having those views, love. You know what they say: "If you're not a socialist at twenty you haven't got a heart. And if you're still a socialist at forty then you haven't got a head!"'

At this moment Art opened the door and all three were taken aback by a huge gust of wind that blustered through into the hallway. In the half hour that Terry had been visiting the strong gusts of that afternoon had accelerated to gale-force speed, and the saplings on the street were bowed almost double as leaves and litter were whisked up and down the street.

'Blimey!' said Art, 'you can't walk home in this, Terry. Let me run you back in the car.' The last thing he wanted to do was get in the car, especially given how much he'd drunk and the fact that he might get blown off the road.

'No, I'll be all right,' said Terry. 'It's only a bit of wind, never did anyone any harm.'

'But it's dangerous,' said Art. 'Why don't you stay and have a couple more drinks until it dies down. There might be tiles coming off the roof and stuff.'

'Ha!' shouted Terry as he made to step off the porch. 'My company tiled the roofs of every street around here for miles.

Quality work, Art, by a quality business!' And with that he marched off into the storm.

'Fat patronising fuck,' said Andrea, venomously, and turned back to the living room. Then she mimicked him bitterly. *'If you're still a socialist at forty then you haven't got a head!* I hope one of his quality tiles comes down and hits him in the neck, then we'll see who hasn't got a fucking head.'

'Andrea!' said Art in admonishment. But she just replied, 'Oh leave it out, Dad. I'm off to bed,' and stomped upstairs. It was still only nine-thirty.

Art spent the rest of the evening alone in the living room, drinking the malt whisky and feeling sad about things in general.

Opining for Democracy's Sake

WHEN MY WIFE and I go to visit my mother and my stepfather they say: 'We don't understand why they're allowing gay people to "get married". It's bloody ridiculous.'

They also say: 'The number of young people out there who can't spell properly and do simple mental arithmetic, it's a bloody scandal.'

It's not much different at the house of my parents-in-law. They say: 'You can't get proper service in restaurants any more. And it's not much better in the shops!'

Or we might be treated to the following: 'We don't mind them having a shop or a takeaway restaurant. It's when they start becoming a burden on the taxpayer or committing crimes that they should be sent back to where they came from.'

They are all over sixty now. It's good that they have views. They have all had views now for several decades, and I should know because I'm forty and I've been listening to those views, at least in the case of my own parents, for several decades too. Those views have barely changed in all that time.

'People who mistreat animals should be stoned in public!'

'People who drink and drive should be made to ride bicycles for the rest of their lives!'

'They should give that mountaineer an OBE; he's done more for Britain than any bloody politician!'

'Why on earth does the Sunday paper need so many damned sections?'

Of course I have long since stopped listening to these views, let alone arguing with them.

'No one in Britain wants closer ties with Europe; it's a complete bloody nonsense.'

What am I going to say? *No one*, dear father-in-law? You mean not a single person in Britain wants closer ties with Europe? You have asked every one of Britain's sixty million inhabitants, have you? And every single one of them said: 'Europe, it's a complete bloody nonsense'?

We had all the arguments years ago when I came back from college filled with the vocabulary of newly raised consciousness – homophobia! bourgeoisification! phallocentric! Bloody great big words, ones that I thought I was the first ever person to learn. At first I yelled and they patronised me. So then I scorned them, and then *they* yelled instead. Over the years the volume fell, as did the strength of my convictions. My stepfather realised that saying certain provocative things related to matters of race and sex no longer ignited me. But he still went ahead and said them anyway. He still does. It must be force of habit.

'It's a fact that there are three working days in every month when women perform well below par.'

Yeah, yeah, yeah.

'I just go along and vote the same as Dave, he understands the issues better.'

Of course he does.

'We should just go in there and bomb the bastard!'

Yes, that will do the trick, I'm sure.

Beat, flog, hang, shoot, bomb, do *something*! Why don't they do *something*?

MY STEPFATHER SAYS angrily: 'These buggers who talk about banning fox-hunting are pussy-footed city ponces who know sod all about life in the country.' My stepfather has never been on a hunt, in fact, he has never ridden a horse as far as I know, but he lives in the countryside so he feels qualified to express his view. This is a democracy. He is entitled to express his view.

Funnily enough, by contrast, my father-in-law says: 'There is simply no case for the anachronistic and barbaric practice of fox-hunting. It's shameful, and these people try to claim they represent civilisation at its most noble peak.' Then again, he has never been a hunt saboteur. It would take him too long to get out of London and at weekends, he's a busy man. But he's entitled to hold his view.

My mother is worried about rising crime, even though she has never been burgled and doesn't know anyone in her peaceful village who has been either. 'All the more reason to be vigilant, it's more than likely that we'll be next!' she says when I seek to reassure her that she is safe in her home.

A policeman came to get a statement from my father-in-law, who had witnessed a car accident. 'You wouldn't believe how long it took them to take that statement, nearly two hours just to write down one page. What a waste of time and taxpayer's money!'

My stepfather, watching a parliamentary debate on the news: 'Why don't they close down Parliament for a year and see how these MPs get on in the real world? I bet we'd see some changes after that!'

Yep, that'll do it.

Sometimes going to see our relatives is like the reading the letters page of the local newspaper, except that we get the un-edited version.

THEN ONE DAY my stepfather goes completely over the top. It is like he suddenly knows that no one has been paying any attention to his views for twenty years, or he understands that reiterating the same little philosophies for the rest of his days is never going to change a thing.

We are having a quiet family dinner when it happens.

'Thanks, Mum, lovely lamb,' I say.

'Yes, Greta, very good, thank you,' says my wife.

'I'm glad you like it, my dears, though it's not every day we can afford to eat lamb, you know.'

Pause.

'Lambs, hose the buggers down!' yells my stepfather. 'Put 'em all in cages and hose 'em down. They taste better that way, you know. And it makes their wool fluffier.'

My wife and I exchange glances. Then I turn to my mother and whisper, 'How long has this been going on?'

'How long has what been going on, dear?' she replies breezily. 'Now eat up your lamb, I've got strawberry pavlova for dessert.'

THAT NIGHT A voice comes to me and says, 'A vacancy has arisen in the ranks of the aged. One of their number has been declared insane and locked away.'

'Yes, that will be my stepfather,' I reply.

'And you have been nominated to take his place.'

'No, no, not me, I'm only forty-one,' I protest.

'Liar!' says the voice. 'You are forty-seven!'

I do a quick mental calculation based on the year of my birth and realise that I must have stopped counting several years ago. The voice is right.

'OK, OK, but that's still too young. I'm not ready yet. I'm still ageing, I'm not fully matured yet. Give me a few more years, please!'

'We've been studying your views lately. You're perfectly ripe. What's more, once nominated, you have no choice.'

'I want to lodge an official appeal against this decision!' I cry, but the voice just laughs.

'You had the chance to protest when you were young and you never took it, so just get old and miserable and sit around moaning with the rest of them.' And with that the voice is gone and I go back to sleep.

I think it has all been a strange dream, until the next morning, and I am reading an article in the local newspaper about a teenage boy who has been fined for breaking a butcher's shop window with an umbrella when he was drunk one night.

'This is outrageous,' I say out loud, to the surprise of my

fourteen-year-old son and my twelve-year-old daughter. 'It's not just that he was drunk at that age, but that he indulged in mindless vandalism too. Where on earth were his parents? And all he got was a paltry fine! They should send him off somewhere where he learns how to behave properly!'

'What are you talking about, Dad?' says my son, Matt.

'This boy!' I say excitedly, holding up the newspaper and pointing to the report. 'Smashing windows when drunk. I expect he goes to your school. Little vandal, and I don't expect the rest of his age group are much better, bloody yobs!'

'Oh,' he says, disinterestedly, 'that's Simon Tyler. He's all right, actually.'

'What?' I shout. 'You think it's all right to get drunk and smash windows, do you? What exactly is all right about that?'

'Calm down, Ewen,' my wife says.

My children are looking at me like I have gone crazy. I want to stop banging on about this stupid butcher's window but I cannot, and continue: 'Imagine you're trying to run a small business and every Monday morning you come into work and find that some drunken kid has smashed in—'

'I'm off, Mum,' says Matt and jumps down from the table and into the hallway to get his jacket and bag and off he goes to school. My daughter follows soon after.

'You OK, love?' says my wife.

I HAVE A free day, so after breakfast I go into town to do some shopping. I have a number of things to get but am having little luck in the department stores in finding exactly what I want. Worse still, nobody is observing protocol on the elevators, standing still on both sides and thus blocking the way for people who want to walk up and down. I stand simmering in my own impatience, although I don't say anything out aloud. At least not until supper-time.

'You wouldn't believe the way people behave on the elevators in shops these days,' I broadcast to my family. 'They just bloody stand there like mules, they've got no manners. They never think about people who are in a hurry.'

'Why were you in a hurry?' asks my daughter, Lilly.

'You know, I had lots of things to do,' I say, unconvincingly.

Everybody laughs except me. They always tease me about my inability to get things done in the time-frame which I, for some reason, always specify beforehand. 'I'm going to have the hallway painted before lunchtime,' I might sometimes announce at breakfast. By lunchtime I am usually still down at the hardware store deciding which paint and brushes to buy.

'But seriously,' I say. 'How come so many people today have absolutely no conception of basic good manners? How come I know perfectly well, and have known perfectly well for years, that you should stand on the right-hand side of the elevator only, in order to allow people to get past more quickly on the left. I mean, it's so bloody simple. Why can't they put public information films on basic good manners on television, before the news perhaps, so that people can learn?'

'I've got some homework to do,' says Matt, and excuses himself from the table.

'Me too,' says Lily, and follows him.

'Are you sure you're all right, love?' asks my wife.

THAT NIGHT THE voice comes back to me. 'Great first day! A stunning debut in the realm of self-righteousness; sweeping generalised theories delivered with all the necessary pomp and peevishness. You have a great future ahead of you, new oldboy!'

'You bastard,' I mutter. 'People like you should be—'

But I am interrupted by derisive laughter, which diminishes into nothingness and leaves me lying in bed with visions of forming a vigilante group against drunken teenage vandals and holding speeches on elevators and receiving loud applause as cowed stair-blockers shamefully step to the right-hand side and let me pass proudly by.

PC Nottingham's Admirer

POLICE CONSTABLE NOTTINGHAM was surprised to find himself being applauded as he wrote down the particulars of the burglar who had just been apprehended attempting to desert the grounds of a house from which he had apparently stolen several fine bottles of forty-year-old malt whisky.

'Bravo, Constable!' shouted the man on the other side of the street, clapping his hands together enthusiastically. It was a residential district and there was nobody else around except for his colleague PC Fringle, who was holding the burglar up against the wall with the help of handcuffs and a knee pointed firmly up the crevice of the man's backside.

'Go steady on him,' said PC Nottingham to his colleague, 'there's a potential witness over there. He's applauding us now but there's no telling when they'll turn against you.' You always had to warn Fringle as soon as things got physical, the lad had been internally disciplined three times now for breaking the bones of people he'd arrested. Well, he hadn't been upbraided for breaking the actual bones, just for having let someone see him doing it. Dolt.

'Don't worry, I've got the bastard in a twister,' said PC Fringle, grimacing as the hapless, halfweight criminal fainted from the pain of having the skin on his arms burned by the well-stacked and zealous policeman. Nottingham sighed. 'Put him in the car and we'll get the rest of his details down at the station.'

'Bravo, Constable!' shouted the man again from the other side of the road. 'What a coup! Lock him up good and proper now so the rest of us can breathe a sigh of relief. Thank goodness you boys can be relied upon to be in the right place at the right time, right at the heart of crime.'

PC Nottingham nodded slightly in acknowledgement of the man's adulation. He was used to people staring whenever he made an arrest in a public place, but this demonstrative exhibition of praise was somewhat unusual. Still, it was better than getting hissed at and being called the filth just because you were doing your job. Like it was you who had committed the crime by arresting someone.

The man was small, in his fifties, with a thin head of dark, greased-back hair. He wore a long blue mac. An unremarkable specimen, thought PC Nottingham, just the kind of guy with decent, old-fashioned values who might appreciate the police going about doing a good job. It seemed like the arrest really had made his day, for as PC Nottingham drove away the man still bore a delighted grin, and was waving manically when he looked in his rear-view mirror just before turning the corner.

PC Fringle appeared not to have noticed the man at all, preoccupied as he was with the bottles of whisky which their captive had been liberating from their previous owner. 'Not bad,' he said, placing one under the dashboard. 'Though I think that one must have got lost on the chase through the gardens, ha, ha, ha.'

THE POLICE OFFICER quickly forgot the man and continued his duties for a number of weeks without further incident. Then one afternoon he was called upon to separate two drunks who had engaged themselves in a brawl in the middle of Sodsworth's pedestrian shopping zone.

It was an unpleasant task, the sort of incident he would prefer to deal with swiftly by sending the violators in separate directions and hoping they would collapse somewhere unobtrusive and sleep it off. But both men were inebriated to the point where they were no longer sensitive to logic, and they stood bellowing streams of offensiveness in each other's faces until PC

Nottingham decreed that the only way to stop them was to place the men under arrest. Upon orders, PC Fringle did so with relish, muttering, 'I love it when they're drunk, they can never remember who kicked them.'

As usual a small crowd of people with nothing better to do had gathered to passively stare at the spectacle in the hope of brightening up their lives and then being able to go home and have something to tell their families across the tea table. PC Nottingham paid them no attention until a voice crowed above the heads of the onlookers: 'Once again excellent work, Constable, my warmest congratulations.' And then the same prolonged solo applause which had heralded the arrest of the whisky thief some weeks before.

PC Nottingham could not help but look up to get a better view of the participating spectator and check if it was indeed the same man as had previously paid obeisance to his crime-tackling skills. Indeed, there was the little fellow in the blue mac, the same expression of marvel across his features, executing the same boisterous arm movements to produce his soundtrack of appreciation. Well, just a coincidence, thought the police constable, although he felt a little less comfortable with the man's obsequiousness compared with the last time, when there had been no other observers of the scene. Briefly PC Nottingham thought to himself, I expect that's what it is like to be famous.

'Superb double arrest, Constable,' yelled the little man excitedly. 'Get this drunken scum off our streets. Why should decent citizens out doing their shopping be disturbed by these beer-guzzling beasts? Thank goodness for men like Police Constable Nottingham here, don't you think, ladies and gentleman? It's men like this mean we can sleep safely in our beds at night!'

PC Nottingham was alarmed to hear his name spoken out loud. He had been about to enter the back of the police van and quiz his colleague about the appearance of a newly made cut above the right eye of one of the arrested men which he was sure had not been there a couple of minutes earlier. Now he stepped back down and turned around and walked over to the little man in the blue coat, who was still applauding and beaming with joy at the sight of the streets being swept of crime before his eyes.

'How do you know my name?' he said to the man firmly.

The man turned around to the assembled shoppers and asked in mock amazement, 'This man asks how do I know his name! Such is the modesty of our town's top crime-quasher! Police Constable Nottingham, the saviour of our streets, the man who bags burglars for fun, the man who has done more for law and order than a thousand home secretaries hamstrung by the paralysis of political systematics, the man who defends the rights of the little fellow like me, who puts his big, brave, blue uniform in front of the forces of disrespect and anarchy to defend the weak against the smells and spuming abuse of those disgraceful enough to be slaughtered on drink by three in the afternoon. Is there any person here who is *not* aware that the baron of the beat who stands so grandly before us now is named and known as Police Constable Nottingham?'

Rather than answer the little man's question people began to walk away, having little clue as to what he was talking about. After a few seconds the two men stood there alone. PC Nottingham was about to tell him to mind what he was saying when the little man said, 'Must go, things to do, and I cannot halt you in your valuable work for a moment longer, Police Constable Nottingham.' And he turned and skipped away.

THE VERY NEXT day PC Nottingham stopped a car for questioning and asked the driver to hand over his driving licence and the vehicle documents. He wasn't exactly sure why he had stopped this particular car, as the driver had not in any way been infringing the law, and there was nothing visibly wrong with the vehicle. It was just a policeman's instinct, possessing that nose to sniff out the putrid and the corrupt.

'How long have you owned this vehicle, sir?' he said to the man in the driver's seat, but before the vehicle's occupant had the chance to answer, a familiar voice rang out from a queue of people waiting for a bus around twenty yards further up the road.

'Bravo, Constable! Nick him, go on, nick the bastard! Search the car, you're bound to find some drugs, or some excess jewellery which just happened to get left over from *a delivery*, I can wager. You know, the sort of garish gold these guys drape around their necks. They're all at it, we all know it, so the sooner he's off the streets and locked up safely inside the better.

'Super PC Nottingham, one-man flood barrier to the tidal wave of alien crime threatening to engulf this once fine British town!'

The driver of the car grinned at PC Nottingham and said, 'Looks like you got yourself a fan club there, man.'

'How long have you owned this vehicle, sir?' PC Nottingham repeated through half-shut teeth. But today the little man in the blue mac was becoming bolder and had ventured so close as to be able to hear PC Nottingham's question.

'Go on, then, answer the officer!' he yelled indignantly at the driver, who continued to smile. 'Although I bet you bloody well can't because I bet you don't bloody well own it, eh? People like you don't come into possession of items like this fine vehicle by purchasing it through the legitimate sales channels, such as a registered automobile dealer. We all know that. Which I think is what Police Constable Nottingham is getting at through his albeit subtle line of questioning, namely how long have you *owned* it, because you can bet as sure as a spade's a spade you don't own it at all—'

'SHUT UP!' roared PC Nottingham at the man, who immediately stepped back. 'I am trying to go about doing my normal duty and I will not stand for this constant interference.' He took a grip of himself and lowered his voice. 'Now, please go away, I have work to do, and I am sure that you too have better things to do than follow police officers round the whole day.'

'Well, well, I never,' said the man in the blue mac, backing off further. 'Well I never, never in all my life saw such a thing. A law-abiding member of the public offering his moral support to the town's best policeman and what does he get for his troubles but a mouthful of abuse. Well, well, well.' And he turned and walked away slowly, ruminating aloud on the reasons why the police no longer enjoyed the trust and support of the British public.

Once the man was a safe distance away, the internally burning PC Nottingham turned back to the driver. 'Now hand over the fucking licence, sambo,' he hissed.

'HAVE YOU NOTICED how there always seems to be that little fellow in the blue mac applauding you whenever you make an arrest?' PC Fringle asked his colleague before salivating over the top end of a kebab and messily savaging the first third of its contents.

PC Nottingham turned slightly in the driver's seat and stared at his sidekick for several seconds, but his intense look of scrutinous consternation was insufficient to distract the youthful officer from his toxic lunch. Eventually Fringle looked at him out of the corner of his eye and said, 'What's the matter?'

Nottingham sighed. 'That *little* fellow,' he said, 'that *little* fellow has been plaguing me for weeks, loudly heralding each and every crime that I have apprehended, applauding like a battery-driven maniac, commentating events with the excitement of a scoop reporter on live prime-time news. And on each and every occasion, and I swear that there have been at least two dozen, you have been standing either close by or directly next to me, at least when you haven't been perpetrating some act of violence upon a suspect. And now, today, something has clicked within your cranium and you have finally perceived the gentleman's constant and aggravating attendance.'

Fringle did not reply, his mouth was stuffed anew with meat and onions.

'Why today, Fringle?' PC Nottingham went on. 'Why not yesterday when we arrested the fourteen-year-old boy for stealing sweets in Woolworth's and the man in the little blue mac was shouting across the aisles: "This man is making Britain great again! Lock up the kids and give 'em a short sharp shock!

Pocketing confectionery, the greatest crime of all, not to mention the most difficult to detect, Mr Holmes." Or why not two nights ago when we booked that elderly lady on Bowery Street for riding her bicycle in the dark without a rear light and the man in the blue mac appeared and screamed, "Hanging's too good for 'em, Constable. Why waste the time and the rope, shoot her on the spot and leave her body in the gutter for the dogs." Did you not, Fringle, find it remarkable before today that we are being pursued again and again by some obsessive nutter with an overactive sarcasm gland?'

Fringle belched, sending a fetid airwave of Tabasco sauce across the car. 'I think it's quite nice that someone is showing some appreciation for our work,' he said. 'It's better than having some long-haired liberal harping on about police brutality and trying to hand the suspect his name and address on a piece of paper pledging to be the do-good witness.'

'This man is not appreciating our work, you dunderhead,' said Nottingham animatedly. 'He's taking the piss, can't you see? And the worst thing of all is that I cannot even arrest the little git, I checked it out with the sergeant, and I even had a letter published on the *Police Review* problem page. As long as he doesn't actually obstruct an arrest or cause a disturbance of the peace there is nothing I can get him on. Every time he pushes me and then just as I'm stretched to my limit and ready to arrest him anyway, he scuttles off and disappears until the next time. And now I've even started dreaming about the bugger – last night he moved into my flat and was waiting at home for me, standing in the kitchen cooking with an apron on saying, "A good hot meal after a hard day's subordinating the populace." I'm thinking of asking for a transfer.'

'Well, I've got an idea,' said PC Fringle brightly, chewing on doggedly.

'Come on then, Fringle, out with it,' Nottingham said wearily.

'What this geezer needs is a good, hard kicking . . .'

*

AS IF HE had somehow overheard Fringle's idea, the little man in the blue mac suddenly disappeared from PC Nottingham's life. For several weeks the officer could not help looking over his shoulder every time he had cause to accost, arrest or question any member of the public. Twice he let drug-carrying suspects on the notorious Whitelaw Housing Estate slip out of his grasp because he could not help looking left and right in anticipation of the loud, deliberate applause together with its verbose, sardonic commentary. Then, gradually, he once again accustomed himself to a quiet life on patrol debagging miscreants with PC Fringle, learning anew to tread that fine line between maintaining civilian order and restraining the latter from going so far as to permanently maim or kill someone.

One day several months later, the two men were sitting in their car smoking cigars and watching some schoolgirls play hockey on a nearby field when they received a call ordering all available personnel to proceed to the centre of town. 'Demonstration outside the town hall. Proceed with caution and break up immediately using any means available,' came the word over the radio.

'Fucking great,' said PC Fringle, wolf-whistling rapaciously out the open window as the surprised hockey players turned to the road to see which car was screeching its tyres so urgently on the tarmac. 'A demo. We don't get many of those in Sodsworth.'

By the time the two men arrived at the scene of the demonstration there were already more policemen than protesters. PC Nottingham immediately recognised the little man in the blue mac who was standing on the steps of the town hall bellowing through a megaphone. Behind him was a large cloth banner hanging limply and crudely scrawled with the words SODS-WORTH ANARCHISTS AGAINST A POLICE STATE. In front of him were thirteen people, mainly young men and women, with encrusted pigtails and mangy black mongrels, waving their fists in the air and cheering every time the man came to the end of a sentence. Around them stood a ring of between thirty and forty police officers, many with Alsatians half-strangling themselves to be freed of the leash, and many of whom had rushed on to duty for fear of missing a momentous day in the town's history.

The little man in the dark blue mac was speaking quite differently today. In tones far removed from his ironic commentaries on PC Nottingham's arrest procedures, he was passionately encouraging his followers to storm the town hall and stage a sit-in to protest at 'the mayor's passive tolerance of a world in which fascist police batons crush the voices of dissent'. It was precisely these words which caused one officer present to yell: 'This is incitement to riot!' thereby instigating a charge of the blue-boys upon the shabby gaggle of schismatics, who were swiftly and conscientiously belted into submission by the happy band of effervescent coppers before a team of ambulancemen promptly dragged away the evidence.

While PC Fringle was delightedly leading the charge brandishing his solid oak truncheon, PC Nottingham had hung back slightly after noticing how the man in the blue mac, pre-empting the imminent massacre, had ducked around the corner of the town hall, nimbly dancing through the pillars undetected by the mass of brutality closing in upon the central target. Nottingham ran around the circle of officers and their eager, punitive sticks and followed the little man. There was nothing behind the town hall except a cul-de-sac and a public toilet. He walked into the men's convenience and booted open the closet doors one by one. In the first were two men engaged in oral sex, in the second sat a clapped-out junky smacking himself up. These minor misdemeanours could be ignored today. For in the third sat the little man in the blue mac who, as the door crashed open, looked up at PC Nottingham, grinned and then took out of his inside pocket a small pistol which he aimed at the officer's forehead.

'THE LADS WEREN'T quite sure what to think when we found you lying on the toilet floor next to some whoopsie with his knob hanging out,' said PC Fringle as he took a seat next to Nottingham's hospital bed. 'It was only when we saw the blood that we realised something was wrong. Bit of a humiliation, eh, having your life saved by some jabber. Still, better than being dead, I suppose.'

'Well, actually, I'd quite like to thank the man,' croaked PC Nottingham, who was irritated by his colleague and wished he had not come to visit. He did not care that he had been saved by a 'jabber', nor that the story had been splashed across *The Sodsworth Sun*. COPPER SAVED BY PLUCKY POOFTER read the headline, with the sub-header GALLANT GAY STOPS PC BEING BLOWN AWAY! PC Nottingham had no recall of the event, but the man had apparently dived across and shoved him out of the way, causing the bullet from the anarchist's pistol to lodge in his flailing knee instead of somewhere in his upper torso. He was just grateful to be alive.

'Well, you'll have a hard job thanking him,' said PC Fringle. 'We nicked the cunt for importuning in a public place. The mayor said that it was a good opportunity to clean up all the scum in the town. We carted him and his mate and the junky and all the demonstrators off to a very safe place far beyond the town's boundaries and I don't think there's much chance we'll be seeing any of them again.' He laughed hard and added, 'And the little geezer with the gun, there was no point making him into a gallant cause for other anarchists to fight for. So he accidentally turned his gun upon himself right there and then.'

PC Nottingham was silent for a long time, too weak to tell his colleague to disappear and never come back. Eventually he looked up at him and said, 'So now the town is cleared of scum, what are you going to do all day?'

Fringle's features glummed up. 'Shit,' he said, 'I hadn't thought of that.' And then the two men sat in silence until the visiting hour was over.

Wendell's End

IT STARTED WITH a roll of the dice, my clumsy throw causing one of the numerically mottled wooden cubes to bounce off the dark green glass surface of the coffee table and straight into the jaws of my Aunt Amy's yelping lapdog, Wendell. Within a few minutes the hyperactive Chihuahua had, much to my uncle's delight, choked itself to death, and our game of Monopoly was over.

'Shit, ain't ever seen nothing like that before!' he exclaimed, slapping his armchair repeatedly as the dog writhed in its death throes, frothing at the lips and gradually weakening to the point where its desperate gasps petered out to one final, slightly reproachful whimper.

Needless to say my Aunt Amy wasn't there when this happened, she was off at her annual stay at the Pancake City Liposuction and Plastic Surgery Health Redemption Farm where, according to Uncle Bob, she was 'gettin' topped up and tucked in'. Wendell wasn't with her because dogs weren't allowed, so she rang every night to check that the pet was in the finest fighting health. In fact, it couldn't have been more than half an hour since Uncle Bob, raising his eyeballs to the ceiling for my benefit, had assured her that Wendell had eaten a full dinner and was in perfect fettle, 'jumpin' around like a coyote on cocaine'.

At sixteen, abroad for the first time, in awe of a man in charge of a company employing one hundred and fifty people and a house at least ten times bigger than the one I'd lived in all my life, I did not feel it my place to heroically spring across the room, dangle the dog upside down and dislodge the die that was the object of its expiration. Besides, I wasn't particularly grieved to finally see the undisciplined pooch come to rest – ever since I'd arrived five days earlier the creature had increased my deep sense of discomfort by plaguing me with its nagging nips, its high-pitched piping and its ceaseless attempts to bound into my lap and dribble on my t-shirt. On the other hand, although I had yet to meet my Aunt Amy, I already had the feeling we were heading for trouble.

My uncle's beam, as if sensing my worry cloud, evaporated and a stern expression crossed his normally jocose features. 'Boy, your aunt's gonna raise hell when she finds out we let Wendell croak on a goddam die,' he said. 'That yappin' mut was the kid she never had.' He rubbed his chin contemplatively and added, 'Guess we're gonna have to make it look like somethin' else.'

Aunt Amy's patently plastic smile stared out from a multitude of frames on sideboards and sills throughout the house, mostly portraits taken with Wendell being forcibly held at the neck so that its boggle-eyes would face towards the camera. I can't say I had been looking forward to meeting her in the flesh even before tonight's main event. She'd been pestering my mother to send over her 'Brit nephew' for the best part of a decade, and now that I'd finally been plonked on a plane to come and spend two valuable weeks of my school summer holiday in the outbacks of Alabama in 'our modest twenty-three-room mansion' (as she wrote to my mother) it turned out she was off having her face pinned back and her thighs sucked out.

She wasn't due back until the following evening so Uncle Bob took the next day off work ('You can do that when you're the company president,' he said proudly, winking at me), and so it was I found myself standing at the side of the deserted road which ran past the bottom of the house, holding Wendell's limp body at arm's length while my uncle drove towards me at around thirty miles an hour.

'Can't we just bury him and *say* he got run over?' I'd asked at breakfast time when he proposed this scheme. My uncle chuckled, like that would have been far too logical.

'Your aunt's gonna have to face a long period of mourning,' he explained. 'That don't just mean sittin' at the side of a grave and weepin' for five minutes and puttin' a bunch of flowers on there once a year. She's got to bathe and dress the body like it was her own flesh and blood. Last dog we had that died had a full autopsy and an hour-long funeral service in an open-topped coffin. Hyacinth. What a name for a hound. Buried down the bottom of the garden someplace. So unless we make it look like an accident she's gonna insist on a report and she'll find out how the dog choked and we'll be in *deep* trouble.' I didn't like the way he emphasised the word 'deep' in such dark tones, nor the fact that he used the collective 'we', so I reluctantly consented to help him restage Wendell's demise.

The first two times my uncle tried to hit Wendell I jerked the body back at the last minute and he missed. I knew the dog was dead but I still felt queasy at the thought of his bones getting crunched, not to mention the distinct possibility of getting spattered in blood. When I yanked him out of line a third time my uncle screeched to a halt, stuck his head out the car window and yelled impatiently: 'Hold the critter in place, can't you? What's the matter, boy, they breedin' softies over there these days? No goddam wonder we had to bale y'all out the war!'

Stung by this affront to my national pride I managed to hold Wendell in place on the fourth attempt. Although I flinched, the front bumper resonantly thudded against the Chihuahua's head and he flew out of my hand and several yards further up the road. Uncle Bob got out, looked down at the gashed cranium and pronounced the operation complete.

I joined him and together we stared at the corpse for a few moments more, half-expecting it to bound back to life and start snapping at our trouser legs. Then I said, brightly, trying to make up for my poor performance: 'Why don't we dump it somewhere then tell Aunt Amy that it ran away?' But Uncle Bob just looked at me like the know-nothing limey teenager I was. 'Listen, boy,' he drawled as he walked back to his car and started wiping off some traces of blood Wendell had bequeathed to his headlamp, 'if you want to spend the rest of your holiday searching every last inch of this county, day and night, for a dog you know you ain't gonna find, then you just go ahead and do that. But it's all right for you, in ten days you can get on a plane back to limey-land. *I'll* be out searchin' for the rest o' my livin' days.'

We wrapped Wendell in the black towel my uncle had brought from the bathroom closet and laid him down in one of the outhouses. It was still early, but Aunt Amy's imminent home-coming hung over us for the rest of the day and we could not settle down to anything. Uncle Bob paced around the house, starting tasks and then abandoning them immediately, while I flicked nervously through the 137 cable channels, unable to alight on a single programme for more than twenty seconds at a time. Although I had been bored mindless for the first few days of my holiday, I now pined for their simple routine – filling out the hours watching TV, taking a ten-minute swim to cool off in the debilitating heat and wandering around the huge house until my uncle came back from work. Then he cooked us a steak for dinner before we settled down to play board games to cover up the fact we had nothing much to say to each other. Now I would have given every cent of my untouched forty dollars pocket money to have that old lethargic monotony replace the terrible, stretched-out tension in which we were anticipating my aunt's arrival.

Eventually we just sat in silence as dusk descended, and although it was the sound we had been listening out for since late afternoon, we both jolted upright when we saw the beam of the headlights on the living-room wall and heard the sound of Aunt Amy's car droning up the driveway.

'Say nothing. Let me handle this,' my uncle ordered grimly, standing up and turning on the lights. As I blinked in the sudden brightness my Aunt Amy appeared at the doorway between the kitchen and the sitting room, put down her suitcase and placed her hands on her hips. Even though the excess had apparently been pumped out of her frame she was still a pretty imposing figure, but much more striking was the profound furrow of her brows and the glint of naked suspicion in her eyes.

'Where the hell is Wendell?' she demanded.

So, no eager enquiries about the younger sister who had gone off to study in England twenty-five years earlier and never come back, and not even a token introduction for the long-awaited 'Brit nephew'. Wendell's absence had usurped all formalities.

'Honey, you'd better sit down,' my uncle said mournfully. 'There's been a terrible accident.' As he began to tell her the story of Wendell's hit-and-run death I saw that he was trembling, and was genuinely afraid of my aunt's reaction. Yet at the end of the story there were none of the expected dramas and histrionics, just the stone-cold statement: 'I want to see him.'

They both went out to inspect the body. Within the next few minutes I half-expected to see Aunt Amy's tail-lights disappearing down the driveway, and that I would go out to find her bludgeoned spouse lying next to the avenged Chihuahua. But just as I was getting crazy thoughts about arming myself with a kitchen knife and going to investigate they came back, only it was Uncle Bob that appeared to be in most distress.

'I'm so sorry, my honey, I feel like it's all my fault,' he whined. 'How I wish, wish, wish there was something I could do to bring him back. I'll do anything to make it up to you, honey, I swear I will.'

Aunt Amy looked stunned, but there was also a resolve there which seemed to stop her from breaking down, maybe because she didn't want to create a spectacle in front of me. 'I'm going to bed, you two,' she said mechanically, the first acknowledgement that I was even there. Then, turning to my uncle, she said, 'I need to be alone, I'll sleep in one of the spare rooms.'

When she had gone Uncle Bob looked at me and shrugged: 'Shock. There'll be much worse to come.' And then he followed her upstairs.

The next morning I slept in and came downstairs to find the

house empty. Uncle Bob had presumably gone to work, but as I stood at the sink filling the coffee jug I noticed Aunt Amy involved in some kind of frantic activity down at the end of the vast garden. I went out to see what was happening, and as I approached her it became clear that she was digging a hole in the long grass and that there was also a small black bundle at her feet. I started to turn round, not wanting to interfere in her grief, but she looked up and saw me and called out: 'Hey, nephew, come here!' I dared not disobey the rock-hard imperative.

She was perspiring heavily and short of breath, but when I reached her she still had the verbal energy to demand: 'How did he kill her?' I began to stutteringly relay my uncle's hit-and-run tale but she quickly interrupted by screaming: 'Tell me the truth, kid!'

I did, immediately, right down to the finest detail.

'Son of a bitch,' she hissed. 'I always suspected he poisoned Hyacinth, but that vet who did the autopsy was his buddy from the Rotary Club so I never was sure I got the real story.' Then she handed me the shovel and said, 'Do me a favour, boy and finish the job up. Put him in nice and deep, another two feet or so.'

'It really was an accident, Aunt Amy,' I said in an unconvincing attempt to belatedly reverse having betrayed Uncle Bob. She stared at me with an expression of disapproval I recognised well from my mother. Then she boomed: 'You did wrong not to help that dying dog, but you did right telling me the truth, boy. If you're lucky God will see that as some kind of recompense.' Then she turned away, walked back up the garden into the house, and by the time I'd developed half a dozen blisters from burying Wendell in the bone-dry earth she had long since packed and left.

Me at Xmas, 2049

'THIS IS NO use to me,' I say, dropping the hand-held cardiograph into the pile of wrapping paper already discarded next to the leather chair's right arm.

Everybody stops what they're doing, which is opening presents (except for Lena, who is eating, of course) and stares at me expecting some elaboration. They wait, I wait. Then my second eldest, Katrin, says, a little impatiently but resigned to the fact that I will never pick the thing up again, 'But, Dad, you told us that was what you wanted.'

'Wrong model,' I mutter. 'Too complicated. How do you expect a man of my age to work out something like that? The one in the advert was easier. Didn't have all those stupid lights and buttons.'

'But the man in the shop said it was the simplest model they had, and it tells you . . .' but then she shrugs and gives up and goes back to showing her grandson (my daughter, a grand-mother!) how to attach two plastic bricks together. At ten months he's more interested in the promotional leaflet which came with the plastic bricks. Meanwhile everyone else returns to their activities, ripping off the wrappings and uttering bogus exclamations of joy, except for Lena, who grinds her gums over another hazelnut coated in chocolate, her hand already gouging the packet for the next one.

One of my grandsons, I forget which one, Jens, I think (half the time I can't remember them any more either), opens up a parcel and takes out a football shirt and lets out a loud whoop. He holds it up for everyone to see. A few people emit a semi-interested wow of acknowledgement to appease him before he rips off his t-shirt and dons the new garment. He looks around for more approval but already everyone has looked away again, gone back to their parcel-shredding, so I call him over.

'What team's that, son?' I ask.

Jens looks at me like I'm stupid. 'It's Europe, Granddad! There only *are* two teams, everyone knows that. And I'm not likely to wear Asia and Americas, am I?' He talks to me like I am a complete imbecile.

'In my day every town had its own team,' I start. 'We used to go and watch games live, every week . . .'

Jens has already walked away. First, he's not interested in anything but the World League (a league, with two teams!), and second, he's heard it all a million times before. I once overheard him snickering with two friends, imitating me talking about football in the twentieth century, and music, and food, and standards of common courtesy, and how we all used to have real cash notes in our wallets, and when he got to the line, 'It's all been corrupted!' he and his two friends laughed on cue and repeated the line themselves, so it was obviously not a one-off impersonation.

Out of the ridiculously towering heap of presents, the hand-held cardiograph is the only gift I have received so far. Every year my daughters ask me what I want, and every year I shrug my shoulders, and every year they complain how difficult it is for them to find me something. I tell them not to bother but that is not protocol and so they buy me crap. I have piles of unread historical and reference books that they will one day inherit. I tell them, 'I prefer novels,' and they tut condescendingly and tell me no one reads novels nowadays. There's too much knowledge to acquire and novels aren't knowledge.

Now it occurs to me, as the pile of presents begins to noticeably diminish, that this year they have taken me at my word and I feel immensely hurt. To annoy everybody I light up a cigarette.

'Dad!' says Viola, my eldest daughter. I am like a persistently annoying child. 'Where on earth did you get *that* from!' Suddenly everyone is groaning in exasperation at the old man, opening windows, turning on extractor fans, running for ashtrays. Even Lena momentarily employs one of her paws to loosen a latch within easy grabbing distance before diving back into her sweetie poke. Smoking is something else that people don't do any more, at least not in the west. A friend's son got me these on a trip to Mongolia. Cost me a week's pension for two packets, but it's worth it when you get a reaction like this.

'What about his heart?' says my son-in-law, Harris, as all bustle around him. He never asks me direct questions any more, not like the time he grovelled for my consent to marry Viola. He puts the query to Viola like I'm not there, like it's not his place to ask me a personal question, but he has to express his thoughts on the matter, just like he always has to express his opinion. On absolutely everything. And because he ekes out the tiny knowl-edge that he possesses over such a wide area everyone can see, even poor Viola, that he is an ignoramus.

Luckily everyone ignores the question, like they usually ignore Harris. An ashtray is produced, and I say, 'Wouldn't mind a brandy seeing as I'm not getting any presents.'

Fi, my littlest, puffs up my cushion behind my back and yells out, 'Someone get Granddad a brandy, and bring him a present for God's sake.' She's the only one that will come near me when I'm smoking, although she blows the smoke away from her face and puts a small plastic windmill on the table next to the ashtray. 'Smoke Guzzla!' it says on the base. She turns it on and the arms go round and round, but that's just for show, the real device is on the back, discreetly swallowing most of my pollution before the remainder goes through the windows and the extractor fans. Everyone escapes a horrific death through passive smoking and I am so distracted by the fuss that I forget to inhale properly and actually enjoy the thing.

Kids today are taught that smoking is more evil than Hitler. In fact they have no real clue who Hitler is. The first thing they'd probably ask about Hitler is, 'Did he smoke?' And if you say, 'No, and he was a vegetarian too,' they'd say, 'Oh, well he can't have been that bad then.' When I smoke, my grandson Charlie, who's fourteen, stands and stares at me like he can't believe what he's seeing. 'Smoking's a killer,' he says sternly. 'No,' I say. 'I'm eighty-four and I'm still alive.' One time he answered this with: 'Not for much longer according to my dad.' His dad is Harris, of course. Viola overheard this and belted him round the head with such force that she had to spend a month in prison as a result.

It was a funny incident. I was all for hushing it up. After all, the kid deserved it. But it was Viola turned herself in. She was so full of remorse that she rang up the police and they came round and took statements and took her away and the state provided a home-help for a month to look after me and the kids. They took photographs of Charlie's reddened cheek, which the next day already looked perfectly normal. No one would have known unless Charlie had filed a complaint. Which was always possible with him, he's a disgusting kid, far too much like his father. If it wasn't for the stupid Smoke Guzzla! I'd blow some clouds his way to take that reproachful glare off his face.

When Viola got out of prison she was so subservient to him that I couldn't watch and spent the next few weeks in my room. 'My mum hit me and had to go to prison,' Charlie'd tell anyone who came by, and she accepted her punishment like it was perfectly just and natural. Maybe it was the only way she could purge herself of her guilt.

If I still had the strength I'd have hit the little bastard too.

Harris has 'forgotten' to get any brandy, the cheap bastard. 'There'll be some wine at dinner,' he says. Dinner is still hours away, and I know that one bottle will be made to stretch between nine adults, most of whom nip at their glasses and barely touch the liquor anyway, they just do it because it's part of the lingering Christmas tradition, to have alcohol with the meal. I still remember last year, joking about finishing the bottle of brandy and saying to Harris, 'You've got a year to get me a new one!' He ignored me.

A present lands in my lap. 'To Granddad, From Lena, Jonathan and Harvey.' I'm not getting excited. Sure enough, even though Lena's present now comes from not only herself but her husband and my great-grandchild, it's the same thing that she gives me every year. Chocolates. 'I don't eat chocolates, Lena,' I say, holding them back out to her, and she has the effrontery to look surprised, and then delighted that she is getting the package back. It annoys me so much that I say, 'I told you that last year, and the year before. Don't you ever listen?' She stops before she gets to me, her hand in mid-air in anticipation of the chocolates to come, and looks at me and I see the tears well up in her eyes and then out the room she storms, wailing loudly, the poor blubbing, blubbery teenage mother, the token festive hysterics. It's come a little earlier than usual this year, although there's no guarantee there won't be more.

'Dad!' chorus Fi, Viola and Katrin in irritation, and the latter runs out after her daughter just like she's been doing for years. It's funny the way taboos change. Lena weighs a ton, yet no one is allowed to even allude to it, let alone suggest that she might cut back on her chocolates. Although ninety per cent of westerners are vegetarian (including everyone under the age of thirty), and healthy living is shoved down our throats from the day we are born, it's considered Corporeal Authoritarianism (to give it the official title) to comment on somebody's size, and it carries an even heavier prison penalty than slapping your child.

My great-grandchild Harvey suddenly hankers after the ample milk-pales of his newly absent mother and starts to wail. Around him there is a fierce argument over possession rights between Charlie and Ambrose, Katrin's youngest son. There have been so many presents opened that nobody knows who received what any more. Or from whom. Viola started a list, but got distracted gushing insincerely over the (in my opinion garish) jewellery which Harris gave her. Now there'll be all hell to pay when the thank you messages go out. And then in the middle of it all Harris' mother (who thank God couldn't make it this year because she had a spine transplant) appears on the Telescreen demanding to know of each child individually what they thought of the presents she had sent them.

'Has Charlie opened his parcel from me yet?' she says hectoringly. Viola doesn't know, you can tell, but she replies, 'No, I think it's still under the tree, Lettie.' Harris' mother admonishes her, 'Well, get him to open it. I want to see his face. It wasn't cheap, you know.' She looks up and sees me smoking a cigarette. 'He's smoking!' she yells. 'With all those children in the room!' Like she can smell it herself over the Telescreen. What an accursed invention. You can't turn the thing off once someone's been connected, so only when Lettie decides to hang up will we be rid of her for the day.

For years Lettie complained about nothing but her bad back. When the spine operation was pronounced a complete success we were all relieved that the phrase, 'Oooooh, me spine's killing me slowly' would never have to be endured again. Only now that it's not hurting, and despite the fact she still has to lie on her back for twenty-three hours a day until the thing has set properly, Lettie has developed other interests. One interest, to be precise. Her family. That was what she was like before her spine started to hurt, an interfering matriarch of the old order. Like her son, always having her say. The first time I ever met her she confided in me that Viola was not the sort of girl she had had in mind for Harris. I replied that she was not the sort of mother-in-law I'd had in mind for Viola. Ever since, unadulterated detestation reigned between us, and never for one second had I seen anything in this woman which didn't make me wish to attend her funeral at the earliest possible date.

'Merry Christmas, Lettie. How's your spine?' I shout across the room. She opens her mouth like she's about to say, 'It's killing me slowly,' but then she remembers it's not any more, so she ignores me and says to Harris, 'Viola can't find Charlie's present. You look for it, Harris. Make him open it. It's good stuff, not cheap rubbish, you know.'

Harris rummages around under the remaining presents, looking at all the labels, but can't find Lettie's present to Charlie. Lettie
is peering through the screen, desperate to be there in the room
giving orders. 'Charlie! Did you open a present from Grandma?'
Harris yells at his son. Charlie doesn't bother reading the labels, so
shrugs and says, 'Dunno. Might have.' Which causes Lettie to
implode at the other end, 'It wasn't cheap, child! Why don't you
show a bit more gratitude? I'm a sick pensioner, you know!' Two
nurses appear in the background and mercifully exhort Lettie to
calm down. One of the nurses turns to the screen and explains that
they're going to cut the connection and that Lettie will ring back
later. Lettie's wrinkled grimace is blanked.

Lena and Katrin come back into the room. Lena is still
snivelling. Her husband Jonathan, who as far as I can tell has
never spoken a word in his life so I cannot describe him, hands
her Harvey to be fed, and the box of chocolates they gave me for
Christmas to keep her occupied while she weans the porky infant.
'Dad, *please* apologise to Lena,' says Katrin.

'Sorry, Lena,' I grunt.

Fi smiles at me and says, 'Good, now you can have another
present.' And she gives me a small soft parcel which turns out to
be a tie. 'I haven't worn a tie for forty years,' I note, dropping it on
top of the hand-held cardiograph.

'Well now's a good time to start again,' she says cheerfully,
picking it up and trying to put it round my collar.

'Why the hell would I wear a tie?' I ask, pushing her away
slightly. 'I never go out. And nobody wears ties these days.'

She gives up and stands back with a loud sigh before lighting up
in her usual fashion: 'Well, that's exactly what you were complaining about the other day! No one looks smart any more, you
bellyached. No one even wears a nice tie, you moaned. Well here's
a nice bloody tie and I went a long way to find a nice bloody tie
because no one sells them any more, so just . . . just . . . oh for
Christ's sake, Dad, you're impossible!'

I'm used to this from Fi so it doesn't bother me. She may have a chronic temper but she has a good conscience too, so always comes back later to put her arms round my neck and apologise. Jens looks up from some supra-virtual pocket screen game and says grinning: 'For Christ's sake! For Christ's sake!' But no one bats an eyelid. All the other kids join in too – Charlie is particularly loud now that his voice has just broken – until there is a chorus of 'For Christ's sake! For Christ's sake!' and all the adults laugh except for me. I wonder what Lettie would have said if she'd still been on the Telescreen.

HARRIS FELT HE had to grovel for Viola's hand because I had lent him £100,000, interest free, to start his own small publishing house, and he'd completely messed it up. He went bankrupt within eighteen months. I didn't really mind, it wasn't like I couldn't afford it, and it had been a genuinely noble attempt at a worthy project. He wanted to publish completely unknown young writers, preferably with a leftist bent, and for that he had my full backing. It was just unfortunate that there weren't many such authors around, and those he published nobody wanted to read anyway. The press wouldn't review the books and The Book Shop wouldn't stock them. He advertised in literary magazines and a dishearteningly minimal number of mail orders trickled in. Some days he didn't even know whether the postman had been or not.

Harris vowed that he would pay me the money back, but twenty-five years later the debt still stands. He also vowed he would stand by Viola, which I suppose he has if you don't take into account the two years she was in a psychiatric hospital after he allowed his lover to move into the basement flat where I now live. It became quite common a decade or so ago for married men to have a live-in male lover. It was just that not all wives, like Viola, for example, were sophisticated enough to cope with the emotional consequences of this prevailing sexual trend. The bloke died of an intake of strychnine one sad night, but they could never prove who had spiked his drink. There were too many candidates, including the guy's six other paramours, although everyone (even

Lettie, who was 300 miles away at the time) came under suspicion. Shortly after that I moved in downstairs, ostensibly to support Viola when she came back from hospital, but really because I had been lonely ever since my own beautiful wife had died. And I've been a pain in Harris' side ever since the day they took his lover's body to the morgue and I stood at the front door grinning at the stretcher saying, 'He came with a stiffy and left as a stiff!'

I actually once liked Harris. He was an imaginative, quixotic but also easy-going young man. When he came to me with melodramatic tears bathing his cheeks and begged me to let him marry Viola I said they could do what they wanted, it was nothing to do with me. He looked a little put out at this, like he could have saved himself the humility. Perhaps it was the memory of this undignified performance, or perhaps it was to cover up his broken promise and his failure to reimburse the money, but soon after the wedding he stopped speaking to me. That way we never had to discuss paying the money back. I wanted to explain to him that it didn't matter, that he should forget about the money. I'd earned most of it by luck or inheritance (which is the same thing), so it wasn't like I'd sweated for it. But soon not speaking to each other became a habit and now it's too late to retract. He became a much more ruthless businessman, and, after his failed publishing venture, made money out of poor people in poor countries instead. It leaves a bad taste in the mouth when you remember his earlier ideals, but when his business went bankrupt so did his conscience, and he realised that he had to do something to nourish and clothe his responsibilities.

Harris says to Katrin's son Grikka, 'Here, give your granddad this present.' He can't even bring himself to hand me it, he uses his nephew as a go-between. Grikka, who is eleven, comes towards me awkwardly holding out a parcel which is obviously a book and says, 'Here, Granddad.' Grikka is the only grandchild I like. Poor sod was named after a Latvian pop star who was very popular for about six months in 2038. I got him under my control when I told him that vegetarians rarely live to be older than twenty. 'But

Mum's a vegetarian and she's forty-two,' he said defiantly. 'Yes!' I whispered: 'That's the secret! To eat meat while nobody's looking! They all do it!' Ever since then he's come to see me a couple of times a week and we sit in my room eating salamis and hams and leftover roast pork and chicken sandwiches with mayonnaise. All stuff I make at great expense in my little kitchenette because I refuse to touch their vegi-muck. 'It makes me pooh different,' he said at first, but that doesn't stop him turning up for our forbidden carnivorous feasts, even if he has to pay the price by looking at my old photo albums and listening to me rattle off ancient family tales from the golden age of battery chickens when there was a slaughterhouse in every town.

'To Dad, From Viola, Harris, Charlie and Jens.' Such a love-laden note to go with a gift. How did Viola think of something so original? Tears well up in my eyes as I read it back again and again, moved utterly speechless by the obvious deep thought and care which has been invested in the festive label prose.

'To Dad, From Viola, Harris, Charlie and Jens,' I read out loud. 'That's amazing, Viola, what a beautiful message. That's very touching. Did it come to you in the middle of the night or did you all sit round as a family and compose it as a collective effort of familial affection? I really don't need to open the present, the label itself is rewarding enough.'

'Jesus, he even complains about the label,' Harris says to Viola.

'Why don't you just open it, Dad?' says Viola indifferently. She is as used to my chuntering as we are all used to Fi's temper or Lena's chocolate guilt crises.

I open it without any measure of great anticipation, which is just as well because it is a compendium of vegetarian recipes. I close my eyes for a minute feeling suddenly very tired and old and apathetic. The book slips to the floor and lands cushioned by all the other uselessness.

'Dad?' says Viola.

'Ignore him,' says Harris, which is easy for him to say as he's been doing it himself for nearly twenty years.

Viola says, uncertainly, 'We just thought it was time you caught on to modern culinary thinking.' Interpreting my locked eyes as a call to justify the superfluous volume, she continues, 'You know, you should just try some of the recipes, I think you'll be surprised how good they taste!'

As if she has not told me these things five thousand times before. As if I have not already received well-intentioned meatless tomes for the past forty years. As if I am old and stupid and don't know what's best for me. I rally myself a little and open my eyes. I know that it's Christmas and that my eldest daughter is a neurosis waiting to happen on such days when she's bearing the responsibility for all the customary Yuletide events, but I cannot prevent myself from saying, 'Just why do people insist—'

But then I do actually stop myself. For although I have heard Viola's vegetarian persuasions five thousand times, I become aware that I have heard my own answer five thousand times as well. I am just as sick of listening to myself as I am of listening to explications of red bean virtuosity. Is this why so many old people end up saying nothing? That's it, I think, from now on I'm saying nothing. I've said it all before. They've heard it all before. Saying it again will not change a thing.

'Thank you for the book, Viola, Harris, Charlie and Jens,' I say instead, brightly. 'Maybe I *will* try some of these recipes.' It's a lie, but at least it's different. Viola actually looks pleased, though neither Jens nor Charlie are listening, and Harris grumbles lowly, 'Sarcy old get.'

I decide right now not to ever get bothered about Harris again. He's not worth it and I've got too little time left anyway. The heart's going. My doctor has offered me a plastic heart and reckons I could live another thirty years. He says I'd be in and out of hospital the same day. I've been considering it, but now I realise that I don't want to see another thirty Christmases like this one. I don't want to see Harris every day for another thirty years. I don't want to bore my grandchildren for three more decades with stories of football teams and slaughterhouses in every town. The average death age for a male in our country now is 102. It's a disgrace. Not because people should not necessarily live quite happily until 102, but because in other countries of the world, still laughably called developing nations, we have made no such endeavours to raise the average death age and it remains exactly what it was sixty years ago. The hand-held cardiograph was to give me some idea of how my ticker was performing and whether I should go ahead and get it replaced. Now I don't want it, extra buttons or not.

We sit down to dinner and Viola tries to put the bib on me that I've had for the last few months because I've started dribbling heavily when I eat. I tear it off like a baby and fling it to the floor. I get my token turkey leg while all around me munch on various combinations of beans and nuts and split yellow peas. I make sure I eat every last bit of fat, scoffing like a pig and dribbling copious juices down my shirt front. Harris lets out a distasteful tut. I drain my wine glass in one and reach over to Katrin, who is sitting opposite me, and grab her glass too. 'You never drink, Katrin, spare some for your old man,' I say, and before she or Fi or Viola can react I've slugged hers too. '*Dad*!' they all cry again. No one drinks like that any more, but I'm enjoying myself too much to care. 'Did I ever tell you how we *used* to celebrate Christmas?' I ask jovially, and again they all chorus: '*Yes!*' All the grandchildren too. Only Jonathan gazes glazedly into his grey nutloaf. 'But what about Harvey?' I ask, pointing at the ten-month-old infant sitting in his high chair sensibly throwing his pulses to the floor. 'He hasn't heard my stories yet!' And I turn to Harvey and address him directly and there is nothing the rest can do but listen, because they have nothing better to say themselves.

'Now when I was young we used to have twinkling lights and cribs with dolls and Jesus and Santa Claus and crates of beer and a great huge turkey which had been raised on a farm to make it as fat as possible . . .'

It's nearly time to go, but I'm not in a hurry. I'll make the most of it on my way out. I pause from my little story to Harvey and pick up the empty wine bottle, waving it at Harris. 'Hey, you tight git. Get us another bottle and we'll write it off the hundred grand you still owe me!' And I laugh and dribble and my great grandson Harvey laughs and dribbles too.

The Crossing

IN THE EUROPEAN city where I used to live it was forbidden by law for pedestrians to cross the street when the lights were against them. There were signs at each light warning those on foot that they were liable to prosecution and a heavy fine should they transgress, while illustrated notices just above depicted a mother and a child and the imperative: 'Always be a model example to children!' Nevertheless, being unaccustomed to such stringent restrictions on my movements, I would often ignore the red light opposite me and walk across the road if there was not a car within killing distance.

There was, however, one crossing in the city where it was impossible to contravene the regulations. Just beyond the main shopping precinct on the way to the post office was a particularly wide highway embracing a double, two-lane carriageway divided by tram lines. The citizens were not deemed capable of judging the distance safely themselves, so as well as the usual lights a small man in a green jacket was posted to monitor the crossing and penalise all whose limbs did not move in line with legality.

Except for very late at night the man was always there. Unless his holidays corresponded exactly to mine, I do not believe he ever took a vacation or a weekend off. But long hours did not blunt his vigilance, and each time you reached the crossing he would stare at you suspiciously, daring you to step out into criminality and force him to employ his tools of justice – a pen, a notebook and the world's shrillest and most frightening whistle.

Of course the latter came into operation when somebody –

usually some out-of-towner unaware of the man's reputation for carrying out his job to the last colon – walked against the light. You could see the look of worry on peoples' faces when this happened, anticipating the scene to come. Many covered their ears in readiness for the cranium-piercing pitch they knew was about to follow. And after the blast came the public official's anger and hysterics, the demanding of personal papers and the issue of a fine (if the criminal had humbly apologised) or a court summons (if he or she had in any way remonstrated or attempted to protest their innocence). People shouting desperately that they were late for job interviews or trying to catch the last post with an urgent letter were deliberately detained for a lengthy lecture or a rigorous interrogation.

If things were quiet the little man even worked beyond the bounds of his remit. One evening I was standing passively waiting for the green light, despite the fact there was only one car visible in the distance coming towards us. I was the only person waiting to cross and was subject as usual to the challenging glare from the green-coated watcher on the pavement opposite. Then, right at that second, we were distracted by the screeching of car brakes. The driver who had been approaching us had suddenly executed a U-turn, driving across the tram lines in the process. This was also against the law of the land and the guardian of the pedestrian beacons blew his whistle and sprinted comically down the street in the direction of the retreating automobile. Realising that his little legs were not powerful enough to compete with a BMW engine he gave up and contented himself with writing down the car's registration number, checking his watch for the exact hour of the misdemeanour.

I meanwhile had exploited the situation to cross the road against the lights. He turned around in time to see me reach the other side, blew his whistle, and once more gave chase, but I was young, thin and fit at that time and had no problem outrunning the hopelessly red-faced little figure waddling in my wake. He shouted after me several times, but as I had no number plate attached to my back (much to my pursuer's chagrin, no doubt) he was impotent to prevent me escaping the scene without penalty.

Then one day shortly after, the strangest thing happened. I was on my way to the post office with a letter to my parents in my pocket. I had been carrying the letter around for days, but every day I came home, hung up my coat, and realised with annoyance that I had forgotten to buy a stamp and post it. Today, though, my memory had functioned at the right moment and I was close to my goal, standing at the crossing opposite the post office where the little green man stood in his familiar place. The pedestrian light, however, was on red.

But this was the funny thing. When the pedestrian light was on red, so were the traffic lights for the cars. Absurdly, the cars and the walkers were static simultaneously, then when the lights both changed to green the cars and the trams charged forward and the only way to cross the road was to risk your life.

Gradually a crowd began to materialise on my side of the pavement. There were a few mutters of dissent at the way the lights were working, but people waited, assuming that there had been some kind of electronic malfunction and that soon the lights would again work correctly, or that a traffic policeman would appear to direct us until the fault was past. Yet it didn't matter how many people began to crowd the pavement, no one dared to cross the road when the lights were on red, despite the fact that the traffic was stationary and there was absolutely no danger. Because all could see the man in the green coat, poised with whistle and notebook.

I was at the front of the crowd, standing right on the kerb. I considered leading the way when the lights next changed. Only I didn't. I confess that I was too cowardly, afraid that the massed ranks behind me would fail to follow my example and that I would receive a fine that I could ill afford, or maybe even a court summons if he recognised me from the night I had run away from him. In fact, the man seemed to be staring right at me, willing me to have a go, and I became convinced that he had not forgotten my face and the fact that I had once professionally humiliated him.

More and more people were wanting to reach the other side of the road. Strangely, there was nobody on the other side, the little man in green stood solo, but held the upper hand by dint of his public status. One or two people said out loud, 'Come on, let's just go!' But you could tell by their tone that they only meant it half-heartedly, and still no one moved. Then, as patience began to erode, a chant evolved and everyone began to shout in unison, 'We want to cross! We want to cross!'

At this the little man blew his whistle decisively and from around the corner and out of the entrance to the post office swarmed several policemen wearing riot gear, holding huge plastic shields, clutching batons, eerily anonymous behind their beetle-head helmets. Of course they had pistols too, that was the norm for policemen in this country. They gathered on the kerb in a rigid formation, three lines thick, still and waiting. I swear the little man was still staring straight at me, only for the first time ever he wore a smile – an ugly, contemptuous grin.

A few people tried to turn round, judging that to cross the street today was just too risky. But such was the density of the crowd behind us now that they could no longer battle their way back through. In fact, so many people had now built up behind us – many of whom could not see the riot policemen and probably had no idea what was happening at the front – that the pressure finally became too great and the crowd surged forward on to the road.

The advance came at a moment when both lights were still on red. As we moved forward the little man blew his whistle dementedly and the police on the other side drew their guns and opened fire. To make matters worse, the traffic lights then turned to green and the waiting cars, as was their right by law, moved forward mercilessly, knocking over pedestrians and running over people who had already been killed or injured by bullets. The only vehicle to stop was the tram, whose driver sat there with his head in his hands, horrified at the massacre before him. The last thing I remember before I lost consciousness was the sight of the man in the green coat slamming his hand on the driver's door, shouting at him, 'Move! Move! The light's green, it's your right of way!'

I was lucky enough to escape both bullets and automobiles, and I came to my senses at the side of the road thanks to an old lady who was slapping me with one hand while holding an open tin of catfood beneath my nose with the other. There was no sign of the riot police, and all of the bodies had been moved from the road. The lights were working normally, and already people were walking back and forth to the post office as if nothing had happened, the blood on the tarmac drying quickly in the midday sun. I thanked the old lady and walked home dazed before going to sleep for the rest of the day.

The next day I remembered that I still had not posted the letter to my parents. I walked towards the post office and reached the pedestrian crossing. The little man in the green coat was on the other side, but he looked much happier than before. Now he was perched on a little stool, directly behind a mounted machine-gun, which he swung carelessly from left to right and back again.

Coming in from the Wilderness

WHEN MY BEST friend Manny lost his temper he used to expectorate at Jehovah's Witnesses. They'd call round at his front door and he'd invite them in, all friendly and offering cups of tea, genuinely convinced that through rational argument he could make them see that there was no God. No human mind was unsusceptible to the power of logic, he used to argue. But after several hours of futile debate, during which the messengers had failed to yield a single gospel of their beliefs, he began to shout at them for being so stupid. When they anxiously rose to leave he realised that he had lost and became so furious that the power of speech began to fail him, and at this point he would shower them in spittle and they would run for the door and trot off down the street, dropping copies of *The Watchtower* in their wake which Manny, still in pursuit, would pick up and shred until he had worked off his anger.

It wasn't just Jehovah's Witnesses he picked fights with. I'd seen him steeped in verbal battle with Seventh Day Adventists, Scientologists, New Catholics, old Catholics, Moonies, Zionists and (usually white) Muslims. Any religious pundit handing out a leaflet or holding a speech in public Manny deemed fair game for conversion to the ranks of the unsaved. Even the harmless old duffers from the Salvation Army who sold *The War Cry* in the pub on Friday evenings were taken to one side and challenged with cogent philosophical monologues on the errors of belief, especially if Manny had downed a few beers. Once he ended up in a bloody fist-fight with an enraged Mormon from Salt Lake City, though usually it finished up with Manny resorting to cheap and blasphemous insults while the offended party stormed off promising long-term damnation to my friend's godless soul.

Even his own mother's funeral had provided a platform for Manny to preach his doctrine of arch-rationalism. He had interrupted the vicar shortly after the start of his sermon and stood up in front of the mourners pointing out that his mother had not been a churchgoer, therefore it was hypocritical to mark her passing with texts and prayers which in no way reflected her life or her beliefs. Which was fair enough. But this did not prompt Manny to deliver a speech which actually did reflect her life and beliefs. Admittedly this would have been difficult given that his mother's main hobby in life had been to go shopping. 'I could hardly stand there and say, "My Mum was one of England's best shoppers," ' he said later in mitigation. Instead he castigated all those present for even entering a church in the first place, started to deliver a speech outlining evil deeds throughout history perpetrated in the name of Christianity, and then broke down in tears before being led out of the church by his sister. His mother's death had hit him harder than he cared to admit.

This was all entertaining enough the first few times you witnessed it, but as he got older he became more obsessive, stopping outside churches and ranting at the walls and the stained-glass windows, deliberately entering Christian bookshops and berating the staff and the customers, picking up tomes from the shelf and picking holes in the first phrase he read out. He was a brilliant orator, and from a non-believer's standpoint his arguments were faultless, but he insisted that it was a waste of time speaking to people who already agreed with you. Instead he chose audiences who were either incapable of understanding him or who refused to understand him, and he failed to win a single atheist convert. When someone pointed this out (it may have been me) things got worse and he focused his entire life on achieving the transformation of a single believer into a disbeliever. He gave up his job, bought a sturdy milk crate and spent all day at various junctures of the city calling on people to burn down the churches. A few Christians complained at first, but gradually people got used to him and he became a minor local celebrity. Of course some said he was mad, but he wasn't as mad as they thought – beneath the shouting you could still make out the common sense if you waited around long enough to listen. Nevertheless, maintaining a friendship with him proved impossible and our contact was reduced to a mutual wave when I hurried past him on his soapbox.

In the meantime I had landed a job as features editor at the local newspaper after several years of working my way up from a junior sub. I often thought about doing a profile of Manny and his place in the city because I wanted to convey to people that he was not just an eccentric, but that he really was an articulate and intelligent man who had something to say. But the paper's editor deemed there was no point as everyone in the city knew him already and besides, he added, 'The guy's nuts, and if we profiled everyone in this city who was nuts we'd have to add sixteen pages to the issue every night.'

One day this same editor threw down two tickets on to my desk and said, 'Dora Wallis the spiritualist is coming to town tonight. Take some girl along and show her a good time then write it up for the early edition if you can.' I rang my girlfriend who, despite being a keen student of her star sign, was reluctant to come along.

'Come on,' I reasoned. 'Spiritualism, astrology, it's all part of the same con game.'

'I'm not going to argue about this now while I'm at work,' she said frostily. 'Why don't you take that mad friend of yours along instead? He'd be sure to cause a stir.'

'He's not my friend,' I replied, but she'd already hung up, and when I thought about it for a while it didn't seem such a bad idea. There was little point in writing a piece about the sad, deluded dupes who usually turned up at these things and stood there nodding credulously as Dora told them she was talking to their dead cat. Manny, however, was bound to stand up with some pertinent quotes and disrupt proceedings enough to make a good story before he got thrown out by security.

I felt a little awkward about approaching Manny as we had not talked for some years. He was standing outside the town hall, one of his regular spots, being generally ignored while explaining the parallel between the rise of literacy and the official policy of atheism in post-revolutionary Russia. Some boys were throwing empty Coke cans at him, which he beat away with one fist while shaking the other in the air. I kicked one of the boys hard in the backside and told them to beat it. 'Fuck you, mister,' he hissed, but they ran off anyway and I walked up to Manny.

'Hey, that was my audience you just chased away,' said Manny sardonically. Or maybe he was being serious. He was certainly looking at me sternly enough. 'Do I know you?' he said.

'Manny, it's me, Robin,' I said. 'Remember?' I didn't really know how best to describe our time together in order to nudge his memory. I could hardly say, 'Hey, remember me, we were drinking partners before you went nuts.' He really didn't look too well from close up and I began to wonder whether this was going to be such a good idea, after all. He was unshaven and his eyes were red and his formerly attractive dark curls looked flat and oily. But I was just thinking how, as a conscientious journalist, I owed it to myself and the paper to persevere, when Manny replied, 'Of course I remember you. I was attempting to be funny, thinking of all the times you've scuttled past me over the last few years like I had leprosy. You're always in a hurry these days, Robin, you must have an important job. Or maybe you started going to church. Or maybe you didn't want to show that mousy little brown-haired girlfriend that you once associated with the town nutter. So what is it now? She gave you the axe and you want to go for a few drinks to talk about it? Or is it just a favour of some kind?'

I blushed profoundly. I decided to hurry on with my task and handed him one of the tickets. 'I thought you might be interested in coming along to this,' I said. 'It's Dora Wallis, the famous spiritualist.' The name had an immediate effect on Manny and he ceased to reproach me, staring at the ticket and emitting a kind of angry, low-breathing snort. 'The worst kind of charlatan,' he muttered, almost to himself. 'The basest, most bogus exploitation of the weak and the vulnerable.' (I made a mental note of the phrases, they would sound good in the piece). Then he looked up cheerfully and said, 'Sure, I'll come, though first you can buy me something to eat.'

It was already early evening, so Manny picked up his milk crate and we adjourned to a nearby pub, where Manny ate three plates of stew and downed four pints of Murphy's, which was OK because it would all be going on expenses. He was on good form, and was much better briefed on Dora Wallis than I was. He didn't seem to mind when I started taking notes while, in between mouthfuls of stew, he ran through a list of British spiritualists since Victorian times whom, he said, had been practising with impunity the same old tricks on the same kind of defenceless people. I trusted that he would stand up later and repeat it all in front of Dora Wallis and her auditorium.

Yet when we took our seats in the theatre Manny became strangely subdued. I thought it was maybe because he wasn't used to the closed-in, formal atmosphere. After all, it must have been years since anyone had taken him out anywhere. Or perhaps the beer had made him a little soporific. I had been afraid that he would start holding forth the moment we sat down, looking around him and seeing so many people, none of whom would be able to escape his sermonising by ducking into Woolworth's. But he sat down and stared at the seat ahead of him, oblivious to the throng of mainly old, grey-haired women who were bustling around us attempting to work out their seat numbers.

When the aged spectators had settled down a man came on stage and asked everyone to be quiet. Dora required total silence during her performances, he said, otherwise she could not tune her psychic ear to 'the people beyond'. Then Dora herself came on stage and sat at one of two chairs. She leaned back pensively for a while and eventually asked, 'Is there an Alice with us tonight?'

Of course there was an Alice with us and she doddered up to the stage and heard Dora tell her all about what her husband Derek had been up to since his death a few months back. Alice was delighted and moved and asked him some questions ('Have you got an allotment up there, love?' 'Yes, he says he has,' Dora assured her). Then came Lizzie, whose husband Roger had also recently passed away (I wondered if Dora Wallis was a close student of our obituaries column), and who said he was still playing golf and was missing Lizzie's baked apples.

'I never made him baked apples,' said Lizzie, uncertainly. 'Oh, I'm sorry, love, I misheard. He says he's met his mother and *she's* making him baked apples,' said Dora smoothly. 'Oh, that's lovely,' said Lizzie and beamed out at the audience and then returned happy to her seat.

All the while I was waiting for a move from Manny. I couldn't believe that he wasn't reacting to this blatant hocus pocus and every moment I expected him to rise and renounce both Dora and her gullible patrons. I glanced at him surreptitiously. He seemed to be frozen backwards into his chair, totally tensed, almost like someone was holding a gun to his head. Then I heard Dora say, 'Do we have a Manfred here tonight?'

Manny jolted and tensed further still. Dora said, 'I can feel it very strongly, very, very strongly. Don't be afraid, Manfred.' There was a few seconds' silence. 'There is a voice calling urgently for Manfred. It's a voice of love, Manfred, it wants to talk to you. Don't be afraid, love, come on up.'

He stood up and there was a little gasp around us. Many people recognised him, of course, from his street speeches. But instead of bellowing his customary polemics and exposing Dora Wallis as a fraud I heard him whisper, 'It's my mum!' and he pushed past me into the aisle of the theatre, his eyes transfixed on Dora, and he walked on to the stage and sat down.

Indeed it was his mum, apparently. Manny got to ask her all kinds of things, including whether she had forgiven him for wrecking the funeral (she had, of course), whether she had really loved him and his sister (again, an affirmative) and what the shopping facilities were like 'beyond' ('Excellent. She says they have everything there,' Dora cooed). I waited and waited for Manny to snap out of it, to stand up and reveal that he had been playing along the whole time, to pontificate angrily against the perils of superstition. But in the end he just started to weep uncontrollably and got down on his knees and put his head in Dora's lap while she comforted him by stroking his hair. Around me the old biddies started crying too at this miraculous turn-around until it seemed I was the only person there not dabbing my eyes with a paper tissue.

I got up and left. It wasn't what I had hoped for, but at least I'd got a story.

Breakfast With a Dullard

IT WAS EARLY on Saturday morning and Reinaldo was enjoying a peaceful breakfast in a deserted café when an acquaintance he knew only as George entered in a state of agitation. Reinaldo could tell George was going to sound off about something. He'd already seen George approaching the café in a determined stride and with a heavily furrowed expression on his face, and Reinaldo had been hoping that George's plan was to walk right past the café and straight back out of his Saturday morning. But George, with a grubby yellow courier's bag slung over his shoulder and wearing a windcheater zipped up to the neck, had banged through the café door, causing its glass pane to judder loudly, allowing both the noise of traffic and the cold early spring air to intrude upon Reinaldo's hitherto relaxed rumination of the morning paper. Clearly George was about to let off steam and Reinaldo was going to have to listen.

'I am deeply annoyed, Reinaldo,' George announced without preliminaries. He dumped his bag on to a chair and came and sat right down at Reinaldo's table. He jolted the table leg with his right knee, causing much of Reinaldo's coffee to splosh on to its saucer, but he did not apologise because he didn't even appear to notice. 'I wasted my entire Friday night *waiting*.' He turned to the counter and ordered a bacon sandwich and a coffee, which, much to Reinaldo's relief, George was going to take away. He could weather the imminent rant until George's sandwich had been dispatched, order another coffee, then relax back down to the pace at which he had previously been mentally sauntering through the morning.

Not only was Reinaldo glad that George would not be staying, he also took some satisfaction from the fact that he barely knew who George was or where he'd first met him. This meant that if George really did have some kind of serious problem, he wouldn't feel in any way obligated to help. Hopefully he'd just have to hear him out.

'I had this taxi ordered to come round and pick up a grand's worth of gear,' George elaborated. 'He was meant to come round at six o'clock yesterday evening because the stuff had to be over in Newham by half-past nine, otherwise no deal, see? By half-past six the taxi hadn't come, but I thought, no sweat, still plenty of time. So I rings the geezer up and he says, sure, the taxi's on its way right now. But still it don't turn up, right, so I ring up again at half-past seven, and I'm telling you, Reinaldo, I'm starting to get seriously annoyed by this time. But the bloke says sorry about the delay, we had a problem at our end but it's definitely on its way now, so I said OK, but at quarter-past eight it still ain't there, so I phone again and he says the same thing, and finally I phone him at nine and he tells me sorry, but the taxi ain't coming at all. I tell you, Reinaldo, I am very annoyed, I am a very annoyed person who lost one thousand pounds worth of business because at that time on a Friday night you ain't gonna get anyone to take that gear down to Newham in half an hour, no way.'

Reinaldo shrugged. He was idly wondering why, if it had been so important, hadn't George phoned up another taxi company to take the 'gear' earlier, but he didn't care enough to ask. He vaguely speculated too on what sort of 'gear' and 'stuff' had been involved, but was again insufficiently curious to post an enquiry. He wished that George's bacon sandwich and coffee would hurry up and come.

But it didn't and George continued: 'I said to this bloke, 'I'm gonna put you out of business for this.' I'm telling you, Reinaldo, I am. I'm gonna phone their number again and again so that it's constantly engaged and no one can get through to order a cab. I tell you what I'm gonna do, Reinaldo, I'm gonna *employ* someone to sit by a phone every Friday and Saturday night for a month, right at their busiest times, and get him to phone their numbers again and again and again. What's that gonna cost me, eh? I'll just have to pay someone forty quid a night and the costs of the phone bill, so maybe no more than £500. I tell you that's gotta be worth it to put these people out of business.'

'I don't think you ought to bother doing that,' Reinaldo ventured, just because he still hadn't actually uttered a single word to George since he'd stormed in. And, of course, it was a patently ludicrous idea, which George would doubtless forget once he'd cooled down. How was he going to phrase the job advert? 'Wanted, one person to phone cab company every Friday and Saturday night for a month. Must have good telephone dialling skills, high boredom threshold and ability to cope when the calls are traced and the police come round to ask what exactly is going on.'

'I tell you, Reinaldo, it's worth that £500 to put that firm out of business and I'm gonna do it,' George reiterated. He was half-way through repeating the entire episode, when his coffee and bacon sandwich were placed on the counter. George stood up, picked up the two items and paid, then left the café without even saying goodbye. He left so suddenly that Reinaldo was afraid George would be coming back again, but gradually silence reasserted itself and he began to relax once more.

Reinaldo ordered another coffee and reflected on what he was going to with his day. He had nothing planned, and the thought of several empty hours stretching out before him absolutely void of tasks, demands or responsibility made him feel immensely content for a few seconds. He already knew he wouldn't do anything worthwhile with his day. He would watch television all afternoon. He would end up in the pub that evening, have a few casual pints and a cigar, chat to a few regulars, watch the football, go home to bed. Since his wife had walked out on him more than a year earlier the novelty of this vacuous existence had still not worn off.

Though Reinaldo recognised that he was a laid-back character, even he had been mildly surprised at how unruffled he was when his wife told him that she was leaving him for another man. This reaction had provoked a sort of delighted fury in his wife, who screamed at him that this just vindicated her decision, he obviously didn't give a fuck about her or what she did or said or thought. That had been the second marriage to end in such a way, and Reinaldo decided that he didn't want any more wives. He didn't really need them, they just seemed to stir the equilibrium. The fact that, after seven years of marriage, he hadn't missed her for a single second since the moment she'd left the house told him that maybe he was more suited to living alone.

'We've wasted seven years,' she had wept. He thought wasted was a funny word. He would probably have lived them in exactly the same way whether he had been together with her or not. They had lived seven years together and now they were living apart, it was as simple as that, Reinaldo thought.

He was deriving a gloomy satisfaction from this uncustomary delve into the recesses of his mind, so was slightly annoyed when music started to come out of the two speakers above the café's counter. It wasn't loud, and had there been some more people in the café it would have been barely audible, but as he had found the silence after George's departure so pleasing, Reinaldo asked the girl behind the counter if she could please turn it off. After all, he was the only customer in the café, so he didn't see why he shouldn't have his way.

The feisty Londoner who had brought him breakfast objected violently to his request. 'Listen,' she said. 'I have to stand around 'ere for two hours every bleedin' Saturday morning before anyone turns up. To tell you the truth I'd prefer to 'ave some work to do than just standin' 'ere starin' into space, it makes the time go quicker. Blimey, it's not like it's loud or anythin', I mean, I could 'ave put on some bleedin' techno or hip-hop or somethin', then you'd 'ave 'ad somethin' to complain about.'

Reinaldo said nothing. The girl stared at him and said,

unpleasantly, 'Why don't you go down the road and sit in that poncy place where they serve croissants an' that? You don't get any bleedin' music in there.'

She disappeared into the kitchen. Christ, Reinaldo thought, why is everyone so uptight this morning?

Herr Junker and His Philippine Bride

APART FROM HIS foul, kitchen-bin breath, his stale body odour and his abusive racist remarks there wasn't really much to say about Herr Junker. I saw him at first as someone to be avoided in my life if at all possible. The problem was that he lived across the landing from me, and somehow I never seemed to be able to leave my flat without bumping into him. This would not have been too critical had we not both been heading for the same cramped lift that would take us down twelve floors to the exit of our building. In we'd get, down we'd go, and a journey which would normally last around forty-five seconds seemed to stretch out like an evening in a crowded right-wing bar.

'Bloody Albanians, eh?' Junker would say to me, following a regular pattern by which he cursed a particular category of foreigner, asked for my concurrence, but didn't bother waiting for an answer. He often gave no reason for his oaths. Sometimes it was just that there seemed to be a lot of them about, like the Albanians. Sometimes it was because he was convinced there were soon going to be a lot of them about, like the Chinese. Occasionally he'd read in his paper that a foreigner from a certain country had been convicted of theft, pimping or drug-dealing, and this provided a cue to damn the criminal's entire nation of origin. He seemed either not to notice or to care that I too was a foreigner, though he never expressed an opinion on my own country, and I never felt inclined to ask.

I was at least able to avoid Herr Junker's eye when we were in the lift together, even if his acrid smell and his fulminating rhetoric made it impossible to forget that I was very much in his immediate presence. He was approximately just over four feet tall and walked with his head permanently leaning to one side, so his gaze was always fixed somewhere to the left of my belly button. He was well over sixty years of age and did not seem to have a job. So often did we seem to meet on our way across the landing that I began to harbour a suspicion that he had nothing better to do than look through the spy-hole in his front door and wait for me to emerge. Sometimes I waited until it was dark before going out, so that I could sneak across the hallway without turning on the light and steal down the stairwell rather than calling the lift. But then in the evenings he even started appearing at the bottom of the lift when I was returning from work.

Herr Junker would greet me as if we were old friends who'd arranged to meet for a drink for the first time in five years. Herr Johnstone, he would say, how are you doing? How was your day? Just going for the lift? I'm just on the way up myself. And then as we waited he would begin to tell me a tale of how he'd been out walking down the street that day and he'd seen this black guy, as black as a raven, and the black guy had had the cheek to come up and tell him he was an African student who didn't have any money, and could he, Herr Junker, give him a few coins so he could get some food. By the time we reached the twelfth floor Herr Junker had long since explained what an outrageous assault this had been on his personal liberty and was outlining a scheme to throw such people out the country and stop them ever entering again. But, he lamented, there just weren't the politicians around these days who had the backbone to come out and say that was what needed to be done.

It was strange that Herr Junker started to fashion himself as my big friend, because my part in the conversation rarely consisted of more than the odd monosyllabic response. I often looked at his pitiful, stooped body and decided that there was nothing to be gained from entering a debate with him on race relations in modern Germany. One time, after he had denounced the Turkish people as nothing better than a race of kebab-munching scoundrels, the damned lot of them, I said to him, 'You obviously feel pretty strongly about this.'

At this Herr Junker turned red, clenched his fists and said with a vehemence a few octaves above the tone of his normal ravings, 'Yes, I feel *fucking* strongly about this, *fucking* strongly.'

One night I came home to find him waiting for the lift as usual, and he greeted me in his customary cordial manner as I looked in my mail-box. But instead of choosing a race of the day upon which to heap his hatred, Junker said, 'So, anything interesting in your mail today?' I was immediately suspicious of his tone, which was so insinuating as to suggest that he knew exactly what was in my mail box, that he had already raked its contents and found something deeply personal. So I ignored his question.

But when we entered the lift I realised why he had brought up the topic of mail. It seemed that Herr Junker himself had that day received in his post-box something very interesting. It was so interesting that it was preventing him from launching into his customary xenophobic tirade, but he wasn't going to tell me what it was. Instead he ventured that I might like to come round for a beer later and check it out. Herr Junker had a feeling that it might just interest me as well. He grinned, he leered, and he half-cackled as he said this, accompanied by a fat knowing wink. I said I might come by later if I had time.

UNDER NORMAL CIRCUMSTANCES nothing would have induced me to voluntarily pay a social call on Herr Junker. But the truth is that I was not living under normal circumstances. I had been working in a strange and unfriendly city for seven months in a job I hated, and I had made absolutely no friends. The only times I had been out I had sat on my own in bars and been ignored by all those around me. Staying in had usually turned out to be the less miserable option. For what it was worth, Herr Junker's invitation to pop round and view his mail was the first attempt that anyone in this city had made to reach out. That he was the least desirable human being among the city's 600,000 population, who perhaps just wanted to show me the latest translation of *Mein Kampf*, could not disguise the fact that he was also the first to say to me, 'Come on round for a beer.'

Still, it was hardly worth getting in the bath for and pulling on some decent clothes. While eating my dinner I decided not to go, then changed my mind about seventeen times. I was curious that for the first time today Herr Junker had refrained completely from blaming non-Germans for the state of the universe. Yet what was I going round there for? What could Junker possibly have received in the post that would be of any interest to me? What could it be that was not in some way sinister or offensive? Whether I was looking to answer these questions or looking to fill a few hours of my empty life I don't know, but after dinner I ended up knocking on Junker's door clutching a few bottles of beer I'd bought at the local kiosk.

In fact I never got the chance to knock on his door because he had obviously been keeping an eye out for me through his spy-hole. He opened his door before I was half way across the landing. Reaching out to grab my bag of beers, he said, almost triumphantly, 'I knew you'd come,' and ushered me into his spartan flat.

There were no pictures or photographs hanging on the wall of his flat. It was big enough to house bookshelves, but Herr Junker had no need to invest in such furniture when he did not apparently possess a single book. He had a television, two yellow sofas and a standing lamp in his living room. There was a pile of old newspapers in the corner. There was an overwhelming smell of his sweat, which seemed to tie in with the tatty yellow of the walls and the furniture. The glasses he brought out for the beers and placed on the scratched wooden coffee table were covered in fingerprints. I said I preferred to drink out of the bottle.

Junker at least did not hang around with the social small-talk before getting to the point of my visit. After he'd taken the bottle-tops off the beers he disappeared into his bedroom and came back

---

clutching a magazine. He was red in the face and looked very happy, like he'd just a heard a plane-load of asylum-seekers had been flown back to face torture and imprisonment in some distant police state. For a moment I was convinced he was going to wave some obscene publication in my face and ask me to take part in some onanistic ritual. And certainly the pages contained numerous women, but thankfully they were all clothed. Furthermore, they were all oriental. And they were all for sale to eager buyers like Junker.

'Just look at these,' he cried jubilantly, as if the whole catalogue was about to come rushing through the door and declare their eternal devotion to him. 'This is it! This is all we have to do! Get one of these each! We'll be made for life!'

I disliked my inclusion in whatever seedy project it was he had in mind, so asked him what on earth he thought he was talking about.

'It's a catalogue!' he exclaimed stupidly. He was so excited he barely seemed able to articulate himself. After a few more seconds he stuttered, 'It's full of women. You just have to go over there and meet them, fling some cash their family's way and bring them back here. Hey, for a couple of single men like ourselves it's perfect! We can go over there together, find ourselves a nice wife each, then bring them back here!'

I avoided Herr Junker's eye by pretending to study the catalogue with intent. The women were all from the Philippines. Beneath each picture was a number and a name, and a short statement from each of the women. 'I am very pretty and obedient,' said one. 'I promise that I will bring you love and happiness. I like animals and housework.' I turned the pages, but there was little variation, just row upon row of young women promising to be beautiful and dutiful. At the back were the conditions. You paid your own fare over there and 10,000 marks to be split between the agency and the girl's family if a successful match was made after the introduction. If it didn't work out, presumably if your bride turned out to be insufficiently pliant, then you only lost your airfare.

'I'm afraid I don't have this kind of money, Herr Junker,' I said. 'Besides, I don't need a bride, I'm engaged to a girl back in England.' Both of these lies were enough to momentarily disappoint Herr Junker. I wondered whether, in fact, he had enough money to make the trip. I also wondered whether there was any girl in the world who would want to come and live in this miserable flat with this nasty little fascist, at any price. I wondered if he was just incredibly lonely, and the catalogue was merely a ruse to tempt me to his pad to keep him company for a few hours.

'That's very disappointing, Herr Johnstone,' Junker said. He looked wistfully at the Philippine women. 'Such young, lovely faces. What a pity they don't have girls like that in Germany any more. Their heads are filled with rubbish here, these young women. But these girls are what women should be.' Declining to say exactly what women 'should be', Junker merely turned round and surveyed his flat. 'Need someone to clean this place up. It's a mess. It's about time I got married.'

We fell silent for a few moments and drank our beers. I was drinking quickly because already I wanted desperately to leave, though I could only have been there for around five minutes.

'I was hoping you would come with me, Herr Johnstone,' Junker said. 'It would have been nicer for the wives, you know, they could have kept each other company here in the flat while we were out drinking in the evenings.'

I remained silent. The spectacle he was painting was too absurd to absorb any observation I might have wanted to make. Eventually I asked him when he planned to go. He said he didn't know yet, that was what he had wanted to discuss with me, he had felt sure I would want to be included in his plans because he had never seen any women leaving my flat, and, quite frankly, the news that I was engaged already had come as a bit of a surprise to him. The woman had not visited me, had she, and I didn't seem to leave the flat long enough to make any trips across to Britain. Perhaps he could see a photograph of the lucky betrothed.

I was incensed both at this egregious intrusion upon my privacy and by the fact that Herr Junker had seen so easily through my lies. Yet something prevented me from storming out of his flat and telling him where to go. For much as I was beginning to seriously loathe him, I sensed that it was better to be on good terms with him rather than have him as an enemy. So I compounded the lie with some far-fetched story that my girlfriend was on a year's study leave in the US, and that we planned to marry when she returned in a few months' time.

'Well,' Junker said odiously. 'If that really is the case, in your place I'd be making the most of my last days of freedom and getting some extra shagging done!' At this Junker punched me heartily on the arm and laughed and laughed. I returned a weak smile, hating myself for my cowardice in not telling him what I really thought of him. But then he stopped quite abruptly, snatched up the magazine and said crossly, 'It's just your loss, just your loss,' and took the marital prospect parade back to his bedroom.

When he returned Junker sat on the yellow sofa opposite me and began whistling idly. I was approaching the end of my beer. Then he said: 'You're probably looking at this flat and wondering how come this guy has 10,000 marks to spend. Well that's just it! I haven't wasted a penny for forty years! It's easy when you get in the habit of it. Look at you, you brought round six bottles of beer tonight. If you leave now you'll be too polite to ask to take them back, I know you English. So I come out with a profit of four bottles!' And at this he laughed hysterically too. I stood up and said wanly, 'Well, you're right there, Herr Junker, because I do have to go now.' I walked towards the door and said I was sure we'd bump into each other again soon. He just sat there laughing, a sound which followed me across the landing until I had shut the door of my flat behind me.

I went out on to my balcony to lean on the ledge and meditate over the view of the city for a few minutes. I looked downwards to see a young, attractive but earnest-looking man standing on the balcony directly below, talking into a cordless phone. I'd never seen anyone below me, so I nodded in a casual greeting when he looked up and caught my eye. Instead of returning the greeting he stared at me harshly and marched inside, failing to reappear for the remainder of the time I stood there.

MY ENCOUNTERS WITH Herr Junker in the lift became no less excruciating. But his conversation had changed from outlining his final solution to the planet's racial problem to a graphic description of just how much sexual action he was going to be getting when he returned from the Philippines. It seemed he had booked his ticket, selected a suitably subservient-looking morsel from his catalogue, and was now intent on rubbing my nose in the fact that I would be sitting all alone in my flat while he rocked the building to its very foundations through long nights of carnal activity.

As if this wasn't bad enough, the neighbour from the balcony below began to get in at the eleventh floor. My hopes that he would prove a new target for Junker's lecturing proved immediately groundless when he turned to me the morning after I had greeted him from above and said sternly, 'You're disturbing my privacy when you lean over your balcony and look down on mine. You are in an unfair position in that you can see down on to my balcony and everything I do there. I'd appreciate it if you kept your eyes away from there in the future.'

I was too surprised to reply, but Herr Junker did the honours anyway: 'You know you're quite right to say that. I too have noticed that Herr Johnstone here has a habit of keeping an eye on his neighbours. You know, barely a day passes that he does not get into the lift with me. Sometimes I think he looks through his spy-hole and waits for me to come out and catch me in the lift just so he can keep up with what I've been doing lately!'

The young man said nothing in response to this. He didn't seem that interested in Herr Junker. He was busy glaring at me. Meanwhile I was staring at Junker in amazement, waiting for him to clarify his comments, or look up and laugh and admit he had only been joking around. But Junker kept his crooked gaze as usual to the left of my torso and began to ask the neighbour if the volume of music from my flat had been disturbing him at all because he, Herr Junker, had just about had enough and was going to complain to the concierge if something wasn't done soon.

'But my stereo's barely audible,' I protested weakly, just as the lift hit the ground floor.

'Well,' said Herr Junker, 'you should fucking well hear it from my flat!' And he stormed out of the lift and downstairs to the washing-machines in the basement.

This marked the start of a new phase in our relationship. After rejecting his offer to accompany him on his great Philippine trip, I was now more an object of scorn and pity in contrast to the big friend I'd previously been. No longer did he greet me with deference at the bottom of the lift in the evenings when I came home from work, rather he launched into a résumé of how many days it was until he flew to Manila, how long it would be before he clinched the deal, how much cash he was going to have to part with, and most commonly, how much sexual intercourse he was going to be indulging in compared with luckless me.

'Of course, you have your girlfriend returning from the United States to look forward to,' he would say sardonically. 'How long now is it until she comes back?' Without waiting for a response he began to answer his own question.

'Now let me see. You've been here for eight months now. Assuming that she went to the US the same time you came to Germany – and as she never came over to visit you here from England that must be the case – then at the very most you still have four months to wait.' He would stop and look into the distance, as if making more mental calculations. 'Well, all things being equal, I should be up to my ears in Philippine fanny juice in around four weeks' time, so I don't have to wait quite as long as you, Herr Johnstone!' I winced at his crudity, willing the lift higher, faster. But there was always time for him to point at any mail I was clutching in my hand from the post-box and say, 'I note no long-distance letters again today.' And then he'd chuckle.

Then a couple of days before he was due to depart for Manila, Herr Junker began to turn on the charm again. He once more uttered the words 'Herr Johnstone' without the parturient sarcasm of the previous few weeks. All references to my sex life, or rather lack of it, were dropped in favour of sympathetic enquiries as to my state of health, whether I had been working hard, how I was adapting to life in Germany. I had given up trying to figure out his behaviour patterns and was merely grateful that he had ceased to furnish me with previews of his imminent fornications. Then, on the eve of his departure, I discovered the reason for his latest transformation.

'Herr Johnstone, I couldn't help but notice that you are running an automobile,' he said as the lift began its climb. 'If you're not doing anything tomorrow evening, could I possibly ask you to run me to the airport for my flight to Manila? It's just that for a man of my age to carry a heavy suitcase on to the underground, and what with all the crime that goes on there these days . . . I just thought you could do me the favour.'

There was an almost pathetic tone in his voice, and even though I absolutely did not want to give Junker a lift to the airport I still consented straightaway. I preferred his ingratiating persona to his vicious one, even if I neither trusted nor liked him either way, and I was happy to keep his nastiness at a distance despite the fact it meant sitting in a car with him for three-quarters of an hour.

Yet I could already sense as soon as we were under way the next evening that my favour was being taken for granted, and Junker once more began to mock me for my sexual abstinence and my lack of social life. 'Though your girlfriend must surely be coming over to visit you soon, Herr Johnstone,' he pointed out after making his customary comparison of a man of his age (just about to have large amounts of sex), and a young man in his prime like myself (seemingly happy to stay in every night and do without).

He paused for a while, before saying. 'You know, it wouldn't surprise me if your girlfriend was coming very soon, right after my departure for the Philippines. Then she will leave again right before my return, and you'll be able to tell me all about it, but I won't be able to check up on whether she was actually here or not!' Then he roared with laughter, while I sat red-faced concentrating on the road in front of me, mad inside that somehow he had guessed exactly what I had been planning to tell him.

As we drove toward the airport we passed through a number of districts containing high-rise blocks, areas known to house a large number of foreign settlers. Junker for a while forgot about me and returned to some of his older themes. As he railed against refugees from the former Yugoslavia I am ashamed to admit I was actually relieved he had found another focus for his warped mind. I felt not even the slightest inclination to disagree when he pronounced that Germany had taken in all of these people who were merely fleeing a hell of their own making. And how did these second-rate citizens repay their civilised and benevolent hosts, Herr Junker wanted to know? They peddled drugs, they robbed old ladies, they cheated the social security system, that's how!

It occurred to me that it was dark and that if I wanted to I could drive him out to the woods south of the city and finish him off in no time for the sake of mankind. But I weighed this up against the possibility that he would somehow get lost in the Manila crowds and never find his way out again, standing ignored and unseen fulminating against the foreigners swarming around him in a language they were too 'uncivilised' to understand. This image kept me amused and kept me from murder until we finally reached the airport. Then we stopped in front of the terminal and I dashed out of my car, grabbed a trolley, put Junker's case on it, then almost yanked him out of the passenger seat before placing him in front of the luggage wagon and wishing him a pleasant trip. He was too surprised by my speed to react, and within seconds I was back in my car and pulling away. About fifty yards further on I fell in behind the queue of taxis waiting to leave the airport area. I looked in my mirror and there was Junker still looking after me, almost dwarfed by his trolley and suitcase. He looked already helpless and alone, just liked I had wanted him to be in Manila. I was astonished to find tears in my eyes and pity welling up inside me. I turned the radio up loud and drove away far too quickly when the lights turned to green.

When I returned home I went straight to bed and didn't wake up again until three the following afternoon. As it was Saturday, and this was Germany, it meant that the shops were already closed and that I had no chance of buying any groceries for the weekend. But I didn't care, I felt suddenly so rejuvenated. The thought of walking out on to the landing and knowing that Junker could not possibly be peeping at me through his spy-hole, that he could not possibly join me in the lift and either abuse me, interrogate me or flatter me, made me want to leave my apartment immediately and go up and down the twelve storeys twenty times over. Even the thought that I might be joined by the miserable complainer from the floor below did little to dampen my spirits. He could stand there and reproach me for whistling too loudly on my balcony for all I cared, but at least Junker would not be there to substantiate his accusations by adding, 'You know you're absolutely right, I can even hear Herr Johnstone whistling on his balcony from my flat!'

Then I did a bizarre thing. I went to the airport again. Well, not so bizarre, really, it was the only place where there was a supermarket still open. But in spite of what I told myself, I wasn't really going there to buy groceries. I came straight out of the basement car park, past the supermarket and up the stairs to the Lufthansa information desk. I was the son-in-law of a Herr Junker, I explained, and my wife was concerned that her father, whom she had not been able to accompany to the airport personally, had made it safely on to his flight to Manila yesterday. It sounded daft, but could she just check, 100 per cent for me? The information assistant begrudgingly brought up the relevant data and confirmed that Junker had indeed made his flight. But I couldn't actually see the screen, so I asked her if she would be kind enough to swing it round so I could just see for myself. She rolled her eyeballs in clear contempt for my mistrust and almost whacked the monitor round on its pedestal so that I could read Junker's name – after Jochimsen and before Krupp – and finally feel that I would be free of his presence for two whole weeks.

I went to the supermarket and bought food, but mainly beers. I went home and started to drink them while watching television, all the time feeling the kind of elation you would normally associate with the highest degree of success in life, like finding your dream job, your dream girl, becoming the father of healthy twins. It was a sad reflection on my quality of life that I was floating on high just because my mad neighbour had taken off on holiday for two weeks. Yet here I was, even laughing at the jokes on Saturday night German television.

After I'd downed several beers I took out a bottle of whisky and began to drink stupendously. I woke up in the middle of the night on my sofa, the television blaring out a multi-explosion action movie, my head splitting me in two. I turned off the television and went to drink some water. I could still hear the action movie, and wondered if it had embedded itself into my sub-conscious while I had been asleep. I went to my bedroom, but the noise just seemed to get louder, explosions and shouting and sirens fusing to form a single unwatchable, unlistenable, trash culture experience. But it wasn't in my head, it was coming from my direct neighbour's, the one whose flat separated mine from Junker's.

I had bumped into Junker around three times daily over the previous six months, but I had only ever seen Bernd Hecker once, shortly after I had moved in. We introduced ourselves awkwardly on the landing one evening, made small-talk for two minutes. He never made any noise, he never made any complaints, he never got into the lift with me. He looked undistinguished, around thirty-five, his thin and curly blond hair receding, and even after two minutes of conversation I instinctively knew that we would be keeping our contact to a minimum. It was as much as he could do to squeeze out the customary inquiries as to my job and my land of origin, and as soon as the first silence offered an opportunity to close the conversation he seized it and scurried into his flat so quickly that he had bolted his door shut even before I'd got my house key out of my pocket.

But tonight his television was uncommonly loud. I presumed that he too had stayed home drinking and had fallen asleep in front of junk TV. Maybe his life was so sad that he was celebrating Junker's holiday as well, for God knows what reason. I decided to chance on my own still drunken state and see if I could fall asleep anyway, but I tossed and turned and my head felt like its blood channels had hit rush hour. Eventually I got up and knocked on the wall. A few minutes later I knocked on the wall again. When that had no effect I knocked on the wall and shouted, a process I repeated three times until I pulled on my dressing-gown and went into the hallway.

I rang Bernd's doorbell repeatedly, but there was no response. Then I hammered with my fist until there was blood on my knuckles from the hard wood. I had to, because I realised that I had locked myself out, and that when Bernd finally awoke I would have to persuade him to let me use his couch for the night or phone for an all-night locksmith, which in Germany would be the equivalent of taking a large gold bar and throwing it into the Rhine.

My whisky-fogged brain dredged up the possibility of Bernd lying there either dead or comatose. I turned round, resigned to having to wake some other doubtless disgruntled neighbour and explain everything. Then the door opened. There was no bleary-eyed Bernd staring uncomprehendingly, though, in fact, I could see him in the background tied to a chair, naked except for a large piece of black tape across his mouth. In the foreground stood a woman clothed in shiny black leather, brandishing a cat of nine tails and holding a mask in her right hand.

'As you may have guessed, Bernd can't come to the door right now. Can I help you at all?' she said.

'Er, perhaps you could turn the television down a little?' I said.

'The television has been turned up very loud at Bernd's request,' she said, 'in order that his neighbours cannot hear him scream while I whip him. However, now that I have placed some tape over his mouth I guess it could be adjusted.'

'Thank you,' I said. I began to turn round, then I remembered that I had locked myself out. 'There's another problem. I left my house key inside and now I've shut the door on myself. Could I come in and use Bernd's phone?'

Then the woman began to cry, and her sarcastic and authoritarian tone dissolved into a whimper. 'Oh please,' she said. 'Please do come in and have a cup of coffee with me.'

THE WOMAN IN leather gear was not unattractive, probably mid-twenties, long black hair, a body you could sleep with. But the second she transformed herself from spiteful sadist to wearied whore her entire demeanour took on the burden of multifarious facial lines which seemed to age her by at least ten years. There was also a bruise around one eye, semi-disguised by make-up, and a number of raw red marks on her neck. We sat in silence in Bernd's kitchen, drinking coffee as she sobbed steadily. I could see Bernd's foot, but no longer the horrified expression which had greeted me as I walked into his flat, and which had then steadfastly stared at the floor in order to avoid my eye for the time it took me to make it into the kitchen.

I had no idea what to say, so I absorbed the contents of Bernd's kitchen and what I could see of his living room. He lived in classic bachelor fashion, sleek but style-shy black furniture adorning the space in front of a huge television screen with stereo speakers and pseudo-erotic posters of half-shaded, naked women on the walls. The kitchen was clean but sterile, all the latest gadgetry looking apparently unused bar the microwave standing adjacent to a mini-tower of instant meal packages which were prostituting a range of culinary cultures. Meticulously pinned to a notice-board were the phone and electricity bills. If Bernd had ever received any postcards, he certainly wasn't making a show of them.

My headache remained in place, the coffee serving only to speed up slightly the thudding inside my skull. I wanted only to lie down in my bed, a tantalising few meters away behind the living-room wall, and fall into a deep sleep like the one I had enjoyed the night before on the back of Junker's transfer to another continent. But I could hardly turn in for the night by blithely sloping across to Bernd's sofa while he sat there naked and tied to a chair and his companion for the night shed mascara-stained tears over her tightly-zipped black attire.

But now she had stopped crying and was staring vacantly at the kitchen table. Finally I said, 'Perhaps I could phone a locksmith or something to come and get my door open.' A couple of minutes later she replied, 'You won't get anyone in this country at this time on a Sunday morning to come and open your door. I once locked myself out of my flat at four o'clock on a Sunday morning. I'd been working all night, I was exhausted. I tried to phone some places from a call-box, but all I got were answering machines. It was cold, so I did a few more customers in their cars until it got light around eight o' clock. Then I phoned my pimp Marco up. He came round and opened my door with an axe and then hit me for waking him up too early on a Sunday morning.'

I was too discouraged to offer another suggestion and we continued to sit without a sound. She went over to the coffee machine and made more. Then she said, 'Bernd rescued me from my pimp three nights ago. He was beating me up in the concourse of the railway station, accusing me of not handing over enough money. It was right in the rush-hour, dozens of people walking past, ignoring my screams. Because I'm just a fucking tart. Then Bernd came by and took Marco by the arm and told him to stop. I've never seen anyone talk like that to Marco. I thought he would kill Bernd, but he looked confused, then worried, and he let go of me, and Bernd asked me if I wanted to come with him, and I thought why the hell not.

'We went to my flat and picked up some stuff and got a taxi over here. Bernd said I could stay here until I picked myself up, sorted myself out. I told him, of course I'm a drug addict, I'll probably sell your TV and stereo the first chance I get and disappear. So he gave me enough money to be going on with and asked me if I really thought I could do rehab, and he would arrange it for me, and I kept asking him why he wanted to help some junkie whore and he said people like me deserved another chance, and that every night on his way home from work he walked past junkie whores and wondered what life-paths had brought them there, and he wanted to do something, at least once in his life, to counter the impotence he felt every time he looked in our worn, desperate faces.

'Yes, Bernd waxed bloody poetics about his concern for junkie whores. Bernd took me in to give me another chance and to salve his own conscience about the suffering he saw every night before he came back to make himself comfy in front of his wank posters. But it only took Bernd a couple of days before he started getting other ideas. Maybe he was already concerned that he wasn't getting much of a payback for the money he was giving me for drugs to stop me stealing his precious TV. And while he was so gallantly sleeping on the sofa and letting me sprawl unmolested in the pimp-free luxury of silk sheets on his big double-bed, Bernd was letting his fantasies take control. His very own whore in his own flat, lying there unused, what a waste. So my chance to start again and get myself sorted out lasted until this afternoon, when Bernd came back from shopping with this shiny leather gear and this age-old device for cutting red weals across his body while he sits there helpless, fastened to his yuppie leather chair, getting thrashed by the junkie whore he wanted to rescue and rehabilitate to become a normal member of society, just as fucking normal as him, I'm sure.'

She paused for breath, her mounting anger subsiding to make way for the collapse of her features, allowing once more the predominance of the lines in her face. There were no tears left.

'Perhaps I should just stay here and be his live-in prostitute,' she sighed. 'It's relatively safe compared with out there. He's not such a bad guy.'

I went over to the coffee machine and picked up the jug to pour some more. The prostitute went into the living room and took the tape off Bernd's mouth. He had fallen asleep, and had pissed himself too. 'Oh, Bernd,' I heard her saying. He woke up as she untied him and I moved out of view, embarrassed in case my eye met his. I heard him groan a little. A few minutes later she reappeared in the kitchen to get some cloths to clear up the mess. 'I put him to bed,' she said.

When I began to pour some more coffee in her mug she said, 'Not for me, I need something a bit stronger.' She assembled the whole drug-melting apparatus and then injected the result into her arm. I was expecting her to lean her head back and sigh in relief or something, but it didn't appear to have any affect on her at all. She continued to stare at the table much as she had done before, taking little notice of me. After finishing my coffee I got up and said I would try knocking up the janitor as it was starting to get light and see if he could break into my flat for me. She just looked up and said, almost cheerfully, as if she had just had a really bright idea, 'Next time I tie Bernd up I'll gag him. Then when he shouts there'll be no need to turn up his television because he'll be stifled.'

I thanked her and left.

AS IT TURNED out, I would have preferred the noise of the television. For Bernd, oblivious to any embarrassment he might have felt over the revelation of his secret lodger and her profession, now had a nightly session with whips and leather which lasted long after my normal bedtime. His junkie whore too had come to terms with the fact that rehab and a new life as Bernd's compliant housewife were perhaps not really meant for her, and had decided that getting enough money to score drugs and live in a warm, safe flat in return for giving Bernd his nightly thrashing was not such a bad thing. But from my side of the wall the sound of a swishing whip cracking against human flesh was as loud and clear as the Saturday night action movie had been on Bernd's first night of self-punishment, while his pain was evidently so intense that even a tightly-bound gag failed to muffle the tortured yells he emitted every time he took a new blow to his body.

A few nights into the first week of Junker's absence I noticed one evening that there was a conspicuous silence next door. I wondered if the novelty was already wearing off, or whether Bernd had been hospitalised with severe bruising at the very least. Then there was a knock at the door, an unusual event. I opened up and there was the junkie whore, but she was looking at me as though she really didn't recognise me. The woman who had poured out her heart to me was as business-like as a door-stepping salesman, offering me a hand job for forty marks, oral sex for sixty and full sex with condom for a hundred. I asked her if she didn't know who I was and she suddenly peered worriedly at my face, stepping back a couple of paces, as if searching her memory for some abusive police official, or perhaps a distant debt-seeking dealer or a jilted pimp. 'Saturday night, remember I locked myself out,' I said.

She looked blank, and then said, 'Oh yeah, I didn't recognise you without your dressing-gown.'

We stood in silence for a few moments before she said, 'Er, well . . . are you interested or not?'

I replied that I wasn't, and asked her where Bernd was this evening.

'He's got a business meeting,' she said. I waited a while longer, then she blurted, 'Well, you needn't bother complaining to the janitor about all this because I'm fucking him too,' and turned and walked quickly away, over to Junker's apartment. I watched her as she knocked. She sensed this and turned round and said, 'What are you fucking staring at?'

'Herr Junker is away at the moment,' I said helpfully. 'And I believe he is newly married too.'

She turned away and flounced down the stairs. 'Doesn't mean he won't want to fuck a whore,' she muttered.

Junker's absence had become a matter of indifference to me in the face of Bernd's noisy activities with his new lodger, and I even became curious to see how he would react to his additional neighbour upon his return. After all, if I could hear everything from the sound of the junkie whore's zip sealing her frame inside her tight leather outfit to the final roar of Bernd's orgasm, then there was no reason why Junker, who lived on the other side of Bernd, should not hear the same, and I couldn't imagine him keeping quiet about it. What sort of an impression would it make upon a virginal Catholic girl from the Philippines, promised a life of sophistication in the great civilised West, if the first thing she heard from her new neighbours was the sound of sado-masochism reverberating around the block? Well, maybe her illusions about life in the West were already shattered the moment she set her eyes upon Junker and his sweaty fist full of deutschmarks.

As the end of the second week approached, I finally had to confess to myself that I was looking forward to Junker's return. In fact, I was thinking about little else. However much I had dreaded his standing next to me in the lift and his demeaning enquiries as to the contents of my post-box, there was no escaping the fact that, apart from my co-workers who seemed incapable of discussing life in terms of anything which existed beyond the office walls, he represented my sole interaction with the world around me. It was unpleasant interaction, certainly, but at least it wasn't television.

I became so restless on the Sunday at the end of the second week that I couldn't even concentrate on the latter medium. I mindlessly surfed the fifty-seven channels from across Europe which came to me through a plug in the wall. I watched a soap opera in Spanish, failing to understand a word but still easily grasping the plot. I watched a Swiss handball match to the very end, even though the side from Aarau was way too far in the lead for the side from Luzern to have any chance of catching them. I watched seven different versions of the news, even though apparently nothing had happened in the world over the previous twenty-four hours. German dancers slapped their lederhosen and grinned stupidly to the sounds of the accordion, on MTV rappers furrowed their brows and threatened to blow some motherfucka's head off, the two-man bobsleigh team from Austria lifted a gold medal, surrounded by happy day-glo ski-suits popping champagne. Looks like the French are in for some milder weather, while the Italians have just launched a breakfast cereal called 'Crappio!'

I called the Lufthansa desk at the airport and asked if there was a flight on its way from Manila. Indeed one was due to arrive, via Dubai, in around six hours' time. The woman could not or did not want to tell me whether a Herr Junker was on board or not, but I needed to get out of the flat anyway and decided to take a drive, although it was already getting dark. Perhaps I would end up at the airport around the time Junker's flight got in.

Junker was genuinely delighted to see me for a number of reasons. First of all I was proof to his new bride that he had at least one friend. Second, he didn't have to splurge out on a taxi-fare. And third, his new bride apparently spoke no German but fluent English, therefore he urgently required my services as a translator.

'Herr Johnstone! What a wonderful surprise!' For one horrific moment I thought he was actually going to embrace me. But he ended up just holding his arms in the air as if hailing a sighting of the Virgin Mary, his grin so wide that it barely made it through the double doors of the arrivals area. Next to Junker was a moving trolley piled high with brand new suitcases, the one I had left him struggling with at the drop-off point two weeks earlier right at the bottom. Behind the pile was his purchase, the newly-wed girl dressed almost totally in white who tried to greet me with an air hostess smile but didn't quite manage to pull it off. For a second I thought it maybe was an air hostess just helping Junker with his luggage, she even had the red necktie, but then he introduced her to me as Sarah. I didn't know whether to kiss her on the cheeks or shake her hand, but she solved the problem by curtseying on one knee and holding out her hand. I kissed it and Junker roared with laughter. 'It's because you're British,' he said excitedly. 'She probably thinks you're a member of the royal family.' I looked to see how she would react to this put-down, but she didn't appear to have registered the remark, and it was here that Junker explained the language difficulty and how I was figuring in his future plans to help her out.

'You see, you can give her German lessons!' Junker exclaimed, as if he were doing me a wonderful favour with this suggestion. I didn't respond, pretending to preoccupy myself with the luggage and looking for our passage to the underground car park. 'None of these girls bother to learn German because they all hope some rich Yank or Brit is going to pick them up, and they figure that a lot of Germans speak English anyway.' I thought of suggesting that Junker learn English instead, but faced with the prospect of teaching his teenage bride or him I decided to keep quiet on the off-chance he would take me up on it. And although I was peeved that he was thrusting this idea at me without giving me much opportunity to refuse, I was already thinking that it might be rather pleasant to have her company in the evening. For I don't think that I have mentioned yet that as well as being young and Philippine, Sarah was attractive enough for most people to look at her standing next to Junker and immediately understand the situation.

We walked down to the car park as Junker ranted against the German customs men who had made Sarah unpack every last suitcase, who had quizzed him extensively about the marriage certificate, and who had finally waved him through by commenting, 'German women not good enough for you, eh?' Junker had been enraged, but so relieved at finally getting through the gate that he had said nothing in case they'd decided to call him back. 'And the only reason they stopped us is because Sarah is foreign!' he exclaimed.

Sarah remained more or less expressionless the whole time that Junker talked. She didn't seem that fascinated by her new surroundings. I wondered if I was supposed to translate anything for her, and I thought about asking her some questions, but couldn't think of anything that wouldn't sound either condescending or intrusive. 'What does it feel like to be married to an ugly little vindictive snake like Junker?' was the query foremost in my head, but I thought I could save that one for later when we knew each other better.

I began to unload the suitcases into my car boot. Junker lamented the amount of money he had had to spend on one shopping trip in central Manila the day after the wedding. 'She just kept pointing and pointing and saying, "Much dearer in Germany," like it was some kind of threat, so I felt I had to buy there or I would have ended up paying out more. Of course their eyes lit up over there when they saw good hard Western currency. Anything could be done in a matter of minutes the moment you uttered the words "dollar and deutschmarks". Ha!' he triumphed, 'religious convictions and bureaucratic conventions simply swept to one side because of these little bits of paper!'

We couldn't fit all the cases in the boot, so Sarah had to cram into the back seat with the remainder of her luggage. As she sought to make space for herself her buttocks faced out towards us through the passenger seat door, and the moment I had been dreading arrived. Junker turned towards me with a lewd grin and was just about to speak when I interrupted him and said, 'No, Herr Junker, I won't tolerate that kind of talk in the presence of ladies, no matter how much of it they can understand.' He looked totally astonished, but apart from some muttered remark about the prudish Brits he surprisingly kept his mouth shut and climbed into the car.

As we drove along and Junker told of his heroics in bargaining down Sarah's family to the lowest possible price (at least he wasn't trying to pretend it was love) I periodically looked in the mirror to try to catch a glimpse of Sarah. Each time I saw her staring mindlessly into the dark embankments aside the motorway, then at the blocks of flats where the Yugoslavs lived, then at the city centre itself.

When we crossed the river I slowed down and said to her in English, 'You can get a nice overview of the city from here.'

But before I could gauge her reaction Junker frantically said, 'What's that you're saying to her? What did you ask her? You two can't speak in English without telling me what you're saying, do you hear? Now come on, what did you say to her?'

I protested that it had been an innocent observation on the landscape and the fine view of the city offered by the vantage point of the bridge. Junker looked at me, his face taut and suspicious, then hissed under his breath, 'You lay a single fucking finger on my wife and I'll break your neck. From now on you only speak to her in English when I ask you to, right?'

I didn't answer. We completed the journey in silence, and when we got back Junker disappeared into the lift with his wife and his suitcases without even wishing me goodnight.

THE VERY NEXT night, however, Junker came back round turning on the charm. He hoped he wasn't intruding on my time, but he and Sarah were having one or two communications problems due to her difficulties with the German language, and the need for her to learn a few basic phrases was becoming quite pressing. Would it be OK if we started the lessons tonight? As usual I had nothing better to do, so I said that would be fine. Did I have any beers in, he asked? Yes, I did, he would not need to bring round any of his own. And within two minutes he was back round with Sarah – who once again curtsied and offered me her hand without looking me in the eye – and a clutch of spanking new German grammar books and a dictionary.

I had never taught anyone anything in my life, and was not really sure where to start. Junker was sitting in the armchair expectantly, already supping my beer. I sat on one of my dining-table chairs, while Sarah was perched on the front of my sofa clutching her knees and staring at the floor as though she only intended to stay for a very short time. Junker burped noisily, expressed himself satisfied with the brew, and then announced,

'We have to teach her what she has to say when she goes shopping. It's no use my having a wife if she can't go shopping for me. We went this morning and I told her the right words but she was absolutely hopeless, and by this afternoon she'd already forgotten everything I taught her. So I have to tell you the phrases in German and you have to teach her them by telling her what the English translation is so that she understands what she's learning.'

I looked at Sarah, who was now intently looking at the grammar book. I explained to her what we were going to do in English. She asked me if she could have a pen and paper to write the sentences down, and Junker's eyes immediately lit up in anger in case this was the start of some secret communication. But before he could say anything I jumped up and said to him, 'She just wants something to write it all down with,' and walked over to my desk to get her a pen. Junker relaxed a little and began to tell me the phrases he wanted me to teach her. Over the next two hours Sarah learned how to ask for a kilo of diced pork while her husband sat drinking beer and listening intently to the English in case he spotted a nuance in our speech that suggested we might be broaching any other subject besides a trip to the market.

I explained to Junker that we should set up some mini-dialogues, as if I was the shopkeeper and Sarah the customer, so that she might be able to understand any questions she might get asked, or know approximately how much she should pay. Junker begrudgingly agreed. But even when holding a direct conversation with me, Sarah steadfastly refused to look anywhere except straight down at the coffee table in front of her. It wasn't like she was nervous or afraid. Her features betrayed more a steely endurance, a determination to get through this desperately dull domestic language lesson.

'Could you please tell me where I find the beer?' Sarah said to me.

'It is on the far side of the shop, near to the bread counter,' I replied.

'How much it costs?' Sarah asked indifferently.

'Twenty-five marks for twenty bottles, including deposit,' I said.

'Thank you,' Sarah said.

Junker looked delighted that she had half-mastered this particular conversation, and promised to test her on it once again in the morning. Now, however, it was time for bed, and that was something he looked forward to more and more these days, he said, looking at me with an ugly and boastful expression. He stood up and gestured to Sarah as if he were hurriedly coaxing a dog out of the door. From next door at this moment came the sound of slapping leather followed by Bernd's customary stifled groan of pleasure, or whatever it was he was experiencing. At first Junker was too preoccupied with a lack of speed in Sarah's response to his gestures to notice anything, but the second crack and cry were far louder than the norm and Junker immediately became alert.

'What the fuck was that?' he exclaimed.

'Oh, I forgot to tell you, Herr Junker. While you were away finding a wife, Herr Hecker next door took in a destitute whore to offer her shelter. All she has to do in return is tie him up and whip him every night. It can get quite noisy. I've met the girl and she's quite nice, though she confessed to me that she is a drug addict. There's not much we can do about it, though. She also told me that if we complain to the janitor it would be a waste of time because he receives sexual favours from her in return for saying nothing to the landlord about her presence in the building.'

Junker's temperature quickly soared to the extent that he could barely emit his profanities. He then marched out of my flat and immediately began to pound on Bernd's door, shouting, 'This is an outrage. Stop it at once! I am a respectable married man, I cannot live next door to low-life druggies with Aids and syphilis! Open up now, NOW! NOW! NOW!'

He began kicking the door so hard I feared he was going to break through it. For a man of his stature he seemed to possess remarkable reserves of energy. Somehow the image came into my head of a small, stinking yellow ferret sinking its teeth into my calf muscle. I shuddered, then I turned round to look at Sarah, but she was still sitting on the sofa vacantly gazing at her German grammar books, as if nothing was happening. This would be a very brief chance to talk to her, I realised, but with Junker in his current state of apoplexy possibly a bad move. In any case, I couldn't think of anything to say to her, and the junkie whore, in full leather regalia, had finally answered the door. She had not even bothered to take her mask off.

'What the fuck is your problem, you sawn-off little piece of shite?' she sneered at Junker, towering above him with her whip in one hand, looking as though she could easily swat him off her doorstep. But Junker too was in the mood for getting straight to the point. 'My problem,' he shouted, 'is that you are a fucking whore, you are the dregs of this fucked-up nation, you spread disease and immorality. I am a family man, trying to live here quietly with my wife. We want to bring up children in this flat, but I don't see how we can do that when syphilitic drug-snorters are hanging around here spreading their filthy, perverted ways!'

'Listen here,' she retorted, pointing her whip down at Junker's nose. 'Any children you have, and I pray to fuck you don't, are going to spend too much time worrying about whether they turn out to be half-developed runts like their pathetic father to care about the moral tone of the fucking neighbourhood. Now kindly stop making so much noise or I might be tempted to call the police!' She slammed the door and there was silence. Junker stood there, seemingly crushed by her audacity. Then he turned round and brushed straight past me, yanked Sarah violently off the sofa and told her to get to fucking bed now or he might not be responsible for the consequences. On his way back past me he stopped and said: 'Goodnight, Herr Johnstone. Perhaps we could have another German lesson tomorrow night. Unless of course your girlfriend suddenly turns up from the United States.' But the slight did not bear its usual vituperative tone and contained the pathetic air of a man trying to claw back some ground after the humiliation he had just suffered. So I said, 'I do not have a

girlfriend, Herr Junker. I lied about the whole thing. Goodnight.'
And I closed the door on him and his wife and went to bed.

NEXT MORNING BERND'S dominatrix called round while I was
eating breakfast. She looked tired, ageing fast, and said she was
sorry about last night and about the noise, she hadn't realised I
could still hear everything so clearly. Bernd wanted it to be known
that she wouldn't be tying him up any more and that he was going
to start seeing a sex therapist. He was going to pay for her, the
junkie whore, to go to college and learn a new profession, not that
she thought she was any good at anything. She also asked me to
tell the little old man across the corridor she was sorry for any
trouble she had caused and that he would have no further cause
for complaint.

'What's your name, actually?' I asked her. 'Ever since my first
conversation with you in Bernd's kitchen that night I just think of
you as "junkie whore".'

She shrugged and said that was probably the best name for her.
'My real name is ugly, I hate it. My street name I suppose I should
put behind me.' I waited for her to say more, but that was it. She
slipped back through Bernd's door, in every measure the opposite
of the woman who had looked like she was going to thrash Junker
down the stairwell just twelve hours before.

JUNKER AND SARAH continued to turn up almost every evening
for Sarah's German lessons. At the start I had hoped Junker would
get so bored he would leave us alone once or twice. I had already
thought a thousand times what I would do in such a scenario, and
every time I had come up with a different outcome. Sarah still
looked so inscrutable that I had no idea how she would react if I
either plied her with questions or if I attempted to seduce her. She
sat there passively repeating the phrases I taught her, caring little
for Junker's praise or scorn, which were delivered according to her
accuracy and pronunciation. Meanwhile the content of the lessons
became gradually more degrading as Junker decreed that it was

not really important for Sarah to be able to speak the language that well, she merely had to be capable of comprehending the stream of imperatives through which he gave her instructions to clean, fetch and carry. And the more humiliating the instruction, the more he chuckled as he demanded its repetition in English. Embarrassed, I told her that ludicrous orders barked in German by Junker such as 'Cook my dinner, now!' actually meant in English 'Please could you start on the dinner soon, dear, if you have nothing better to do.'

One night he had clearly been drinking before they came round, I could smell the whisky on his breath. We all sat down and he announced that every sentence we had learned over the previous week now had to be appended by the words 'you lazy slut'. He shouted at her: 'Do the ironing now, you lazy slut!' and then began to laugh. 'Go get me my paper, you lazy slut!' he went on. 'Come on, Herr Johnstone, tell her what it means in English. The lazy bitch seems to think that she has come here on a free meal ticket. She can't seem to understand that there is no money to go clothes shopping every day, or that there is supposed to be a hot meal on the table every evening!'

I told Junker that I was not prepared to repeat such obscenities to Sarah, but was then interrupted as he stood up, waved his arm at me dismissively and said he needed to use my toilet. 'I'm not going to listen to any self-righteous moral lectures from some British loser who can't even get himself a girlfriend,' he announced and disappeared into the bathroom. I looked over at Sarah, expecting her to spend the next two minutes analysing the thread of my carpet, but instead she looked up at me straight away and whispered, 'I am living in a hell. My family has sold me to a monster. I don't expect you to help me, but please, however much he insults you, don't stop these lessons. They're the only chance I ever get to see anyone but him or the checkout girl in the supermarket.' I leaned across and took her hand. She looked at me terrified, but didn't take it away, at least not until she heard Junker rattling the door of the bathroom. Our body contact lasted for around three seconds, and by the time Junker had reappeared in the living room I was sitting back in position in my chair, a decent distance from his wife.

It would probably have been OK if she hadn't started to cry. Perhaps it was the culmination of repression, but her determined endurance of the previous weeks was all of a sudden shattered. She didn't just cry, she wailed and fell on to the floor and curled up into a ball. Junker began to shout at me: 'What did you do to my wife while my back was turned? Did you molest her, you fucking pervert? Couldn't you keep your hands off her for two seconds? Why don't you get yourself a girlfriend, why do you have to sniff around my wife, eh?'

Just as Sarah's resolve had collapsed into hopeless hysteria, so I came within a whisker of taking Junker's head under my arm and battering it into the wall. After absorbing his insults and insinuations for the best part of a year, my passivity was in seconds comprehensively swamped by a well of anger which saw the only solution in terms of violence unlimited by considerations for law and order. But Junker for once came to my rescue by collapsing with what later proved to be a minor cardiac arrest, and I phoned for an ambulance instead.

As Junker lay groaning on the floor, Sarah realised something was amiss and gradually ceased to sob. I was putting a cushion beneath Junker's head and generally attempting to hide my complete lack of medical knowledge, or how to react to an emergency, when I looked up to see her now standing and coldly observing her suffering husband. 'Why can't we just let him die?' she asked. Any temptation such a proposition might have awakened in us subsided with the arrival of the emergency services. As they efficiently fastened him to a stretcher I told them that his wife spoke no German, so it would probably be better if I accompanied him to the hospital. I told Sarah I would come by later or ring her with a medical update, then went downstairs with the crew and climbed into the back of the ambulance.

At the hospital I waited around for a few hours until a nurse told me that he was in no danger, but that he would have to stay in the hospital for a few days under observation. I said I would come back with his wife to visit tomorrow, then went straight home, where I found Sarah waiting for me in my bed.

THE NEXT DAY I phoned in sick at work and we went in my car to visit Junker. He looked exhausted and not particularly pleased to see me. I offered to leave him alone with his wife, but he said, 'No, you have to translate for me.' He told Sarah that he was going to be here for a couple of weeks, and that during this time she had to stay home and look after the flat. Under no circumstances was she to come round to my flat for German lessons. He was going to have a phone brought to his bedside so that he could check up on her. He would be back up on his feet as soon as possible, and if there was any 'trouble' during his time in hospital she could be sure he would get to hear about it and that she would have to take the consequences at a later date. But his orders lacked their usual aggressive tone and his threats seemed pathetic and empty. Once I had relayed everything to Sarah she said to me, 'Tell him I hope he dies and rots in hell.' Suddenly I felt incredibly worried by her new-found boldness. I said to Junker, 'She says she'll do just as you ask.'

Junker then tried to threaten me in case I should get any wrongful intentions into my head with regard to his wife, but I cut him short and said, 'Calm down, Herr Junker, remember that you need to relax. We'll come round again tomorrow evening after work.' I looked at Sarah and said, 'Could you just kiss him goodbye for the sake of appearance?' But she just stood up, said, 'Never again,' and walked out of the ward.

When we got back into the car I said to her, 'What are you doing? Remember this man is your husband, you're living with him.'

She looked at me sharply and said, 'I don't ever want to have to touch that evil little reptile again. You must be able to imagine what I have been through.'

'But, Sarah, legally you're his wife. You could get into all kinds of problems if he realises you slept with me.'

'What do you mean that I could get into problems?' she said, her voice rising. 'Don't you mean that now you are worried that *you* are going to have problems?' She turned away from me and looked out of the passenger's window. 'You didn't have any problems sleeping with me last night, did you?'

I began struggling for words. 'But . . . but, Sarah, that was just one night. What I mean is, what are you going to do if you leave him? You can't speak the language or anything. I mean, where would you go . . .' I tailed off, feeling awkward and knowing that I was going red in the face. We drove along in silence for a few minutes until she spoke again.

'Last night I said I didn't expect you to help me. Then a few seconds later you took my hand. It seems I falsely interpreted that. Clearly I am just a naïve little nigger girl from the third world who let herself be sold into slavery because her family wanted hard German marks and who doesn't understand your sophisticated Western love ways. So,' she said wearily, 'just forget it, forget it, forget it.'

Actually, there had been very little sophistication in my love ways the previous night. We had been incapable of staging any kind of sexual union because she was not only extremely upset but also, apart from whatever doubtless passive role she had played in Junker's bed, wholly inexperienced. On my side I could not get it out of my head that no matter how attractive she was, Junker's foul breath and wizened, stunted body had been there before and I was unable to deflect a feeling of repulsion every time I began to let my hands roam.

As we drove on I tried to explain to Sarah that I could not possibly make her any kind of commitment after just one night, and in order to try to make her feel less rejected began to adumbrate all kinds of bogus reasons relating to my work, my family and a desire to return to Britain. Just as I was feeling slightly ashamed about fabricating a terminal illness for a non-existent brother she interrupted me once more and said, 'Forget it! Did you not hear me the first time?' And she stared ahead, her look of hard resolve fixed firmly back in place.

When we got back to the flat we bumped into Bernd's whore going up in the lift. She looked different, fresh-faced and in casual but smart dress. She smiled at us. She was clutching a batch of folders and some text books, and explained that she had enrolled on a course to learn secretarial and administrative skills. This was her first week and it was going well. In the afternoons she was going to the rehab clinic and was trying to wean herself gradually off drugs. In the evenings Bernd brought her flowers home and then took her out to dinner. I said I was glad it was going so well for her. She looked at me and smiled again, almost too widely. 'Yes, it is going well. I wonder how long it's going to last?'

When we reached our floor Sarah stormed out of the lift and straight into Junker's flat. Although I feebly called after her she slammed the door and locked it from the inside. For the next two weeks she refused to answer, even when I went round to offer to take her to the hospital. Once I put a note under the door, but by the time I had walked back across the landing to my door she had slipped it back out with the words FORGET IT scrawled on the other side.

I presume that Junker returned by ambulance, but I never realised he was back until he began to pound furiously on my door at around ten o'clock one evening, yelling that he knew I was in there and that I should open up immediately. I wasn't surprised. It had been far too quiet during the fortnight of his absence, and I'd sensed that upon his return there would have to be some kind of dramatic showdown. It was almost a relief now to hear him fulminating on my doorstep.

As soon as I opened up he stormed in, dragging Sarah behind him into my living room. As if on cue I heard from next door that Bernd had once again succumbed to his need to be tied up and abused by his live-in secretarial student. Junker began screaming at me, clearly disregarding medical instruction. 'Herr Johnstone, would you kindly tell my wife the English for "Get your clothes off." She seems to have forgotten and is now incapable of getting undressed.'

'I could not do that, Herr Junker,' I said. 'It is far too personal a matter and it's something you will have to sort out between yourselves.'

Junker threw the by now weeping Sarah on to my sofa and put his contorted, crimson snarl as close to my face as he could. 'Well, it wasn't too personal for you to fuck my wife while I was lying in hospital, was it, Herr Johnstone? That didn't seem to disturb your great fucking principles about interfering in other peoples' family business, eh? So why don't you tell my wife that I want her to get her fucking clothes off?'

As Junker hissed his piece it became increasingly difficult to ignore the sounds coming from Bernd's apartment. Even by his standards the noise was loud and I thought it could only be a matter of time before the neighbours below complained. More worrying were Bernd's sexual groans, which allowing for masochistic pleasure sounded more and more like a man howling under the duress of severe torture. I brushed Junker aside and went out to rap on Bernd's door. When this elicited no response I tried Junker's tactic of kicking hard, but had to break off when I heard Sarah screaming. I rushed back into my own flat to find Junker attempting to rape her on my sofa, yelling, 'You fuck my neighbour and you run up a 1400-mark phone bill to the Philippines and now you won't even let your own husband have you, you foreign slut!'

I pulled him off her and wrestled him to the floor. He wriggled around beneath me, his eyes tight shut with determination, then he attempted to bite my fingers, which were holding his shoulders down. 'Calm down, Herr Junker,' I said, myself breathing heavily from the effort of keeping his wiry and obstinately squirming frame nailed to the floor. 'You don't want another heart attack, do you?' But Junker didn't have time to lose his life like that. His heart stopped shortly after Sarah came up behind us, pulled me off him and thrust my kitchen knife into his chest. She did it just once, and I had neither the chance nor the inclination to stop her. It killed him outright.

For the shortest of moments there was a complete silence. Even the noise next door had stopped. Then Bernd's leather-clad whore appeared looking dazed, and said, 'My real name is Ursula Trautwein. I think I just killed Bernd.'

Behind Ursula Trautwein several curious neighbours from the flats downstairs had gathered on the landing and were peering into my apartment. 'Aha,' I thought, 'at last I'm going to get to meet the other people in the building.'